HEAT

A LESBIAN AGE GAP ROMANCE BOX SET

EMILY HAYES

SURGEON

PROLOGUE

The hustle and chaos that was the Emergency Room, normally left Dr. Katherine Ross feeling excited and energetic. The E.R had a way of turning someone from being dead tired on their feet to feeling more alive than they had ever been. When she was a surgical intern, she would sit around just waiting for a major car pile up, or a similar crisis, just so she could experience the chaos over and over again. Both Katherine and the other interns used to question what type of people they must be that they would be hoping and praying for a major accident just so they could have the chance to fight to scrub in on a cool surgery.

They would race down the hallways to try and get to the E.R first. To the public, it was the Emergency Room, but to the hospital staff it was the Pit. Why? Because you never knew what could fall into a pit, could be nothing, could be everything. In a pit, things could get swallowed whole.

Throughout her time as a surgical intern, then

surgical resident at Forest Vale Hospital, Dr. Katherine Ross had experienced many ups and downs of the career she had chosen. However, one thing became very clear, very quickly, she loved the human heart. There was nothing more satisfying, nothing more powerful, than holding a beating heart in your hands. Taking something that controls your very life and restoring it. The more complicated a case was, the more dangerous the surgery was, the better it was for her. She loved a challenge. She loved doing what everyone said would be impossible. It didn't matter to her if the surgery took twenty hours, she was there from the first cut until the last stitch was sewn.

Surgery was her world. She loved it and wouldn't want to do anything else. She thought her life was complete, she couldn't imagine how her life could possibly get any better. All of that changed when she met the most amazing woman one day, years ago, sitting in the Pit.

Melissa Freemond had come in with a broken wrist and had been waiting for an x-ray. Katherine wasn't sure what it was about her, but she couldn't help but go to her. Melissa had this vibrant long wild red hair, so vivid across the room. She was thin, petite, and her hair was a big statement on a small woman. She was drawn to her, as if there was an invisible string attaching her to this beautiful stranger. She had to go over there to speak with her and it had nothing to do with her injury. Her injury was boring, she wouldn't even need surgery. What was interesting, was how she got the injury.

"I'm Doctor Ross," Katherine said as she arrived and with a clipboard ready for notes. "Do you want to tell me what happened?"

Melissa looked up from her place on the edge of the

bed, wide green eyes more alive than ever and dirt on the side of her face. "I was playing flag football with some of the guys and made a dive for the runner. I totally got the flag though and we won the game!"

Katherine smiled, enjoying Melissa's animated retelling of the game and examined her wrist carefully.

"Well done for winning the game. Did you happen to put your arm out as you fell do you think?"

"I think I must have, yeah." Melissa's legs were tiny in her short shorts and her wrist was delicate in Katherine's hand.

Katherine had done something then, that she hadn't done before. She took Melissa down for an x-ray and then she put on the cast herself. It was something a first year intern would do, not a resident, but she wanted to spend more time with Melissa. She wanted to learn everything she could about this tiny woman who plays flag football with men. As it turned out, Melissa was a new teacher at an elementary school. She spent her days teaching and shaping the minds of second graders. To Katherine it sounded like a circle of hell in Dante's Inferno, but to Melissa there was nothing that made her smile more. She loved what she did and that was something Katherine could understand completely.

Katherine could never have imagined that one day she would meet the woman she would marry, sitting in the Pit with a broken wrist, but it happened. They quickly started to date, then fall in love and within eighteen months they were married. Katherine couldn't believe it. She swore she would never marry, especially not while she was still in her residency. Her work schedule was insane, she was constantly working and studying. But, they made it work.

Melissa knew what it felt like to be busy, she was often busy with her lesson plans and grading tests, getting report cards ready. She was always trying to help her students and find new ways to teach them in a fun and creative way. They would often spend their nights on the couch or at the dining room table both working, but they shared that time together and it made it better. They were happy. Really really happy.

They spent ten years married and each and every single one of those years Katherine had loved. She loved being able to wake up in the morning to her beautiful wife and to be able to come home to her arms after a difficult day. As Katherine's career had progressed, the hours hadn't really eased. Katherine's determination to become one of the most renowned cardio thoracic surgeons in the world was all consuming.

Katherine never expected that there would come a time in her life that standing in the Pit would be something that brought crushing pain to her. It started off as a normal day. She had just finished a successful twelve hour surgery and was on her way home. She never expected to get a call that her lovely wife had been in a severe car accident.

She turned and drove straight back to Forest Vale. She ran into the ER and stood there, for a second she was frozen to the spot. The place that used to bring her such joy, such a rush, only filled her with dread and she made her way through the chaos to where her wife was being treated. She followed the pull of that invisible string right to her wife. She couldn't believe what she was seeing.

Lying in an ER bed, covered in bruising and blood, was her wife. The woman that had changed her life. The woman that she had fallen so deeply in love with, almost instantly. The woman who was her soulmate was currently lying in a hospital with machines hooked up to her and a swarm of doctors around her. Katherine's eyes immediately started to read the monitors to gauge just how bad her injuries were. She could tell that there was an issue with her breathing and her heart rate was too low. Something was wrong.

"We need to get her to surgery immediately. Page Cardio and tell them we have a hot one coming in." The lead Doctor, Mark White, said.

"She's my wife." Katherine suddenly came back to life. "Mark, she's my wife. What are her scans coming back as?" Katherine demanded, finding her voice finally.

Everyone in the room turned, recognising Doctor Ross's voice straight away. They were so busy trying to keep their patient alive, they didn't even notice that they had company. Dr. White stepped forward and spoke.

"Katherine, I am so sorry. You aren't a doctor right now. You are patient's family. We will do the absolute best we can for her."

"What are her scans? I demand to know!" Katherine demanded again.

"Get her to the O.R right now." Dr. White ordered before he turned back to Katherine. "Scans are indicating that there is a tear in her left subclavian artery. Jackson will do the surgery."

"He isn't good enough." Katherine said, as she watched them wheel out her wife and take her away. She wished with everything in her to be able to have a moment with her to tell her how much she loved her, but she knew she couldn't. With her type of injury every single second counted, stopping to tell her she loved her could cost her life.

"I'll do it. Let me scrub in." Katherine snapped straight back to professional mode.

"Katherine, please, you know you can't do this. You cannot operate on a loved one, it's a rule for a reason. I'm sorry, but all you can do right now is wait."

"Jackson isn't good enough. He will kill her. We need a different surgeon."

"Katherine," Dr. White took her hand and looked at her kindly. She was a surgeon, she didn't need his pity. "You know as well as I do that there is no time to get anyone else in. You know we cannot let you anywhere near the O.R. for her surgery. Jackson is her best chance right now. You have to wait."

And with that Dr. White was gone and Katherine was left standing there in the E.R. Staff she knew and staff she didn't know were staring at her. Jackson Myers was not a good enough surgeon for this, she knew he wasn't. He was old, he had never been the best and he was always resistant to new techniques, new equipment. She made a conscious effort not to work with Jackson where she could, hence why he was often on opposite shifts to her. She knew they would never let her do the surgery herself, they were married and it went against the rules. You couldn't treat a family member and you most definitely couldn't operate on one. It was set that way to ensure the surgeon's mind was clear. If a surgeon's mind was compromised and their judgment was questionable they could make mistakes. Some of them rookie mistakes and others devastating. A surgeon could go too far, push the surgery on too long because they feared their loved one dying on their table. Doing more harm than good. She couldn't stop going through the surgery in her head. She could do it. She was the best. She could save Melissa. She took a deep breath. She couldn't believe her wife's life was literally in Jackson Myers's hands.

Katherine let out a shaky breath as Ellen Lau came over to her. Ellen was a kind and efficient E.R. nurse that she had always got on well with.

"Dr. Ross. I am so so sorry. Let me come and wait with you." She took Katherine's hand and walked with her towards to O.R. waiting room. "Do you want me to get someone for you?" Katherine thought for a moment. There was nobody she was really close to at work. She had always kept a professional distance. She was so career focussed.

"I need to call my sister." Katherine's mind was going a mile a minute. Thinking about what the surgery would be and how difficult it could be if the tear was large in size. She could bleed out almost instantly when they opened her chest. Even if she did make it, Katherine knew her beautiful wife had a long road ahead of her. Having open heart surgery was not an easy thing to recover from. Her chest plate would have been cracked open and closed with wires to hold it in place while the bones healed. She would need to have the wires then removed later on once the bones started to heal. She could have lasting damage from the surgery and that was if everything went right. There was no telling what could happen if complications came up.

Katherine sat in the waiting room with Ellen, just hoping to hear anything on Melissa. She had called her sister when she arrived in the sad room and Aimee quickly arrived to meet her and replace Ellen. All they had were each other, after their mother who had raised them on her own died when Katherine was at medical school. She had quickly explained what she knew and that they could be in for a long wait, assuming everything went well. Katherine knew she didn't want to see Jackson any time soon. If the surgical team were still in the O.R., that meant her wife was still alive. It was hours later when Jackson walked into the waiting room. He was dressed in blue scrubs with his surgeon's cap on, he looked exhausted. Katherine and Aimee both stood waiting to hear the news. Katherine was a little worried that he was out here already.

"Dr. Ross, I'm so sorry. There was too much bleeding, we couldn't get it under control. The tear in her artery was as extensive as any I have seen. I couldn't save her. I am sorry for your loss."

Katherine couldn't hear anything. She was numb. All she could hear was I'm sorry for your loss. She had said the words herself plenty of times. During your intern year you are taught how to say it, you get to say it all the time when a patient dies on the table, even if it wasn't your fault. Your teachers get you to say it over and over again so you can learn how to do it properly and how to become numb to the endless reactions that could come from a family member. Never in a million years did she think she would be the one standing in a hospital and hearing those words and feeling nothing. Jackson's voice was calm and controlled, she knew the tone, she used it herself plenty of times. But she realised just now how little it did for the one hearing it. It did nothing to stop the pain that exploded in her chest. It did nothing to ease the sudden loss of her wife. And it certainly did nothing to ease the guilt that was tearing away at her very soul at knowing her wife was dead, and convincing herself that if it had been her hands working on her wife's heart, maybe she would have survived. Maybe she wouldn't be standing here feeling like there was a gaping hole in her chest.

She had lost the woman she loved. She had lost her soulmate. The only woman to ever truly make her smile. The only woman to ever make her feel alive and special. She had lost her heart and she was never going to get it back.

1

Katherine sat in a coffee shop with her sister just around the corner from the hospital. She was on a quick lunch break and Aimee wanted to catch up with her. Katherine had been pretty busy the last few months with her department. She was the Head of Cardio Thoracic Surgery at Forest Vale Hospital now. She had been promoted three years ago and as a result she had plenty of work to handle both with patients and on the administrative side. Over the past five years since she had lost her wife, Katherine had thrown everything she had into her work. She refused to date, not even thinking about being with anyone other than Melissa. To Katherine, there was no one in this world that could ever compare to her.

"So, have you given it a try yet?" Aimee asked.

She had been trying to get Katherine to date for the past year. She knew her sister was grieving the loss of her wife, but after four years she thought it was time for her to get back out there. She didn't want her to be alone for the rest of her life. She knew she would never find anyone like

Melissa again and chances were she would never get married again, but she wanted her sister to not be alone for the rest of her life. She needed to remember how good it felt to be with someone. To have someone there in her life that she could talk to and have some fun with. Aimee knew without a doubt that Melissa wouldn't want her wife to be alone and miserable for the rest of her life. She needed to find some joy again and she needed to get away from the office. It wasn't healthy for her to spend every waking hour working, she needed to get a life again.

"Yes, I joined the app. And no, I haven't met anyone off it yet!"

Katherine had joined the dating app six months ago when her sister refused to stop talking about it. It was an app where she could set her profile to 'interested in women' so she wouldn't have to deal with every guy hitting on her and trying to convince her she wasn't truly gay. She had lost count in her life how many times she had been told by men, "You aren't really gay, you just haven't met the right man yet." The arrogance of the average straight, white guy never ceased to amaze her.

She had been messaged by a few women, and matched with a great deal of them. She hadn't messaged any back, but then one woman caught her eye. Sophia. Sophia was a lot younger than her, only twenty-four, but she she had these enchanting blue eyes that drew Katherine in. Enchanting blue eyes and dark hair. Instead of the other messages that she received that all either said some version of hey to let's hook up, Sophia had welcomed her to the app and told her some great spots to visit in town, because Katherine had said she was new to town, and offered to show her around as a friend.

It was different and came across very friendly. They

had started to text each other after that, never meeting in person. Katherine hadn't listed her job on the app, because she didn't want to be hit on for her prestige and her salary. If she was going to entertain dating someone, it would be because they liked her for who she was and not what she had to offer. Sophia hadn't mentioned what her job was either and Katherine didn't ask. The one thing she did like about Sophia, she had made it very clear she wasn't looking for commitment. She was only interested in a friends with benefits type of arrangement. Nothing but fun without any responsibility. She was very confident in herself and what she wanted or was capable of and Katherine could understand that. She realised suddenly that she was looking for the same thing. The thought of having someone to be close to, but none of the pressure that came with dating seemed like just what she needed.

"Do you plan on it?" Aimee pressed.

"I don't know, maybe. There is this one woman who I've texted back and forth for the past couple of weeks. I might meet up with her."

"You should. That's good. That is so good! You should meet her for like coffee or something. In a public place so there are no worries about her potentially being crazy. If you don't like her in person you can easily walk away."

"Yeah, maybe. I'll think about it." Katherine's eyes gazed into the distance.

"So what is going on at work? Anything new coming up?" Aimee asked, sensing that her sister needed the change in topic.

"New set of interns are starting next Monday. That's always entertaining."

"Are you going to be nice to any of them?" Aimee asked with a smirk.

"Only the smart ones that show promise. I've yet to discover an intern that I could look at and say, ok this person will be a great doctor one day. Everyone wants to be a surgeon, but the reality is, most will end up switching specialties or being just an average surgeon. I don't want average. If I am going to teach someone everything I know to make room for the next generation after my time has come, then they need to be special. They need to be someone that I know can handle the pressure and has the drive to want it. I haven't found that yet."

"I would have thought lots of people would be interested in cardio."

"It's a specialty that sounds cool, but in actuality there is a lot of pressure involved. Much like neuro. A lot of people will stick with plastic or general surgery. Less risk of death and it's not as stressful. It takes a lot to cut into someone's brain and potentially change everything about someone and it takes a lot to hold someone's heart in your hands. Knowing that, with a single wrong cut, you could kill them. It can be a lot and as cool as the title sounds, most will never have the skills required for this type of surgery."

"Well, maybe someone in this next group will surprise you." Aimee said with a warm smile.

In truth, Katherine was always hoping that she would find an intern that held a real interest in cardio and had the potential to be really great. She would love to have someone that she could teach and pass down her own knowledge. The heads of the departments all had their star pupil, but she still had no one special. She knew she could be cold and come across as distant with people. She was confident in her abilities and knew that that sometimes came across as arrogance when it was a quality found in a woman. She was one of only a handful of female surgical heads in the country. She didn't get there by being sweet and easy going. She was tough and demanded the best of the people who worked within her department.

As a result their department was very well known and had patients coming from all over the country and sometimes the world for their chance to have Katherine operate on them. Sometimes she did, and sometimes there wasn't anything even she could do for them. It was those cases that got to her the most. Science had come a long way, but it wasn't perfect. Some hearts she couldn't repair and trying to repair them would only cost the patient what little time they had left. Sometimes she was confident she could fix them and still the patient died. Every time she had to turn a patient away or she lost them on the table, she felt like she was failing Melissa all over again.

She hadn't got over the death of her wife and the guilt she still felt over it. She would never stop feeling like she wished she had had the chance to do the surgery herself. Maybe her hands could have saved her wife. It was a decision that still haunted her dreams.

KATHERINE COULDN'T BELIEVE she was sitting in a bar that Friday evening waiting to meet a stranger from a dating app. She had no idea if Sophia even looked like she did in her profile pictures. She had no idea if the intensity of those blue eyes that had drawn her in would be there in person. She had heard about it more than enough just from walking the halls in the hospital about people using fake profile pictures on dating apps. She didn't understand the point of it, it wasn't like they weren't going to notice the difference when you showed up for the date. Why set yourself up for failure when your date was obviously going to notice that you lied?

Katherine had decided after her lunch with Aimee that she was going to ask Sophia to meet in person. They had never talked about it before and Katherine had no idea if Sophia would even agree to meet, but she had. Katherine couldn't help but feel a slight tingle of excitement creep up her spine. She was excited to meet her, but also a little nervous at the same time. She hadn't done something like this before, not even before Melissa. She had never gone on a blind date in her life and she had no idea what it would be like.

Katherine looked up from her phone to see Sophia walk into the bar. She couldn't help but smile at the sight of her. She was petite, in tight black jeans and a sheer floaty top. Katherine could see her black bra through the material and it excited her. Sophia's dark hair was down and she was wearing a small amount of makeup. Katherine always hated it when beautiful women covered their face with makeup, so she liked that Sophia hadn't. Sophia easily found Katherine and gave her a warm smile, as she headed over to the table. Katherine stood, unsure if she should shake her hand or not, but that was resolved when Sophia pulled her in for a hug as she spoke.

"It's great to finally meet you."

"You too. Can I get you something to drink?" Katherine asked, as they pulled back.

"No, I'll get it. What would you like?" Sophia said with a warm smile. Her blue eyes were just as intense and direct as they had been in her profile pictures.

"I'll have another glass of Merlot please."

"Sure." Sophia loved Katherine's confident response.

Katherine watched as she headed over to the counter and ordered her drink. After a moment she came back over with the Merlot and a white wine for herself and sat down.

"So, it is lovely to finally meet you. You look just like your photos." Sophia admired Katherine's honey blonde hair and steely grey eyes. Sophia had always had a thing for older women. Katherine wore smart trousers, heels and a blouse. She was clearly accomplished and confident in herself. A businesswoman, Sophia thought. A high powered business woman. She wouldn't ask her about it, ultimately, it didn't matter. But there was something about high profile, confident older women that always had Sophia weak at the knees.

"Refreshingly, so do you. I have heard all sorts about online dating. It isn't my usual scene. What is a girl like you doing on there? You are stunning. Surely you can meet women anywhere?" Katherine took a sip of her wine.

"Ah, you see I don't want the commitment of women who want to date me. What I love about the apps is I can be completely open from the start in that I just want a casual arrangement. I don't want to be being pushed to commit. I have other priorities in my life. How has your week been?"

"Good, thank you. A lot of paperwork, but it goes with the job. I work a lot. So your 'arrangement', if it is something you would like to explore with me, is something that intrigues me. It is something I could fit into my life. My work is my priority, I have no need for a relationship that will in any way complicate that."

Sophia looked at her intently, glad they were on the same page. "It is something I would like to explore with you, yes." Their eyes met, both intense and straightforward in their desires. Sophia's mouth on the rim of the wine glass drew Katherine's gaze.

Katherine liked this bold, young woman. There was something about her. About her straightforward, confident nature. She reminded Katherine a little of herself, twenty years ago. Katherine looked again at Sophia's black lace bra under her top.

"Well, this will be my first 'arrangement' of this type. I'm assuming we don't make polite small talk about each other's work and families?"

Sophia smiled. "No, I think we discuss the finer points of our 'arrangement'. So far, I have: No commitment. No discussing work or family. We call each other when we want company and sex and if the other is keen and available, we meet up. No dating. What are your limits?"

"Sexually?" Katherine raised an eyebrow.

Sophia laughed. God, Katherine was hot. "I mean, I meant in terms of the 'arrangement', but sure, sexually is relevant too!"

She was enjoying this conversation with Sophia. She was young, but she didn't act like a normal twenty-four year old. She was mature and intelligent, she seemed like someone who would be capable of having a conversation that could stimulate her. She could feel a spark between them, there was chemistry and it surprised Katherine. She didn't think she would ever have chemistry with another woman again, certainly not one so young.

"I'm pretty open sexually. I'm not afraid to experiment, although it has actually been quite a while since I had sex, I am not short on desire suddenly since meeting you.

Outside of that, I like honesty, openness, and respect. I don't expect you to only sleep with me, but I don't really want to hear about what else you get up to. Your time with me will be just about the two of us. An escape from real life. If there is ever anything we aren't comfortable with, sexually or otherwise, we just say 'arrangement' and everything stops and we have a chat about it."

"Like a safe word?"

"If you like. I think that is important. Consent is always at the core of everything. Sexually or otherwise. Either of us says 'arrangement' and we can re-negotiate."

"Sounds fair to me. I have to be honest, I share a house. Do you live alone?"

"I do."

"Are you happy to use your home or would you prefer we meet in hotels?"

"My home will be fine." Katherine felt desire pooling between her legs.

"Close by?" Sophia said with a flirty smile.

"Ten minutes."

"Then, what are we still doing here?"

Katherine hadn't come here tonight expecting to sleep with Sophia. But in the short time they had been in the dimly lit bar, Katherine had found a lust awaken within her.

Katherine gave a smile as she spoke. "Let's go then."

Sophia smiled and she got up. They headed out onto the street and hailed a passing taxi. This could be the beginning of something great for the two of them.

2

They arrived at Katherine's house and Sophia couldn't help but take a moment to look around. Sophia lived in a shared apartment with two roommates and at times it felt very cramped. Her new job wouldn't pay that much, but she would be able to make more money as her career progressed. In time, she would be able to afford her own place.

Katherine's home was stunning, modern and clean. Sophia could tell that Katherine preferred to have things organised and her home clean. Sophia's place had a more lived in feel to it. None of her roommates cared if they left dishes in the sink overnight, they could simply wash them the next day. They didn't care if there was a coaster down on the coffee table or if they sat on the couch and ate dinner while watching tv. That was normal to them, that was comfortable. They had a dining table, but it was just covered in books or papers. Katherine's place was clean of any clutter or slight mess.

She turned around and gave Katherine a warm smile. "Your home is beautiful."

Katherine smiled. "Your body is beautiful."

Sophia felt weak at the knees.

Sophia could tell it had been a little while since Katherine had done anything like this. She couldn't see any photos from where she was standing, but that didn't mean that Katherine hadn't been married or wasn't still. She was older, so it would make sense that she might have been with someone for a while. There was a slight indent in her ring finger, but no ring. It was hard to tell if it was recent or old. A wedding ring had this ability to shape the finger of its wearer. A symbol of ownership. An indelible sign. No matter. Katherine's history was irrelevant to her present.

Sophia could tell she was slightly nervous by the ever so slight crinkle in her forehead. She was clearly a very capable woman, but maybe this was slightly out of her comfort zone. Sophia was good with nervous people though, she had been nervous plenty of times in her life and would be many more before it was over. Sophia also knew that the best way to get over being nervous was to get to the task that was making you nervous. Waiting longer never helped and when you started to do that task that was making you nervous eventually you stop being nervous and just focus on what you need to do.

Sophia walked over the short distance to Katherine and ran her hand down the buttons of her blouse. She met her hard grey eyes. "So, where's the bedroom?"

Katherine could see the smirk on the young woman's face and the light in her eyes and she knew that Sophia wanted this, wanted her. Katherine allowed herself to stop thinking about everything. To stop thinking about the past. To stop thinking about what she should be doing at work right now. She allowed herself to just focus on this moment, on this beautiful young woman in front of her. It was time she allowed herself to have some fun and that was exactly what she was going to do.

Katherine went over and pulled Sophia in for a heated kiss. Sophia easily returned it as he hands moved to Katherine's jacket, pushing it off from her shoulders. Katherine felt it everywhere. She had almost forgotten what passion was. But here it was, overwhelming her. Katherine pushed Sophia back as she continued to kiss her, guiding her over to the hallway. She took her hand and lead her upstairs to her big bedroom.

Desire overtook Katherine. Everything that had been missing for so many years suddenly felt so real. She kissed Sophia. She liked that Sophia was smaller than her. Delicate, like a bird. Her hands were hungry as they stripped Sophia's clothes from her. She was wearing a thin black lace bra and black lace panties. She looked like a dark angel standing in front of her and Katherine felt a heated lust she had never known.

Katherine pulled her own clothes off quickly. She removed Sophia's bra and pushed her down onto her bed. Katherine then removed Sophia's thong. God, she wanted her. Her body laid in front of her was perfect. Small breasts pert and small nipples hard. Sophia smiled and spread her legs confidently.

"Like what you see?" Sophia said.

"Very much so." Katherine said smiling. "You look incredible. I can't wait to taste you."

Katherine got down onto her knees and spread Sophia's legs open further, pulling her to the edge of the bed. Sophia wanted to pull her legs from her body to give Katherine greater access to her burning core. Katherine grabbed her slim thighs and gave a long lick between her folds and Sophia moaned.

"You taste so sweet." Katherine said.

"I taste sweeter the more you do it." Sophia tipped her head back onto the bed and pulled Katherine closer to her.

"I'll be the judge of that."

Katherine went back to give Sophia another long lick, loving the taste of her on her tongue. It had been so long since she tasted a woman and she had forgotten the life that it breathed into her. She had forgotten what it felt like to have this type of power over someone. To know that you were the one that made the other feel that level of pleasure.

Sophia. Sophia. Sophia.

Katherine moved her tongue to Sophia's clit and gave it a suck and a little nip, causing Sophia to moan. Goose-flesh appeared across her body.

"You like that?" Katherine asked with a smirk.

"I like a little pain, sometimes, done in the right way. I like... er... I like it rough. I want you to be rough with me." Sophia said, suddenly a little shy.

Katherine could feel herself pulse knowing that she could be rough with her. She had forgotten how alive being dominant made her feel. How naturally it came to her. How much of a rush it gave her.

"Oh, I can be rough with you. Are you adventurous?" Katherine asked, as she slowly inserted one finger, and then another, into her heat.

"Yes. You can do whatever you want with me.....Oh fuck." Sophia moaned as Katherine started to slowly finger fuck her and lick at her clit.

Katherine inserted another finger and started to seek Sophia's g-spot. She knew she hit it when Sophia let out a long moan and arched her back pushing onto the fingers. Katherine started to lick and suck more at her clit and she moved her fingers faster inside of Sophia. Sophia was moaning and writhing on the bed very quickly and Katherine knew she was close to orgasm.

"Come for me. I want to feel your orgasm."

Sophia felt heat build inside her and that incomparable feeling. Her world shattered into a million pieces as she came for Katherine's tongue and fingers.

Sophia lay on the bed in quiet recovery.

Katherine smiled to herself for a second. She had forgotten this feeling. This indescribable feeling of being able to give this level of pleasure to someone. To take her body and play it like a musical instrument. To have her come alive for her touch.

Sophia came back to life slightly and Katherine ran a hand lazily up Sophia's thigh. Sophia shivered with excitement at her touch and felt a need begin to burn again.

Katherine watched her body begin to respond again as she trailed her fingers almost disinterestedly across Sophia's body.

"I... er.... I want more. I need to feel you inside me again."

Katherine smiled. "What do we say Sophia? Where are your manners?"

"Please. Please. Please fuck me some more. I want to come again."

Katherine didn't need asking twice. She stood up and pulled Sophia up. She turned Sophia around so she was facing away from her and roughly bent her over. Her hands possessive on Sophia's hips. She began to spank Sophia, her hand hard against Sophia's ready ass. Vibrations ran up her arm as she hit Sophia. "Do you remember your safe word Sophia?"

"Yes. I remember."

"Do you like me hitting you Sophia?"

"Yes. Yes. Please don't stop."

Katherine spanked her again. And again. Harder. More. Tension ran out of her body. Anger. Frustration. All of it, she found her release in Sophia's body. She took Sophia's small hip in her left hand and pushed the fingers of her right hand roughly inside her wetness. Sophia gasped and yelped.

"Oh, you can take it Sophia, I'm sure you can." It hurt slightly as they entered her and stretched her, but Sophia's body relaxed, her desire flooded out of her when Katherine spoke to her like that, when Katherine treated her body like that.

Katherine's left hand fisted in Sophia's hair as she pushed her face down into the bed. Her ass was high as Katherine fucked her hard. Sophia had wanted something like this her whole life. She had always asked for rough, but never found a woman who could give it as rough as she wanted it. She felt alive in every cell of her body. She felt more desire than she had ever imagined was possible. She wanted more. More of Katherine. More pain. More fucking. Just more.

She screamed wildly as Katherine took her as hard as she had dreamt of. Maybe harder. She lost herself to it. She heard noises coming from her mouth that she didn't recognise. When she orgasmed she clenched hard around Katherine's fingers. She gushed and her whole body throbbed. She collapsed forward onto the bed. Spent.

Katherine smiled as she gazed at the beautiful girl on the bed in front of her. There was really something between them. A magical connection. A chemistry she had never imagined. Her darkest desires were becoming real with Sophia's body. There was so much she wanted to do to her.

She went to her ensuite bathroom and washed her hands. She came back to the bed room and Sophia still lay in a mess. Her eyes opened.

"Are you ok?" Katherine asked.

"Yes. Oh, god yes. That was incredible." She rolled onto her back.

"Sophia?"

"Yes."

"What do you say?"

"Thank you. Thank you SO much," she laughed.

"That's better. Now why don't you come here and get your pretty little face between my legs and show me just how grateful you really are?"

3

It was Monday morning and Katherine was sitting in her office getting ready for the new flood of interns that were about to take over the hospital. She was supposed to be focused on her work and getting ready for the interns that she was going to be stuck with on her service for the week. Intern and residents are not allowed to pick a specialty until they are in their third year of residency. So they would float around from one speciality to the next, building their skills and understanding of the human body. It was important that they had experience in all aspects of surgery so they would know what to look for should a situation come up unexpectedly. They needed to have a strong understanding of general surgery so they could build those skills and be able to take them and implement them into their area of focus.

That is what Katherine was supposed to be focused on, but all she could think about lately was her time with Sophia. After that incredible first night, Sophia had headed home. Neither of them wanted a sleepover. Katherine couldn't get her mind off Sophia though. How

hot she had been, how her body responded so enthusiastically to Katherine's every touch. They had text each
other the following day, and a couple of days later
Katherine had invited Sophia over, an invitation that
Sophia was happy to take. There had been more hours of
rough sex in Katherine's bed. More desire. She tied
Sophia's wrists to the headboard with silk scarves. She
pulled her legs apart and tied her ankles to the feet of the
bed. She blindfolded her. She took her like that. On top of
her. Her fingers thrusting inside her. She felt so powerful
over her. She gave her four fingers, made her stretch to
accommodate them. She saw Sophia's face wince as they
entered her. She saw her breathe deeply and relax
through the pain, then she saw the pleasure overtake her.
She was heady with her power over Sophia. As she felt
Sophia's bound body orgasm hard underneath her, half
her hand inside of her, she came herself, hard, her clit
pushed against Sophia's thigh. This was it. This thing with
Sophia. This was sexual chemistry at its finest.

Her obsession with Sophia's body almost scared her.
There was so much she wanted to do to her. She loved
hearing Sophia beg to be fucked. Making her plead for
fingers inside of her. Making her beg to orgasm again and
again. She was insatiable. They both were.

The nights she hadn't spent with Sophia, she had
fantasised about what she might do to her and touched
herself to orgasm.

Sophia had woken something up inside of her and
now that the beast was awake, it was not going back to
sleep anytime soon. Katherine had every intention of
using Sophia as long as she was willing.

Katherine looked at her clock and saw that she needed
to head down to meet the interns. She grabbed her things

and headed out to greet them. She was not looking forward to it, but it was something she needed to do. She did hear that this year the intern group was smaller. More and more they were going to different hospitals all over the country. They would focus on their ideal city that they'd want to live in and apply for intern positions there. It made sense to Katherine, and not something that was often done when she was an intern.

Katherine headed down to the main area of the hospital and saw how young they all looked. They were in their fresh white coats and they had hopeful eyes and big dreams of being the next top surgeon. In reality most of them would flunk their boards, switch specialties when they realised how hard it was, and then whoever was left would either get fired for making a huge mistake or the lucky ones would get to move on to their residency. Katherine knew that chances were slim that they would succeed in their surgical career.

Katherine took in the interns and she felt her heart stop when her eyes landed on the one person she never expected to see. There amongst the crowd of fresh white coats was Sophia. Her Sophia. She had her glossy hair up in a ponytail and had on the blue scrubs and her own white coat. She was an intern and she was an intern here at this hospital. Katherine couldn't believe it. At first she wanted to think that Sophia must have sought her out for her position here, for her name of being a department head. But she quickly pushed that thought away. There was no way that Sophia would have known who she was. She only used her first name, not her last, she didn't have her job posted anywhere and it had never come up in conversation. Sophia also never revealed her job either.

Katherine couldn't believe this was happening. It

wasn't that people didn't know she was gay, she never hid
it, and every one knew her wife had died. But Sophia was
now an intern and she was her superior, they couldn't do
anything together ever again. It was against the rules and
she could be in trouble for it. Her career could be placed
on the line, her reputation. She could be accused of
favoritism, of taking advantage of an intern. There was too
much risk with it and as a result their time together would
have to come to an end. And that hurt a lot more than
Katherine wanted to admit at the moment. What her and
Sophia had was just fun, but that was the point, it was fun.
For the first time in so many years she was finally having
fun again. Sophia had woken up a beast inside of her and
it was now craving Sophia every second of the day. She
felt so alive again. She had no idea how she was going to
focus on doing her job and teaching her. Every fibre of her
being just wanted to touch Sophia. To take her there and
then.

Katherine headed down the stairs and headed over to
where the other department heads were. She could tell
the moment Sophia saw her as her eyes went wide with
shock before she quickly recovered it. They would need to
have a conversation about their situation, but that couldn't
happen right now. First they had to get through this
welcoming ceremony and then find out who got which
interns to start with. Afterwards, they would then hopefully be able to get a private moment together so they
could talk and get everything straightened out. Katherine
had no idea how to say it. She was an intern now so she
would understand that Katherine's reputation was on the
line. Katherine was really hoping that Sophia would
understand.

As the welcoming ceremony went on all Sophia could

do was try to not look at Katherine. She had no idea that Katherine was the Dr. Katherine Ross that she had heard so much about from her intern roommates. They were obsessed with her skills and wanted the opportunity to learn from her. Sophia didn't have a specific specialty in mind yet, when it came to surgery. She wanted to get a feel for them first and see which she felt suited her best and felt right to her. She was a firm believer that you didn't pick the speciality, the specialty picked you. The last person she ever expected to see here today was Katherine.

As much as Sophia tried not to watch Katherine, she just couldn't help herself. She watched Katherine's inter-action with the other doctors. Watched how she spoke to them with an air of superiority around her. At first Sophia had found it hard to believe that her Katherine was the Dr. Ross she'd heard so much about, but the more she thought about it the more sense it made. Katherine was brilliant and she had said that her job was very demanding and time consuming. Katherine looked in the general direction of the interns and Sophia turned away quickly. She felt undressed by Katherine's eyes. She felt lust pooling in her. She wanted Katherine's hands on her body.

She knew realistically that it was over. It was very likely that it would be against the rules for doctors and interns to have any kind of intimate relationship. There would be too many complications involved. Sophia shook her head at the unfairness of it all.

The welcoming ceremony ended quickly and some of the interns split into groups talking about what they wanted to specify in. Sophia was still unsure about what she wanted to specify in but she knew that cardio was definitely out of her options. Katherine was head of cardio thoracic. Picking cardio would mean that they would spend a lot of time together and Katherine would have to teach her. Just thinking about working with Katherine and watching her hands on a scalpel, on a human heart made shivers run down Sophia's back as scenes of them in bed together flashed through her mind. Sophia felt wetness between her legs.

"Do you think Dr. Ross is a nice person? She looks kind of scary to me."

The whisperings of two of the interns caught Sophia's attention. She'd noticed them at the beginning of the ceremony, giggling together. They were probably friends from Medical School or roommates.

"She looks very strict. And very hard to please." The second one said after watching Katherine for a minute. Sophia thought about pleasing Katherine with her mouth. With her body. She wanted so badly to please Katherine.

"I heard that she's a lesbian" the first one said, her voice even lower than before, as though she was revealing a dirty secret.

Sophia heard the second one chuckle

"That explains why she's so uptight. I guess she had to work hard since she couldn't fuck her way to the top."

Sophia looked at the two of them in disgust. She couldn't believe they'd talk like that about a person they didn't even know. She fought off the urge to confront them and turned to look for her roommates instead. They'd come to the hospital together but they'd been separated before the ceremony began. She hadn't seen them since it ended.

"Sophia." Sophia turned to look and she saw her roommate Sara.

"Sara, hi." Sara pulled Sophia into a quick hug

"I've been looking for you everywhere"

Before Sophia could speak Sara continued.

"Did you see Dr. Ross? She's so confident and beautiful and oh my God, she was talking to Dr. Davis and she didn't even look flustered. I've heard she bats for the other team but still, she could've had some type of reaction."

Sophia listened to Sara's rant with a small smile on her face. Sara had been so excited to come to the hospital today that she'd barely slept and the happiness on her face made Sophia happy. The hospital was probably everything Sara had been expecting and more.

Dr. Davis and Dr. Ross were Sara's role models. They were both cardio thoracic surgeons and Sara had been so excited to work with them since she got accepted as an intern at the hospital.

"Yeah, she's very beautiful and he's very handsome. I'm sure she's used to seeing him since they've worked together for so long." Sophia said, her heart beat faster as she looked at Katherine. Sara nodded her head.

"Yeah, you're right. That's probably why she didn't react the way I would've."

"Have you seen Jenna?" Sophia asked

"No. She's probably talking to some of the other interns and getting to know people. I'll call her when we're ready to leave so we can all go home together."

Sophia nodded and turned her attention back to Katherine. She tried not to look but she just couldn't help it.

She couldn't stop picturing Katherine on top of her. Pinning her down. Fucking her. Looking at her intently with those hard grey eyes. Katherine caught her eyes and she could tell they were thinking of the same thing. She sighed. This was bad. They were already too attracted to each other. There was no other option than to end their relationship now before this attraction got both of them in trouble.

Katherine watched Sophia walk out of the hospital with her little intern friends in tow. They were laughing about something and Sophia was watching them with a small smile on her face.

She watched Sophia's slender body sway as she walked and she couldn't help but remember how that body had felt. How it had looked splayed out in front of her. How Sophia sounded when she came. This was bad. Of all the hospitals in the country why did Sophia have to be an intern in this one? Their relationship that had barely started had to come to an end.

Sighing, Katherine dialled Sophia's number. She picked up on the second ring.

"Hello," her voice was calm and devoid of emotion. Katherine guessed that she'd already figured out that they couldn't continue their relationship.

"Sophia. Hi. Do you think we could meet at the coffee shop close to the hospital?"

"Sure. But I think we both know why you want to meet." She'd guessed right. Katherine was glad that they were on the same page. Maybe they could still remain casual friends.

"I think it's rude to end a relationship over the phone. I'd rather do it in person"

Sophia chuckled and Katherine's stomach did a slow back flip. Should they just end it over the phone? They were both on the same page already. Did they really have to meet up? Yes, they did because as much as she didn't want to admit it Katherine wanted to see her again. Not as

an intern but as the woman that had made her feel alive
again.

"I guess you're right. I'll see you soon."

The call disconnected. Katherine took a deep breath
and got ready to leave the hospital.

Katherine was already sitting at a table when Sophia
walked in. There were two coffees on the table. Katherine
had presumptuously ordered for her. She liked it. Sophia
could see that Katherine was twiddling her thumbs. Was
she nervous?

"Did you order for me or were you just really thirsty?"
Sophia said as she got to the table.

Katherine shot her a smile and nudged the cup
towards her.

"I guessed you were a flat white girl."

Sophia returned her smile and sat down. She took a
sip of her coffee before she spoke.

"You guessed right. So you are actually Dr. Katherine
Ross?" she said.

"I'm sorry. I should've told you about my profession or
I should've at least told you my last name."

Sophia shook her head.

"It's fine. There's no way we could have known this
would happen. I didn't tell you about my job either."

"Well, that's true."

Katherine hadn't thought it would be this hard to end
what they had together. They weren't even in an official
relationship so she couldn't call it a break up but it was
hard to bring up that part of the conversation. Both of
them knew that was the point of their meet up but they
were both reluctant to bring it up.

There was a lull in the conversation and they met each
other's eyes.

Sophia's gaze was heated and Katherine knew some of that heat started to show in her eyes too. They were supposed to be ending things but all she wanted to do was kiss Sophia. To take her, right here in the cafe.

"It's a shame that this has to come to an end so soon." Sophia said, and Katherine nodded in agreement as she took another sip of her coffee. It was a damn shame.

4

———

"Are you going to meet up with someone else from the app?" Aimee asked from her spot on Katherine's couch.

It'd been over a week since she met Sophia to end it in the coffee shop. It had got easier to see each other at work. They rarely spoke to each other but they acknowledged each other with a nod or a smile sometimes. Some days were better than others. She watched her sometimes. From a distance. On some days it was all Katherine could do not to pull Sophia into an empty room and have her.

She was surprised that she was still so attracted to her and affected by her. It'd been so long since she'd been interested in anybody, yet, here was Sophia, like nobody else on earth.

"I don't know about that. I haven't been attracted to anybody. Nobody really compares to her." Katherine told Aimee swirling the wine in her glass.

"So there's nobody that interests you at all?" Aimee asked.

"There's no one Aimee. If there was I would definitely tell you"

Aimee sighed and flopped on her back.

"I just want you to be happy."

Katherine understood why Aimee was so eager for Katherine to start dating again. Ever since she'd lost Melissa she had lost a part of herself that she knew she wouldn't ever get back. She knew she wasn't the same as before and she understood that it made Aimee worry. However, she couldn't force herself to feel what she didn't.

"I'm alright, Aimee. Don't worry too much about me."

Aimee nodded her head and let the conversation end but Katherine knew they'd revisit this topic the next time they spoke.

"I NEED GOOD COFFEE, or I'll collapse and die," Jenna said dropping herself into a chair in the cafeteria.

"There's coffee right there." Sophia said pointing her head in the direction of the pot of coffee that was brewing.

The look Jenna shot her made her chuckle. The coffee in the hospital was terrible. Jenna and Sara had said that it tasted like dirt and despair.

"Just go to the coffee shop. It's your lunch break anyway. I'm sure if you hurry no one will notice you're gone."

Jenna groaned. "I can't go. Dr. Davis has me doing scut work for three nurses as punishment for coming in late this morning."

Sophia understood Jenna's frustration. It was bad enough doing scut work for one person not to mention three.

Scut work was basically all the work that no one else liked to do. It was all the menial, unfinished tasks that the professionals left for the medical students. Things like drawing stat labs, delivering reports, running errands and putting in orders for the nurses.

"Why were you late? You were awake when Sara and I left."

Jenna shot her a sheepish smile.

"I stopped for a coffee run on my way here. There was a long line but I didn't leave."

Sophia shook her head and Jenna thudded her head on the table.

"Jenna, I need you on the third floor."

It was a nurse Sophia didn't recognise. She was pretty. Sophia could tell she was older than them and that she was tired. She had dark circles around her eyes. She looked like she was one yawn away from falling asleep.

"I'll be right there, Claire."

Jenna shot Sophia a pleading look and Sophia sighed.

"Alright, I'll go get coffee. You guys look like you really need it."

Claire smiled at her and the skin beside her eyes crinkled.

Sophia walked out of the cafeteria with them and they split up.

The walk to the coffee shop was short. Sophia opened the door and the little bell at the top of the door jingled. The smell of freshly ground coffee and milk surrounded her. Thankfully, there weren't many people in line. She would be back at the hospital in ten minutes at the most.

She joined the queue and pulled out her phone to keep herself occupied. She scrolled through the applications on her phone trying to decide between playing a game and replying her texts. Her phone dinged then with a notification from the dating app. She had a new match. She hadn't checked the app in weeks. Not since she and Katherine ended things.

She touched the notification and the loading page popped up on her screen. For some reason, she was hesitant to check who she had matched with.

If she had to guess, she'd say it was probably because she wasn't ready for another relationship. Purely sexual or otherwise. She barely had time for herself and she didn't need the added burden a relationship would bring. She didn't think she would find someone again who would bring the fire to body her like Katherine had.

But she checked the match anyway. She had been matched with Andrea, 32. A pretty thirty two year old banker with hazel eyes and long, wavy brunette hair. She had written on her profile that she wasn't looking for anything serious and that she enjoys reading and watching the sun set.

A banker would definitely understand how busy she was so she wouldn't be too demanding and she wasn't looking for anything serious. She was beautiful and closer to Sophia in age. She was a good fit for Sophia, but still she hesitated.

Her finger hovered over the message icon. To text her or not?

The lady she had been standing behind left the line, a cup of freshly brewed coffee in her hand. Sophia was next. She put her phone away and focused on placing her order. She had to be out of here in five minutes. She would debate texting Andrea later.

"Sophia. Hi." Sophia looked up and there was Katherine. Honeyed hair perfect, grey eyes glinting dangerously.

Sophia was used to seeing her in the hospital but they rarely spoke and were never alone together. She was just getting used to that, yet here was Katherine, smiling at her, a bright look in her eye. Sophia wasn't sure what it was about, this woman that commanded all of her attention. Sophia returned her smile.

"How are you?" Sophia asked.

"I'm alright. Just on a quick coffee break. I just got out of surgery. As you know, I can't drink that awful coffee at the hospital."

Sophia wanted to ask why she seemed so excited. She wanted to know what had caused the bright look in Katherine's eyes. She wanted to buy Katherine a coffee, listen to her talk and then go home with her and take all of her clothes off. But she couldn't do any of that.

"That's great. I can tell it went well. I'd love to stay and catch up, but I have to go. My lunch break is almost over."

Katherine nodded her head in understanding. "We'll catch up some other time then."

Sophia shot her one last smile and left. The thought of texting Andrea already forgotten.

On most days, Katherine didn't pay much attention to her phone. Ever since Melissa died, she didn't have much use for it. She had social media but rarely used it or interacted with anyone. She didn't play games or take pictures. Her phone was mostly for calls and text messages. And yet, here she was, sitting alone on her bed, staring at her mobile phone.

She hadn't been able to stop thinking about Sophia since they ran into each other at the coffee shop. The interns would be cleared to leave work in an hour or two. She could invite Sophia to her house. Not even to have sex, but just to talk. Katherine knew that that wasn't the nature of their relationship. They hadn't agreed to be friends after they'd ended things. They barely even spoke to each other. They had agreed to be friends with benefits but while their deal lasted it had been more of benefits than the actual friendship. But now that deal was off so maybe they could come to another agreement?

Earlier today Katherine had wanted to sit down with Sophia, have a cup or two of coffee and talk to her. She had been so happy earlier because she had successfully completed an aortic dissection repair on an eighteen year old girl. The girl had had multiple heart problems since birth. But this one could easily have killed her. And after six hours, give or take a couple of minutes, they'd completed the surgery and it had been successful. Just the thought brought a smile to Katherine's lips.

If Melissa were still alive, they'd celebrate. First with a dinner date at their favourite restaurant, then they'd come home with a bottle of red wine. Then they would fuck. A good surgery high always made Katherine want sex. It used to, and now Sophia had awoken it in her again.

Katherine's smile was bittersweet now. What was she doing? She couldn't actually be just friends with Sophia and she knew that. They were too attracted to each other. It wouldn't work. She threw her phone so it landed on the right side of the bed. Loneliness was clouding her judgement. She rubbed her eyes with her hands and lay down. It was a little early for her to sleep but if she stayed awake she might cave and text Sophia, and besides, she needed the rest.

Her doorbell was ringing. The consistent sound of it

roused her from her sleep. Confused, Katherine searched for her phone under the blankets. When she found it she checked the time. It was a little after midnight. Who was at her door? She knew it wasn't Aimee. Aimee would've called beforehand.

She flung the duvet off and walked out of her room, into the hallway, down the stairs and to the door.

She was still half asleep but she remembered to check the peephole. She didn't have lights on the porch so she had to rely on the lighting from the moon. She squinted trying to see the face of the person standing outside her door. Just then the person looked in her direction. Sophia? That woke her up fast. Sophia was at her door.

She unlocked the door and pulled it open.

"What are you doing here? It's past midnight."

At first Katherine assumed something was wrong but Sophia didn't look like something has happened to her. She had a wanting look in her eye that sent delicious shivers down Katherine's spine.

5

Katherine was going to ask why Sophia was at her doorstep again but she couldn't because Sophia was kissing her. Her thoughts faded away, pushed to a faraway place in her mind that she couldn't access.

They stumbled further into the house and she swung the door shut.

Sophia tangled her fingers in Katherine's hair and she moaned into their kiss. She knew they shouldn't be doing this but she couldn't bring herself to stop. She didn't realise till she had Sophia in her arms again just how much she had yearned to touch her again.

"Please. I want you. I need you." Sophia gasped breathily.

Katherine's hands were exploring Sophia's body under her top. She trailed her fingers up and down her slender back, tangled them in her hair and teased her nipples with her thumbs. Sophia moaned into the kiss pulling herself even closer to Katherine.

Sophia broke the kiss and trailed her tongue down

Katherine's neck. Sucking lightly on the skin just above her collarbone. Katherine couldn't stop the moan that slipped from her lips. Sophia held Katherine against the wall and continued to nip and suck the skin on her neck while pushing the straps of her flimsy nightgown down over her shoulders.

When Katherine's breasts were bare Sophia went straight to her nipples and sucked them one by one into her mouth. Katherine's reaction was instinctive. She moaned her approval and her eyes slid shut. She was still half asleep and happy to be in this dream world. Her fingers found Sophia's hair and she pulled it eliciting a moan from Sophia's lips.

Sophia kissed her. Her mouth, her neck, her shoulders, her breasts. Sophia fell to her knees and kissed her stomach, the curve of her hips.

Katherine had missed this. The feeling of being so desired.

"I want you so much." Sophia's face was to her pubic mound. The thin silk of her nightdress was the only thing between Sophia's mouth and her burning core. She breathed the words through the silk. The words sent vibrations running right through her body.

"We shouldn't be doing this" Katherine breathed back. Even as she said it, she knew nothing could stop them from being together tonight.

"So, stop me then. Safe word." Sophia said as she pushed the silk nightdress up around her hips.

They were still in the hallway. The tiles were cold under Sophia's knees. She didn't care.

Sophia put her mouth to Katherine's sex. Licking, lapping, sucking. Worshipping at her alter. The moan that escaped Katherine's lips was gratifying.

It was what Sophia had been wanting to hear when she had decided to pay Katherine a visit. During the drive she'd considered the possibility that Katherine would turn her away. That the attraction she was feeling was one sided. But judging by the wetness coating her mouth that clearly wasn't the case.

"You're overdressed" Katherine said and Sophia smirked a little before pulling her shirt over her head leaving her half naked as she hadn't bothered to wear a bra.

With Katherine's help she pulled off her jeans and threw them to the side.

Katherine leaned against the end the couch and Sophia knelt before her. Katherine's thighs parted on their own accord.

"Show me with your pretty mouth, exactly how much you want me." Sophia felt electricity run through her with Katherine's request. Demand. Request. Either way she was desperate to pleasure her.

Sophia ran her mouth up the inside of Katherine's thigh. Slightly teasing her with her tongue and teeth as she licked and nipped the skin. She had planned to tease her some more but the smell of her arousal made Sophia impatient. The smell of Katherine's wetness was intoxicating her leaving her heady with lust. Unable to resist, she darted out her tongue and lapped again at Katherine's wetness. The taste on her tongue was made sweeter by Katherine's moans and groans of approval.

"Fuck." Katherine growled as she grabbed Sophia's head and pulled it closer.

Sophia made her tongue work faster. Licking. Sucking. Wanting. Needing..

Katherine's hips thrust forwards as she held her head

so she could grind into Sophia's face. It was at times like these that Sophia found it hard to believe this woman who was filled with so much passion was the same stoic surgeon who rarely smiled real smiles or spoke to anybody.

Katherine's breathing quickened and her hands held on tightly to Sophia's hair. Loud moans left her lips as she orgasmed, coating Sophia's face with her release.

Sophia straddled Katherine and kissed her, letting her taste her own arousal. Katherine moaned and her eyes slid shut.

"Wow," said Katherine. "I think I need a drink. Will you join me?" She lifted Sophia from her and stood up, naked and on slightly wobbly legs and headed to a wine rack. She chose a Rioja and passed it to Sophia. "There is a bottle opener and glasses in the kitchen. Would you?"

Sophia returned shortly with two glasses of red. She only had her panties on. Her pert little breasts were alert in the air. Katherine was lounging, naked, on the sofa with her eyes closed. So beautiful in repose, Sophia thought. She wished she could photograph her exactly like that. Katherine sat up as she heard Sophia.

"A lovely Rioja, Dr. Ross. Can I get you anything else?" Sophia served the wine to her as though she was working in a classy cocktail bar. Aside from the fact she was in a state of undress.

Katherine smiled at this amazing girl before her. She couldn't quite believe what was happening. "Why, thank you, Ms Sophia. Please take a seat and enjoy your wine with me."

Sophia sat next to her and took the wine glass. There was a fruity acidity to it as she put it to her lips.

"I had a distal aortic dissection repair today on an 18 year old girl. It was the worst tear I have seen."

"God, did she survive?" Sophia knew the girl's chance of survival wasn't good.

"Yes! I did a beautiful repair. I wish you had seen it. She had lost a lot of blood. She nearly died in the ambulance. Then again, we nearly lost her as soon as I got her on the table. But I controlled it. I got her back. I did the perfect surgery. It was beautiful. You would have loved it." Katherine's eyes lit up as she spoke about her brilliance. Surgery was the love of her life. Surgery was what she lived for. The power of holding a human heart in your hands. Being god. Being the difference between life and death. Sophia wanted that for herself. She would be an exceptional surgeon like Katherine one day.

"Wow. I wish I had been there. I can't wait to get on my cardio rotation and learn from you. She was lucky to have you today. To have your hands working on her. The girl. A lesser surgeon and she would have died. Now she has her whole life ahead of her." Katherine watched Sophia's adoration and it made her feel warm.

"Yes. There will be some recovery. And she may not be without further issue as she gets older. But for now, she is alive. She has every chance."

"What is it like? Honestly? To be that powerful. To literally hold life in your hands." Sophia was a curious student and Katherine loved to teach.

"It is incredible, Sophia. It is a rush like nothing else. An honour. To be able to save a life is an honour."

"What is it like when you don't save them? When you try everything, but they just don't survive?"

"It is the deepest pain that there is. Some deaths affect

me more than others, but I am always aware that as long as I hold life in my hands, I also hold death."

"What do you do with the pain?"

"Oh, Sophia." Katherine smiled wryly. "I push it into the darkness and I work harder. I become a better surgeon. I work to increase my survival rates and save more people."

Sophia sipped her wine thoughtfully.

"I want to be like you. One day."

"Oh Sophia, you only think that you do. Where's the use in being like me? I save people, yes. And then I come home, alone to my big house. I can't even get a dog because I work too much. There is an emptiness in being me."

Katherine looked thoughtful for a moment.

"But, if you want to be a great surgeon, work hard and learn. Then go back and work harder. You are smart, Sophia. I see that. Take the opportunities presented to you. There are some great surgeons for you to learn from at Forest Vale."

"I will. I promise, I will. I want to be the best. I am the hardest worker." Sophia's face lit up.

Katherine looked to her. She wanted her. She reached her hand across to her. She ran her hand up Sophia's thigh, to her waist, pulling her in.

She leaned in to her. She kissed her deeply using her hand to pull Sophia's head closer.

Katherine trailed her fingers down Sophia's body stopping between her legs. She ran her fingers under the red lace of Sophia's panties and through her slickness, enjoying the way Sophia's moans slid into her mouth.

The smell of arousal permeated the room. Katherine felt intoxicated by it. Intoxicated by her. Katherine slightly teased the sensitive flesh between Sophia's thighs, trailing her fingers through Sophia's folds before she thrust her fingers into her.

"Fuck. Katherine. Fuck me. Please. I need it, so badly." Sophia moaned, she threw her head back and flexed her hips, leaning back on the arm of the sofa. Katherine slid in another finger. Sophia's was dripping down her fingers. The faster she thrust, the wetter Sophia became.

Without withdrawing her fingers she rearranged their positions so Sophia was lying on the couch beneath her.

She kept thrusting her fingers into her. Sophia's hips jerked and her legs flailed like she was trying to move away and move closer at the same time. Katherine's left hand pinned Sophia's shoulder down, leaving marks, as she fucked her. Hard. She bit Sophia's shoulder and Sophia cried.

Katherine felt her clit pulse under her thumb and knew Sophia was about to climax under her. As Sophia's body tried to writhe, it was pinned by Katherine's weight. The power Katherine had over her in every way, just made it more and more heady for Sophia.

When Sophia orgasmed, she was breathless. Katherine's name coming from deep within her. Her hips jerked as she wanted more and less at the same time. Her body overrun with the pleasure that Katherine had given her.

They were both breathing heavily. None sure what to say to the other. Katherine couldn't muster the strength to speak. She was spent. She eased her fingers out of Sophia. All she wanted to do was sleep. It seemed like Sophia shared the same sentiment because soon enough, her breathing evened out and her eyes drifted shut. She had fallen asleep and left Katherine alone with her thoughts. Katherine cleaned her up and covered her with a blanket before going upstairs to take a shower. The water ran down her body, washing away the evidence of her sin. She could see red marks on her skin where Sophia had sucked at her in the fogged up glass of her shower. She wasn't sure what tonight had meant to Sophia, but for her it had been powerful. The attraction between them was not one that could be dismissed easily, so she understood why Sophia had sought her out, but their situation remained the same. They couldn't be together. Katherine couldn't let her attraction to Sophia jeopardise her profession. She'd worked too hard to achieve everything she had. She wouldn't let her lust and loneliness cloud her judgement to the point where she tarnished the image of professionalism she'd made for herself. She turned off the water and stepped out of the shower. The chill of her towel contrasted with the heat of her body as she wrapped it around herself. She knew she still wasn't ready for anything serious. She probably never would be. But, what about Sophia? Was she still on that same page?

6

T hree loud consecutive beeps broke through the silence and Katherine dashed out of the bathroom to grab her phone. She had set her phone to beep three times whenever she got a call from the hospital.

"Hello, Dr Ross? There's an emergency. There's a trauma patient who is showing signs of flail chest. We're doing all we can to keep him stable but he can barely breathe. We need you."

Katherine didn't like operating on trauma patients. It reminded her too much of the night she'd lost Melissa. The ER. The bleeding. The distraught relatives. Even now, she still wished she had had the chance to do that surgery. She might have saved Melissa. Being powerless had been the hardest part of losing her. She shook away the thoughts of guilt and focused on the situation at hand. She may not like it but she had to save him. It was her duty as a doctor.

"Apply pressure on the flail segment. Make sure you hold the flail segment in place. That'll reduce the chances of it damaging his vital organs. Prep for surgery. I'll be there as soon as I can."

She cut the call and pulled on her clothes as fast as she could. She had to hurry. She grabbed her phone, wallet and keys and ran down the stairs. She stopped short when she saw Sophia's sleeping form on her couch.

She searched inside her bag for a sticky note and a pen. She placed the sticky note on the nearest wall for support and wrote a quick note. She placed it on the arm of the couch so Sophia wouldn't miss it and then she hastily left the house. It was a little after 3am so there weren't a lot of people on the road. She pushed her accelerator as low as it could go. She'd be at the hospital soon

SOPHIA WASN'T sure what she had been expecting to happen when she'd made the drive to Katherine's house. All she knew was that she wanted her and she didn't want to end things before they'd even gotten a chance to be together. She'd pictured a night of passionate sex and a conversation afterward while they were laying down down together spent from the sex they'd had where they would both agree that they had something too good to just give up. Sure, that was a little too optimistic considering the fact that Katherine had made it clear what their 'arrangement' was.

But what Sophia hadn't been expecting was to wake up naked and alone with a sticky note stuck beside her head. Katherine had clearly scribbled the words in a hurry. She hadn't even bothered to completely spell her words. Sophia had thought that she'd left the house to avoid having to deal with her in the morning until she read the note.

The words Katherine had scribbled floated around in her head "Got to go. There's a trauma surgery. Last night was amazing, but I'm sure you understand that it can't happen again. Help yourself to whatever you want, then let yourself out."

Sophia imagined her saying the words in the same detached way doctor's broke the news that a patient was dead and it hurt her. It hurt a lot. She liked Katherine. It hadn't been in her plans to consider a romantic relationship with anybody and yet here she was falling for the beautiful, brilliant doctor who wanted nothing to do with her.

"Sophia, you're with cosmetic surgery this week." Sophia turned her head towards Maya, her brows furrowed.

"I was there last week. According to the rotation I'm supposed to be with neurology"

They had a rotation system at the hospital for the surgical interns. As interns, they weren't allowed to choose their specialties yet. They were supposed to move from one department to the other so they'd devised a weekly rotation system that allowed them to work in all the departments. This week Sophia was supposed to work in the neurology department. She'd been looking forward to learning from Dr. Carter.

"Well apparently, you impressed Dr. Mitchell. She asked for you specifically"

That eased Sophia's frown. Dr. Mitchell was a petite woman with a bright smile and an even brighter mind. Last week she'd given the Sophia and the other interns are series of tests to test their ability to think on their feet. She'd taken simple questions and twisted them, adding her own situations and conditions. The questions were easy enough to understand and answer, if thought about in a simple way. But a large number of people had thought about the questions too much, thereby complicating the test even further for themselves. Not surprisingly, a lot of people had failed. But Sophia and a few others hadn't and she'd praised them for it, gifting them all apples to celebrate their success. Sophia guessed that Dr. Mitchell had personally requested for all the people who'd passed to join her today.

Sophia thanked Maya and headed for the cosmetic surgery department.

"Can you do it?"

Sophia was sure the look on her face was the same as everybody else's. Dr. Mitchell wanted them to assist her in a full body lift surgery. This would be her first ever surgery. And it was a procedure as difficult and risky as this. Her heart beat sped up.

"You're all very promising interns. There's no need to be scared. I'll be there every step of the way. All you have to do is help me." Dr. Mitchell said.

No one said anything and she sighed.

"There's also the option of leaving my office right now and revoking your internship so people who are actually serious about saving lives and helping others can take your place. I realise that I made the mistake of letting you think you had a choice in this matter. You're doing it. All of you. You are scrubbing in with me. So you better put on your big boy and big girl pants." Dr. Mitchell looked seriously annoyed.

"Yes, yes, I'm in." Sophia was keen. The others followed suit.

Sophia didn't understand what the woman had expected. That because they'd passed her test, they'd jump at the chance of operating on a real person after only a couple of weeks as interns?

Dr. Mitchell walked out of her office and Sophia guessed she was going to prep for surgery and she expected them to follow her.

Okay. Okay. Sophia could totally do this. She recalled Dr. Mitchell's explanation of the procedure and recited it to calm herself.

To lift the lower body, all they had to do was make incisions similar to a bikini pattern to tighten the abdomen. Sophia knew that they may have to make use of liposuction in order to achieve the desired outcome. Deep sutures and skin tapes or clips would be used to close the skin incisions. When it was broken down that way it didn't seem so scary. Sophia made herself calm down then she went about prepping herself for surgery.

After she scrubbed in, she couldn't help but pause before she entered the O.R. She wasn't a religious person at all, but she said a prayer to steel herself and then she walked in as though the O.R. was where she was born to be.

"Congratulations on your first ever surgery!" Sara screamed from the phone. She smiled wildly and stuck the camera close to her face.

Sophia couldn't help but think that she had got lucky in the roommate department. She'd responded to an ad that they'd put on social media. She'd been desperate for an apartment and their offer had been perfect for her. They each had their own room and they all contributed to the rent and other bills. The best part was that they were all surgical interns so they got each other.

Sophia liked the fact that neither of them were overly dirty or overly crazy. They had no significant drama or baggage. They just wanted to be surgeons. She'd heard stories about people having crazy roommates so she'd been hesitant to move in with strangers, but thankfully everything worked out.

Sara and Jenna had known each other since their high school days. They'd been best friends for years. They had been through medical school together. Sometimes Sophia joked that they'd probably get pregnant at the exact same time, so their kids could be born on the same day.

Sophia laughed at Sara's antics and raised her glass of wine so Sara could see it. They were in Sophia's bedroom, celebrating her first ever successful surgery with a bottle of fine white wine. She hadn't been the one in charge but she had definitely done her first cutting on a live person, and that in itself, was worth a celebration.

"Thank you. I really wish you were here so you could celebrate with me."

Sara was at the hospital working a night shift. Sophia didn't understand how she could stay so energetic.

"I'll drink a glass of wine when I get home on your behalf." Sara said and Sophia smiled at her.

Jenna leaned on Sophia's shoulder and clinked her glass with hers.

"Now spill. Did Travis really vomit after you guys were done?"

Sophia chuckled a bit at that. Travis had walked out of the operating room looking green and unsteady but instead of bending over and vomiting like she had expected him to he'd leaned against the wall and got himself under control.

"No. He did look a bit green but he kept the contents of his stomach to himself."

They talked for ages. Sophia gave them details of the surgery. She told them how Dr. Mitchell had had her make the first incision. Her hands were shaking so badly, then she'd recited the procedure in her head and steeled herself. It hadn't been easy but she'd done it. And she had been worried that the patient's anesthesia would wear off and she'd wake up and start screaming in pain. First surgeries were nerve wracking. Sophia wasn't sure how she'd handle her first solo surgery when the day finally came.

Jenna talked about her first surgery too. She told them how she'd been so scared the patient would stop breathing that she kept monitoring the vitals like some kind of maniac.

Sara was nervous for her first surgery. She didn't say it in so many words but Sophia knew that Sara felt like she'd mess up her first surgery. Sophia made a mental note to talk to her about it later.

"I have to go. The others are probably wondering where I am by now."

"Alright then. I'll have one more glass of wine for you" Jenna said with a wink. Sara laughed and waved goodbye before disconnecting the call.

"One more glass then we'll go to bed okay?" Jenna asked and Sophia nodded her head in agreement.

They refilled their glasses, saluted each other and then downed the drinks. They'd had enough wine for the night. Anymore and they'd both have hangovers at work the next day.

Sophia flopped on her bed and Jenna left the room with a goodnight thrown over her shoulder.

Sophia snuggled under the covers and it didn't take long before her eyelids started to droop. All the thoughts of surgeries and wine silenced as she drifted off into a peaceful sleep.

7

Katherine had known this would happen eventually. She knew that the interns had some sort of rotation system so they could learn from all the different departments. She'd known that eventually she would have to teach Sophia. Katherine knew she could be professional about it but she wasn't sure Sophia could. Ever since that night at her house Katherine was sure Sophia had been avoiding her on purpose. They never ran into each other anymore and on the off chance that they did, Sophia didn't acknowledge her, she simply looked away. It was hard, but Katherine understood that she was hurting. But now, they would have no choice but to work together, she was curious as to how Sophia would behave or react. They were going to spend the whole week together and Katherine would do her job regardless of the issues between her and Sophia.

But at the same time Katherine understood Sophia's standoffishness. She would be unfriendly too if she'd been treated in such a way. Katherine had felt bad about it at first. It didn't sit right with her that she'd left nothing but that rude note. She hadn't even apologised. She knew she'd hurt Sophia but it was for the good of them both. Sophia now wanted nothing to do with her.

A knock sounded on her door, pulling her from her thoughts.

"We're all here, ma'am," the intern said, she could tell he was a little nervous by the slight break in his voice and Katherine smiled a bit. The interns had convinced themselves that she was strict and mean, so they were a little scared of her. She didn't mind it though. If they felt that way then there was no way they'd disrespect her or act nonchalant in her presence. She pulled herself up from her chair and adjusted her clothing. She'd instructed the interns to wait outside till they were all present and now they were. That meant that she was about to see Sophia again.

How would Sophia handle things this week? Was she capable of being professional, or would she let her emotions control her?

Katherine sighed in reply to her questions. She didn't know Sophia well enough to guess how she would behave. There was only one way to find out, and it was to face the situation head on.

"Alright. You can all come in."

She walked to the front of her desk and sat on it as the interns filed in. There were six of them in total and Katherine noticed that Sophia had been the last to walk in. Her head had been dipped, but Katherine caught sight of the frown that marred her lovely face.

"Good morning. I'm Dr. Katherine Ross, although I'm sure you already know that." Her voice didn't hold any particular emotion. She was watching Sophia to see how she would react.

"We'll be working together for quite a while so I feel it's appropriate for me to tell you my rules."

She felt unease spread through the room. She could practically hear them whispering it to each other *the rumours were true. She is strict!* Sophia's head shot up at that. Katherine guessed that she was used to responding to her.

"I have just two rules. They're not difficult to follow. The first is that I require obedience. Do whatever I tell you to, and we shouldn't have a problem. The second is more of an expectation than a rule. I expect you to be diligent and hard-working. I do not appreciate people who are lazy or nonchalant. If you're working with me, then I expect nothing but your best and then some. Do you understand?"

A chorus of replies ranging from *yes* to *yes ma'am* echoed in her office and Katherine nodded her head in satisfaction.

"I've been paying attention to your performance in other departments and I have noticed one thing that you all have in common."

There was an uncomfortable pause like everyone was trying to guess what they had in common with the person they were standing next to. Sophia tried to look unbothered but Katherine could see her tension in the stiff way she stood.

"You're not pushing yourselves."

The confusion was easy to see. They were all wondering what she meant. Even Sophia didn't try to hide her confusion. Her brows were furrowed and her lips were flat.

"In the departments you all do scut work and assist in surgeries when you're needed. You do what you're ordered to, which is good. But only to an extent."

Katherine had Sophia's full attention now. Her face was alive again. It was something Katherine decided she liked about Sophia. Regardless of their personal involvement Sophia didn't mind learning from her. She wanted to listen and improve.

"When I was an intern, I used to spend most of my free time in the ER. The pit." Katherine couldn't help the passion that slipped into her voice. She could tell she'd got their interest.

"Whenever there was an emergency we'd rush down and offer to assist in any surgery. We were determined and knew what we wanted. But you," she made sure she met each of their eyes letting them know she was talking to them directly, before she continued, "you shy away from surgeries because you're scared or you're not confident in your abilities. And it's pathetic."

She knew there was even more tension in the room now. They were probably offended. But she couldn't bring herself to care.

"You all plan to be surgeons someday. One day you're going to be the only thing standing between a patient, and death. You are going to hold life and death in your hands. What are you going to do then, if you are too scared to assist in a surgery now?"

They knew she wasn't wrong. The embarrassed looks on their faces said it all.

"You came here to learn, but most of you seem satisfied with the scut work being given to you. If I'd been satisfied with the scut work I was given I probably wouldn't be here today. So what I need you to do is, seize every opportunity to improve your skills and prove to

yourself and everybody else that you're capable. Get yourself in an O.R. whenever and however you can. Okay?"

Replies were chorused and Katherine nodded her
head and stood up.

"Well then. Since we're all in agreement. We should
get to work."

SOPHIA HAD ACTUALLY LET herself believe that the attraction she felt to Katherine was fading away. But she'd been
wrong. So very wrong. She'd avoided seeing her for a
couple of weeks, telling herself that the less she saw her,
the quicker the attraction would fade. And yet, as soon as
their eyes met, Sophia had felt fireworks going off in her
stomach all over again.

She'd locked eyes with her and all those emotions
started coming back. Memories from the nights they'd
spent together had played in her brain like a slideshow.
She remembered their conversations from when they
matched on the dating app. Katherine had been so polite
and unemotional at first, then she'd eased into the conversation, into light chatter with Sophia. Sophia remembered
how shocked she'd been when Katherine had made a
joke.

She found it hard to believe that the woman she knew
was the same as this one. This unemotional professional
surgeon. The only time Sophia had heard something that
could be passion in her tone of voice was when she was
telling them about the pit and her days as an intern.

As she was talking, Sophia had imagined them talking
about it further over dinner. She could see those days had
meant so much to Katherine. It wouldn't hurt to hear her

talk about it. She might even learn a thing or two. As quickly as the thought came she had banished it. Katherine had already made it clear that their relationship was to be strictly professional. And to be honest, Sophia was still upset about the note Katherine had left her.

She wouldn't be able to bear it if she invited her to dinner and she got shot down like that again. And besides, Katherine had probably already moved on from her. Katherine didn't even seem to be affected by her presence today like she used to be. She didn't notice Katherine's eyes roaming her body, like she used to. While she had been warring with all her emotions and thoughts, Katherine had been stoic. Or was she just that good at masking her emotions? Sophia couldn't tell. She didn't know her well enough to guess that. It really was an unfortunate turn of events that she was interning at the same hospital Katherine worked at. She would have loved to see how their relationship would have worked in another situation. Would they have kept to their 'arrangement'? Would their relationship have grown into something more on its own?

Her questions, of course, remained unanswered and she sighed. There was no point in dwelling over this. She had other things to do, like finishing her pasta before it went cold.

"Sophia, hi." she looked up and her eyes met with Travis's.

He was the intern who'd almost vomited after the surgery last week. She knew he was very intelligent, and he had always been friendly towards her.

"Hi. Travis, right?"

"May I?" he asked gesturing to the seat across from her.

She nodded her head and he sat down. She caught a whiff of his aftershave.

"So um..." He stroked his eyebrow with his finger and chuckled a little. He was clearly nervous and Sophia found it kind of cute.

"I was wondering if you'd like to have coffee with me sometime."

If Sophia was into guys at all, she might have said yes. Travis was handsome, tall and brilliant.

"Travis, I'm not into guys." She could tell she'd surprised him by the confusion on his face.

"Really?" he asked and she nodded her head in reply. Normally she'd have given a sarcastic response but she wasn't feeling up to it.

"I wouldn't mind having coffee with you as friends though." Travis smiled at her

"I'd like that. Dr Mitchell has been singing your praises. I'm betting I could learn a thing or two from you."

Travis was a welcome distraction. He was funny and attentive and he truly was brilliant. They stayed in the cafeteria for ages and they talked about everything from their time in medical school to the high school parties they went to and Sophia was grateful, because not once did she think of Katherine.

8

"Are you going to be my doctor today?"

Sophia was a little startled but she looked up at the little girl and nodded her head. One of the doctors had an emergency and had to leave the hospital. Sophia had offered to monitor her patients till she got back.

She hadn't expected the girl to be awake when she walked in. She'd expected the girl to be asleep like all the other patients she'd checked on earlier.

Hospital rooms all looked the same to Sophia. The white paint. The occasional flowers and cards from well-wishers. The white sheets and the constant smell of anti-septic and medicine.

"I'm Katie."

"I'm Sophia."

"You have a princess name." Katie said and Sophia smiled at her.

"Thank you." She went back to checking her vitals. She had three other patients to do and mercifully they were all in the same ward.

"I fell off my bike." Katie announced suddenly.

"Did you?" Sophia feigned surprise.

She'd read the girl's file. She'd fallen off her bike and bruised her ribs. The fall hadn't been too severe so they hadn't broken but they'd been bruised badly and she'd been in a lot of pain.

"I did. My mom said I fainted."

Sophia laughed at the way she said it like it was an achievement.

"How's the pain?"

"It's gone. It went away while I was asleep."

Sophia nodded and shot the girl another smile.

"I'll be back really soon. Okay?"

"Okay." The girl's eyes widened like she'd just remembered something, then she whispered conspiratorially.

"If you're coming back, will you please bring me chocolate." Sophia pretended to think about it for a minute, then she nodded her head. The toothy smile the girl rewarded her with was blinding.

"That was good." Katherine said and Sophia was startled again. She hadn't noticed her standing there.

"What was?" She asked. It was weird to be having a conversation in the hospital. They rarely spoke to each other now, so why was she doing this?

"The way you spoke to her. Some doctors have a hard time relating with the young patients, because they're so busy or they're thinking of something else. But you handled it well. Don't lose your way with patients as you get more responsibility heaped upon you." Sophia understood Katherine's point but she didn't understand why Katherine thought it was important to talk to her about it. Could it be that she just wanted to have a conversation?

"Thank you. I'll keep it in mind." It irked Sophia that

Katherine didn't look affected by her presence. Or maybe she was just a fool to keep believing that she and Katherine had some kind of magic between them. Even now, she was imagining sneaking off to an empty closet or office so she could see Katherine's real desire for her.

"Something else you need to learn is how to control your facial expressions."

Sophia furrowed her brows at that. She'd never heard of doctors learning to control their facial expressions.

"Really?"

"Yes. You can't make faces when you see things on people's bodies that you're not used to seeing."

That made sense. It would be bad for a doctor to make faces in or out of a patient's presence.

"I understand."

"Good. Now when you're done with the other patients I'd like you to come to my office. I want you to scrub in on my surgery with me."

Sophia was stunned, but she nodded her head keenly and walked away.

She hurried off to check on the other patients on her list so she could scrub in on Katherine's surgery.

Katherine clearly wasn't feeling the same way she was. It was time to move on. Sure Katherine was captivating, beautiful, smart, confident and successful, but there were loads of women like that. She just had to find the right one. She would go through her matches tonight and find a suitable partner for herself. She remembered Andrea the banker. The match she had gotten at the coffee shop that she had never messaged. She would text her tonight. Maybe they would hit it off and Sophia would finally start forgetting about Dr. Katherine Ross.

KATHERINE RECLINED IN HER CHAIR. Her thoughts centred around the surgery she'd just been in with Sophia assisting her. The first couple of hours into the surgery had been the easiest. Everything had been under control. The patient's vitals had been normal. Then, everything had changed. The patient's heartbeat had gone out of control. The patient had started hemorrhaging. Blood had started spilling out of the chest cavity, over the table, over her hands, over the floor. So much blood.

Katherine had had years of experience so she'd stayed calm and thought of the best possible course of action. The interns however were green. They'd been terrified. Katherine could see the question in their eyes. "Is the patient going to die?"

Sophia had looked at her with that determined look in her eye that sent shivers down her spine. There had also been fear in her eyes. Fear that Katherine understood. Katherine had had the insane urge to hold her, till the fear in her eyes disappeared. Even now as she replayed the situation in her head she felt the need to hold her. Katherine found it a bit funny that she'd been worried about Sophia being unprofessional but here she was imagining holding her in her arms.

She couldn't help it. Sophia had surprised her in the O.R. She'd been scared but she'd put behind her fear and focused on her determination to complete the surgery successfully.

"Do you need a chest tube?" Sophia had asked in a calm voice that Katherine had not been expecting. In that moment Sophia had proven to Katherine that she was going to be a great surgeon. She had the temperament for it.

The surgery had been a success. They'd drained the blood and continued the surgery normally. The blood loss had been as severe and they had used a lot of blood to save the patient. Katherine had left the nurses with instructions for the medication of the patient. Everything had turned out alright but Katherine couldn't seem to get the surgery off her mind. She reasoned that there were several reasons why she was thinking of it. Maybe she had forgotten to do something vital and she was subconsciously trying to remember or maybe it was on her mind because she had nothing else to think of. Perhaps it was because of Sophia and fear Katherine had seen in her eyes even after the surgery had ended.

There had been no traces of the fiery determination that Katherine loved to see in her eyes. There was just fear. Katherine had wanted to speak to her. Comfort her. Hold her. But their relationship was professional. Comforting or holding Sophia would have led to them rekindling their relationship and she couldn't allow that happen. She just couldn't.

Katherine was restless. She stood up from her chair and walked around her office. First she walked in circles then in a straight line back and forth. Then she walked to her window. She wasn't sure if she could call it fate or a sign from God but right outside her window, walking out of the hospital, was Sophia.

Her head was bent and her shoulders were hunched. Katherine guessed that she was either going to the coffee shop or taking a walk to clear her head. She was walking slowly, her slender body swaying as she did so.

It was possible that Katherine found everything this woman did attractive. Even walking.

Before Katherine could talk herself out of it she grabbed her phone off the table and called Sophia. She heard the phone ring twice. Sophia stopped walking and fished her phone out of her pocket.

Katherine realised that Sophia could choose not to pick up. She could hang up now and save herself the embarrassment that would follow if Sophia actually cut the call, but she forced herself to stay on the line.

"Dr. Ross, did something happen to the patient? Is everything okay? I stepped out for a quick break but I could come right back." Sophia rushed out the words before Katherine could even say hello. She was obviously very worried that the procedure had gone wrong. Katherine understood the fear. Sophia had never seen that kind of hemorrhaging before. Especially in a situation like the one they'd been in. Even Katherine who was far more experienced than Sophia knew how close they had been to losing that one.

"No. Nothing happened to the patient. I just... I wanted to talk to you." The silence on the line was deafening. Sophia's confusion was evident.

"About what?" Sophia said slowly like she wasn't sure she wanted to know the answer.

Katherine cleared her throat.

"I wanted to ask if you were okay."

Sophia's voice was shaky when she responded.

"I'm alright."

Katherine realized her mistake now. After the way she'd treated Sophia, it wasn't really surprising that she didn't want to talk to her about the way she was feeling. It was easier to deny that she wasn't okay over the phone. Katherine internally scolded herself.

She sighed.

"Alright then. Just, a surgery like that is tough. It is ok to feel weird when you see that much blood. When you nearly lose them. I just wanted to say." There was silence from Sophia, Katherine felt awkward. "Anyway, sorry to bother you." She hung up. She rested her head on the glass of the window and she wanted to kick herself. She could have handled that so much better, but she'd fucked up. She watched Sophia put her phone back in her pocket and continue her walk and then she made up her mind.

She grabbed her bag off the table, threw her phone into it and walked out of her office. She hurried into the elevator before she could talk herself out of what she was about to do.

9

The coffee shop was one of Sophia's favourite places to go. She liked how warm it felt. The pleasant aromas of coffee and milk. The constant chatter. Even the little bell at the top of the door. She liked the waiters. They were nice. Sophia wasn't sure she'd ever seen anyone frowning in here and she didn't want to be the first so she made sure her feelings didn't show on her face. She had chosen to sit at a table facing the window so she could watch people come and go.

Sophia had so much on her mind that she wasn't sure what to think of first. She wasn't sure should think about anything at all. She felt like she would burst into tears at any moment.

She was overwhelmed. Every time she closed her eyes she saw blood. So much blood. On the patient. On the table. On the floor. On her hands. Sophia knew the surgery had been successful but she couldn't help but think that it almost wasn't. They nearly lost the patient. There had been so much blood. She'd barely been able to stay calm but Katherine hadn't even batted an eye. Is that what would be expected of her too? Would she be expected to remain completely stoic even if a patient flat lined? What would she do if that happened?

She would have blamed herself so much if the patient had died. It wasn't even her patient. What would she do if or when her own patient died on her operating table? If someone's heart stopped beating in her hands?

Tears pricked her eyes and she took a deep breath and closed her eyes. She had to calm down.

"I thought you said you were okay."

She looked to see Katherine standing over her, a kind smile on her face.

Sophia wiped her tears away and averted her eyes.

"I am okay," she insisted

The last person she wanted to see her like this was Katherine. The ultimate professional. Katherine probably thought it was pathetic for her to feel this way.

"It's okay, you know. You don't have to be okay right now."

That surprised Sophia. She was sure her surprise was showing on her face but she didn't mind.

"Did you ever feel this way?" she asked. Katherine sat down before she answered.

"The first time I saw a man die, I almost quit. I vomited after the surgery. Right in front of the doctor in charge. I still think I got a little bit of vomit on his scrubs. I cried for days and shut myself inside. I refused to eat or see anyone."

Sophia's eyes went wide. She couldn't believe what she was hearing.

"I don't know if I should feel insulted by the surprise on your face," Katherine said making Sophia chuckle, despite all she was feeling.

"I'm sorry. I just didn't expect you to open up to me this way."

"Well, you looked like you needed to hear it. It's not weak or stupid to feel this way. The day it stops hurting to lose a patient or to almost lose one is the day you should quit."

Katherine said the words with so much conviction that Sophia couldn't do much but look at her.

"I know how scary it is to see something like that so I completely understand how you feel right now."

Sophia wanted nothing more than to be held. She wanted to crawl into Katherine's arms and stay there for hours. Tears were building up in her eyes and she knew Katherine could see them.

"Let's get out of here. You need to cry and I want to be there for you. Come with me."

KATHERINE'S ARMS WERE WARM. It felt like her embrace was the only thing holding Sophia together. They were cuddled up on Katherine's couch. The same couch where they'd had sex. The same couch that Sophia had fallen asleep on.

Sophia held on tighter to Katherine and wept. She cried till her eyes were red and snot was dripping out of her nose only then did she feel better.

Katherine's fingers were in her hair massaging her skull. It felt good.

"Do you feel better?" Now that she'd cried and got tears and snot all over Katherine's shoulder she was embarrassed, so instead of talking she nodded her head.

Katherine grabbed a box of tissues from the table.

Sophia collected it from her and mumbled a small thank you. She felt like a child.

Sophia blew her nose and cleaned up her tears. She was sure her eyes were swollen and her nose was red, but maybe she didn't look that bad because Katherine was staring at her with so much heat in her eyes.

Katherine had been the one to put an end to their relationship. She'd made herself very clear with the note she'd left behind. So, what was this now?

Why was she looking at her like that?

She moved to get off her legs but Katherine held on to her.

Sophia could see what she wanted in her eyes and she was sure her eyes mirrored the same request.

Suddenly, they were kissing. Katherine was kissing her tears away. Kissing her pain away. Their tongues tangled as they kissed. Sophia couldn't prevent her hips from moving. She moved her hips against Katherine's legs and moaned. They lost themselves in each other. They lost their pain in each other.

10

Sophia sat up on the chair. She was spent. Her body was slick with sweat and she could barely feel her legs. She was grateful to Katherine. She felt much better than she had before. She could close her eyes and not see a sea of blood threatening to drown her.

"You're not going to fall asleep on me this time, right?" Katherine asked and Sophia shook her head. She'd been wondering what would happen after the sex. Sophia had been naive to think that this meant that they were going to be together. Clearly, it had just been another hookup to Katherine. She blamed herself for this. She was weak and couldn't control herself. She'd known somewhere inside her that this changed nothing. She'd allowed herself be used by Katherine. Sophia wanted to blame it on the emotional state she'd been in but she knew the truth; if Katherine made a pass at her she would agree regardless of her emotional state. She eyed her clothes scattered on the floor and decided it would be better to leave before Katherine told her to "see herself out" she made a move to get up but Katherine's hand on her arm stopped her.

"Don't leave"

The sincerity in her eyes was staggering.

"I don't want you to leave." Katherine said again.

"You're going to want more sex tonight?" Sophia asked. Katherine laughed and Sophia's brows furrowed

"I guess I deserve that," she sighed, "I'm not asking you to stay because I want sex. I'm asking you to stay because I like you. I want to talk to you. I want to be around you. I want to look after you."

Sophia was stunned into silence. What was going on? Was this some sort of joke?

"I honestly won't touch you if you don't want me to. I just want to have you here. I want you to stay."

"But what about the note you left me, and our jobs? What happened to being professional? I'm just so confused." That note still pissed Sophia off whenever she remembered it.

"I can deny it for as long as I want to, but the connection between us is magnetic. There is magic between us."

"But... you've been so cold. I thought I was the only one who had developed feelings." Sophia was seriously stunned. She hadn't been expecting this at all. After the way Katherine had treated her and the way she was in public, she would never have imagined that Katherine would be saying these things to her.

"I'm so sorry about that note and the way I've been acting too. The truth is it was never just about being professional, that was just what I told myself because I wanted an excuse to push you away."

"What does this mean for us now?"

"Well, it means that we have a relationship now. If you'll have me if course. I won't push for any kind of commitment. I just want to be with you." Katherine lowered her eyes and Sophia could tell she was nervous and maybe a little bit embarrassed.

Sophia climbed onto her and captured Katherine's lips with her own. Neither of them tried to slip their tongues into each other's mouth. The kiss was sweet and tender. It was the beginning of their relationship.

Katherine smiled. "Let's go and take a shower," she said after they broke the kiss. Sophia nodded her head.

They walked up the stairs, still naked and into the big beautiful bedroom. Katherine's home was beautiful. Sophia loved the modern decor. It was all so smart. Katherine had put up album covers from her favourite musicians. She had a bookcase too. Upon further inspection Sophia realised that the books were contemporary romance and crime novels. It made her happy to know that Katherine's whole life didn't revolve around surgeries and the hospital. Of course there were also a couple of science books arranged neatly on her table. It would've been weird if there weren't any. She realised they didn't know each other at all. She wanted with all her heart to know Katherine.

A photo frame of a beautiful woman with a delicate face and wild red hair on Katherine's nightstand caught Sophia's attention.

She moved towards it and picked it up.

"She was my wife." Katherine said before Sophia could ask.

Sophia knew Katherine had been married. But Katherine didn't wear a ring so she'd guessed they were divorced but now she was having second thoughts. Why would Katherine keep a picture of her divorced wife on her nightstand? It was possible that she hadn't been the one who filed for a divorce and she was still in love with the woman but if that was the case then what was Katherine doing with her?

"She died during surgery."

"Oh god. I'm so sorry." Sophia said and Katherine waved her condolence away. "She was so beautiful."

"She was amazing. We were so happy."

"She had been in a car accident. She'd been rescued and rushed to Forest Vale. She'd needed surgery, it was a left subclavian artery tear, and they wouldn't let me operate on her. She died on the table for Jackson Myers. He just wasn't good enough. If I had been the one to operate on her I'm so sure I could have saved her. I feel so so guilty that I didn't try harder to get in that O.R."

She replaced the frame and stood up. She could see that it had taken a lot for Katherine to say what she just did. Sophia didn't want to point out that there was a possibility that she wouldn't have been able to save her either and if she'd died while Katherine had been operating on her then her death would've been even more tragic because Katherine would blame herself even more.

She moved closer to Katherine and held her. Katherine buried her face in Sophia's shoulder.

"She is why I was pushing you away." Katherine whispered. "I felt guilty because it felt like I was trying to replace her."

"I'm not going to replace her, Katherine. There's no way I can."

They held each other for a few more minutes and then Katherine broke the silence.

"It's kind of weird that we are just standing here hugging while we're both naked" Sophia laughed and let go of her.

"Let's go and shower then."

Katherine's bathroom was just as beautiful as the rest of the house. Sophia liked the way everything looked under the blue light. Including them.

Katherine stepped into the shower and twisted the knob for hot water.

The water cascaded down her body, flattening her hair and dripping off her fingertips.

Sophia wouldn't have been able to take her eyes off Kathrine if she'd tried. The woman was a sight to behold. Her body swayed as she turned to pick a body wash. She squeezed the body wash onto a wash cloth and gently scrubbed Sophia's body. She washed her neck first. Then her chest, her breasts, stomach, arms, legs. It was the most sensual thing she had ever felt.

They switched and Sophia scrubbed Katherine's back with the wash cloth. She took her time with it. She bent down and washed her ass as well. She used her fingers to knead her ass as she did it. Katherine moaned a little and Sophia moved on. She washed her legs carefully. Her arms. Her breasts. Her stomach.

Katherine squeezed shampoo in her hands and washed Sophia's hair as though she was a child. Her gifted fingers massaging shampoo into Sophia's scalp felt blissful. They took their time. They kissed. They held each other under the water. It was the most intimate time of Sophia's life.

$\sim$

"I HAVE GRANDMA FINGERS," Sophia said, wiggling her pruney fingers.

Katherine laughed and tossed her a large shirt.

"You're so silly. Just get dressed and come cuddle with me." Katherine said as she slid under the covers

"So you wouldn't cuddle with me if I was naked?" Sophia asked and Katherine shot her a look that made her chuckle.

"I wouldn't be able to keep my hands off you if you were naked."

"Alright, alright." Sophia threw on the shirt which was big and loose and reached midway to her knees and climbed into bed too.

She laid her head on Katherine's breast and listened to her heartbeat. She couldn't help but fear that tomorrow this Katherine would be gone and she'd be left with the stoic one that didn't care about her. She feared that she'd wake up and be all alone again.

"Stop thinking so hard. You're chasing my good night sleep away."

Katherine held on to her tighter and used one hand to play with her wet hair.

Maybe everything would be alright after all. Maybe she'd wake up and this Katherine would still be here holding on to her just like this.

SOPHIA WOKE up to the sound of an alarm clock ringing. She stuck her hand out and tried to turn it off but it wasn't in the usual spot. Did someone move her alarm clock? She'd have to tell Jenna and Sara to stop moving her things.

The alarm clock turned off and then she felt someone kiss her neck. Her eyes shot open and she came face to face with a sleepy Katherine. Then she remembered, the patient, the coffee shop, the sofa, Katherine's wife, the shower and most importantly, the fact that they were in a relationship now.

"Good morning," Katherine said, placing another kiss on her collar bone.

"I really don't want to leave this bed." Katherine said and she placed her head on Sophia's chest.

"Sophia, could you call in sick? I can call and say I have a personal errand to run but I'm available for an emergencies."

Sophia couldn't believe what she was hearing. Where was the professional surgeon? It wasn't like the change was a bad thing but she'd changed so quickly. Sophia couldn't see any traits of the woman that she knew from the hospital. Was Katherine that good at pretending?

"Oh shoot. We can't call in sick. We need to check up on our patient from yesterday."

"I guess we'll just have to leave then." Sophia said but even as she said it she tightened her grip on Katherine.

Katherine wiggled and Sophia unwillingly let her go. She took off her shirt that she'd put on after their shower the night before leaving her stark naked. Katherine went about selecting clothes. When she was done she turned around like she knew Sophia would be watching her. Sophia watched her dress slowly and carefully. It was erotic.

Sophia found herself chuckling alone in the room. Katherine totally had been putting on a show. Sophia tossed the covers off her body and took off her shirt. She hoped with everything in her that this Katherine wouldn't leave.

11

G etting to work hadn't been an issue. Katherine had driven them both. She'd been planning to drive into the garage so they could go their separate ways there but Sophia had reasoned that a lot of other people would be there too so Katherine had dropped her two blocks away.

Katherine had kissed her before she'd left the vehicle and when she was standing on the side walk she blew her a kiss before driving off.

Sophia felt reassured that Katherine wasn't going to go back to being unemotional and distant. She knew that they would obviously have to maintain a professional relationship at work so they wouldn't stir up any questions but outside work was where she got to see the real Katherine. The one with real emotions and beautiful smiles. She smiled to herself as she walked down the street to the hospital. Scenes from the night before flashed through her head. Katherine apparently was a sleep talker. Sophia had heard her mumbling some things about scalpels and surgery. Ever the doctor.

She could see the hospital now, so she walked faster.

She was curious and kind of scared to see what the day would be like. She was interning in the pediatric department that week and the week after that was the general surgery department, the week after that was neurology department and then cosmetic. She wouldn't get to see Katherine unless they met up during her lunch break or after work. Katherine could request for her specifically but if she did it more than twice in a row it would be suspicious and Sophia wouldn't learn as much as she should from the other departments.

She hospital doors slid open and she walked in. The smell of medicines and antiseptic floor cleaners hit her almost immediately and she smiled to herself a little breathing in the air. She knew at least that this would always be consistent.

KATHERINE WAS HAPPY. She'd been in and out of surgeries all day, her back and feet were killing her but she was happy. She couldn't stop thinking about Sophia. She couldn't stop remembering their time together. She hadn't realised how much she'd missed being cuddled till she had woken up with Sophia's warm arms around her.

If she had the option of staying in bed with her the whole day she would've taken it.

The day was almost over and Katherine still hadn't seen Sophia. They hadn't been able to text or meet up because of how busy they both were.

It was nine o'clock now. Katherine guessed the interns didn't have much to do anymore so they'd leave by 10. She picked up her bag and fished out her phone.

She had three texts from Sophia. The first one was a

text asking her if she was free for coffee. She had apparently asked around and realised that Katherine had been in surgery at that time because her second text read "just found out you're in surgery. Good luck!" Katherine smiled at the message and checked the third.

"Is it normal for me to miss you as much as I do?"

Katherine didn't know if it was normal but she knew she missed her too. It was funny how much she did because they'd been together just that morning.

Katherine texted her back.

"I'll be free for coffee tomorrow if I don't have any emergencies."

"Thank you! The surgery was a success and the patient is in recovery"

"I don't think it's normal but if it's any consolation, I miss you too. So, will you come over to my house tonight?"

Katherine knew that she could've just replied the last text but it irked her when she texted three things and only got one reply. She was right about the interns not having much to do because the three dots that showed Sophia was texting her back popped up on her phone screen.

"Text me if you're free. I'll bring the coffee to your office. Maybe I'll even seduce you while I'm there." Katherine chuckled at Sophia's reply. She'd never done anything that wasn't work related at the hospital and yet here she was considering having sex in her office. Sophia was clearly a bad influence.

Sophia agreed to come to her house and then they texted back and forth till it was almost ten. Katherine stood up and stretched. She felt the tightness in her back and her knees ached.

According to their plan. Sophia had left first. Sophia was going to walk till she got to the front of the building where Katherine had dropped her off in the morning and Katherine would pick her up from there and take them both to her house.

During the drive, Katherine told Sophia about the surgeries, the procedures and the risks. For every risk, she gave Sophia gave a solution or prevention and Katherine had pulled over to kiss her.

"What was that for?" She had asked when she had continued driving.

"Your intelligence is attractive," she replied and she could've sworn she saw Sophia blush.

When they got to the house they both trotted up the stairs. Katherine fell face first into her bed and groaned. She really was tired.

Sophia laid down beside her and their eyes met. They did nothing but look at each other. Katherine was thinking about how pretty Sophia's eyes were and how much she needed a massage and a bath. Sophia was thinking of taking a bath too. It kind of surprised her how quickly they'd gotten used to each other. They didn't argue over their schedules and neither of them were annoyed with the other for not being able to see each other earlier today.

"Do you want to share a bath?" Katherine said and Sophia nodded, but neither of them made a move to get up.

"I really, really like you. You make me happy," Sophia said.

Katherine smiled weakly at her,

"You make me believe that I can love again."

12

T he first few months of their relationship could only be described as blissful. Sophia had been so happy that she could've burst. After the first couple of weeks they settled into a routine. In the morning, they'd get ready for work. Sometimes if they woke up early enough, they had sex. Then they'd bathe or shower and Katherine would drive them to work. Instead of blocks away from the hospital, Katherine started dropping her at the coffee shop. Sophia would order coffees for them both then take it back to the hospital. She'd go straight to Katherine's office and they would spend what time they could drinking coffee and talking.

By the time they were done, a lot of other interns would have arrived, so Sophia would kiss her and they'd make plans to meet later in the day before she left.

Whenever Sophia interned in Katherine's department they always snuck away to have sex in on call rooms, because Katherine couldn't resist the lure of her.

The first time they'd had sex at work Sophia had been the one to initiate it. It had been a little after Sophia's lunch break. She'd gone to Katherine's office to give her an update on a patient she'd done surgery on and Katherine had looked so sexy rattling off medications that Sophia just had to kiss her.

"I love it when you talk doctor to me." Katherine had laughed at her silliness but Sophia hadn't been playing.

"I don't have any underwear on."

"Sophia, we can't."

"Yes, we can. I said I was going to seduce you. Remember?" Sophia had said and then she'd kissed Katherine again. Katherine had flicked the lock on her door and they had made love right there on her office floor. The thrill of having sex at work knowing the risk and knowing that anybody could knock on the door had turned them both on so much.

They had sex at work many more times after that. Sometimes in an on call room or in Katherine's office. Whenever they did Katherine would say they were in their honeymoon stage so this behaviour was expected from the both of them. Of course, if they had got caught, that excuse wouldn't have helped them in any way.

Her roommates were the first people she'd told about her relationship with Katherine. They'd been wondering why she barely slept at home and why she was so happy all the time and she wouldn't have felt right to lie to them so she'd told them the truth.

Sara had screamed and Jenna had been shocked into silence

"No way. No fucking way. Dr. Ross!?" Sara had screamed holding her head in her hands as she bounced around the room.

"You hit the fucking jackpot!" Jenna said finally,

joining Sara to jump around then they'd both turned to her and flicked her forehead.

"That was for not telling us earlier." Jenna had said.

"This is so great. I'm so happy for you!" Sara had wrapped her in a hug and she felt herself flood with relief. She'd been worried that they would take it badly or that they'd think she was only with Katherine so she could use her for her career or that they would think they could use Katherine through her to further their careers. She should have known better. Sara and Jenna weren't like that.

After she'd told them she'd taken some of her things and headed to Katherine's house where she stayed for the next couple of days. Their relationship was beautiful and there was nothing that made Sophia happier than knowing she was going to go home and be with Katherine.

BUT THEN, everything changed.

Sophia could feel that something was wrong. She'd been gossiped about before so she knew how to spot the signs. People were whispering around her and when she walked in a room the conversations suddenly died.

It went on for most of the day. During her lunch break she found Sara and Jenna and asked if they knew what was going on.

"I haven't heard anything." Sara said and her brows furrowed.

"Neither have I. Why would they be talking about you? You don't think they found out about Dr Ross do you?" Jenna asked her eyes wide.

It was the first time Sophia considered that possibility. Her heart started beating faster.

"You guys didn't tell anyone. Did you?" She asked and they both shook their heads.

"You know we wouldn't do that."

Sophia nodded her head and apologised.

"I'm sorry. I know you guys wouldn't do that. If you hear anything about what's going on let me know okay?"

"We will. You should try to calm down. Maybe talk to Katherine. She might know something." Sophia nodded her head and went to find Katherine.

She was just about to step into the elevator when Travis stopped her.

"Sophia. Hi. I wanted to talk to you about something."

She turned to him and he led her away from the elevator and towards a room she guessed was a supply closet. They didn't enter the room, they just leaned on the wall beside it.

"So um, are the rumors true? You know, the ones about you and Dr. Ross?" Sophia blinked up at him and he shot her a sheepish grin.

"I already know you're a lesbian and we know she is too and you do seem to spend a lot of time together."

Sophia was looking at him but she couldn't hear the words coming out of his mouth. How had they found out? They'd been so careful. Except for all the times they had had sex at work. Oh God, had someone seen them after all?

Travis misunderstood her silence and kept talking.

"It's not like I have a problem with it. I'm not homophobic. Live and let live you know? But I was just wondering, if you could talk to her for me. Maybe she could give me some 1:1 time? Maybe you can get me in on one of her surgeries?"

Sophia turned on her heel and walked away from him.

This was what Katherine had been trying to avoid. How did they find out, for God's sake?

She hurried into the elevator and tried to keep herself calm. Maybe this wasn't all bad. She got off the elevator and walked as fast as she could to Katherine's office. She would have run, but she didn't want to draw even more attention to herself.

"Katherine, I don't know how-" she stopped short, because sitting right there in front of Katherine's desk was a man. Sophia knew immediately that this was the hospital's president. Just leaving the office, was another intern. Sophia recognised her. She was the one who had been shit talking Katherine on their first day here. It made sense that she was the one to rat them out.

Sophia stepped further into the office and closed the door behind her.

"I'm guessing you're Sophia," the president said.

"Yes sir. I am." Sophia replied

"Good. Well you may not know this but this isn't the normal procedure we take here when there's a personnel issue. There's usually a conference and we talk to the vice presidents as well so we can come to a conclusion. However, Dr. Ross is a good friend of mine so I decided that I'd rather speak to her directly."

Sophia hoped they weren't going to fire Katherine. It would be terrible if everything she'd worked for her whole life was taken from her.

"Please don't fire her. I'll leave the hospital instead. Just don't fire her please."

"I'm not going to fire her," he said and Sophia nodded her head. Through all this she hadn't been able to read Katherine's expression. She didn't know what she was thinking or what she was feeling.

"I am, however going to ask you two for a favour." The president said and Sophia's heart beat sped up a little.

"Relationships between doctors and interns, sometimes are unavoidable and it wouldn't be right to fire good doctors for feelings that are beyond their control so instead of doing that, I have personally decided that my good friend, and exceptional surgeon Dr. Ross, should be able to date who she so pleases."

"Thank you so much Mr Ryan. We will be so much more discreet. I am so sorry for our indiscretions." Katherine answered quickly and smiled.

"Thank you so much." Sophia couldn't quite believe it.

He waved away their thanks and stood up.

"Please keep the intimacy between you two away from the hospital." The president finished and Sophia nodded her head.

"We will. We're so sorry for any trouble we've caused." He nodded his head and stood up.

"Thank you for the courtesy you showed me. We will be so much more discreet in future."

Mr Ryan left and Katherine smiled at Sophia. "I can't believe it. I was so sure he was going to tell us we had to end it. Sophia, that's it. We can be together properly now."

Sophia smiled widely. Her intense blue eyes met Katherine's. This was really the beginning of something special.

"My surgeries for the day are done." Katherine looked to her excitedly. "Want to get out of here for a bit?"

"I'd love to."

THE END

. . .

FIND out what happens next for Katherine and Sophia in the next Forest Vale Romance The Doctor's Rival.

It is a standalone Enemies to Lovers Romance but Katherine and Sophia feature as side characters. (And they have a couple more really great sex scenes!)

FOREST VALE HOSPITAL BOOK 2

The second book in the Forest Vale Series also features Katherine and Sophia alongside a new Age Gap Butch-Femme medical romance. Check it out to catch up with Katherine and Sophia and more from Forest Vale Hospital:

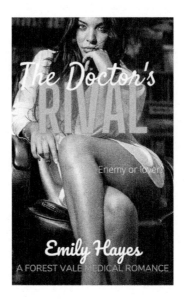

Click the Link or type into your web browser: getbook.at/TDR

HEADMISTRESS

A LESBIAN ROMANCE

1

Megan's fingers drummed against her steering wheel. She was so late, beyond late, the one thing she couldn't be today. The morning did not start off as well as she had hoped it would. Her daughter, Lola, would not co-operate. Megan understood, going to school was not an easy thing to do when you were just five years old, and normally she would have handled it better, but today was a big important day for both of them. After working minimum wage jobs, sometimes more than one just to make rent, today Megan had the chance at a real job with benefits, a good wage, and decent hours. Hours that she could work while Lola was in school, something they'd never had before. This interview had to go perfectly, and she was going to be late.

Finally, parking her car, Megan checked her makeup one more time in the mirror before getting out and heading into Westerville High School. Megan couldn't shake the nerves that were making their way all through her body. Most would think an interview to be a personal assistant would be no big deal, and maybe it wouldn't be if

Megan hadn't lied on her resume to even get the interview. She had zero experience as a personal assistant; most of her experience was as a waitress. Megan figured it had to be at least similar to being a waitress. She followed orders from her boss, she got the customers what they needed, and she did it with a smile. That had to be close to what being a personal assistant was. At least that is what Megan was hoping.

Megan walked into the main office and instantly noticed two things, one there was a beautiful woman standing there. With mocha skin, dark hair, and a tight pencil skirt, this woman was designed to make a person look twice. The second thing she noticed, said woman, did not look friendly. What could have been very warm brown eyes were, in fact, cold as ice. She was staring right at Megan, and she couldn't help but feel like she was being heavily judged. All Megan could do was hope this wasn't her potential boss, but Megan knew that was merely false hope.

Deborah Stewart ran a very strict school, students and teachers, alike. She was known to be an ice queen, but that never bothered her. If her staff were on top of their game, that meant the students would be getting an even better education, and the school would have an impressive reputation. That was all Deborah cared about. The school was everything to her.

She could tell that the woman that stood before her, Megan, was the woman set to have an interview with her. She was late by fifteen minutes, way past acceptable to Deborah. She had already made up her mind that she would not be getting the interview, let alone the job; if she could not show up on time or preferably early for an interview, then she must not truly want this job. Deborah had no interest in having a personal assistant that can't even be bothered to be on time. It was unacceptable to her, and she was telling the receptionist, Kathy, to call and schedule an interview with the other candidates when Megan finally walked in.

Seeing Megan standing there in front of her brought on conflicting feelings inside Deborah. At first appearance, Megan was a beautiful young woman. However, her clothes were old and worn, clearly secondhand. Her golden hair was a long tangled mess. She looked like she had just rolled out of bed and into Deborah's office. Deborah was torn between a spasm of desire at the thought of Megan rolling out of bed and her professional appraisal of Megan looking a mess for an interview. What got Deborah, though, was her blue eyes, they were as blue as the ocean. They were pulling her in, mesmerizing her to the point that she had to force her own eyes to look away for a moment to collect herself. Megan was here for an interview for a job Deborah had no interest in giving to her. But she would let her have the interview; after all, how could she say no to having this attractive young woman sitting across from her for a few minutes?

"Miss. Campbell, I presume." Deborah asked in a cold tone. Keeping all of her emotions from it and off her face.

"Yes, Ma'am, are you Miss. Stewart?" Megan said with a warm smile, hoping it would help to melt her icy exterior.

"My office." Deborah said, turning and heading to her office, not even bothering to make sure that Megan was following her. She knew she would be.

Megan quickly followed Deborah into her office. She only had a moment to look around, but even her office was cold. There were no pictures of family or friends on the walls or on the large desk. The walls were a light beige color, void of any warmth a rich color would provide to the office. Even the furniture in the room didn't say inviting. It was clear that Deborah had no interest in being friendly or welcoming to visitors or fellow teachers.

"Take a seat." Deborah ordered as she sat down in her comfy office chair.

Megan wasn't going to let Deborah's cold exterior stop her though, this was her chance at providing a better life for Lola, and she was not going to screw this up now. Megan sat down and crossed her right leg over her left, making sure she sat up straight and kept her eyes on Deborah. She might not feel confident, but she was not going to show it.

Deborah opened the file that contained Megan's resume as she spoke. "Your resume says you've been a personal assistant for five years now. What happened with your last job?"

Megan could feel the judgment radiating off from Deborah. Almost as if she didn't believe her resume, sure it was completely false, even down to her address, but there was no way Deborah could know that.

"It was time for a change. I had been there for two years, and I felt myself growing comfortable with the position. I wanted to start a new adventure and challenge."

"And you find being a personal assistant to be challenging?" Deborah asked, not being able to keep the unimpressed tone to her voice. To Deborah, being a personal assistant was far from challenging. After all, it was nothing compared to the workload and responsibility she had as a Headteacher.

"I find people to be challenging, not the work itself. Working for someone different will allow me to utilize different skills and be around different personalities. I'm sure you enjoy being around the other teachers and getting to know any new ones." Megan was very proud of herself for the smooth answer. She may only have a high school diploma, but that didn't mean she wasn't smart. She had figured out how to raise a baby all on her own while working multiple jobs. It had taken real smarts to stretch every dollar she had.

"And what skills have you utilized with past employers?"

"I've managed phone calls, emails, handled scheduling, making travel plans and note-taking, of course. I've prided myself on being there for all of my employers when they need me. I know life can be very busy, especially for you as head of a such a successful school. You must have so much paperwork with all of your students and staff. You must be exhausted by the end of the day." Megan said with a warm smile. She was hoping if nothing else, she would get this woman to warm up to her and bond. She learned long ago that if you could get your potential employer to like you and connect with you, you were more likely to get the job. Her charm had come in handy many times in the past.

Deborah simply stared at Megan, as if she had said the dumbest thing in the world. She didn't care for chatty. She didn't care to get to know someone. She was here because she loved teaching, not because she loved being close to people. She didn't want to be friendly with her assistant; she wanted an assistant that could do the job and not complain about it.

"You've used scheduling software and Excel before?" Deborah asked, in a dead tone.

"Of course, and I am a very fast learner for any

programs you might use that my past employers haven't. I'm always learning and finding new ways to do something. I've always been like this, I used to drive my parents insane. Your parents must be so proud of you being a teacher, a Headmistress, you are shaping the minds of the future." Megan said with another killer smile.

She was trying to be cute, Deborah knew that, yet she didn't hate it. She had no idea what was going on right now. She doubted that Megan would be a good match for her. She was messy, late, chatty, and seemed to enjoy knowing things about people. She was the exact opposite of who she wanted to have as a personal assistant. Yet, there was something about her. Something that made Deborah hesitate. Something that made her even entertain the idea of having an interview with her after she showed up fifteen minutes late.

"Can you start now?" Deborah asked. She had no idea how well this was going to go. She would probably live to regret it, but for some unknown reason, she wanted to see Megan in her office more. She didn't want to listen to her talk, but she did want to see her work, preferably in a tight skirt and top.

"I can, yes," Megan said with a big smile. She couldn't believe that she might have actually secured this job. She wasn't going to get her hopes up yet; it could have just been a routine question to see how serious she was about this job. For all Megan knew, there were ten other candidates waiting for their interview behind her.

"There is a three-month contract that you will need to sign. It is a probationary period, where I will be closely monitoring your work. Should I not be impressed, at the end of the three-months, you will be let go. Alternatively, IF you impress me, then you will be hired as a full-time personal assistant. The contract is straight forward; you will need to read it over and then sign it if you agree to the terms." Deborah pulled out the contract from her top drawer, along with a pen.

Megan took the contract and saw that it was three pages long with very tiny print. She did her best to review it quickly. She had never signed one of these before or even seen one. Some of the words were very big and new to her, but she did her best to understand what it was saying. She was too afraid to ask what a word meant in fear that she would be called out as a fraud. She did notice that for the first three months, she wouldn't have any medical benefits, and she would only have five sick days. Something that shouldn't be an issue as long as Lola didn't make her sick. It would only be for three months, and then she would have vacation time, more sick time, and full health benefits. She could make it work for three more months. Feeling confident, Megan signed and dated it before returning it with a warm smile.

"It's all pretty straight forward. I appreciate this opportunity to work for you. I won't let you down."

"Well, we will see." Deborah pulled out another piece of paper and placed it down in front of Megan. Her hands were smooth and brown and perfectly manicured. "This is what your daily tasks will look like. Some will change depending on the day and my needs. This is what I need you to complete by the end of the day. Kathy will show you to your desk and sort out any additional paperwork that you need to fill out. If you do not know something, then ask. I will not tolerate mistakes."

The cold stare that Deborah gave her told Megan that this woman was not going to warm up any time soon. It also meant she would need to be on her A-Game if she was going to be able to keep this job at the end of the three months.

"Thank you. I will get started on this right away."

Megan picked up the paper and headed out of the office. She only glanced down at the list of tasks once she was safely out of Deborah's office. There were thirty different items on the list, some seemed easy enough, while others looked like they were written in another language. She would have to ask Deborah questions throughout the day. She was just hoping the answers wouldn't leave her with even more questions. One thing Megan did know was that today was going to be a long day.

2

———

"Lola, come on it's bedtime!" Megan called out once again to her little five year old.

This was a nightly ritual with Lola and it was starting to become rather overwhelming for Megan. She knew that with Lola now being in school she would want to spend more time with her at night, it was understandable. But now that Megan had to be at work for nine and Lola had to be at school for eight, they couldn't stay up that late. They both needed to be in bed and fully rested so they could get up and get to school in the morning.

"All clean Mommy." Lola said with a big toothy smile.

"Beautiful, now into bed for you." Megan said with a warm smile as she walked with Lola over to her bedroom.

After getting Lola all tucked in and giving her a kiss goodnight, Megan closed the door as Lola curled up with her favorite teddy, her dark curls messy on the pillow. Megan let out a sigh as she headed off to the living room, where her bed was, to see that her roommate, Amber, was back from work. Amber was a godsend to Megan, not only did she pay half of the rent, but she also looked after Lola when Megan had had to work nights. Lola honestly had no idea what she would have done if she had never met Amber. Yes, the apartment was small and rundown, but they had managed to make it work. It was a two bedroom, so Megan slept on the pull out couch they had managed to score at a thrift shop five years ago. It was tight and hard at times, but they always made it work.

"How was it?" Amber asked, handing Megan a glass of cheap red wine.

Megan took it gladly as they sat down on the couch. "Well, I got the job! But it was a lot harder than I thought. I'm fairly certain my boss hates me."

"Congratulations! First days are always rough. You'll get used to what she likes and how she likes things. She can't be that bad, I mean, she is a teacher."

"Head Teacher, as she liked to remind me today. And she might actually be that bad. Every time I did something even a little bit wrong she was a total bitch to me. I mean, it was my first day, you would think she would give me just a little bit of slack."

"Yeah, but you are supposed to have already been working as an assistant. She probably figures you should know how to do everything already. It's a miracle you even got through that interview." Amber said with a smirk. "Your charm never ceases to amaze me!"

"I still stand by what I said, waitressing and being an assistant are virtually the same thing. The only difference is, she seems to be immune to my charming self. Whenever a customer was annoyed, I could just flash them my smile and chat them up. In no time they were happy and leaving me a tip. All I'm getting from her is ice."

"Not everyone is happy like you. Some people take a long time to warm up and some never do. You'll get used to how she likes things and her attitude. I still can't believe you aren't going to tell them about Lola."

Megan could hear the slight judgement in Amber's voice. She knew that Amber wasn't happy with her decision to hide Lola. It wasn't that she was ashamed to be a single mother, how could she be? Lola was the best thing that ever happened to her and if everyone saw it that way then she wouldn't have to hide her. Megan had been to interviews in the past for better jobs and she got told to her face that she couldn't work there and be a single parent. Sure, they didn't put it that way, but basically that is what they said. This personal assistant job was the best opportunity to have something real. To be able to afford her own two bedroom apartment one day for her and Lola. Megan couldn't risk losing it all because she chose to have a child and raise that child.

"I might one day if I am still working there. You know why I am keeping her a secret. I can't risk losing this job. If I can just get through my three month probation and get on a proper contract…"

"I know and I get it. Still, how long can you really keep a secret child from the people you work with? She's going to get sick, she's going to have school holidays where you'll have to work. There's no guarantee I'll be off for them. Eventually, they are going to find out."

"And when that day comes, I'll deal with it then. Hopefully I'll have been working there long enough that no one thinks twice about it. I honestly have no idea how my boss would handle me having a child. Teacher or not, she isn't warm at all to anyone. I bet she HATES children."

"I don't know, Lola is a pretty special little girl," Amber said warmly.

"She sure is," Megan agreed.

If you had told Megan five years ago that she would be this much in love with someone, she would have told them they were crazy. Yet, here she was sleeping on a pull out couch working her ass off all so this sweet little girl could have a shot at having a real life. Megan honestly didn't know what she would ever do if she lost Lola. To Megan, Lola was it, she was everything. She had tried dating since Lola had been born and joined a dating app, but nothing ever came of it. Some good sex, but that was it. Some were running away the second they found out she had a child and the ones that didn't weren't worthy enough for Lola. It didn't matter to Megan though, she had Lola and that was all she needed.

"So, is anyone at the office hot?" Amber said with a big grin.

"That is not what I am there for."

Amber rolled her eyes. "You've got eyes though. Come on, you must have noticed if someone was smoking or not."

"There might be a few teachers that have it going on, but I'm not there for dating. I'm there to work and I am not about to screw up this job over a night of fun."

"Ok, ok, I get it. But what about your boss, is she smoking?" Amber said with a giggle.

Megan gave a flirty smile and Amber giggled even more, causing Megan to start. If there was one thing Megan had to give her new boss credit for, it was that she was stunning. Older, but stunning. Her curves fit perfectly in her tight pencil skirt and button down shirt. She even wore stiletto heels instead of those traditional kitten heels that most teachers wore. It was a shame she was so cold on the inside, because on the outside she was fire. Megan wondered how old she was.

"She might have it going on." Megan answered giggling.

"Might, my ass! She is totally smoking isn't she?! You are so lucky. Even if she is an evil bitch, at least you will have something smoking to look at all day!" Amber whined, her boss was anything but fun to look at.

"Nothing is going to happen, not now and not ever. I am there for work. Not for anything else." Megan said with a serious voice.

It didn't matter how much fun Deborah was to look at, nothing would ever come of it. Megan wasn't going to let her desires take over her. She was there to work and it was just that simple. She could be a nun for a while and then find someone else to hook up with once she was settled in at work. She had spent five years like this so it wasn't anything new. Tomorrow was just going to be another day at the office.

3

I t was day two of her job and once again Megan was running fifteen minutes late. She couldn't believe her bad luck. She had got up thirty minutes early today to get Lola ready for school and at her school on time. Megan thought it was going to be a perfect day, she would get to work on time and Lola would be happy in school. Except, she didn't expect the massive amount of traffic there was going to be between Lola's school and her job. Because of where they lived, Lola's school was on the opposite side of town and at just after eight in the morning the traffic was horrific. It took her almost an hour to get across town to work. She had no idea what she was going to do tomorrow. She had to drop Lola off at eight for the before school care, it couldn't be earlier. So tomorrow, the time would be the same, meaning the traffic would be the same. She was going to have to try tonight and see if there was a different route that might be further in distance, but hopefully less traffic and just might get her to work on time.

Megan rushed into the building and headed straight

for her office to toss her coat and bag down before taking a couple calming breaths and heading into Deborah's office. The look that Kathy gave her did nothing to ease her fears. Megan knocked on the door and waited to be told to enter. Deborah did not like it when you just walked into her office, even after you knocked. She wanted you to wait there until she gave you permission to enter, something Megan found out yesterday in a not so pleasant way.

"Enter." Deborah said in a tone that made Megan cringe.

Megan walked into the office and Deborah didn't even bother to look up at her. She already knew it would be Megan. Deborah continued to work on the paperwork in front of her, without giving Megan any attention.

"Ma'am," Megan started, but was quickly silenced by a raised hand.

Megan had no choice but to stand there and wait for when Deborah was ready to speak with her. She did her best not to slouch or roll her eyes at the whole show. Yes she was late today, but it was the traffic, that wasn't her fault. She even got up thirty minutes early just so she would get to Lola's school on time. She couldn't be held accountable for traffic. After five minutes Deborah finally stopped writing and looked up at Megan. Deborah didn't speak right away, instead she took in the young woman in front of her. Despite her young age and appearance, she was not very fashionable. Megan's clothing was on the low quality end, something that could have easily been found in the thrift shop. It instantly made Deborah wonder just what this woman spent her money on. Being a personal assistant might not pay as well as being a doctor, but it was above minimum wage. There was no ring on her finger, so it didn't go to a spouse. Deborah couldn't help but maybe think Megan spent her money on alcohol or drugs, it would certainly explain how she was always late and looked a mess, despite it being a new job.

Though, if Deborah was honest with herself, there was something about this young woman that intrigued her. Enough to make her pick her over all of the other overly qualified candidates that she had for this position. There was something about those blue eyes, an intensity, a spark, she dreamt about them last night. She couldn't help but wonder what they would look like when they were flooded with pleasure. It was a desire that would have to stay in her mind only. Megan was her employee and that is what she would always be. Not once in her entire career had she ever slept with an employee and she was not about to let this messy blonde girl ruin that now.

"Ms Campbell, please explain to me how it seems to be impossible for you to show up on time." Deborah said with an icy tone.

"I'm sorry Ma'am. I live on the other side of town, I left forty-five minutes early, but the traffic was insane." Megan made sure she threw in as much remorse in her voice as possible.

"Then leave an hour early. I don't care if you have to leave two hours early, you will get here on time tomorrow or you will not have a job. Do I make myself clear?"

"Yes Ma'am." Megan knew she had to say yes. The problem was, she had no idea how she was going to pull it off.

"Your list has been updated. You need to upload the new schedule within the system for the students to show the changes to their timetables. There was a glitch and now everyone is showing up at the wrong time and at the wrong classes."

"Yes Ma'am, I will get right on that. How do I go about making the change in the database software?" Megan hated having to ask her anything, as it didn't go over so well yesterday whenever she had a question. Despite being a teacher, Deborah really hated questions.

"I showed you where it was yesterday. Surely you are not that stupid that you can't remember where something is." Deborah said, not impressed at all and already reaching her limit for the day.

"No Ma'am, it's just that you showed it to me briefly and you didn't go over everything that entailed within the software. As it is a new software for me, I was hoping for just a quick explanation. You would know it better than anyone." Megan said with a charming smile, but once again it had zero effect on Deborah.

"If I did everything myself there would be no need to have you. Which might be the better option if you are this incapable of figuring something out. Get it done, and I expect it to be done right the first time. No more little stupid mistakes like you made yesterday. You claim to be a professional and have experience in this field, I suggest you stop acting like a rookie and show me you are capable of doing this job."

"Yes Ma'am. I will handle it for you." A smile plastered on her face once again, though this one was very much fake.

"Kathy has files that you need to organize and file properly," Deborah said before she went back to work and Megan had been dismissed.

"I'll get right on it Ma'am." Megan said with a smile, even though Deborah didn't see it.

Megan headed out and over to Kathy to see what the files were.

"Those boxes at your desk are the files. They all need to have new labels placed in accordance with what Ms Stewart wants, then you need to refile them alphabetically. She needs it done by the end of the day along with your other duties." Kathy said with a knowing smile.

Megan looked over at her desk. The boxes had been there yesterday as well so she didn't think much of it. Now, she was not looking forward to going through them. There were ten paper boxes and all of them were full of files. It would take her hours, plus she had her other tasks that she needed to complete. Megan couldn't stay late, she had to pick up Lola. All she could do was hope that she could get it done today.

"Thanks Kathy." Megan said with a warm smile. It wasn't her fault that Megan was going to have to work through lunch.

"Good luck."

Megan headed over and got started on the first box, today was looking to be another long day.

It was nearing lunch hour when Megan stretched her arms above her head. She had been sitting hunched over her desk going through the endless number of files. She hadn't moved at all in three hours. Now it was almost lunch time and she was in desperate need of caffeine. Megan got up and headed to the staff lounge where she could grab some coffee to have with her lunch back at her desk. The staff lounge was not busy at all, as most teachers were finishing up their class before lunch would begin. There was one man in the lounge by the coffeemaker. Megan hadn't seen him before, not too surprising really.

The man was very good looking. Megan could see through his suit jacket that this man had some muscles to him. He was looked Spanish, with dark brown hair and brown eyes. He turned around and when his eyes landed on Megan, a warm smile graced his features.

"You must be the new assistant to the Ice Queen."

"Is that what everyone calls her?" Megan asked with her own warm smile, walking closer to the coffeemaker.

"That tends to be her nickname. I'm Juan Garcia, Head of Languages." Juan said, holding his hand out to Megan.

"Megan Campbell. It's nice to meet you." Megan said, shaking the offered hand.

"How has your time been?" Juan asked, as Megan got her coffee.

"It's been difficult, but nothing I can't handle. She is not my first difficult boss, they all warm up to me eventually."

"I bet they do." Juan said with a flirty smile.

Megan gave him a smile in return, but she was not interested in starting anything with anyone, especially in this school. She was here to work, it was just that simple to her.

"I'll see you around I guess then." She said, as she grabbed her coffee.

"Oh you can count on it."

Megan headed out of there and went right back to her desk. She pulled out her packed lunch and got back to work. She had to get these files done today and the clock was ticking.

～

IT WAS NEARING the end of the school day and Deborah found herself once again watching Megan from her desk. No matter how many times she had told herself to ignore the young woman. She was supposed to be focused on her marking and yet, every few minutes she was looking over at Megan. It was an intense sexual attraction and Deborah knew she would need to do something about it to remove this attraction. It had been close to a year since she had been with anyone, perhaps it was time she found a one-night stand to play with. Someone that could take the edge off and then she would be able to focus without imagining what her assistant would look like spread open on her desk.

Deborah let out a sigh and began to pack up her things. There was no way she was going to be able to focus on her marking with Megan sitting over there. As she was all packed up she saw as Juan walked into Megan's office with some roses in a vase. Deborah was instantly inter-ested in what was going on. She saw the big warm smile Megan gave Juan and the one he gave her in return. She took the vase and smelled the flowers and Juan continued to speak. Deborah couldn't make out what was being said, but it looked very friendly, too friendly in her opinion. Megan had only been here two days and she was already looking to mess around with someone. Deborah couldn't ignore the surge of jealousy that flooded her body. She wanted nothing more than to go over there and shove those flowers in Juan's face. Juan gave Megan a hug before he turned and left the office.

Once he was gone, Deborah was out of her seat and moving to Megan's office before she could even register what she was doing. She didn't bother to knock, and gave Megan the coldest look yet.

"If you are going to be sleeping with the faculty, keep it out of my office."

"Pardon?" Megan asked, slightly confused as to where this was coming from.

"You are here to work for me. That does not include you having visitors coming by and bringing you flowers. Whatever you have going on with Mr. Garcia stays out of my office. You wish to see him it will be on your own time and not the time I am paying you for. Do I make myself clear?"

"Yes Ma'am. Though, you are mistaken. I just met him at lunch in the staff lounge. He brought me the flowers as a welcome gift. There is nothing going on between us. Even if he is interested, I couldn't be less so." Megan said completely serious.

Deborah squinted. Garcia was an infamous ladies man around the school. Good looking and charming. And yet, Megan was entirely believable when she said she couldn't be less interested. Curious and curiouser thought Deborah. Megan was a curious little thing. What were her secrets?

"Well, keep your personal life out of my office. Have you finished your work?"

"I have almost all of the files completed. There are just two more boxes for me to finish up tomorrow."

"They needed to be completed today. Perhaps if you spent less time fraternizing, you would have had them completed. You can leave when they are done. Kathy will be here as well finishing up her work and she will inform me when you leave. She will also be checking to make sure you have done it correctly before you leave. Get it done." Deborah demanded.

"I can't stay late Ma'am, I have to get home."

The very last thing Megan could do was not pick up her daughter in the next thirty minutes. She didn't have long for after school care. She had to go and get Lola.

"Do you die if you are not home at a certain hour?" Deborah asked, clearly getting more upset as this conversation continued.

"No Ma'am."

"Then what could possibly be more important that you need to do then finish your work? Or perhaps you don't need this job. If that is the case then you don't need to bother coming tomorrow."

Megan could tell she was serious. If she didn't stay she could kiss this job goodbye, something she couldn't afford. If she lost this job there was no telling what would happen to Lola and her. She would have to go back to taking on multiple jobs to pay the bills and those bills would only increase because she would have to find a babysitter. There was no choice, she had to stay.

"My apologies Ma'am. I have no problem staying." Megan said with a warm smile.

"Get it done." Deborah demanded before she turned and headed out.

Megan let out a deep breath, she couldn't believe this. She thought having this job would mean that she could be home with Lola every night, now it was looking like that might not be the case. She didn't have a choice right now though and sitting here wallowing in self-pity was not going to solve anything. She pulled out her phone and quickly sent a text to Amber explaining what was happening. Amber had to work the night shift tonight, so she would need to be home by seven, doable if she rushed non-stop through the files. With confirmation from Amber, Megan got back to work.

4

It was six-thirty the next morning and to say that Megan was exhausted would be an understatement. She had stayed at work until just after six before rushing to get home so Amber could get to work. Then she had to handle Lola, who was very excited and hyper at seeing her. When she finally got Lola down for bed it wasn't for long before her night terrors started. Lola had been having them for a few years now, no doctor could ever tell her why. They all said the same thing, sometimes it just happens. That was normally followed by the lovely comment about how if her life was unstable it could cause stress and anxiety in Lola's life, triggering the night terrors. So not only did she have a child that screamed most of the night at the monsters that only she could see, Megan got to feel like a complete failure that her new job was stressing Lola.

They both only got a few hours of sleep and normally Lola could sleep all day, but she had to go to school because Amber only had six hours off before she had to go back into work. Which meant Lola had to go to school and she had to go to work to deal with the Ice Queen herself. A door opening had Megan turning to see who it was. She was surprised to see Amber making her way down the hallway, rubbing her eye.

"What are you doing up?"

"Forgot to close my blinds and now I need to pee. I didn't get a chance to ask, how was work?" Amber asked, as she leaned against the kitchen entrance.

"Oh great, right up until the part where my boss lost her shit because another teacher brought me welcome flowers to my office. Or her office as she pointed out multiple times." Megan rolled her eyes.

"What? Does she hate flowers?" Amber asked confused as to why someone would have such an issue with it.

"I think it was more to the fact that it was a male teacher doing it. She automatically assumed I was sleeping with him or trying to sleep with him."

"Oh, is he cute?" Amber asked, slightly more awake now.

"He's a fine piece of Spanish delight. But I'm not interested. I mean, the older I get, the gayer I get right? I get it, he's a huge flirt, but she didn't have to just jump to conclusions. And what is the big deal about leaving some of the filing for me to do today? I mean she's off in her office marking when she isn't teaching, why can't I be working on filing old files when I have the spare time? It's not like they are going anywhere and why the hell are they not in some database somewhere?"

"I don't know, schools are funny that way. They like to keep their paper records in case something ever gets deleted and destroyed. You are right though, it's not like they were of a high value that it had to get done. You could have easily done it in your free time. Sounds to me like your new boss likes to be in control of everything. This could be her way of making sure you are at her mercy and you know it."

Megan had never thought of it like that before. She took a moment to really think about it and what Amber said did make sense. In the two days that she had been working for Deborah she had made multiple comments about her not being qualified, and all the things she did wrong. She told her multiple times that she wouldn't have a job if she didn't get this or that done. Of course, two of those times was because she was late, but the rest were taken to the extreme.

"That actually makes a lot of sense. When I got there yesterday, after she allowed me to come into her office..."

"Wait, what do you mean allowed you?" Amber asked, cutting Megan off.

"Oh, that's one of her things, and she does it with everyone. You have to knock, no matter if she's busy or not. If that door is closed, which is always, you have to stand there and wait for her to tell you to come in. Then when you are allowed in, you have to stand and wait until she deigns to speak to you. Not that anyone told me that on my first day and I got reemed out like you would not believe."

"Wow, that takes a special kind of person. So what happened today when you got granted permission to enter the castle?" Amber said with a slight eye roll.

"She was doing some kind of paperwork, she didn't even look up. I swear I stood there for like a solid ninety seconds before I went to speak and she silenced me with her hand. I had to stand there, quietly, until she finished whatever she was doing before she addressed me. So I could totally see how she is dependent on the whole control aspect. I mean, even my charm isn't working and I've been putting it on pretty good."

"Well, there have been people immune to your charm. Look, some people in this world are just cold and bitchy, it's in their blood. You can't fix it, all you can do is try and work around it. So keep being your sweet and lovely self and then hopefully she will just get used to you. Who knows, maybe you'll rub off on her." Amber said with a shrug.

"Maybe. I gotta get Lola up and ready for school. I can't be late again today or the Ice Queen is going to turn into the Dragon Lady and eat me."

"Well if it's the fun kind of eating there are worse ways to go," Amber said with a flirty smile.

"Maybe that's her problem. She needs a good lay to warm her up." Megan giggled.

"You should volunteer your services."

"Oh, I doubt very much that she is gay."

"You never know, she just might need the right persuasion. After all, aren't you her personal assistant?" Amber said with a wink before she turned and headed off to the bathroom.

Megan couldn't help but shake her head. Even if Deborah was gay, Megan would bet every dollar she had that her pussy would freeze anything that came near it. Softly chuckling to herself, she began to wonder if she was curious, if she sort of liked how hard Deborah was on her. Deborah intrigued her. Deborah was beautiful and powerful, like the epitome of stylish femme power dyke.

Megan headed over to Lola's room to get her ready for school. She was hoping it wouldn't be too bad to get her up and dressed, but she knew it was going to be a challenge. If there was one thing Lola loved, it was her sleep. It had been a blessing when she was younger, but now that she was having to go to school it was quickly becoming a curse.

"Lola baby, you gotta get up," Megan said, as she sat down on the edge of the bed.

Lola rolled around and groaned at being woken up. "No up, sleep," she whined.

"I know baby, but you got school today. You can't stay home, Mommy has to go to work. Come on baby, it won't be so bad and tonight after school you can sleep as long and as much as you want." Megan promised.

She got up and opened the blind, bringing the sunlight right into Lola's room. Lola made a groan once again, but she at least sat up so Megan was taking it. She gathered clothes for Lola to wear and helped to get her very sleepy child dressed. Once she was all dressed it was time for her to go pee and then Megan did her hair. With Lola looking beautiful they headed off to the kitchen where Megan popped in some frozen waffles into the toaster while Lola sat at the small bistro table in the corner.

"Did you have fun at school yesterday baby?"

"It was ok. I like being home with you."

"I know, me too baby. But Mommy has to work so we have a nice place to live and yummy food in our bellies. You'll get used to school and before you know it you will love it. You'll be upset when it's the weekend," Megan said with a warm smile as she brought the cut up waffles over to Lola.

"Never," Lola said in her stubborn voice.

Megan knew better than to try and argue with that tone, so she left Lola eating so she could get ready herself.

She was just finished putting her makeup on when she got an email from Lola's school. Instantly her heart sank, the school had a pipe burst and it was closed down while repairs took place. They suspected it would be three days before the school could be reopened. Megan couldn't stop the panic from taking over her. If Lola couldn't go to school, there was nowhere else for her to go. She wasn't old enough to stay here alone and Megan couldn't take the time off from work to stay with Lola. If she worked at the diner, maybe she could switch enough shifts to make it work, but she couldn't with this job. There was no one that could cover for her and Amber needed to work today just as badly as she did. They were both struggling with the rent each month.

Before Megan knew it, her eyes were flooding with tears and she was fighting to control her breathing. She didn't know what to do. She had been struggling and fighting every single day since the moment that plus sign showed up on that test. She thought the guy she slept with would at least do the right thing and be there for Lola. She didn't care to be with him, she didn't need his love or his support. She just needed him to do the right thing and be there for Lola. Help her provide for her and be in her life. But instead she got told to have an abortion and leave him alone. She could have taken the easy way out, but she refused to give up her baby. She knew it was going to be hard, she knew she was going to be missing out on a lot of sleep, but she also knew when she looked at Lola's inno-cent little face that it was all worth it.

For five years now she had been struggling to make the rent payment and be able to feed and clothe Lola. She had gone without food herself just so she could get that pack of diapers or can of formula. She had worked a hundred hours a week just to pay the bills. Working jobs where guys would grab her ass and she was treated like crap. She finally had the opportunity to get a real job, one which would enable her to care for Lola properly and that she could be proud to tell people about, and now it was looking like she was going to lose it. All because of a fucking pipe bursting.

Megan only allowed herself a few minutes to cry and freak out before she forced herself to stop. This wasn't going to help her. She had to figure out what to do and the only thing she could think of was taking Lola with her to work. She knew Deborah had a busy day, maybe she could hide Lola behind her desk with some toys. It was a ridiculously long shot, but she could hope. Maybe it would be okay? If Deborah had an issue with it, then she would just tell her about the pipe and maybe tomorrow Amber would be able to switch shifts with someone so she could be home to watch her. If she showed up on time today and did an amazing job, then maybe that would please Deborah enough that she would overlook the fact that there was a five year old in her office. Or she was going to be fired right there on the spot in front of her daughter. Either way she had to go and just hope it wouldn't be too bad.

5

Megan sat in her car outside the school and let out a long breath. She was early for once. The downside was her beautiful daughter sitting in her car seat next to her. Normally that wouldn't be a downside, but it was in this situation. She had no idea how she was going to sneak Lola in and keep her a secret throughout the whole day. Even if she did by some miracle manage it, how the hell was she going to do it for another two days if Amber couldn't swap shifts? Megan let out a long sigh, there was nothing she could do about it right now. For now, she had to get to work and just pray that her boss wasn't that big of a bitch to fire her in front of her daughter. Megan grabbed her purse and Lola's backpack that was filled with things to entertain her with. She got out and got Lola out of her seat. They walked towards the main doors, while Megan spoke.

"Ok baby, remember that Mommy has to work today. I can't play with you. I need you to play with your toys and color while I am working. Then afterwards when we get home tonight we can play as long as you want. Deal?"

"Deal Mommy. I'll be a good girl." Lola said with a big toothy smile. Lola was delighted to going to work with her Mom.

Megan could only hope that this would go over well. They walked through the school and the halls were pretty empty, as it was still early. Megan quickly snuck Lola into her office and was glad that Kathy was not at her desk. She got Lola sitting down on the floor behind her desk with her backpack, while she quickly got herself sorted. She got a glimpse of Deborah before her door was opened and her boss was standing right there, skirt tight around her hips. An expensive white shirt tight and immaculately pressed.

"Good morning Ma'am. Did you have a good evening?" Megan asked with a friendly smile.

"Here is the list of what needs to be completed today before you leave." Deborah said, handing over the list.

Megan took it with a warm smile. "I'll make it happen."

Deborah went to turn and head to her office, when she caught the face of a little girl poking out from behind Megan's desk. Deborah turned to give the little girl her full attention. The very first thing she noticed was that she was enchanting. She had warm big dark eyes and messy wavy brown hair. She was very cute but she also didn't belong here. Deborah turned around fully to give the little girl her attention. She looked exactly like Megan, but at the same time nothing like Megan with her caramel skin and dark eyes and hair. Megan seemed to catch on that something was going on. She looked down to see that Lola had poked her out of the side of her desk.

"I can explain," Megan instantly said, as the panic was welling up inside of her.

"And what is your name?" Deborah asked Lola in a kind voice completely ignoring Megan.

The tone of her voice was a foreign one to Megan and she was surprised her voice was even capable of sounding that kind.

"Lola. What's you name?"

"My name is Deborah. How old are you?"

"Five." Lola said, as she held up one hand.

"I'm sorry. She's normally in school, but they had pipes bursts and there's water everywhere and my roommate has to work so she can't watch her. I don't have a babysitter and I just found out this morning. She will be very good and you won't even know she's here I promise." Megan said with a rush.

This was the worst thing that could have happened. She knew it would be impossible to hide Lola from Kathy, and realistically she knew that Deborah was bound to find out, but she was hoping it would be closer to the end of the day and she could have proven that Lola wasn't a distraction to her work.

"Schools tend to have that issue, especially if they are older. The winter causes the pipes to freeze and then they burst when it gets warmer out. Lola, I could really use a little helper today. Do you think you could help me?"

"I'm a good helper." Lola said, as she stood up on her sturdy little legs.

"You look like a good helper. Come on, let's see what fun we can have." Deborah said with a smile, as she held her hand out for Lola to take.

Lola quickly went over and placed her tiny hand in Deborah's and they headed out of Megan's office and over to her own. Megan couldn't help but stand there, confused. She had no idea what the hell had just happened. To begin with, she had never seen Deborah have anything that resembled a smile on her face. She thought her face would break if she actually cracked a smile. Now she had just taken Lola to her office to hang out. She didn't give Megan any trouble about having brought her child in to work with her. Megan knew that Deborah was a teacher, but she taught teenagers and not kindergarteners. There was a difference in teenagers and a little five year old girl and yet Deborah didn't even hesitate to steal her away. Megan let out yet another sigh. There wasn't anything she could do about it right now. At least she still had a job, at least she thought she still had a job. Deborah could be waiting until tonight to fire her. That was something she could worry about later. Currently, she had a long list of things she needed to complete if she was ever going to get out of here on time with Lola. Putting her worry aside, she picked up the list and got to work.

6

D eborah sat in her office with Lola sitting in a chair right beside her at her desk. When she had walked into Megan's office that morning, the very last thing she ever expected to see was this beautiful little girl hiding behind a desk. Deborah knew she was cold on the outside. She knew that she came across as someone who didn't care about other people. But, she really did love children. She had always wanted to have children, but her ex-wife had zero tolerance for children. She loved to have the house perfectly clean and organized. She loved being able to go out to fancy restaurants and on vacations whenever she wanted. To her, she couldn't do any of that if they had a child. Then it would have to be family friendly restaurants and vacations. To her that wasn't romantic and that wasn't a life she wanted. So Deborah settled for not having children, even though she desperately wanted one. She had even tried to bring up the option of adoption for an older child. One that would still be young enough to bond with them, but old enough that they wouldn't lose sleep every night over or have to deal with changing diapers. Her ex-wife still wouldn't budge and ultimately it was one of the many reasons things ended between them.

She never expected Megan to have a child. She didn't seem like the type to have a child, and yet when Deborah thought about it it did make sense. Why she was always late in the morning. Why she seemed to have lower quality of clothing. Why she looked exhausted every day. She was busy raising a five year old child and the fact that she didn't mention having Lola's father watch her today, she was clearly doing it on her own. Deborah could understand why Megan would hide having a child and being a single parent. She didn't know first hand, but she had friends that were single parents when they were younger and they often got passed over for jobs they were qualified for because of it. So Deborah didn't blame Megan for keeping this a secret. She knew it wasn't a reflection of how much she cared and loved Lola, but more so she would be considered equal when applying for a job.

Deborah and Lola were working on some simple math problems that Deborah had created for her. Lola was a very bright little girl that was very curious about everything. That was what Deborah loved about young children, they were always curious. In her early years of teaching Deborah had worked in the primary grades. Most teachers, especially in this school, hated being stuck in the younger grades, especially kindergarten and grade one. To Deborah though, they were the best eight years of her life. She loved being in a room surrounded by hyper five year olds running around, because to her, that was real teaching. It was pure curiosity and excitement to learn. Deborah became a teacher so she could show children how amazing learning could be. She wanted to unlock all of that curiosity and watch it come to life. It was something she missed greatly since making the switch to this school. Working with teenagers was different. They didn't tend to ask why, but rather just copy down what was written and memorized it. They were more focused on what the future would be and what grades they needed to get into the University they wanted. Their curiosity was gone and it was a real shame. Getting to spend the day with Lola was a dream come true to Deborah.

"Very good Lola. You are a very smart little girl." Deborah said with a warm smile as Lola was able to answer all of the math questions.

"Thank you." Lola said with a giggle.

"Do you like your school?"

"It's ok." Lola said with a small shrug.

"Just ok? Why just ok? What about it do you not like?"

"Ms Wilson, she is always busy and it's not very fun."

"Not very fun, well that's not good. Why isn't it very fun?"

Deborah was very interested in learning more from this little girl. She always thought that learning should be fun for kids, especially in the younger grades. They needed that fun so they would enjoy school and want to go every day.

"It's boring sometimes. We sit and write our letters or we sit and Ms Wilson reads to us. We go outside, we have snack, we have lunch, then we do numbers. Same thing every day. Boring."

"That does sound boring. What about art? Do you make anything?"

"Sometimes, but never for fun. Mommy and me do it for fun." Lola said with a smile.

"Do you? What kind of art do you do?"

"We make a big mess in the living room or kitchen. We get paint everywhere. Or we make slime." Lola said with a massive toothy smile. It was clear that she loved being creative and getting her hands dirty.

"Slime eh? You know, I've never made slime before. Is it hard?" Deborah said, with a warm smile. She was truly enjoying spending the time talking with Lola.

"Super easy, just three things. Mommy even gets food color and we make it rainbow."

"Oh rainbow, that sounds very pretty. Do you make sticky slime?"

"Ya and fluffy. They look like clouds."

"Maybe you could show me one day how to make it."

"I can do that!" Lola said very excited to teach someone something.

Deborah couldn't believe how adorable this little girl was. She could tell that she was Megan's daughter. They looked identical with the exception of Lola's skin being mocha like Deborah herself and her hair and eyes dark and not pale and blonde like Megan. She had that same charm, beautiful eyes, big smile and messy hair as her mom. Deborah couldn't help but wonder where Lola's dad was and if he wasn't in the picture, then why wasn't he?

"So it's just you and your mom?" Deborah asked, trying to see what she could get out of the little cutie.

"And Amber."

"Who is Amber?"

"Mommy's friend. We live with her."

"Oh, is that a new thing?" Deborah asked. She was very curious about who this Amber woman was. Was

Megan gay? Was Amber her girlfriend? Deborah was very interested in these answers, more than she cared to admit.

"No, we've always lived with Amber. She watches me when Mommy has to work."

"Do you like your Mommy's new job?"

"I don't know. I like that Mommy is home with me at night now. She can read me a bedtime story and she's there in the morning. I like that."

"She wasn't there before?" Deborah asked. She knew that some personal assistants had to work pretty crazy hours, but she had never heard of one having to work overnight.

"Not every night. Mommy worked hard, she had two jobs."

"Two jobs? Wow, she must have been working a lot."

"Mommy worked a lot at a diner and a bar bringing people their food. Now she works while I go to school and she picks me up and we get all night together. I like that part the best."

"Your Mommy was a server before this job, was she?" Deborah said with a smirk as things clicked in her head. She had a feeling that Megan was not that experienced in the personal assistant area, but her resume said very differently. Now it all made sense why she wasn't very good at some of the simplest of tasks. She had never done this before. She was a waitress and lied on her resume to get a better job.

"Mmhmm." Lola answered, as she started to draw on her paper.

"And now your Mommy gets to drop you off at school and pick you up." Deborah stated, as she could see how much that meant to Lola.

"Yup, we get more time together with this job. So, I guess I do like it."

"That's good. Well, I think it's time for lunch, what about you? Are you hungry?"

"Starving."

"Well, let's grab Mommy and I know the perfect place for us to go to sit and enjoy some yummy food." Deborah said, as she stood up.

She held her hand out for Lola to take, which she did easily, and they headed over to Megan's office. They walked in and Megan instantly looked up and smiled at them both. They looked scarily alike. With their similar colourings, Lola could have been Deborah's daughter.

"Hey baby, how are you?" Megan asked from a desk covered in papers.

"Deborah said it's lunchtime and she knows a great place to eat our lunch. Come on Mommy."

Deborah fixed Megan's blue eyes with her own eyes, dark and intense. She looked at Megan with a hunger and Megan felt it wash over her and pool between her legs. Deborah smiled at Megan for the first time.

"Ok, I'm coming." Megan said with a warm smile, as she picked up her and Lola's lunch.

Megan followed them out of her office and she had no choice but to follow Deborah and see where she was leading them. She was a little surprised to be heading outside of the school. Megan figured that they would be going to the lunch room. Deborah led them across the parking lot and then across the street, through some trees and then they arrived at a little hidden park that Megan had no idea existed. The park was surrounded by trees, but it was rather large. There was a playground, with monkey bars, and a swing set. Along with multiple picnic tables for people to utilize. No one was there and Lola instantly gave both of them a huge smile.

"Can I go play Mommy?"

"Let's eat something first and then you can play baby."

They all went and sat down at one of the picnic tables and got their lunches out. Lola took a big bite of her ham sandwich as she swung her legs back and forth. Deborah ate her own lunch, but watched as Megan's lunch seemed to consist of just a few pieces of fruit. It was clear that a lot of love and effort had been put into Lola's lunch and Megan's was just whatever they had left over. Deborah kept the conversation to a minimum as they ate and just allowed them all to enjoy the warmth of the sun. She found herself watching Megan with her child, a loving mom. When Lola had finished eating she took off running for the playground with Megan and Deborah right behind her.

Megan wasn't sure what to make of any of this. She never expected Deborah to be ok with her having a child, much less having the child here at her work. Yet Deborah didn't hesitate to chase Lola all around the park. She left her heels by the picnic table and even in her tight pencil skirt, she was still playing with Lola and running round with her. It warmed Megan's heart to not only see Lola having fun, but also to see a softer side to Deborah. She had no idea that Deborah could even smile, much less laugh and have fun. It was a warming sight to see. Something else nagged at Megan too. A growing sexual desire to be taken by Deborah. She found herself more and more turned on by the control Deborah asserted over her at every opportunity.

They continued to play for thirty minutes before they needed to head back to work. Lola didn't even complain, which surprised Megan as she normally hated having to leave a park. It was as though she sensed Deborah's natural authority too. They all headed back inside and as Megan went to bring Lola with her into her office so Deborah could work, Deborah quickly dismissed the idea and brought Lola with her once again into her office. Megan had no idea what to make of any of this, but she didn't have the time right now to think about it. She had work she needed to complete before she would be able to take Lola home at the end of the day.

IT WAS FINALLY the end of the day and Megan was proud of herself for getting everything on the list completed and without screwing anything up. She was feeling very good about herself. Her door was open, so Deborah walked in, but without Lola. Megan turned to see where her daughter was and saw that she had Kathy's attention as she told one of her famous Lola stories. Megan turned her attention back to Deborah, ready for a lecture from her.

"I'm sorry about bringing her here today. I truly am," Megan spoke first, hoping it would ease whatever lecture was bound to come her way.

"She's amazing, a very curious little girl," Deborah said warmly.

"She is. She's always asking people why this or why that. It can frustrate some people and I know her teacher wishes she would stop."

"Never let her stop. Curiosity is the best part about learning. Kids are often curious from a very young age, but it is beaten out of them by the educational system. When they reach high school they stop wondering why and just focus on what they need to know so they can pass. Embrace her curiosity and maybe she won't lose it. She also seems very creative. She's got lots of stories in her."

"She does. She loves art, but she doesn't get it much at her school. I try to foster it at home in any way that I can. It seems like the only time she sits still long enough is when she is coloring or painting. She's not short on energy." Megan said proudly.

"Creativity is a wonderful thing. It's good that you allow her to embrace it and express herself. Most parents wouldn't. Don't worry about school, she can be here until it is open again. She's no trouble to have around. And I'm sure Ms Jackson would love to have her in an art class."

"Really? Are you sure, because I can try and find a way for her to stay home. I don't want to cause any trouble."

Megan could not jeopardize this job. She knew that Lola being at home would be tricky, especially if Amber couldn't switch her shift. Megan would have to do the one thing she swore she would never do, and that was leave Lola with a babysitter. She would do it though if it meant she wouldn't lose her job.

"She's no trouble at all. She's a breath of fresh air. And she really is quite the helper. I got plenty of work done today thanks to her. Bring her until the school is repaired. Now it's the end of the day, and it is time to head home. I'm sure she is going to sleep very well tonight after all of this excitement." Deborah said with a small kind smile.

"One can hope. I'll see you tomorrow Ms Stewart." Megan said with a warm smile.

"Don't be late." Deborah warned sternly as she turned and headed off to say goodbye to Lola.

Megan couldn't help the small chuckle at that. It was

ok to bring Lola, but it would not be ok for her to be late. Well, Megan could live with that. Megan packed up her and Lola's things and went to save Kathy from a very long story. Today had gone better than Megan could ever have imagined and hopefully the next couple of days wouldn't be so bad either.

7

I t was Monday morning and Megan walked into work feeling pretty good about herself. A spot had opened up in Lola's before and after school care program for an earlier slot. She was now able to drop Lola off at her school at seven thirty in the morning instead of eight. Which was great because now she had an extra thirty minutes to get to work and she got to avoid the heavier traffic. All of this meant she would have to get up at five thirty in the morning to get Lola up and ready and herself ready for the day and to get to the school for the drop off time, but it was worth it when it meant Megan would get to work thirty minutes early. This would allow her to get settled in, be there before Deborah and get a jump start on some of the routine things she had to do during the day.

Megan walked to her desk, coffee cup in hand, and started to get some of the files organized that she needed to finish going through. She hadn't got them done on Friday, but Deborah had insisted that they could be finished on Monday and to go home with Lola. Lola's school had sent out an email Saturday letting the parents know that the pipes were fixed and it would be open Monday morning. That was a huge relief to Megan. She knew that Deborah said it was ok for Lola to be at work when she needed, but she also didn't want to abuse that privilege. She knew that Lola could be a handful and she didn't want Lola to cause any problems for Deborah. During those three days Deborah had been amazing with Lola. She had taken her around school to show her everything and the classes. She even got Lola to sit in a couple of the art classes with Ms. Jackson, which was Lola loved. She went home Friday with six new paintings she had done. Ms Jackson had come by her office Friday closer to the end of the day to drop them off now that they were dry. Ms Jackson couldn't stop raving about how amazing Lola was and that she had some serious talent already with a paint brush. She had gifted Lola with a set of pastels for her to experiment with and Lola had spent the whole weekend covered in pastel making multiple masterpieces. One of which Megan had to promise to bring with her today to give to Deborah. Lola had not stopped talking about Deborah all weekend. Strangely enough, Megan had not been able to stop thinking about Deborah either.

Since the very first day Lola had been at Megan's work, she would not stop talking about how amazing and fun Deborah was. She would talk all night about the cool things Deborah had taught her and that she couldn't wait to go to work with her again tomorrow. She actually went to bed early just so she would be properly rested for Deborah the next day. It warmed Megan's heart to see her daughter take so well to someone. She normally took a little while to get warmed up to someone. The only exception was Amber, and that was because Amber had been there since she was months old.

Megan looked up when she heard someone approaching her office fifteen minutes after she arrived. She saw that it was Deborah and not Kathy.

"Good morning Ma'am." Megan said warmly.

"Good morning. You are early and without Lola. Did you leave her at home?"

"No, the school is open again and a spot in the earlier before school care became available so I was able to get Lola into it. She now gets dropped off at seven thirty instead of eight, which is great because then I get to avoid all of that traffic." Megan said with a smile.

"She would need to wake up earlier though, she does not come across as a little girl who likes to be up early." Deborah said warmly.

"She loves her sleep and she can be a night owl, but she's gotten better with having to be in school. She'll get used to it and she still has the weekend to sleep in. Also, I have something for you. Lola wanted to make sure I gave it to you."

Megan pulled out the pastel picture of Deborah, Megan and Lola and the park playing. Deborah and Lola with bold black hair. Megan distinctive with messy yellow hair. She handed it over to Deborah and Deborah gave a big smile at seeing it.

"She is very good at drawing."

"She is. Ms. Jackson gave her some pastels to try and play with. She spent the whole weekend with rainbow colored hands." Megan said with a chuckle.

"Tell her I love it and I am going to frame it and put it up in my office. This is perfect for when I am feeling stressed. I can look at it and remember what an amazing little girl there is in the world." Deborah said with a warmth that could only come from someone who was born to be a parent.

"I'll tell her. She'll be very happy."

"If I may ask, where is her father?" Deborah asked cautiously. She was not sure what Megan would be comfortable talking about and what would be off limits.

"He's not in the picture. He was a chef at a diner. We had slept together a few times, nothing serious, but I ended up pregnant after a stupid drunken night. I told him and he didn't want me to have the baby. I suppose I could have had an abortion, but I couldn't do it. I know it might sound silly, she wouldn't have been anything more than a pea, but the second I saw that plus sign, I fell in love with her. I let him off the hook and I never heard from him again." Megan said with a shrug.

"That doesn't sound silly at all. Some people are born to be parents and you were clearly born to be a mom. I'm sorry he wasn't there for you, it must have made it difficult for you." Deborah said sympathetically.

"It was. I ended up moving in with Amber, she's an amazing woman and my best friend. She's helped me with Lola from the time she was only three months old."

"She is your girlfriend?"

"God, no! We are just friends."

Deborah leaned against the door frame and looked behind her slightly to see if they were still alone. She was pleased to see that they were.

"You don't have a desire to date someone though?"

"I tried a long time ago, but whenever the girl found out I was a single mom they tended to take off. Or they weren't as interesting as they seemed in the beginning. It is a lot, I guess. I don't really look like a mom and I guess it is kind of a lot for someone to take on, me and Lola. I kind of gave up on dating for now." Megan said with a small shrug.

"The girl?" Deborah asked, that was the only thing she picked up, it was the only thing that mattered to her. Deborah was pleasantly surprised to hear that Megan wasn't straight.

"I tend to be much more interested in women. I spent wasted time when I was younger, getting drunk and having meaningless sex with men. But I do prefer women. I only date women." Megan asked, she didn't want to make Deborah uncomfortable at all.

"I'm gay myself, so you don't have to worry about that. I was just surprised."

Deborah was doing her best to ignore the heat that was flooding through her at the prospect that Megan was also into women. She had been attracted to Megan since the moment her eyes landed on her. Those wild ocean blue eyes. That body that was made for sin. But it was one thing to be attracted to someone and know that you would never get to be with them and to be attracted with the chance that you could be with them. Deborah's mind was already thinking about all of the things she would love to do to Megan. She wondered what sounds Megan would make underneath her, and it would be underneath her. Deborah was not a woman who gave up control for anything, especially in the bedroom. She liked to be the dominant one in the relationship. She loved control and power play and she loved knowing that she could bring someone to a level of pleasure that they had never reached before. She would love nothing more than to get Megan spread out on her desk, begging for release.

Megan could see the heat ignite in Deborah's eyes and

she knew then, for sure, that Deborah wanted her. Megan was surprised that Deborah found her attractive. Deborah was clean and put together, whereas Megan was messy and wild. Megan was also a lot younger. They came from two different worlds and Megan couldn't help but think that she didn't belong in Deborah's world, that she wouldn't ever understand how Deborah's world worked. Still though, she couldn't help but wonder what it would be like to be with Deborah. To be on her knees for Deborah. She wanted to know what her touch felt like. She wanted to know how her lips would feel against her own. Megan came around her desk and leaned against it.

"Why the surprise?" Megan asked with a flirty smirk.

"You have a daughter, that normally means you prefer men over women." Deborah said, as she moved closer. She felt like there was a bungee cord attached between her and Megan. Something that was bringing her closer to Megan. A heat and intensity that had been burning more and more since they first met.

"Things happen when there have been a few shots of tequila in the night. It's been almost six years since I've been with a man. And there hasn't been a huge amount of women since." Megan said with a shrug.

"No one catches your interest?" Deborah asked, closing the gap between them.

With Megan half leaning, half sitting on her desk, she had to look up to Deborah and she could see the heat get even hotter in her eyes. Oh yes, Deborah did like to be in control, of that Megan was certain. Megan had never before let someone take complete control over her, yet she found her nipples getting hard and wetness seeping between her legs. Before Deborah, she had never met anyone she wanted to give complete control to.

"There might be someone, but will she do something a little reckless? Something very against the rules?" Megan challenged.

Deborah smirked as she started to lean in even closer to Megan. The heat between them was pulsing and they both wanted nothing more than to close the small gap between their lips and finally get a taste of the other.

"She might surprise you." Deborah said softly as she hovered her lips right over Megan's.

"I like surprises." Megan whispered back. She thought she might explode.

Deborah closed the very gap between their lips and touched her lips to Megan's. The second their lips made contact Megan let out a soft moan. She couldn't believe how soft Deborah's lips were. Megan pressed harder against Deborah, but Deborah was not about to give up any control. She moved back slightly to stop Megan from pressing harder into the kiss. Only when she had control did she press harder against Megan and she brought her hand up to Megan's throat and just placed it there lightly, keeping her in her place. Megan moaned at the weight of Deborah's hand against her throat, she wasn't squeezing, she was just placing it there as if she owned her, and that was enough to make Megan's panties soaked. She felt Deborah's tongue licking at her lips and she gladly opened her mouth to let it in. She couldn't believe how good it felt to have Deborah's tongue in her mouth. Megan didn't try to fight for dominance, she allowed Deborah to take it freely and she was well rewarded with a passionate kiss.

Megan was so caught up in the kiss that she missed the sounds of someone on the outside of the main door. Deborah caught it just in time to pull away and move back as Kathy walked into the office with Ms Jackson right behind her. Megan was breathing heavily and she could feel her nipples as hard as pebbles inside her bra. She looked at Deborah and she could see the passion was still inside her eyes. She didn't want to stop, but they had to. Deborah was not about to get caught making out with her assistant.

"You need to get the list done by the end of the day. Don't disappoint me." Deborah ordered with a hard voice as she turned and headed out of Megan's office.

Megan just gave a smirk, as she knew then for sure that Deborah did it on purpose. She had to keep up appearances. She couldn't let people know the things she really wanted to do to Megan. She couldn't let people know that she actually cared. Megan didn't mind, she would be thinking about that kiss for the rest of the day. Hell she was certain she would be feeling that kiss on her lips for the rest of her life. What might have been a simple kiss was the most seductive kiss that Megan had ever felt. Deborah's power was the ultimate seduction to her. She couldn't wait for the opportunity to get more. It had been a long time since she had been touched and she desperately wanted Deborah to take her entirely and touch her everywhere.

8

Deborah had been sitting in her office for the majority of the day. She had a light teaching day and normally she used these days as a way to get caught up on all of the marking or paperwork that she needed to do. And she certainly had a lot of it to get caught up on after spending three days with Lola in her office. Not that she didn't love every second of it. To be able to spend three days with a smart little girl, it was like a dream come true to her. She wanted to spend more time with Lola. She wanted to teach her everything she knew so she could embrace her curiosity and learn while having fun. Deborah looked over at the picture she had placed on her desk, the one that Lola had made for her. She could see that, even at five, Lola had some natural talent when it came to drawing, something that should be cherished and nurtured. It warmed her heart to see the drawing and it would be a great addition to her office, especially on the days when she was feeling down or stressed. It was a little reminder of why she has always loved teaching.

Deborah had been trying to focus all day long on her

work, but every chance she got, she found herself looking out of her window and across the office into Megan's office. She couldn't get that kiss out of her mind. She had no idea what had come over her. She never acted like that, on impulse and her basic dominant desires. Yes, she had when she was younger, but she wasn't young anymore, she knew better. If there was one thing she learnt from her failed marriage is that she needed to be in control. She had to have control and keep not only her partner at a distance, but her own feelings as well. She couldn't allow herself to care about another woman again, she couldn't go through that pain and heartache again. She refused to be vulnerable and she refused to let another woman hurt her like that again. Megan was messy, she was charming, she was a flirt and she was everything that Deborah had no interest in. Her ex-wife was much like herself. She was put together, well presented, educated and kept her emotions in check. Megan was the exact opposite of that. She was a wild child. She was messy, she lied to get a job, she had a child from a drunken mistake. She was everything that Deborah should be avoiding and yet her body was screaming for her. She wanted to make Megan hers. There was this primal need deep inside of her to claim Megan as her own and Deborah was having a hard time keeping that urge down.

It was the end of the day and everyone was packing up to leave. Deborah noticed that Megan was still sitting at her desk and was slowly putting things away. Normally she was quickly running out of here to pick up Lola. Yet today she was not in any hurry at all. In fact it seemed like she was trying to wait until everyone was gone. Deborah went to work on getting her own desk cleaned up and she saw Kathy leaving and then Megan stood to collect her things. Deborah sat back in her chair and watched as Megan left her office, but she turned to look at Deborah as she did. Deborah raised her hand and called Megan over. Megan walked over and opened Deborah's office door.

"Yes Ma'am." Megan asked.

"Close the door." Deborah ordered.

Megan did as she was told and stood there waiting to see what Deborah wanted.

"You are normally rushing out of here to get to Lola, not tonight?"

"Amber picked her up today. She didn't work today and wanted to spend some time with her. A friend of hers works at an art studio and she lets Lola go in and play with all of the supplies." Megan answered with a warm smile.

"That's nice. So not in a hurry to get home." Deborah stated with a smirk.

"No Ma'am."

"Put your bag down." Deborah ordered.

Megan did as she was told and then Deborah spoke again. "Take your shirt off."

Megan was slightly surprised by the directness of Deborah, yet why, she wasn't sure. This had been building. They both wanted this. Deborah clearly loved to be in control. Megan turned slightly to the open window in the office.

"No one will come in. Take your shirt off, now." Deborah said with a harder tone, she didn't like to be disobeyed.

Megan removed her jacket and then slowly began to unbutton her pink dress shirt. Once it was all unbuttoned she removed it, revealing her lacy white bra underneath.

She wasn't sure what she was expected to do next, so she figured she would go with the flow and do as she was told.

"Now your shoes and skirt." Deborah ordered.

Megan removed the items of clothing and stood there in nothing but her matching thong and bra set.

Deborah looked her over appreciatively. Megan's body was lean. Her breasts were big and full, Deborah couldn't help but notice them around the office. Her ass was deliciously round. There was absolutely no sign that she had had a child. Her stomach told no tales. Megan's body was built to envy or desire. Megan's body was built for sin.

"Come here, now." Deborah ordered, as she turned her chair slightly.

Megan walked over to Deborah, she was not shy at all. She knew her body was hot. It always had been, she had literally been blessed with it. She had taken great care of it over the years, one of the few things she had in her life that was actually all hers. Once she was in front of Deborah, Deborah ran her hand along the back of Megan's thigh up to her ass and reached between her legs, her hand startling against the lace of her panties. Megan shivered with excitement.

"So wet already. But you'll have to wait. You've been a very bad assistant, Megan. And I know you lied on your resume. I could have had any number of better assistants. Now, bend over my desk."

Megan leant forward across the desk. Her breasts pressed into the neat piles of paperwork.

"I'm sorry, Ma'am."

"You will be, Megan." Deborah watched appreciatively as Megan was bent across her desk, her ass raised in it's white lace thong. Nothing excited Deborah more than Megan's absolute obedience. Megan's willing capitulation to her desires. There was so much potential for where that could be taken.

"Megan, you will say the safe word, 'RED' if at any time with me you are uncomfortable and want to stop. Do you understand? I will stop immediately, but only if you say RED."

"Yes, I understand." Shivers ran through Megan's body as she anticipated Deborah's touch.

A sharp slap rang out as Deborah began to spank Megan. Her hand sharp against Megan's round ass. Megan yelped. Deborah kept spanking her, rhythmically. One cheek, then the other. One, then the other. She watched the cheeks heat and redden beneath her slaps. She watched Megan moan and her body moving as she began to accept the pain. Megan submitting willingly for her. This, this was what she truly loved. She increased the power with which she hit Megan. She wanted to see how far she could go. She knew Megan would be bruised up in the morning. She wanted to see the bruises.

Megan winced, but she continued to take it, her body began to relax into it, the endorphins did their job. Deborah saw how saturated the white lace was. Deborah saw the trickle of desire on Megan's inner thigh.

Deborah ceased the spanking when Megan was in a real daze, both cheeks red and beginning to purple in places. Deborah ran her fingers across the heat of Megan's sore ass. She got close to Megan's pussy and then moved away, Megan gave a whine.

"Please," Megan begged.

"Please what?" Deborah asked, continuing to trail her fingers around.

"You know what," Megan whined.

"Say it," Deborah ordered.

"Touch me, please. I need it," Megan begged, as she was already breathing heavily.

"Where? I want to hear you say it, Megan."

Megan felt her cheeks blushing against the desk. "My cunt. I want you to touch my cunt, please, Ma'am."

"Ok, but you must ask permission before you orgasm. Do you understand, Megan?"

"Yes," she gasped. "Yes."

Deborah ran her fingers up and down the lace, teasing her. Toying with her. Deborah enjoyed Megan's embarrassment, she enjoyed the lace. She enjoyed lingerie. She pulled the thong to one side and ran her fingers up and down Megan's wet heat. Megan nearly jumped off the desk as she felt the electricity of Deborah's touch where she needed it most. Her ass burned from the spanking. She felt so close to something incredible.

Deborah pushed two fingers deep inside of Megan. Megan let out a long moan at the invasion, but her hips rocked for a moment and she tried to get the fingers to go deeper. It was everything she wanted and needed, Deborah's fingers deep inside her. Deborah felt Megan's body responding to her as she caught her G spot. She began to fuck Megan with her fingers. She had wanted to do this for so long. Megan's body was trembling from the pleasure that was surging through her. She had never felt anything like this level of intensity.

Deborah began to hit her ass cheek again with her free hand, whilst fucking her with her fingers and her thumb started to slide against Megan's clit.

Megan screamed. "Oh god, I'm going to come. Please can I come?"

"No, Megan. You need to learn some self control."

Deborah wound it all back, slowed her fucking, stopped the spanking, removed her magical slippery thumb.

She began to build again gradually and Megan felt the heat building again.

She asked again, "Please Ma'am, please let me come."

She was denied again.

Deborah continued her controlled dance, taking Megan to the brink and then bringing her back, never quite letting her go. Megan's whole body shook and sweat beaded on her. She had never felt intensity like it.

Deborah built the intensity again, she was learning Megan's body. She knew what to do.

"Please, Ma'am, can I come?" Megan begged again.

"Yes," came the response. "I want you to come hard for me Megan. Come as though your only purpose in life is to submit to me."

Her words sent Megan tumbling right over the cliff, like nothing ever before. She gushed hot and wet over Deborah's hand and down the inside of her legs.

Deborah smiled to herself. Megan's orgasm was the sweetest thing.

Deborah gave her a minute collapsed over her desk to recover. She watched Megan's beautiful body breathing deeply, the cheeks on both her face and her ass bright red. She was the most beautiful thing Deborah had ever seen.

"Get on your knees, Megan."

Megan responded as quickly as her body would allow and was soon on her knees on the floor, feeling the wet patch she had created on the carpet.

"Now, clean my fingers, Megan. You made a mess." Deborah stood above her, still immaculate in her expensive outfit. She held her hand out to Megan's mouth, still sticky and wet with Megan's pleasure. Megan closed her eyes and allowed the fingers to penetrate her mouth, she licked, she sucked, she cleaned with her tongue, the taste of her own sex powerful on her tongue.

"Get dressed." Deborah ordered.

Megan slowly moved her shaky body and slowly got dressed. Once she was dressed, Deborah pulled her in for a heated kiss. Deborah was desperate to taste Megan from her own tongue. She kissed with intent and the taste of Megan's sex was potent. Deborah pulled away satisfied. Megan's hair was just as messy as usual.

"See you tomorrow." Deborah said with a wry smile, and with that Megan was dismissed.

9

Megan closed Lola's door behind her as she made her way out into the kitchen. She needed a drink, desperately after the day she just had. Amber was already sitting down on the couch waiting for her. She had picked up on Megan's energy when she returned home to a very messy Lola. Lola had a blast at the art studio like always. After a few long bath, having to change the water twice, Lola was finally clean, fed and into bed. Megan walked into the living room with two glasses and a bottle of cheap whiskey. Amber knew that if Megan was hitting the whiskey, it had been one hell of a day.

"Has your boss gone back to being the Dragon Lady with Lola no longer there?" Amber asked, as Megan poured them each a drink.

"Nope. I did something stupid, or I did something that felt unbelievable, but it most definitely was stupid."

"What did you do?"

"No judgments." Megan said with a pointed look to Amber.

"Never, you know that."

They have never had judgments between them. They could tell each other anything, and they had, plenty of times. That was what was great about their friendship, they could tell the other that they had murdered someone and the other would ask if they needed help to bury the body. They had each other's backs and they always would.

"I had sex with her." Megan admitted, looking right at Amber.

"Hello!" Amber said shocked.

"Over her desk." Megan added.

Amber opened her mouth and was completely shocked. She had no idea where this had come from. Last she heard, they didn't even like each other, but Megan was making it work.

"You dirty slut." Amber teased as she slapped Megan's thigh and giggled. Megan yelped.

"Oh, Amber, you need to take a look at this." Megan turned and rolled down her pyjama trousers exposing her red raw ass.

"OH MY GOD! What the fuck?! Are you ok? Was this consensual? What a kinky bitch!!"

"Totally consensual. And yes, she is such a kinky bitch."

"Oh man, so the Dragon Lady's got some game. How was it?" Amber asked, very interested in that part. If there was one thing Amber loved to talk about, it was sex. She wanted all of the dirty details.

"It was amazing. I can't even lie, it might have been the best sex I've ever had in my life," Megan said with a huge smile.

"Girl, you better start talking and I mean right now.

How the fuck did this even happen?" Amber asked, as she turned so she could get comfy and settle in.

"She came into my office this morning and we got talking. She asked about Lola and her school. I gave her Lola's picture. She asked about Lola's dad and I explained then I had made a comment about being with girls and it turned out she was gay. I was half sitting on the front of my desk and she came over to me and words were said, then she kissed me."

"Words were said? What words? Like sexy words?" Amber pressed, dying for more details.

"I had said that there was someone that caught my interest but she was too control to do anything. Next thing I know she's closing the gap and said she might surprise me. I said I liked surprises and then she kissed me. I mean, we were alone in the whole office, school hadn't started yet, but still, she kissed me. And let me tell you, the second her lips touched mine it was like this fire took over my entire body. I had never felt like that from a kiss before. It was amazing," Megan said with a dreamy smile.

"Lucky bitch. So you kiss and then what? Went about your business like nothing happened?"

"Someone was in the hallway and we pulled apart before Kathy and Ms. Jackson walked in on us. Then yeah pretty much, we went about the day like normal. At the end of the day I wasn't moving very fast to get out of there. I knew you had Lola and I was curious to see what would happen. After Kathy left and she didn't leave her office, I got up to head out. I looked over at Deborah and she called me into her office. And that is when everything changed."

"Oh my God, tell me right now and don't spare me any

of the dirty details." Amber asked, with a big excited look on her face.

"She ordered me to put my bag down and then to remove my clothing, piece by piece. There is a window in her office that you can see from the hallway outside, but she said not to worry about it. Then she told me to bend over her desk because I was a bad assistant. She gave me a spanking like nothing I have ever known. It hurt, a lot, but then, honestly, the longer I took it, the better it felt. It felt intense and freeing."

"Holy fuck." Amber said, as she fanned herself with her hand.

"Then she made me beg her to fuck me. Then she made me beg to be allowed to come. Then after all the begging, I just exploded. Then she made me clean her hand with my mouth. Then, she kissed me and just casually said 'See you tomorrow.'."

"Holy mother of fucking god. Shut up! Shut up right now! You guys just left? Like nothing happened?" Amber asked, beyond excited for this.

"Pretty much. Now I have no idea what is going to happen tomorrow when I go back in."

"You let her do it again obviously." Amber said, like it was the most obvious thing in the world.

"It's not that simple, and you know it. She's my boss, she could fire me at any moment if she wanted and then I would be screwed, in the not so fun way." Megan was honestly worried about that the most. If Deborah had enough of her, she could easily fire her and then what would she do? She didn't want to have to go back to working two jobs as a waitress just to be able to pay rent.

"She's not going to do that, plus if she did, you could also claim sexual harassment. She'd have to have a valid excuse to fire you. It had to be good though, the cold ones are always amazing in bed." Amber said, not yet ready to give up on the sex talk.

"It was amazing. She is so dominant. Yet, I don't know, there was something really sexy about it. I have never been more turned on before in my life. The way she ordered me around, it was like nothing I had ever felt before. The more she ordered me to do, the wetter I was getting."

"Well that makes sense. A lot of people love being controlled, in the right environment. That's not weird at all. She likes to be in control and you enjoy how she does it, so embrace it. Have some fun with it. It's not weird at all."

"I've never felt like that before. I've never wanted to be controlled before in any aspect of my life."

"Yeah, but sometimes it takes the right person to bring something different out in you. That doesn't mean you are always going to want to be controlled, it just means that you like it when she does it. There will be times where you still want to be in control in the bedroom and with a different person you may find that you don't like being controlled. It all depends on the person you are with and how they make you feel. Don't overthink it, really."

Megan let out a sigh as she took the rest of her drink before she poured herself another one. She had no idea what to think about any of this. She knew that she loved everything that Deborah did to her and she couldn't wait until they could do it again. She wasn't going to stress over it and this time around she was going to take Amber's advice and just roll with it. She would see what would happen in time, for now she was going to allow herself to feel good and have some pretty hot dreams tonight.

10

It had been a week since that day in Deborah's office and to say the week had been filled with sexual tension would be an understatement. They both desperately wanted to touch the other, but they weren't able to. With people always coming and going in the office and with Megan having to leave right after work to pick up Lola, they hadn't had the time to do anything with each other. Now it was Saturday night and Amber was able to work the day shift today so she could watch Lola that night. Megan was running all around the apartment trying to get ready for her date tonight. She had no idea where they were going, she just knew they were going to dinner and then hopefully back to Deborah's place for some fun.

Megan wasn't sure what restaurant they would be going to, so she put on one of her best black dresses, a short cocktail dress, but also not too short to be inappropriate either. She had done her hair, leaving it down in messy waves and she put on some makeup. What she didn't put on was any underwear at all. That would be the nice surprise that Deborah would have for later. She was almost ready when there was a knock on the door. Amber went to answer it as Megan went and gave Lola a kiss good night as she was already in bed.

Deborah was surprised that this was where Megan and Lola were living. She had taken her address at work yesterday, but she didn't think much of it. When she started to drive through the area her heart sank. There were drug addicts, pimps and prostitutes all over. The buildings all looked rough and rundown and there wasn't a single park in the area. It was a drastic change to the area her own home was in. She was in the rich area of town, surrounded by greenery and large extravagant homes. Walking through the building didn't help her either, as it looked just as bad on the inside then it did on the outside. The door opened and a woman, who she assumed was Amber, gave her a warm smile.

"Hi, you must be Deborah. Come on in." Amber said with a warm smile, as she moved back to let Deborah in.

"Thank you, you must be Amber." Deborah said, as she walked in and took notice of the apartment.

It was just as rundown as the rest of the building was. The kitchen was small and old, there was a pull out couch in the living room with sheets thrown on it. The whole apartment was rundown just as badly as the outside. It was a mess, but it had homely touches.

Megan came around the corner looking absolutely stunning in a little black dress and more make up than she wore to work. Deborah was taken aback by her beauty.

"Hey, sorry I was saying goodnight to Lola," Megan said.

"It's fine, are you ready to go?"

Megan gave a nod and said goodbye to Amber as they headed out. Once they were down in the car Deborah couldn't help, but place her hand on Megan's upper thigh.

"You look delicious," she said.

"I taste delicious too," Megan said with a sexy smile, as she moved Deborah's hand higher so she could feel that she wasn't wearing anything underneath.

Deborah moaned when her fingers made contact with Megan's wetness. In that instant, Deborah changed her mind, they could order food in later. She was taking Megan to her house and they were going now. She set off driving through the dark streets.

"Turn and face me." Deborah ordered.

Megan did as she was told, but it was awkward with her legs.

"Spread your legs wide open, I want to see you."

Megan moved her legs so her left was hanging into the back section of the car, making them fully open for Deborah. Deborah reached into her purse and pulled out a small finger vibrator and handed it over to Megan.

"Put it on. Play with yourself, but you are not allowed to come," she ordered.

"Yes Ma'am." Megan said with a husky voice.

She put the finger vibrator over her two fingers and turned it on. She placed it against her clit and let out a moan at the contact. She made sure to look right at Deborah as she enjoyed the sensations buzzing through her body.

"What are you thinking about?" Deborah asked.

"You fucking me. I can't wait to feel it. I want you so deep inside of me, I want you to fuck me so hard and deep that I won't be able to sit down at work on Monday."

"Put your own fingers inside yourself. I want to watch

you fucking yourself." Deborah's eyes flitted between Megan and the road. Megan pushing her fingers inside herself, her legs splayed open for Deborah's pleasure. Who was this girl? Where had she come from?

"Of fuck, yes." Megan moaned, as she closed her eyes, the vibrator still buzzing on her clit.

"Do not come. I mean it," Deborah ordered.

"Yes Ma'am."

Megan had to remove the bullet to keep herself from orgasm, but she was a good girl and listened to Deborah's orders. When they finally pulled up to Deborah's house, Megan was so close. They got out of the car and headed inside, Deborah's usually calm demeanour was almost urgent with desire for Megan.

Inside the house, Deborah lead Megan to the living room.

"On your knees," Deborah commanded. Megan dropped straight to the floor with an obedience she would have never have imagined in herself. Between her legs, she was literally throbbing with desire. She waited for Deborah's next instructions. Deborah slipped out of her dress and sat on her wide sofa in just her underwear, Megan looked up, desperate to see her.

"Do not look at me!" Deborah ordered. Megan's gaze dropped to the floor immediately.

"Come to me. On all fours."

Megan began to crawl slowly and obediently across the luxury living room carpet to Deborah. Deborah watched her and smiled to herself. Megan's breasts swayed in her dress as she crawled. Her messy tangle of bed hair was perfect for grabbing.

"Good girl." Deborah said as Megan reached her feet and knelt there demurely awaiting further instructions.

"Tonight, my pleasure is your priority. Your orgasm is not a guarantee, but mine is. You will work to pleasure me, and if your work is good enough, I'll think about fucking you. Do you understand?"

Megan nodded. "Yes Ma'am."

"Take my foot and massage it." Deborah's heels were off and she raised an elegant smooth caramel pedicured foot to Megan. "With your hands. And mouth."

Megan was shocked for just a second. She had never considered putting anyones foot in her mouth. But, here, with Deborah, she didn't hesitate. Her mouth went straight to work, her eyes closed in concentration. Deborah's toes in her mouth as her tongue slipped and slid between them. Of course, Deborah's foot was scrupulously clean. But Megan realised she would have done it anyway. Megan realised in that moment that she would do anything for the woman above her.

Deborah smiled as Megan worked on her foot. One foot, then the other foot. Hard at work for Deborah's pleasure. Deborah felt tingles spread through her body. Fiesty, wild Megan had taken to submissive life like a duck to water.

Deborah spread her legs and moved closer to the edge of the sofa. She put her hand to Megan's face and raised her chin, looking her in the eyes. "Now to the real work, Megan." She took a handful of Megan's tangle of golden hair in her hand and pulled Megan's head in between her legs to her hot, wet core.

Megan pushed her face into Deborah, tasting her, her tongue, her mouth, working hard. Deborah had a neat thatch of thick dark pubic hair. Immaculately waxed underneath and around the edges leaving a neat thick square. It tickled Megan's nose as she worked.

Deborah looked down at Megan's lovely face, intent in concentration as she worked. Deborah felt her tongue hot and wet between her legs. Deborah felt turned on beyond belief. She knew it wouldn't take long. She grabbed the back of Megan's head and pulled it into her. She ground against Megan's face and orgasmed hard. The release ran through her body as her head tipped back and her eyes closed. This is what she had needed since the day she first met Megan when she was late for her interview.

This is what she had needed for years.

11

It was Monday morning and Deborah made her way into Megan's office. She had thought long and hard last night on what she was going to do about Megan. She had found herself drawn in to caring for the woman and her daughter and to Deborah that was unacceptable. She couldn't allow herself to get caught up with another woman, especially one so much younger than her, who worked for her and had a young daughter. Being with Megan could make everything messy and change her life, that was something Deborah couldn't allow to happen in her life. She had to cut all ties with Megan and Lola outside of work. Their relationship had to be strictly professional. She couldn't believe she had broken her own rules around professionalism at work. She wasn't going to allow herself to fall in love with someone, she refused.

Deborah walked into Megan's office and closed the door behind her. Megan gave her the biggest smile Deborah had ever seen yet and it only made the butterflies in her stomach grow. Deborah pushed it away and schooled her features. She wasn't going to risk everything for Megan. She had done it once with her ex-wife and it had almost destroyed her.

"Hey. How are you this morning?" Megan asked with a smile.

"We need to talk. As of this moment you will only refer to me as Ms. Stewart or Ma'am and I will refer to you as Ms. Campbell. Our relationship with stay strictly professional. There will be no more sexual activity or contact outside of work. And I expect you in the future to utilize a babysitter instead of bringing your daughter here. This is a place of business and it is not a daycare center. Do I make myself clear?" Deborah said in a cold tone.

"What happened? I don't understand?" Megan crumbled before her eyes.

She had begun to get feelings for Deborah. Deborah had taken her to places she had never imagined. She had found a submissive side of herself that she had never known existed. She had so many questions. She had seen a softness in Deborah's eyes, she knew Deborah felt for her too. She couldn't believe that Deborah was now backtracking and going to act like none of it even happened.

"It was a mistake to do anything with you. I am your boss and I will remain as your boss. Nothing will ever happen again, do I make myself clear?" Deborah demanded.

"Sure. Is that all Ma'am?" Megan said with tears in her eyes.

She was devastated and she wasn't going to pretend like she wasn't. But she needed this job desperately so she would have no choice but to take this shit and continue on. It wouldn't be the first time she spent an amazing night with someone and then they didn't want anything to do with her. Deborah had looked at her like she cared and like there might be something more there, but apparently it was all a lie. Just another person who wanted her for her body and then cut off cold and moved on and pretended like it never happened. Well if that is what she wanted, Megan would have to give it to her. This was why she rarely dated, people only let you down.

"Don't you dare pout at me or question me or you can pack your things and leave. This is the list, I expect it to be done by the end of the day." Deborah said with a deadly edge and she placed the list down on the desk and walked out.

Megan picked up the list and couldn't believe that this was happening. She had been so happy this morning. She couldn't believe Deborah could do this to her. The worst part was knowing there was nothing she could do. She needed this job, so she had no other choice but to shut up and take it.

It was Friday afternoon and the week had been one of the longest weeks of Megan's life. Deborah had been brutally cold; the Dragon Lady was back with a vengeance. Every time Megan didn't get a task done within a reasonable amount of time, Deborah was right there to remind her how she was under qualified for this job and that she should have stuck to waiting tables. When she wasn't belittling her, she was giving her icy glares from across the office. Even when she had a question, Deborah would now make her stand in her office and wait until she felt like answering the questions. Part of her games still, no doubt. She was still getting off on her dominance over Megan. There hadn't been a single day that week that

Megan wasn't crying in her car after work on her way to pick up Lola.

Megan hated how pathetic she had become. She had reached a whole new low and spent the previous night, after Lola was in bed, eating a pint of cookie dough ice cream. She was miserable and she was hating herself for ever allowing herself to care about Deborah, for ever allowing her heart to fall for her.

Megan walked into the teacher's lounge to get some much needed coffee. Lola was once again having night terrors and had barely slept at all last night. Megan had no idea what she was going to do about it. She was feeling like a failure as a mother and as a lover and as a personal assistant. Megan leaned against the counter, waiting for the coffee maker to finish brewing. She felt someone coming up behind her and placed their hand on her hip. Megan opened her eyes and turned to see that it was Juan that was touching her and not the person she was craving.

"Don't touch me," Megan snapped. She didn't know what was Juan's deal, but he seemed very interested in her sexually and that was the last thing she wanted.

"Sorry, I was just checking to see how much longer the coffee was going to be. You look awfully tired, did you have a long night?" Juan asked, moving back slightly.

"Yeah," was all Megan said. She was not in the mood to deal with Juan. She wasn't in the mood to deal with anyone, today. She just wanted to curl up in bed and sleep for the next twelve hours.

"Not very talkative today. Maybe you just need a good night out and have some fun." Juan said with a sexy smirk. "I would be happy to take you out and show you a good time."

"Oh god. Please stop. I'm gay Juan. I'm seriously not

interested." Megan looked right at Juan, hoping he would finally give up and focus on someone else.

Juan laughed. "You can't be that gay. How do you have a daughter?" Juan asked invasively.

"I got drunk and slept with an idiot like you. Ironically, Lola is the best thing in my world, but I have no intention of making any more drunken mistakes." Megan reached over to pour the coffee.

"Maybe you just need the right man to show you how good it can feel. There's plenty of liquor at my place." Juan said, as he moved his hand to the small of Megan's back.

Megan on one hand couldn't quite believe his persistence, but on the other hand, she had met many men, like Juan, who just wanted her for her body. She didn't want to live like that any more.

"Get your hands off me!" She pushed him off. "Wow, that says it all right there doesn't it? You are really that desperate that you need to get a girl drunk just to sleep with you? Well in that case, go to a bar and pick up the drunkest girl, because it's never going to be me." Megan said with an edge to her voice.

Five years ago, she would have probably taken up his offer. Gone out with him, got drunk and fucked him. Tried to fuck away her pain. Especially now, with her pain over Deborah. But, it was a really bad idea and the thought of his hands on her body made her feel physically sick. She had made the mistake of sleeping with someone in the school and she wasn't going to be making that mistake again.

Megan moved back, but turned to face Juan. "Touch me again and you'll be losing that hand." She smiled widely with a cold edge, before she turned and headed back to her office. She was so done with this day.

12

_____

I t was after ten in the morning the following Monday
and Deborah was beyond furious. Megan was late,
again. For the past week since she had called things
off between them, things had been pretty tense between
them, mostly because of how she was acting towards
Megan. She had been treating her horribly with the hopes
that Megan would eventually get sick of it and quit. The
problem was, Deborah hadn't realised that Megan
couldn't afford to quit. She needed this job more than
anyone and as a result she was taking all of Deborah's
abuse. Deborah had seen a few times in the previous week
Megan crying in her car at the end of the day and
Deborah knew she had to change things. She had come in
with the intention of talking to Megan, kindly and finding
a way that they could work together.

There had been many times the past week where
Deborah just wanted to kiss Megan and make it all go
away. To apologize for being so cruel and explain all her
fears around their relationship and take her and Lola
back to her house and look after them there forever. She

had felt herself falling in love with Megan so scarily quickly and that scared the hell out of her. She barely knew Megan and yet, spending that saturday night and Sunday day with her had felt like the most natural thing in the world. She had opened up more to Megan than she ever had anyone else. Everything about Megan was like a drug to her. It was insane how quickly she had fallen for this unlikely girl. This unlikely messy blonde girl that had showed up late for an interview and somehow her deep ocean eyes had made Deborah believe in something. Somehow, Megan's warmth and charm had crept under Deborah's armour and got to her very heart. When she got scared she did what she always did, she pushed away and ran.

You can't get hurt if there is no one there to hurt you.

Now she was taking her anger at herself out on Megan and she knew it wasn't fair, but she couldn't seem to stop. Megan was really late this morning.

Deborah got up and stormed out of her office and over to Kathy.

"Where is she?" Deborah demanded.

"She's not going to be in today or for a long while I'm afraid." Kathy said sadly.

"She quit? The least she could have done is given me two weeks notice."

"She didn't quit. It's Lola, she was hit by a car this morning outside her school. She's at the hospital." Kathy said sadly, with tears edging her eyes.

"What? Is she ok?" Deborah asked, instantly her whole body was consumed by fear.

Deborah broke down. Lola. Lola. Lola. Her big dark eyes and toothy grin. Lola and her messy dark hair and endless curiosity.

Megan would be distraught.

"I don't know. She just called, crying, to tell me that she wouldn't be in and that Lola had to be airlifted to a children's hospital." Kathy said, as a few tears ran down her cheeks.

"Airlifted? It's that bad? What hospital?"

Deborah couldn't believe this. If Lola's injuries were bad enough that she had to be airlifted, then it was bad, it was really bad. She had to get there. She had to get to Megan and Lola.

"Our Lady of Grace in Portland."

"Cancel my classes and meetings for today and the rest of the week. Get cover in wherever you can." Deborah said, as she turned to head back into her office.

She quickly grabbed her things ready to go.

"Let me know how she is please." Kathy had suspected there was something more between the uptight Head-mistress and Megan Campbell, but this confirmed it. She had never seen Deborah more visibly upset.

"I'll keep you updated." Deborah said, as she headed out of the office and quickly ran to her car.

She needed to go home real quick and grab a bag, she was going to be staying until Lola was able to come back home. Deborah couldn't believe this was happening. She couldn't believe how stupid she had been. She had been so afraid of losing them that she pushed them away and now she could lose them because she wasn't there to protect them. She let the fear consume her instead of allowing herself to just be happy. She had to get to them, that was all that mattered.

∾

IT WAS seven hours later when Deborah finally arrived at the hospital. She parked in the first spot she found and then ran into the hospital. After stopping to ask at the nursing station where Lola was, she ran to the surgical waiting room. Just the fact that Lola was in surgery did nothing to stop the fear that was running wild inside of her. Whatever her injuries were, something required her to need surgery. Deborah ran into the waiting room and saw that a few people were there, but she didn't care about them. She only cared about the broken looking Megan sitting in one of the hard plastic chairs. Deborah went right over to her and sat down beside her as she spoke.

"Megan, my love." she took Megan's hand and spoke kindly.

Megan looked up and the second her eyes landed on Deborah, the dam had broken. She let out a heart wrenching sob and collapsed into Deborah's arms as she finally allowed herself to break down. Deborah simply took Megan into her arms and held her as she cried her heart out. She offered some soothing words, but she knew it wouldn't be enough to stop the pain that was flooding through Megan. After a good ten minutes Megan's tears slowed down, but her breathing was still hitched. She pulled back and wiped at her cheeks as she spoke.

"Sorry."

"You have nothing to be sorry for. How is she?"

"She has bleeding in her brain. They have to operate to drain it and stop the bleeding. They don't know what it could do to her. She's also got a broken right leg and four broken ribs." Megan said with a shaky voice.

"She's going to be ok. She's tough and she is going to pull through this."

"But her brain, what if something is wrong? What if

she's never the same again?"

"Then we will handle it. She's young, that means she will heal quickly and she will bounce back. If there is a problem with her mind, then we work with her on it and help her adapt. We will get her back to being that amazing little girl that she is. What happened, how did she get hit?"

"It was my fault. There was no parking at the school so I parked a block away. We were at the stop sign and I didn't see a car coming. Lola was ahead of me and she saw her friend and just ran across the street in front of the car. I wasn't close enough. I couldn't get to her in time. I didn't hold her hand, I always hold her hand, why didn't I hold her hand? I'm sorry, I'm so sorry. It is all my fault." Megan said, as the tears started up once again.

"No, I'm sorry. Megan, I am so sorry. I've been such a bitch to you and you don't deserve it. It's not your fault, you didn't do anything wrong. It was all me. I got scared because of how much I love the two of you and I pushed you away. I shouldn't have, I'm so sorry. You are sunlight itself to me. You are the most beautiful thing that has ever happened to me. I love you, Megan." Deborah said, with her own tears running down her cheeks.

Megan never thought in a million years she would ever see Deborah emotional like she was right now. Megan knew she could hate Deborah for what she had said to her, for what she did to her. But she couldn't bring herself to. She loved Deborah and she wanted to explore a life with her. She was the one that she had been waiting her whole life for and she was not about to let that slip away again.

"I love you too."

Deborah pulled Megan in for a slow and tender kiss.

The kiss was kept short, as they were in public, but when Deborah pulled away she pulled Megan into her arms and held her as they waited to hear news about their little girl.

The waiting.

The hours of waiting.

It was agony.

～

THE MOMENT FINALLY CAME, five hours after Deborah had arrived. A very tired looking doctor walked through a set of double doors and headed straight for them. They both stood up, holding hands as they went over to Lola's doctor.

"How is she?" Megan asked right away.

"She's going to be just fine. She has a long road to recovery though. We were able to repair the bleeding and she does have a shunt in right now to help drain any excess blood. We will remove that in a few days when she is no longer draining any liquid. We are going to keep her sedated until the shunt is removed, just because of her age, we don't want her to be in any pain or pulling on it by mistake."

"But she's going to be ok?" Megan asked, needing to hear it.

"She will be. But like I said, there is a long road to recovery for her. Her broken ribs will be painful for her and with her broken leg it will be hard for her to move around. Normally she would be on crutches, but with her broken ribs she won't be able to use the crutches without causing herself more pain. She will have to use one of the scooters that she can place her knee on and walk that way. Kids actually really love it." The doctor said with a warm smile.

"What about her brain? Will there be any lasting damage?" Deborah asked.

"The injury did take place where her motor skills are. Her writing will be affected and any fine motor skills she has, such as holding a fork, pencil, drawing etc will be compromised. Now, they won't remain that way, she will just need to relearn those motor skills. However, she is young, so you will find that she bounces back very quickly."

"Oh my god." Megan said as she closed her eyes. "I can't take this. Lola. Oh god."

"It's ok, we can work with her on it. I know a lot of great and fun exercises she can do to strengthen her hands back up. Like playing with clay or slime. And she is so young, so she will relearn it very quickly." Deborah said, as she took Megan into her arms.

She knew how important art was to Lola and how much she loved to sit and color or draw. Having the weakened motor skills would be very frustrating for Lola, but they could still incorporate some art into her life that would also help her strengthen those skills again.

"Can we see her?" Megan asked.

"Of course. She is in recovery right now. I'll bring you back there. Again, we are going to keep her sedated until the shunt comes out and it also allows her body the chance to rest and heal up some so that when she does wake up she won't be in as much pain. We will also be keeping her on a low dose of morphine to help her get through the bulk of the pain."

"When will she be able to leave?" Deborah asked.

"That is something we will need to see when the shunt is out. I know she was airlifted here and you are quite the distance away from home. Once she is out of the woods and I can safely say she is ok to be transported. We can airlift her back to your home town and she will probably need to be in the hospital there for a couple of days and then she can go home. Realistically you are looking at two weeks, assuming everything goes well and she doesn't develop an infection."

"Is that a risk?" Megan asked, now even more worried.

"It is always a risk when someone has surgery. It is why she is on an antibiotic IV just in case. But, we are very good at keeping everything clean and monitoring our patients, especially the children. It's safe for you to be optimistic and hopeful. She pulled through the worst of it and now it's just a matter of healing. Children have the best chance of a full recovery with this kind of injury."

"Thank you Doctor." Deborah said on their behalf.

"I'll take you to her now."

They followed the doctor down the halls until they reached Lola's room. Megan clung to Deborah for support. Megan felt her eyes water as she saw the bruising that was already coming through. Lola had a white bandage wrapped around her head, with a breathing tube in her nose. She was also hooked up to multiple monitors and had an IV line going into her tiny hand. Megan wanted nothing more than to scoop Lola up and hold her in her arms and never let her go. The doctor left the two women there with their child. They both went and sat down to the right of Lola and took her hand in theirs. Deborah was heartbroken at seeing this little girl in such a big hospital bed. She didn't belong here and Deborah was going to make sure that both Lola and Megan ended up exactly where they belonged. She was done running.

"It will be ok, Megan. I've got you now. I've got you both. I love you so very much."

EPILOGUE

I t was three weeks later when Deborah was finally
pulling up out front of her school with Megan and
Lola in the car. The past three weeks had been hard
and long for everyone. Once Lola's shunt was able to be
removed three days post surgery she was allowed to be
woken up. She had been terrified when she finally opened
her eyes and they could see that she was in pain. They
both worked quickly to calm her down and it didn't take
long before the pain meds kicked in and she was sleeping
once again. That first week in the hospital had been rough
and Lola had a hard time understanding why she couldn't
go home. When she could finally leave and be airlifted
back to their hometown. Megan was the only one allowed
to go with Lola in the helicopter. Deborah had no choice,
but to make the long drive back home alone. She took
comfort in knowing that Megan was with Lola and she
kept her updated every step of the way.

After spending yet another week in the hospital Lola
was beyond ready to leave and she couldn't have been
happier when they were finally told that she was being

discharged. That day Deborah had loaded Megan and Lola up in her car and took them to their new home, her home. Deborah had been getting everything set up for Lola and Megan to be living with her once she returned from Portland. She had converted her office into Lola's bedroom with a big comfy princes canopy bed, with all of her toys, stuffed animals, and clothes. As well as new ones that Deborah added along with an art desk and supplies and an easel for her to use as well. Amber had spent time with them both helping them move and settle in. She still wanted to be a big part of Lola's life.

Deborah had made space in her own room for Megan. Spending the nights sleeping next to her, she knew it was meant to be. Their connection grew every day.

Lola had taken it really well to no longer living with Amber. She loved living in such a big house, with a pool and a big backyard. She also loved her new room and would spend as much time as she could drawing. Her fine motor skills were returning gradually. Deborah never let Lola think for one second that she couldn't do something or that it wouldn't get better. Deborah had made a point in helping Lola with little fun exercises that she could do to get her hands back up to where they were.

After spending two weeks away from work, on the third week Deborah had reluctantly gone back to work. She had ensured Megan that her job would be there when Lola was ready to go back to school, that she didn't need to worry about it. If she wanted to still work for her of course. Megan was a little unsure at first and not really comfortable with Deborah paying the bills, but she eventually agreed that Lola's health was more important than anything. Megan had made the point of doing the cleaning and cooking while Deborah was at work, to her it was the least she could do to contribute to their household.

"I might come back to work for you at some point. I actually love to serve you. It does things to me. It makes me feel alive."

"That is why you serve me so well at home as well, isn't it? You are a natural. A born submissive."

"I never would have imagined it. But yes. You make me feel safe. You make me want to serve you in every way. Will we be playing kinky games in your office still if I come back to work?"

"Oh, absolutely. I can't wait to have you on my desk again. Every time I sit at my desk I imagine you bent over it and it makes me smile. There is SO much more I want to do with you." Deborah smiled warmly. A smile that was becoming so much more common.

IT HAD BEEN three weeks since the accident and it was the first time that Megan and Lola were going back to the school. They didn't know why they were going to be here, but Deborah had a surprise in store for them.

"You ready baby?" Megan asked, as she got out of the car and over to help Lola.

"Ready Mommy."

Megan helped Lola to get out of the car, while Deborah went and grabbed the scooter for Lola to use. The doctor had been right, Lola loved the scooter and was often using it in the house to race them down the hallways. She thought it was amazing and lots of fun. They got Lola on the scooter, and then they all headed inside. Deborah led them down the hallway to the teacher's lounge. Once they walked in to Megan and Lola's surprise, everyone was there with decorations all over the room and a banner that said 'Welcome Home Lola!'

Megan instantly teared up at seeing all of the love and support from the staff that she hadn't really known all that long. Kathy was the first person to come up to her and give her a big hug before she did the same to Lola. One by one everyone moved in for a hug and offered their words of support. Amber was there too and pulled them both in for a big hug.

"How are you feeling Sweetie?" Kathy asked Lola.

"Better thank you Ms Kathy." Lola said with a toothy smile.

"Thank you so much everyone. Really, I don't even know what to say." Megan said, overwhelmed by the care they all seemed to have for her daughter.

"How about 'yes'?" Deborah said.

Megan turned to look at Deborah and saw that she was now bent down on one knee with a ring in her hand.

"What?" Megan said softly, completely shocked.

"I've been married before, but when I met you, you proved to me that soulmates are real. Love at first sight, or something like that. I believe our souls have crossed many times in our past lives and we have once again found each other. I have no desire to waste any more time. I don't want to spend another minute on this earth without you and Lola by my side. Megan Campbell, would you do me the honor and make me the happiest woman in the world? Will you marry me?"

Megan's eyes filled with tears of joy. She never thought she would ever get married. She never thought she would ever find a decent job with people that cared about not only her, but her daughter. She never thought she would ever find a love like this.

"Oh wow. Yes! Yes of course I'll marry you."

Everyone in the room clapped, as Deborah slipped the engagement ring on Megan's finger, before giving her a deep kiss. They felt little hands on their legs and they looked down to see Lola, trying to give them both a hug. They both bent down and pulled Lola into a hug.

"If there is a wedding can I wear a new dress?" Lola asked curiously.

"Of course, my angel. What colour would you like it to be?"

Megan felt exhausted and happy when she headed home with her family that night.

There was a lot to be said for lying on your resume.

ESCORT

1

——————

"Yes, Miss. Green, I'll make sure the flower decoration has lilies and not roses, so the background looks more fairytale-like."

God, these people nowadays. Do they get married because they want to or just for some Instagram attention? Ashley thought to herself, sighing inaudibly.

Ashley Davidson ran New York City's most prominent event management company and had the world at her fingertips. Who wouldn't want a life like that – except for well, perhaps Ashley herself.

There she was, sipping coffee and looking down at the busy streets from the confines of her office, thinking about what was missing.

Another day was passing in hustle and bustle, but a certain loneliness gripped the evenings. So much to do, but still very little meaning.

She got up from her desk and walked to the floor to ceiling windows of her office, her heels clicking against the hardwood floor.

Coffee in hand, she looked through the window. At

least she had never settled and feigned love just because the idea of it seemed to fill voids and save you from sitting with yourself and your thoughts. That was cowardice. It was an easy way out that so many people took. Just to settle with the nearest eligible man or woman who wanted you. But as long as rich people kept settling, she kept making money. Planning high-end weddings and celebrations was big money.

Another call halted her train of thoughts. Yet another client was asking her to make a day in their lives more memorable. She gave a wry smile at the irony.

She walked out of her office, suddenly reminded of something, and moved to the elevator at the end of the hallway, greeted by her employees along the way.

She walked out of the building, clad in her grey designer pantsuit with a white button-down shirt. Her black wingtips clicked the cemented sidewalk as she took a look at her Rolex.

Knowing she had time on her hands, Ashley slowed down her pace ever so slightly and walked to her destination. The sun had almost set in the horizon, and darkness began surrounding the city.

Nearing her favorite place in all of New York, Ashley smiled as she entered Maison Kayser. It was a midsized cozy French restaurant located near her office building. The doorbell rang as she went inside, greeted by the smell of coffee and chocolate. Ashley walked to the far end of the restaurant, taking a seat at the table next to the window.

"Ms Davidson! It's been a while since you've visited us." A man, clad in a black shirt with the restaurant logo engraving and black pants called out to her.

"Hello, Jamie. Yes, it's been a while." Ashley replied to the man giving him a small smile.

He put a menu in front of Ashley and then left.

Looking out the window, Ashley noticed her reflection staring back at her.

Her brunette bob was immaculate as always. Her light makeup was still sharp; it had lasted all day.

Ashley ordered a cup of coffee and her favorite white chocolate pistachio cookie as she waited for her friend to arrive.

Just as the waiter put her order on the table, Ashley looked up to see Trisha arriving.

"Ash!" Trisha all but yelled at her, grinning from ear to ear.

Ashley got up to greet her friend with a hug and chuckled at her enthusiasm.

"Hey Trish."

"Oh my God, how long has it been? Like years, since I last saw you!" Trisha exclaimed.

Trisha looked flawless in a royal blue silk shirt just as you would expect a CNN reporter to look.

Ashley rolled her eyes at the obvious exaggeration.

"Trish, it's just been a week." Ashley reminded her as Trisha settled in her seat and ordered a drink.

"Yeah, yeah. A week too long. How are you?" Trisha waved her off and asked.

"Nothing new. What about you? How's Kevin? The wedding's still on for this winter, right? Or have you two been fighting again?" Ashley joked, expertly dodging questions about herself.

"Oh yeah, that's very funny. I'm glad something amuses you, even if it is my relationship. And yes, honey, the wedding is very much still on. You're not getting yourself out of this. Can you imagine how lucky you are!? My bridesmaid and event planner for the wedding of the decade!" Trisha stated.

"If you stay together long enough to actually get married." Ashley teased, winking at her friend, knowing it would rile her up.

Narrowing her eyes at her, Trisha huffed and then said,

"Oh shut it. And not a good job at evading my question, okay. Now spill. How are you, Ashley?"

Ashley looked at her best friend.

Trisha Peyton. Daughter of the famous news reporter Donald S. Peyton. He had been her role model in pursuing her current job and passion, Journalism. Her mother was a known fashion designer, Martha Peyton.

Trisha was privileged and spoiled, but Ashley adored her. Her dark skin was incredible, glowing, and line-free, and she never looked a day over twenty-five.

They had been inseparable since school days. Trisha was one of the most down to earth people Ashley knew, despite her background. Ashley could always count on Trisha and knew she could reach out to her for anything and everything. Trisha was the one person Ashley could never genuinely hide from.

"Hello! Earth to Ashley!" Trisha snapped her fingers in front of Ashley, pulling her out of her thoughts.

"Yeah, sorry." Ashley chuckled and then continued,

"I'm doing fine, Trish. It's the same as it has been for the past seven years. Work is what keeps me sane. It gives life meaning, you know."

"Ash, you have to let someone in someday. You can't shut everyone out like this forever." Trisha said softly, her hand reaching out to cover Ashely's, giving it a gentle, reassuring squeeze.

"I'm fine, Trish. I mean it. Stuff like that isn't for me. I came to terms with it long ago. The occasional fuck I get is all that I need. And it's not like I didn't try. I even used your dumb left and right-swiping app." Ashley said to her, rolling her eyes.

"Tinder. It's called Tinder, honey." Trisha corrected her, amused.

"Nobody excites me anymore. I saw a couple of women for sex, and that was alright, but I just don't think I want anymore. They do. I can see it in their needy little eyes. But I don't. I tell you, Trish, most of this relationship thing is just simple peer pressure. People don't want to be seen alone. We equate being alone to being sad, but that isn't true. Seeking happiness in someone else is the saddest thing of all." Ashley continued, her annoyance rising with every word.

"Yeah because nothing screams more meaningful than a new girl every week." Trisha retorted but then sighed and continued, "Okay, okay. You're an adult, and you know exactly what you want and need in life, so I'm sure what's meant to be will be."

"Exactly." Ashley gave her a smirk to which Trisha rolled her eyes.

Clapping her hands together, Trisha's eyes glinted with mischief. "Okay so. Since it has been SO long since I have seen you. Since you are only going to bury yourself in more work and it will be ages until I see you again, we will go to a new exclusive club in town and drink and dance our night away. It is exclusive, its VIP. What do you say?" Trisha finished, wiggling her eyebrows at her.

Ashley let out a short laugh as she shook her head and replied, "Lead the way."

Trisha jumped from her seat, squealing excitedly. Grabbing her purse, she waited for Ashley to pay the bill and dragged her to the car.

"What are you high on these days?" Ashley laughed, nudging Trisha's shoulder.

"Well excuse me for being human and not some workaholic robot." Trisha countered.

"Did you bring your car today?"

Trisha asked Ashley as they walked to her car. Ashley shook her head. She didn't usually drive herself.

"Awesome! We're taking mine then."

Trisha stated, leaving no room for argument.

They got into the car, and Trisha drove to the new club.

～

"WHY DON'T we just turn around and go someplace less.. you know, cramped." Ashley started as they drew near the club.

"Oh no, no, no. We are going to go to this club tonight, and we're having the time of our lives." Trisha said to her.

"You're just dragging me here because Kevin's here, right?" Ashley put her head back on the headrest.

Trisha grinned at her.

MONARCHEE. The big neon sign displayed the club name. Ashley had to admit, it looked amazing.

Trisha handed the car keys to the valet as they got out of the car and made their way towards the club's main entrance.

The glass double doors were huge, and there was

security on each side of the entrance. Trisha walked ahead of her, displaying a gold membership card to the guards as they nodded and opened the doors for them.

From the corner of her eye, Ashley noted teenage girls wearing skimpy outfits moving towards the back entrance.

There is no way they are old enough to get in. Ashley thought to herself.

Shaking her head, she followed Trisha into the club, immediately hit with the smell of alcohol and beat of the music. The party was already in full swing.

The club had a big dancefloor where bodies mixed as people danced their night away. A huge disco ball rested right above the center of the dancefloor, reflecting light throughout the club.

There was a large seating area with luxurious sofas throughout. Ashley noticed a VIP area and an upstairs area. She wondered what was upstairs.

Raised cages were around the dancefloor. Beautiful women in tiny underwear danced in them.

Trisha turned to Ashley and said something that Ashley couldn't catch due to the blaring music in the background. Trisha took them straight towards the VIP area, and she was greeted by a massive figure who enveloped her in a hug. Trisha turned, and Ashley recognized the good looking muscly guy as Trisha's fiancé, Kevin. They had the rockiest relationship Ashley had ever seen. But tonight, at least, they looked to be on good terms. He waved and smiled at Ashley as she returned the gesture.

So much for sticking together and dancing the night away, Ashley shook her head, amusingly.

She moved to the bar and turned her attention to the dancefloor. Immediately a figure caught her eye. An olive-skinned woman in a tight black dress. Curves everywhere. She was moving her body seductively at the music, Ashley couldn't stop watching her.

Her eyes met Ashley's and held their gaze for a long moment. Ashley smirked and then turned to face the bar.

"A Gin Fizz, please." Ashley told the bartender.

"I take it you don't go clubbing very often." Ashley turned, and there was the young woman in the black dress. The young woman with the dangerous curves.

"Well, not a good time to imply I am too old for clubbing." Ashley replied, her eyes taking in her intense eyes, her full lips. Damn, this girl was hot, and she knew it.

"Haha, no. I meant the Gin Fizz isn't good here. You'd think they'd want to perfect their drinks since it's a newly opened club but oh well. Nothing's perfect." The girl carried on.

"Two Vieux Carré, please." She called to the bartender. Then she turned to Ashley and extended her hand.

"Hi, I'm Carol."

"Ah, but it isn't Christmas yet." Ashley teased, shaking her hand.

Carol laughed and shrugged. "Your lucky day then, isn't it?"

Noticing Ashley's office attire, Carol proceeded to ask, "You came from work? What do you do?"

"I own my own company. You might have heard of it, AXEND Co."

"Oh wow! I have read about you in a magazine. I knew you looked familiar. it's really nice to meet you."

"Do you want to come home with me tonight?" Ashley

said confidently, her eyes flashing. She knew she was twenty years older than this girl, but she didn't care. "Just one night. I don't do dating or relationships."

"By tomorrow morning, I'll forget you exist!" Carol retaliated, with a smirk of her own.

Gulping down her drink in one go, Ashley got up, jacket in hand, and looked at Carol.

"Shall we?" Ashley extended her hand to Carol.

Carol smiled, taking her hand, following her out of the club.

"THAT'LL BE $20." The cab driver told the two women.

Ashley paid the driver and gave a tip, and they headed to her apartment building.

Carol couldn't help but admire the beautiful building in one of the most expensive areas of NYC. She remembered the article she had seen on Ashley in the magazine. Ashley was one of the most successful businesswomen in the city. Of course, she lived here.

53 West 53.

The women entered the building, greeted by the doorman, and stepped into the elevator.

Ashley pressed her designated floor, and the ride to her apartment was silent. The elevator doors opened. Ashley pushed her code into the digital security lock, and the doors to her apartment opened. It was a luxury penthouse, the whole top floor. Of course, it was incredible.

Carol stood stunned for a while as Ashley looked at her, amused.

"Like what you see?" Ashley teased Carol.

Carol grinned at her, "I hope the penthouse isn't the

only thing that will impress me tonight." Ashley loved her confidence.

Ashley's apartment was the 47th floor, overlooking the beautiful Central Park, the Hudson River, and Downtown Manhattan. It was huge, modern, and stunning.

The windows were floor to ceiling glass. The main area was open plan, and there was a magnificent glass chandelier in the middle. The floor was polished concrete. There was very little that was personal on display.

Carol went down the few steps to the living room and stood in awe of the place.

Everything was so... perfect.

Ashley grabbed her hand, bringing her back from her thoughts and lead her to the stairs. Ashley lead Carol to a bedroom.

"Nice room." Carol commented, looking around. There was nothing personal in the room. Carol went to sit on the Queen-sized bed, looking up at Ashley.

"Thanks." Ashley replied. This was one of the guest rooms, where Ashley usually brought her one night stands.

Ashley stopped talking. They both knew that they weren't there for talking. She reached to Carol's mid-thigh. The hem of her tight dress. Ashley pushed her back onto the bed and peeled the dress upwards, revealing black lace underwear. Carol looked back at her, eyes wide, capitulating to her. Their eyes connected and held gaze as Ashley pulled down the black lace, down Carol's smooth bronze legs, off over her ankles, taking her heels off with them. Carol didn't close her legs. She knew she looked good. Her dark thatch of pubic curls drew Ashley's eyes. Dark curls on top, smooth olive skin underneath. Soft olive wetness underneath.

Ashley took a deep breath. She wanted her. This was good. This was what she wanted. Beautiful younger women for one night only. Beautiful younger women who she could do as she wished with.

Ashley reached to the bedside table drawer and pulled out a black leather harness and a black dildo. She held them up as a question to Carol. Carol nodded her consent.

Ashley undressed leisurely and replaced her underwear with the harness; Carol watched her as she did. Ashley's body was as Carol expected, lean in the soft light, carefully and correctly kept, as her apartment was.

The black dildo jutted intimidatingly from Ashley's groin. She loved wearing it. She loved the power that she felt with it. She approached Carol, holding her gaze. She pushed Carol's legs roughly apart and put her fingers to Carol's wetness. Running them up and down, Carol's whole body quivered. Her pupils pooled with desire. Her legs widened of their own accord. Carol's body begged for sex for her.

Carol moaned as Ashley pushed two fingers inside her. So wet. So wanting. She added a third and began to fuck her with them. Carol's body responded as Ashley leaned into her, her strong arm going to work for Carol's pleasure, hitting her G spot hard. Carol gushed on the bed linen. Ashley smiled. She removed her fingers and got on top of Carol, the dildo pushing at Carol with intent. It slid inside, welcomed, wanted. Ashley was bigger than Carol. She enjoyed the way her bigger frame was powerful over Carol. Carol's pupils dilated further as the dildo entered her. Ashley enjoyed that it was big. She enjoyed that women knew about it when she fucked them. She enjoyed that women would still be feeling it days later.

She knelt back on her knees and pulled Carol's body

into her, onto the dildo, her hands on Carol's hips. She thrust into her. Out and in. In and out. Carol's body moved, and her full breasts swayed. Ashley loved to watch her. She loved to watch the lovely curves of her body as she moved. The smooth skin and loveliness of youth all displayed before her. All displayed for her.

Ashley pulled out and flipped Carol over. Her hands on Carol's hips again, maneuvering her body where she wanted it, where it pleased her. Carol on all fours, round ass backed up to the side of the bed. Ashley stood behind her and entered her again, her hands on her hips, controlling her. Out and in. In and out. Fucking her. The lovely curve and the lines of her waist to her ass, perfect for watching. Her dark hair a messy mane. The dildo hit her G spot in this position, and Carol went wild for it. Ashley's hands were holding tight on her hips, thrusting into her. Carol squirted everywhere as she came. Ashley smiled smugly to herself, still holding Carol up by her hips, her body quivering in orgasm. This was what Ashley really loved.

∼

THE NEXT MORNING, Ashley called an uber for her. While leaving, Carol passed by a room with a gorgeous hand-crafted oak door. That was Ashley's bedroom, and much like Ashley's heart, it was locked.

2

_____

It was mid-day when the city skyscrapers came into view as the airplane neared New York City. Vienna smiled to herself as she heard the pilot inform the passengers that they were to land soon. She had missed her home.

Vienna prepared herself for landing, gathering the few belongings she had taken out of her small bag and loosening her long golden hair from its band and shaking it out over her shoulders. Traveling first class sure had it's perks though, she thought to herself.

As the plane landed, Vienna could barely contain her excitement. The plane came to a rest, and the doors opened, allowing passengers to exit. Gathering her stuff, Vienna exited the plane, moving towards the small bus that would take the passengers to the airport.

Vienna proceeded to go through the security and grabbed her suitcases from the conveyer belt. She walked out through the airport doors and was immediately greeted by her company driver.

"Hi, Steven!" Vienna greeted him with some vigor despite being exhausted from the long flight.

Oh, she hadn't missed the overcrowded New York, but she was going to be happy to be home.

Steven took her bags and put them in the trunk before opening the car door for Vienna.

"How have things been, Steven? How are Seline and the kids?" Vienna asked.

"They're all good, Miss Rhodes," Steven told her.

"I hope you are not this formal with them, are you?" She quipped.

Steven laughed as they continued their car ride.

101 Park Avenue, Vienna stepped out of the car and felt dwarfed by the buildings.

She took the elevator to the 16th floor to Black Label NYC. Black Label was the escort company that Vienna had employed Vienna since she was eighteen years old. Black Label provided top class escorts for women both in the US and worldwide. Black Label served the richest women in the world. It promised the best, and it always delivered.

Vienna Rhodes was the top-earning lesbian escort on Black Label's books. Vienna had clients all over the world who adored her and were prepared to pay vast amounts for the pleasure of her company and her body.

Vienna nodded to the receptionist as she walked straight past to the office and knocked.

"Come in." a voice called out from inside the office.

Opening the doors, she smiled warmly at the woman sitting at the grandeur desk.

The said woman let out a gasp as she quickly got up and engulfed Vienna in a hug. Vienna laughed and put her arms around her.

"Oh, my God! You're back!" Meredith exclaimed.

"Well, you know me. Couldn't stay away from home any longer." Vienna grinned, pulling back to look at her.

"It's so good to see you, sweetheart. How are you? Did the trip go well?"

"I'm good, Meredith. The trip was amazing. How are you?" Vienna replied.

The two women pulled back and went to take a seat. Vienna sat across the desk from Meredith.

"I'm good, as well. Glad to know the trip was relaxing. You look so well." Meredith looked Vienna up and down appraisingly. Vienna always looked exquisite, Meredith was proudest of Vienna, her own creation. Vienna had a body made for seduction and a face that trod a fine line between sex goddess, smart businesswoman, and inno-cent young woman. Vienna had the intellect to know precisely which version of herself to play at any given time.

"Thank you. I feel great, actually. The rest did me good." Vienna looked back across the table at Meredith Bowes. The CEO of the company was the kind of woman Vienna aspired to be one day. She was strong, indepen-dent, and a woman of unyielding character. She had taken in Vienna when everyone else in life had failed her and given her a chance to grow into the woman she was today. Vienna saw the signs of aging around Meredith's intense blue eyes. She had no idea how old Meredith was, prob-ably older than she could guess. Ironically, as Meredith aged, Vienna grew into her prime. Vienna's hair tumbled in long golden waves. Her green eyes were vivid and bright. Vienna was glorious.

Everything Vienna was and everything she had was thanks to Meredith Bowes. They had had a sometime sexual thing. Rarely now, more often when they first met. Meredith had taught her about her body and trained her to be unshockable and exceptional sexually. Some might say taking advantage of her, but Vienna had never seen it like that. She would be eternally grateful to Meredith for the opportunities she had offered her.

"Vienna. I know we need a new lead client for you. I want you back on retainer. A girl like you shouldn't be job-hopping. You are too good. I don't want to give you just anyone. We will put you forward first for any significant contracts that look good, but it is your choice. You are our best, and you get the best. Meanwhile, I will give you the highest paying ad hoc bookings."

"Perfect. Thank you. I love holiday bookings, meanwhile. The Maldives was SO good. I could live like that!"

The two women sat in the office, sipping coffee, and caught up. An hour later, Vienna took her leave and asked the driver to take her home.

Her lovely house was open plan with a spacious living-dining-kitchen area and a wall of glass and sliding french doors to the garden. Vaulted wood ceilings, beautiful walnut floors, comfortable and quality furnishings.

The beautiful house was the thing Vienna had wanted most with the money she was earning. She had bought it earlier in the year, excited like a child to be able to afford such a place. She had always dreamed of a garden, so it had to be a house, not an apartment. She loved to dance around the house, naked to loud music when she was alone.

She unlocked the doors with Steven in tow, her luggage in hand.

Thanking Steven, she walked him out to the car.

"See you tomorrow!" Vienna called out as he pulled out of her gated driveway.

Vienna's eyes landed on her beloved car as she smiled at the memory when she had first bought it. Her cherry red Aston Martin DBX stood proudly in the garage, glinting in the last remaining rays of sunlight.

Walking back inside, she went to the lounge and plopped onto the sofa.

Dialing the number of her favorite sushi restaurant, she ordered dinner. As she waited for her delivery, Vienna went through her voicemail, laughing at the messages her best friend Chloe had left. She had known Chloe since she started at Black Label. Chloe felt like a sister to her.

Her dinner arrived, and Vienna wasted no time in diving in. Finally, after a long day, Vienna went to her bedroom, taking a shower to relax, and then fell into her big bed and was soon asleep.

"Okay, Mrs. Chopra, we'll send our best girl, and I guarantee you, you will be blown away." Meredith hung up and immediately dialed Vienna's number. When the client wanted a woman, their best meant Vienna. Meredith a range of escorts for her wealthy female clients. Black Label escorts whether male or female or gender-fluid were stunning looking, intelligent, educated, and highly sexually skilled, without exception. Meredith kept a range of different types available; nothing surprised her anymore with clients' requests. Vienna was classically beautiful, but Vienna had a lot within her range. Meredith's most valuable escorts could play any part.

"Yes, okay. I got it. Alright, Meredith. Thank you."

Vienna threw her cellphone on the bed and took a shower before meeting with the client.

It was sometimes tiring. Vienna had only come back from her client trip to the Maldives with Alison Reynolds, a sexually demanding heiress. The beach life suited Vienna. She loved it, and the Maldives were like nowhere else on earth. To keep Alison sexually satisfied was a small price to pay for the holiday of a lifetime. She genuinely liked Alison, and she had had a great time. Vienna wasn't some poor little escort; she was highly paid and loved her work. She was at the top of her industry. She saw clients that she enjoyed seeing and clients that Meredith asked her personally to see.

She put on a plum bodycon dress and straightened her wild hair. A bold red lip completed her makeup. The client had asked for sexy, and in that dress, with those lips, Vienna was dripping sex.

Throwing her phone into her purse, she grabbed her keys and headed off to the Chopra residence.

AFTER GETTING BUZZED through the gates, Vienna parked up and headed to the door of the big house.

The door opened to a woman in a luxurious red silk robe, probably in her mid-fifties, with a wide smile to welcome Vienna. "You must be Vienna. Hi, I am Shweta. Lovely to meet you. Your photos are lovely, but they don't do you justice. You are radiant. Truly."

Vienna had that effect on people. It was as if people were just drawn to her.

"You are beautiful yourself," Vienna replied, fixing Shweta with her green eyes.

"Come on in, please. Make yourself at home. Would you like something to drink before, well, you know..."

"..I pleasure you." Vienna completed the sentence with a smirk and then continued,

"I would love a red wine."

Shweta handed Vienna a glass of wine, and the two women sat down on the living room sofa.

"So, this is my first time with an escort—a woman. I have always wanted to. I have always dreamt of it. I really don't know why I didn't seek it out sooner." Vienna watched her; her dark brown eyes were alive with desire; she was nervous, a little. They often were. But this woman knew what she wanted. She looked at Vienna with a hunger. Vienna noticed Shweta's eyes moving across her body; she knew this woman didn't want small talk. Shweta put her glass down and put a hand on Vienna's leg, softly stroking the skin on her thigh. Vienna looked into her eyes and ran her hand down Shweta's face, teasing her dark hair, cupping her chin, moving her lips closer to her. She kissed her, their lips moving, their tongues exploring. Shweta's tongue was becoming insistent, her kisses desperate for more. She was unleashing a hunger that had been building for years onto Vienna. Vienna's hand ran down over Shweta's collarbone under the silk robe that she was wearing. Shweta reacted, her body shook under Vienna's touch. Suddenly her hands were all over Vienna, touching her ass, her breasts. Touching everywhere her eyes had roamed and wanted.

Pulling back for a second, Vienna said, "You want to continue here, or..."

"Let's go upstairs." Shweta breathed out, still dazed from the kiss.

The two women made it upstairs to Shweta's bedroom,

and Shweta pushed Vienna against the wall for another kiss. Insistent kissing. Desperate kissing. Shweta wanted Vienna's female form like nothing else. Vienna sometimes wondered why they wanted her so much. She was just another body. Just another collection of parts. But, want her, they did. And she wasn't about to complain.

"Your dress...off. Now." Shweta breathlessly told her as Vienna moved to kiss and bite Shweta's neck, making her moan. Shweta went to remove her robe. She was naked underneath.

Vienna pulled back and peeled the dress off slowly, knowing Shweta's eyes would follow her every move. She threw the dress to the side and was left in her black net bra and panties.

"Would you like these off too?" she gestured to her underwear.

Shweta looked at her incredible body. She had never seen anything so perfect outside of porn. She was mesmerized.

"Take them off, please."

Vienna continued the show, tantalizingly undoing the bra and shrugging out of it, her natural breasts high and firm, her nipples erect. She turned around and wriggled her hips as she rolled her panties down and then bent right over as she pulled them off her ankles. It was a move she had pulled on clients a thousand times, and not once did they seem to recognize that it was a show.

Vienna turned and looked boldly at Shweta, sitting on the edge of the bed. All green eyes and red lips and blonde hair. Shweta's eyes traveled to the golden hair between Vienna's legs.

Vienna walked slowly to her and took her face and kissed her again, her hands beginning to roam. She then moved her right hand down between her legs and stroked the smooth brown skin and soft dark hair. Vienna stroked, and her fingers slid through wet folds until Shweta was left a moaning, heavy breathing mess.

Shweta's breasts spilled out from her body as she lay back and enjoyed what Vienna was doing to her. Vienna climbed on top of her, taking a big nipple in her mouth and suckling as her skilled fingers played between Shweta's legs, toying with her, teasing her.

She then lifted her attention to the other breast taking the nipple into her mouth, giving it the same treatment. Shweta's hands fisted into Vienna's hair, pulling her closer to her chest. Her desire for this young woman that she had just met, surpassed anything else she had ever felt in her life.

Moving them to a more comfortable position in the bed, Vienna slowly crawled on top of Shweta and spread her legs apart.

Shweta watched Vienna above her, her eyes taking in this beautiful being as Vienna's right thigh pushed tight to her clitoris. Vienna bent to kiss her neck and her ear, sucking her earlobe, moaning into her ear, her thigh sliding up and down Shweta's wetness.

Shweta could feel the tension building up as she moved her hips in sync with Vienna's leg, gripping tightly to her. Before she could succumb to the incredible feeling, Vienna pulled her leg back and replaced it with her mouth.

She licked and sucked hungrily as Shweta gripped her hair and arched her back, pulling Vienna's face even closer, if that was possible. Vienna thrust two fingers into Shweta, screamed as she clenched her walls around Vienna's fingers. Her body pushed onto Vienna's fingers and tongue.

Shweta was breathing heavily, mumbling incoherent words as she finally came into Vienna's mouth with a scream, squirting. Vienna lapped up the juices, her tongue swirling. Shweta moved her hips against Vienna's face riding her orgasm and then fell back onto the bed, panting heavily.

Shweta pulled Vienna up to rest her head on Shweta's warm, soft belly and stroked her hair as she lay back, getting her breath, her world spinning.

There was a couple of minutes before she sat up and pushed Vienna onto her back smiling seductively and said,

"My turn."

CLIENTS DIDN'T ALWAYS WANT to 'give' to Vienna. Some wanted both; some wanted one or the other. Vienna knew that she had to be incredible at both. The best. She had to put on a show while they fucked her, whether she was enjoying herself or not. Vienna was a gifted actress in that they never knew she was acting.

Shweta had never pleasured a woman before. She made up for a lack of experience with enthusiasm. She was desperate to taste Vienna, to lose herself in Vienna's soft wet folds. As Vienna's back arched and her body writhed and moaned, Shweta just wanted her more. Her fingers were pushing into Vienna, exploratory, new. Vienna's body was responding as though they were hitting her exactly right. As though Shweta was a lover that had taken her body a thousand times and knew her better than she knew herself. Vienna angled her hips slightly so she could stimulate herself on Shweta's fingers. She knew she could make herself squirt like this. Her body shook, and gooseflesh rose across her. Her back arched, pushing her further into Shweta's mouth. She moaned loudly and pulled Shweta's head into her. She gushed, and the walls of her vagina shuddered.

Then her body went limp, her eyes still closed. She scrabbled at Shweta's head and pulled her up her body, lying on top of her. Shweta's breasts were heavy against her own.

"That was incredible," Vienna whispered. Shweta was mesmerized by this beautiful girl, lying fucked beneath her. Vienna's legs still shook. Years of practice had given Vienna the skill to control every tiny movement of her body. Shweta believed her entirely. She believed she had given an orgasm to this goddess.

They lay for a minute, Shweta collapsed into her and nuzzled into her neck. The weight of her on top of Vienna felt strangely nice. Vienna had still enjoyed Shweta. She enjoyed being able to be this magic for Shweta. To make Shweta's fantasy everything and more than she had ever dreamt it could be. Vienna loved being the dream girl. She loved being the best.

Shweta eventually rolled off and lay quietly on the pillow, lost in thought.

"Well, I'll have to go back to pretending with my husband for some more time now," Shweta replied, rolling her eyes.

Vienna wasn't surprised by the mention of a husband. There often were husbands or partners.

"I'm so gay," said Shweta. "Tonight has proven it for

me. You have given me the best night of my life. I am so very grateful to you."

Shweta continued, "In our culture, a woman's sexuality is still a very unpleasant matter to discuss, a lesbian isn't something I could be even though I am. I know now. My social status, my children, my money, and my home are tied to my husband. Without him, there is nothing. " Shweta told Vienna.

"You must be one hell of an actress to fake your whole life like that." Vienna raised on one elbow, her golden hair falling seductively. She saw part of herself in Shweta. She respected her for how she chose to live her life. Using the skills that she had to better herself. Vienna smiled at her and kissed her lightly.

"Well, it is not hard to please a man. He has no idea what goes through my head." Shweta said to her, letting out a short laugh. "You are lovely, Vienna. So so very lovely. You will be in my head for a long time, and I would love to see you again. But meanwhile, if you aren't in a rush to leave, please, could we fuck again?

3

"**O**f course, I'll come! Kevin's parties are like the source of half the clients I have," Ashley said to Trisha over the phone.

"Saying you're my best friend and I would come would have sufficed, but alright," Trisha mumbled sarcastically to Ashley.

Ashley laughed and bid Trisha goodbye.

"Joanna, I'll be out for the remainder of the day, if there are any important calls let me know," Ashley told her secretary over the intercom.

Ashley made her way home to get ready for Kevin's birthday party.

Kevin Marsh was one of the most successful businessmen in New York. He was the co-founder and CEO of Marsh and McLennan. His birthday was celebrated royally every year. Ashley never minded attending the event, not just because Kevin was her friend, but because his parties were a chance to network and pick up as many new and very wealthy clients as possible. Ashley was no doubt the best at what she did. However, her dazzling charm was why people booked her to organize and put on their events. To dazzle the most wealthy people in New York, she needed to be in front of them, and Kevin Marsh's party would put her right there in poll position.

ASHLEY GOT out of her BMW and handed the keys to the valet. The party was held at one of the farmhouses Kevin owned, and the place was decorated to perfection by Ashley's team. The entrance consisted of a golden carpet spread to welcome the guests, with silver columns standing erect towering over the entering guests.

The theme was minimalistic metallics. Several tables with golden linen cloths were scattered neatly around the farmhouse lawn, with Chiavari chairs. Metallic balloons were put around the main table on which the birthday cake was to be displayed.

The party was similar to any other elite party, conversation, canapés, and wine. Free-flowing wine.

Kevin and Trisha greeted Ashley at the entrance.

"You made it!" Trisha hugged Ashley, welcoming her.

"Of course, I did. I told you I'd come." Ashley replied, pulling back from the hug to look at Trisha.

Trisha wore an off-shoulder dark grey long satin dress, and her dark hair was twisted and pinned.

With Kevin at her side dressed in a dark grey suit and gazing at Trisha lovingly, the two looked the perfect couple. Appearances can be deceptive.

"You look amazing, Trish." Ashley looked at her stunning friend in genuine admiration.

"Thank you! You too, Ash. I love you in green!"

Ashley smoothed down the dark green silk shirt. She liked the way it brought out her eyes.

"Happy birthday, Kevin. You look handsome." Ashley wished Kevin, pulling him in for a hug. Handing her gift to him, she smiled.

"Thank you, Ashley. You look beautiful, yourself." Kevin replied, putting the gift with the rest of the presents on the table beside him.

"Enjoy your evening," Kevin said to Ashley as she walked to where the rest of the guests were.

"Oh, Ashley, it's so good to see you again! You came here alone?"

A significant reason Ashley despised these gatherings, was the constant irksome questions everyone had about her personal life.

"Well, Mrs. Becker, my success doesn't count as a legitimate life partner, so yes," Ashley replied dryly.

This was getting too bothersome. She might have to stop attending these events altogether and send her secretary to cover for her. Ashley gulped down her drink and looked at the woman currently on a mission to get on her nerves.

"Poor you. All these riches but no one to share them with. Sad. I know you are a lesbian, dear, and it doesn't matter, you know. There are lots of lovely women out there." Mrs. Becker charged again with her comments. Did this woman not understand the meaning of the word privacy? Ashley thought to herself.

A hand wrapped itself around Ashley's waist, pulling her away from the nosey woman.

"Hey Ash, Kevin wanted to see you. Would you come with me for a minute?" Trisha, the savior, jumped into the painful conversation, saving Ashley. She then faced the older woman apologetically and said,

"Sorry Mrs. Becker, I'm going to have to steal Ashley for a while. I hope you don't mind." Trisha pulled Ashley away from the woman without even giving her a chance to reply.

"You're a lifesaver, Trish." Ashley let out a sigh and then winked at Trisha.

"You're welcome, hon'. I couldn't help but pity you." Trisha laughed at Ashley's murderous glare before continuing,

"That condescending old hag had her paws right in you. She wanted to keep you to herself for the rest of the night. I had to come to the rescue. Oh, and by the way, if it doesn't work out with Kev, you're still my backup." Trisha winked, both of them ending up laughing.

Ashley and Trisha moved to the bar and ordered their drinks before taking a seat at the bar stools. They talked for a while, sipping their drinks before Ashley decided to voice out her thoughts. Who better to confess to than her own best friend?

"You know Trish, maybe Mrs. Becker is right. I don't have someone to share my life with. Perhaps it is lonely at the end of the day, despite all this grandeur lifestyle.

"Really? You don't admit to things like this, normally. I usually have to force it out of you." Trisha looked at her, surprised by her sudden confession.

Ashley let out a laugh at and said,

"I'm joking. I LOVE this lifestyle. All these people can go to hell and take their suggestions with them." She winked at Trisha, taking a sip of her drink.

"You are impossible at times," Trisha replied, rolling her eyes.

"Oh, you love me." Ashley winked at her.

"Yes, I do," Trisha admitted, smiling.

"On a serious note, maybe it would be a good idea, though." Ashley started only to be interrupted by Trisha.

"You sleep with the hottest women in the city! You can have whoever you want. And since you're not looking for a full-time relationship, neither are you settling down, what more do you want?"

"No, I don't mean sex. I mean like a fake girlfriend, you know, for parties like these and to appear publicly with me so wherever I go, I don't get the 'aw you so lonely' chant. Although, I'm not sure I know anyone who would do that without it becoming, you know, complicated." Ashley explained. If people could mind their own business, none of this would be necessary, but as the wealthiest people in New York seemed unable to do that, maybe Ashley needed to address it.

"Oh. Well, I've got just the thing to help you. Come here, let me show you something." Trisha took out her phone, opening a website, she gave the phone to Ashley.

"Really? Porn is your solution?" Ashley asked her, which made Trisha roll her eyes.

"It isn't a porn website. It's an escort agency – Black Label. It is the absolute best there is. I once did a story on them. They exist to serve wealthy women. You could hire one of their finest girls and problem solved- you have a fake girlfriend."

Ashley inspected the website, impressed.

"This sounds good, but will they keep it all discreet? I mean, no one can find out it's a sham girlfriend and not an actual partner. That could dent my reputation big time." She told Trisha.

"Don't worry about that. A lot of their clients are celebrities. Discretion is what they thrive on. You just need to say the magic word, and we can free you from Mrs. Becker's exasperating nagging the next time she sees you."

"Okay, text me the details, and I'll check them out." Ashley was intrigued, handing back her cellphone.

WHEN SHE ARRIVED HOME, Ashley opened the escort agency website that Trisha had sent her. Contemplating for a while, whether or not to do this, Ashley finally gave in and dialed the agency number.

It was a good thing the company had a 24/7 service.

"Good evening, Black Label, how may I help you?" a voice answered on the other end.

"Hello, this is Ashley Davidson. I'd like to speak to a manager." Ashley asked the woman.

"Just a second, ma'am." The voice replied as Ashley waited for her to connect the call with the manager.

"I'm directing your call to the manager, you may speak to him now."

"Thank you." Ashley politely responded as the call connected with the manager.

"Hello, this is Mason Park." A gruff male voice said.

"Hi. This Ashley Davidson. I wanted to speak to you about the escorts. Could you give me some information regarding that?"

"Oh, Ms. Davidson, it's a pleasure speaking to you. Yes. Yes, of course, I can. The company works to provide escorts for pleasure and company. You can hire an escort for as long as you want, of course, with a reasonable fee. Your escort will be able to provide you with whatever services you require while you are paying for their time. We provide male or female escorts, or if you want an escort of less binary gender, please just give us the best description of what you want, and we will provide it for you." The man finished.

"I see. Well, I would like to meet the best female escort you have. I want a long term regular arrangement. The cost is no issue. I need someone feminine, intelligent, educated, and charming. Kindly have her meet me at my apartment for a short interview. I am at 53 West 53. Top floor." Ashley responded.

"Of course, Ms. Davidson. Our top girl is available for a new long term arrangement. Did you want exclusive rights to her or just priority?"

"Priority would be fine. I don't need exclusivity."

"Perfect. We will have her come over to your home tomorrow morning. Is that alright?" Mason inquired.

"That's wonderful. Thank you, Mr. Park." Ashley responded.

"I would like to request the details of this interaction and any future dealings between your company and me be kept extremely private." Ashley asserted.

"We ensure the privacy of every client, Ms. Davidson; you do not have to worry about a thing," Mason replied.

"Alright, thank you once again," Ashley said, ending the call.

Hanging up the phone, she sighed and laid back on the sofa. There was no going back now, she thought.

4

_____

The next morning at 10 am precisely, Ashley buzzed in Vienna from Black Label. As Vienna walked into her apartment, Ashley's eyes widened slightly. This woman, this escort, was stunning. She wore a tight black pencil skirt and heels and a red ruffled top. She had blonde hair, long down her back, and these enchanting green eyes that just wouldn't quit. Ashley had never seen anyone that looked like her.

"Hello, I'm Vienna." The woman spoke, her voice like warm honey, extending her hand.

Ashley recovered from her shock immediately and shook Vienna's hand.

"Hello. I think you're already aware of who I am. Come on in, please." Ashley said to Vienna, allowing her to enter the penthouse.

Ashley was in Sunday morning casual wear, sweatpants, and a white tank top with no bra. Still, Vienna immediately noticed how attractive she was, in an androgynous way and how prominent her nipples were. The penthouse apartment was incredible, but Vienna was used to the homes of the extremely wealthy.

"You have a beautiful home," Vienna said to her, her sharp green eyes admiring the house as the light hit different planes of her lovely, delicate featured face.

"Thank you," Ashley replied as Vienna took a seat on the sofa, putting her purse on the coffee table.

"I'm sure you hear this all the time, but your beauty is dazzling," said Ashley with a certain crunch in her voice.

"Thank you, Ms. Davidson. Beauty is a significant part of what it takes to be the best in the escort world."

"Please, call me Ashley," Ashley said gently. To which Vienna replied with a respectful nod. "So, you are the best, then?"

Vienna nodded again. "Yes. I have worked very hard to be recognized as such. I am so much more than just my face and body."

Ashley smiled to herself. She loved this young woman's confidence.

"Would you like something to eat or drink? It's still fairly early in the morning. Breakfast?" Ashley asked her.

"Oh, no, no. Thank you. Just a glass of water, please." Vienna told her.

Ashley got her a glass of water and then went to sit down on the sofa across from Vienna.

They sat in silence before Ashley decided to break it.

"I asked for this meeting to see if you'd be the right one for the job. I don't need anyone for sex or something of that sort. I can pick up women for sex. I just need someone to accompany me to the parties and events that I attend and be lovely, charming, and convincing as my partner. Being in the business world, you're not spared from these gatherings and certainly not spared when you show up alone." Ashley explained to Vienna. "I want a fake girlfriend."

"Absolutely. I can do that. Do you want me to be educated, confident, and politically aware, or innocent naive insipid hottie, or sex bomb without too many brains? Or, if there are any other character traits you want, please, just specify. I can be anyone you want me to be."

Ashley watched her, her breasts full under the red silk. Ashley was very intrigued by her.

"The first version. I want you to be able to hold your own in intelligent company. But, don't be controversial, keep people happy. Make them love you."

"No problem at all. So dress wise, classy, feminine, and smart?"

"Yes."

"What do you want my name to be?"

"Vienna is fine."

"A long term arrangement?" Vienna enquired, her lips were swollen and red and overtly sexual.

"I have some important events to attend throughout the year, and I must have someone by my side, romantically speaking. I can give you my calendar ahead of time. So, yes. A long term arrangement. If you can commit to that." Ashley elaborated further.

"I see. However, I'm sure you didn't just ask to meet me to tell me all that. You have questions of your own as well. Am I right?" Vienna said to her.

"Yes, that's right," Ashley affirmed, resting against the sofa and then continued,

"Can you tell me more about yourself, your real self?"

Vienna smiled and began, "Well, I'm 28 years old. I'm originally from Detroit. I went to high school there and then moved to New York when I was 18, looking for something better. Meredith Bowes herself took me in, showed me Black Label, and promised if I learned and learned well, I would have an incredible future. She put me through my double bachelor's in philosophy and art history, criticism, and conservation from Princeton University. I like to read a lot, and US and world affairs are things I like to keep myself updated about. My favorite writer is Cormac McCarthy. I like to draw in my free time. Mostly paintings.

Last but not least, my job is something that I take very seriously, and that is why I am the best there is. I love my job, and I love my clients. I am the ultimate professional. You will be more than satisfied with your decision to hire me." Vienna smiled, lovely in the light. "And, if you do change your mind on the sex thing, while you are paying for my time, you are my absolute priority. Anything you want. Just ask at any time." Her voice was like silk.

Ashley looked lost in her thoughts for a while. Vienna had this effect on people almost all the time, but this particular one lasted longer.

"Everything alright?" inquired Vienna.

"Nothing I just thought that–.."

"–That I am overqualified to work for an escort agency?" Vienna chipped in before Ashley could complete her sentence.

"I can charm anyone you want me to. I will be the best date you have ever had. I can make people believe we are in love, but at the same time, I will never overstep. Give me a chance, and you will see." Vienna continued, she was mesmerizing in her confidence.

"If you want me regularly, you will need to fill in this contract committing to paying my retainer. That way, you will get priority on me, but not exclusivity. Will that be ok?"

Ashley nodded and signed the contract that Vienna had displayed in front of her after giving it a thorough read. The papers contained all the terms and conditions of their deal. Vienna signed the documents after Ashley had done so, and they both took a copy.

Ashley walked Vienna to the door.

"I'll have my calendar sent through to you. Please confirm your availability for all dates." Ashley told her.

Vienna nodded and exited the penthouse. The black skirt was tight around her ass.

Ashley couldn't stop watching her ass as she walked away.

Get a grip, Ashley. She's a fucking escort.

∾

THE CELLPHONE RANG TWICE as Vienna picked it out of her purse and answered.

"Hello, Vienna. How are you doing?" Ashley's voice came from the other side.

"Hi, Ashley. I'm good. Just out shopping. How are you?" Vienna replied.

"Good, good. I know my secretary arranged to have you accompany me to the charity function tonight. I'll pick you up at seven if you text me your address. I'll need you to wear something elegant, femme and classy. Nothing slutty." said Ashley.

"Yes. I'll be waiting. See you then." Vienna's voice was positive and warm.

"Splendid. See you tonight." came Ashley's reply as the call ended.

Sparing a look at her watch, Vienna gathered her stuff and headed home from her shopping trip. She had three hours until Ashley arrived, and Vienna had lots of time to look her best for an excellent first impression.

Vienna showered and loved the feel of the water hot on her body. She washed thoroughly. She wrapped a towel around herself and walked to her closet, picking out a long one-shoulder burgundy satin dress. I'll give you classy. She styled her hair retro curls resting on one side. Her makeup and understated jewelry finished the look.

Taking a look at the clock on the living room wall, Vienna sat down on the sofa and waited for Ashley.

Fifteen minutes later, the bell buzzed—Ashley's BMW outside of Vienna's gates. Vienna pressed the button to open the gate and headed outside.

"Hey. You look amazing." Vienna greeted Ashley as she got out of the car to open the passenger door for Vienna, complementing her.

Ashley was in navy blue pants that clung to her ass, and a white button-down shirt with a tight vest over it, and her hair slicked back. She looked dapper in a masculine, feminine hybrid way. Vienna liked it. Vienna couldn't help noticing how the cut of it showed off the strength of her body.

Ashley tried to keep her cool as she looked at Vienna and moved around the car to open the door for her.

Vienna was breathtaking, Ashley thought to herself. Never had a woman had this effect on Ashley before.

"Vienna, you are stunning. The dress is perfect."

"Shall we?" she asked, extending her hand for Vienna to take.

Vienna smiled warmly and took placed her hand in Ashley's, nodding.

"Chivalry isn't dead. Thank you," she said as Ashley helped her into the car.

The ride to the event consisted of Ashley explaining the event formalities to Vienna and telling her about the people she would come across once there. Ashley was all business. This was a business arrangement.

The valet took the car, and the two women headed into the building. Heads turned in their direction as they walked in, and Ashley took Vienna's hand in hers, as Vienna smiled at her. Electricity jolted through her feeling the softness of Vienna's hand in hers.

Looking around, they noticed the lavish arrangements for the charity event.

It was held at Guastavino's. Located at 409 E. 59th Street, this architectural phenomenon was packed full of rich history. With its massive granite arches and Catalan vaulted ceilings, the 15000 square foot venue was the perfect destination for such a luxurious event.

The elite class filled the venue as they drank and busied themselves in fatuous conversations.

Ashley and Vienna grabbed their drinks from a waiter and moved to sit at their designated table.

"After the formalities are over, that's when the mingling with the people begins," Ashley informed Vienna, her voice low.

"We should go through the history of our romance again," Ashley suggested, and so they did.

Soft music played in the background as people chatted when a voice grabbed their attention. "Ladies and gentlemen, as your host for tonight, I would like to thank all of you for coming tonight and donating to such a noble cause. Events like these are a chance to indulge ourselves in the way of helping the less fortunate. I hope you contribute generously to this cause and bring happiness to those in need. Thank you once again, and enjoy your evening."

"That's Tyler Johnson. He's one of the leading businessmen in the country. His father is the former US Supreme Court Judge. Great guy. Always ready to help people. His wife, however, a real bitch." Ashley explained.

"I think that sneer is like something permanent on her face. She probably thinks it's pretty, but it's not." Vienna snickered.

"She always has her nose in my life all the time." Ashley continued.

"If she asks, we have made out several times, and I taste like cherries," Vienna stated, her eyes glinting with mischief.

"Why should she ever ask that?" Ashley asked, amusement clear on her face.

"Well, you did say she was a prying woman." Vienna was used to defending her unabashed humor. Ashley smiled to herself. Vienna was something else.

Sipping their drinks, the two women sat back and relaxed. These events did take a lot of time.

"This is a fancy place."

Vienna said before continuing,

"We're just one murder short of a real-life Agatha Christie novel." She laughed.

Ashley looked at her, surprised, and then let out a short laugh herself.

"You have an interesting mind, I must say." She teased.

Vienna shrugged lightly smiling at Ashley before asking,

"Why do you hate this Mrs. Supreme Court Judge

Daughter-in-law, did one of your girlfriends leave you for her and break your heart or something cliché like that?"

"Her name is Leyla, and no, that is not what happened. We are not seventeen." Ashley replied.

"Funny, we think emotions and heartbreaks are only for seventeen-year-olds." Vienna retorted.

She had always had the mind of a philosopher, behind all the sly humor, and she didn't hide it at all.

"It's just that when you get rich and successful and are openly homosexual, you score yourself some enemies," Ashley replied, her eyes dropping on Vienna's left wrist, noticing a small tattoo.

"I got drunk and got inked. I've got loads of them under this dress." Vienna explained and then without waiting for a reply continued,

"I am joking; it is a Celtic Triskellion. It symbolizes reincarnation." Vienna's emerald eyes flashed wildly under long dark lashes.

"Interesting, so someday you want to leave what you do and begin a new life?" Ashley was showing genuine interest. She couldn't remember the last time she had been so interested in someone.

"Well, originally, I got the tattoo because I did start a new life. Moving to New York, becoming Vienna, the Black Label girl was a reincarnation for me. One that I cannot thank Meredith enough for. I didn't have a great childhood. This job pays me well, and I enjoy it a lot. I get to live a life of luxury that many can only dream of. But, yes, someday maybe I will do something that is more for myself. As they say, more for the soul, you know. There are other things I want to pursue in life." Vienna replied as the conversation flowed.

As the evening progressed, whoever Ashley introduced Vienna to was blown away by her. Vienna was right; she could make anyone love her. The sarcastic humor she showed alone with Ashley was reined right in, and Ashley watched as Vienna quickly assessed each new person and then became lovely and charming and interested in them.

Ashley dropped Vienna home later.

For the first time in a while, Ashley had a good time without caring about how many clients she had picked up. This was different.

What was not though, however, was a text from Trisha asking to meet her the next morning. Ashley replied, telling her to come to the office at 11 am.

"HEY, where do you disappear to at times, are you in a secret cougar society?" Trisha barged into Ashley's office as she always did.

"No, you know me, I have to be surrounded by dumb rich people to get more work," Ashley answered, not matching her best friend's excitement.

"You badmouth rich people a lot for someone worth quite a bit herself." Trisha shot back.

"So, I went ahead with your idea and got a girl to attend these events with me. A fake girlfriend." Ashley told her best friend.

"Oh! Congratulations on your new fake relationship, like always Trisha saves the day!" Trisha quipped, "I am happy it solved your problem, and the old ladies are off your back." She continued with a grin.

"Well yes, but it's not just that, I had fun with Vienna, you know. She is smart, knowledgeable, talks well, is carefree. She's like a younger version of me." Ashley contributed, with a fondness for her pretend partner evident in her voice.

"What is this? Ashley Davidson, the robot I have known for years, finally feels something?"

Trisha had her comeback ready. The witty sense of humor was common between her and Vienna. Ashley thought to herself.

"Yes. It is weird and uncomfortable for me. I don't know how to feel about it. Also, it is her job. She is supposed to make me feel like this, isn't she?"

"So, you know a lot about this girl in one meeting. Do you even know me this well?"

Trisha had made her mind to tease Ashley.

"Stop being so extra, Trish; I know everything about you." Ashley finally retorted, coming out of her bubble.

"Oh, shoot! I better get ready. I have to meet Kevin's parents tonight." Trisha said with a look of sudden realization spread on her face.

"Just don't be yourself, and it will all go well." Ashley teasingly offered advice.

"Ok, I am offended, but I will also take your advice, you just make sure I get to meet this girl of yours soon. We could hang out together at my house it has been a while, just the three of us." Trisha suggested.

"As much as I miss being at your place, you realize she is not a real girlfriend and charges me quite a lot for the pleasure of her company?" Ashley continued the conversation, trying not to let everything out.

"Oh, sweetie, you can pay someone to be nice, but you cannot pay them to them to be interesting."

∾

ASHLEY HAD TRIED to underplay Vienna's effect on her, but deep down even she knew, she was charmed.

Pull yourself together, Ashley. Get back to the reason you have a fake girlfriend. She is good for business. Vienna will be great for business.

VIENNA HAD a relaxed evening completing a painting, stroking the brush artfully on the canvas. Her paintings were always dark. The colors gave flashes of her tragic past—her drug addict mother yelling at her in the dark, messy pit of an apartment that they lived in. But Vienna also found them soothing. She had come a long way. She had clawed her way out from the gutter. She looked around her beautiful home and the life she had created for herself. The light coming through her window changed color as the sun set.

5

A couple of days later, Ashley was in her office, trying to decide whether or not she should ask Vienna to tag along to Trisha's house. She couldn't stop thinking about her. She had never been nervous about anything before. What had changed? Finally, deciding, she grabbed the telephone and dialed Vienna's number.

"Hello?" Vienna's voice came over the phone.

"Hello, Vienna. How are you?" Ashley began.

"I'm doing well," Vienna replied formally.

"Are you free this evening. Sorry, I know it is late notice." Ashley continued.

"Oh, luckily, I am actually. What is the event? You can text me the details, and I'll be there." a usual reply came from Vienna.

"Actually, it's not an event. We are going to see my friend." Ashley clarified.

"Sure, of course, what do you need me to wear? How do you need me to be?" The charm in Vienna's voice was back.

"I mean, just come real casual. Jeans or whatever. I was thinking we just hang out, you know. It's something me and Trisha do once in a while, and I thought maybe you would like to be there too." Ashley explained.

"Oh." Vienna screwed up her face in confusion. "No one has asked me to just hang out with them for a long time now. Paid or otherwise." Vienna genuinely felt surprised.

"Well, if you can't or don't want to, it's fine," Ashley said trying to hide her disappointment, maybe Trisha wasn't the only one wanting to see Vienna like an average person.

"No, I'll be there. It will be a refreshing change for me too. Besides, you are my main client now, and you pay my retainer, so yeah, absolutely, sign me up."

"Great! I'll wait for you at my office, be here for 6 pm. Trish's place isn't far from here."

Ashley hung up the phone, the disappointment in her voice was gone, replaced by her usual confidence.

Vienna bid her colleagues goodbye and drove to her house. She had recently started as a part-time Intern at the New York Institute of Fine Arts. Her work there was very flexible. It had to be given the unpredictable nature of her main job for Black Label.

After showering, she pondered what to wear. This was one of those rare moments where she was confused about how to look and what to wear—hanging out at Ashley's friends. Jeans or whatever. Jesus.

She suddenly realized she had a lot of clients and colleagues, but not many friends.

Outside of work, she usually chose to be alone. The only person she could call a friend was Chloe.

She ended up deciding on some faded denim skinny jeans, torn at the knees, and a plain white Tee-shirt. Really casual. She kept stressing it was too casual, but took a deep breath and got over it.

She braided her hair to one side and applied some light makeup.

Satisfied with how she looked, Vienna grabbed her purse and phone and headed out the house where the driver was waiting for her.

Arriving at Ashley's company, she made her way to the front desk.

"Hi. I'm here to meet Ashley Davidson. Could you direct me to her office?" she asked the woman politely.

"Do you have an appointment?" the woman inquired.

"Yes," was Vienna's response as the lady dialed Ashley's office.

"Miss Davidson, there's a.." the lady looked at Vienna.

"Oh. Vienna Rhodes." She replied.

".. Vienna Rhodes here to meet you. Shall I send her up?"

Vienna waited as Ashley gave the order, and the woman directed her to Ashley's office.

Vienna was impressed by the setting. The working space was spacious and straightforward, furnished by a long desk in dark green and contrasting white chairs. The floor to ceiling windows gave an open and comfortable feel, providing light, and displaying a gorgeous view of the city.

Vienna walked to Ashley's office and knocked.

"Come in." Ashley's voice echoed.

Turning the handle, Vienna walked into Ashley's

office. It was similar to the rest of the floor setting, minimal and spacious. Ashley got up to greet Vienna with a quick hug.

"Hey. Welcome to my office."

"Thank you. It's very nice. I like the setting." Vienna complemented.

Vienna took some time to admire Ashley. She wore a black crew-neck sweater with navy blue trousers. Her short hair was behind her ears; her dark eyes were intense. She looked as well kept and quintessential as always.

"Take a seat, please," Ashley said to her as she walked back to her desk.

"Would you like some coffee?" Vienna's thoughts were interrupted, as Ashley asked.

"Oh, no, thank you. I have had too much of it already." Vienna refused.

"Just give me a minute, and then we can leave." Ashley continued talking while sorting some of the files.

"Sure," Vienna replied, noticing the art and design around her.

Ashley focussed on the files. She needed to finish off this paperwork before they could go. She needed not to be distracted by Vienna. She could smell her sweet perfume across her desk. She was exquisite in jeans and a Tee. On Vienna's body, the simple outfit was striking.

Ashley could feel her desire for Vienna rising.

She shook her head.

For god's sake, Davidson. Stop it.

"Hey! I'm so glad you guys could make it!" Trisha exclaimed, hugging Ashley, then moving to Vienna.

She pulled back and extended her hand to Vienna, making Vienna grin at her antics.

"I'm Trisha Peyton, the person responsible for the keeping this woman sane." she hinted at Ashley and laughed as Ashley rolled her eyes.

"I'm Vienna Rhodes. It's a pleasure to meet you, Trisha." Vienna shook her hand with a warm smile.

"Are we spending the rest of the day here, or are you going to invite us in, Trish?" Ashley smirked.

Trisha rolled her eyes and smiled.

"Please, do come in." She moved aside, letting the two women enter.

The apartment was magnificent with its custom white oak flooring and gracious, European-style casement windows—floor to ceiling windows and a captivating view.

Vienna complemented Trisha's house to which she grinned from ear to ear, thanking her.

"Don't mind her; she's usually high on something," Ashley whispered into Vienna's ear, making her chuckle, as they went to sit in the living room.

"So.. Vienna, thank you for coming here. Please relax. I know the arrangement between you and Ash. You don't have to pretend anything." Trisha continued as they sat down. Vienna was next to Ashley, her denim-clad thigh tantalizingly close.

"Thanks. So, I'll just be myself then?"

"Yes. I wanted to meet you after Ashley went on about you the other day, telling me that she couldn't have a better fake girlfriend. A compliment indeed!" Trisha wanted to go on but was stopped midway as Ashley have her a look that clearly said don't.

Ashley cleared her throat suggestively before speaking up,

"Let's have something to eat first, reporter woman." She continued.

"Oh, that's where I have seen you!" Vienna exclaimed, purposely ignoring the earlier the part.

Although she didn't make it apparent, it made Vienna happy that Ashley thought well of her. She always wanted to please the client, right? There was nothing special about Ashley.

"We do these sleepovers so that one of us does not feel old." Vienna was jolted back to reality by Trisha's crisp voice.

"Please, Trish, you are not much younger than me, you just have this skin that never ages." Ashley continued the banter as Vienna smiled silently.

"Seven years is a lot, but oh well, whatever helps you sleep at night." Trisha shot back.

"You two wait here while I check the oven," Trisha said while moving to the kitchen.

As the two women were left alone, Ashley found herself absorbed in Vienna's perfume; it smelt french, a more potent scent with a subtle rose underneath it. It was driving Ashley crazy, and she was almost leaning into Vienna, quickly drawing back she spoke awkwardly,

"Um, I must tell you Trisha is a big foodie. She will go on and on about what she cooked and how it's made."

Vienna nodded, she noticed the earlier awkward advance but did not mention it at all.

"Oh, this perfume is amazing! Which one is it?"

exclaimed Trisha as she returned and pointed towards Vienna, she knew it wasn't Ashley's.

"Thank you. It's Amouage Jubilation. It is my favorite."

Ashley logged the name in her brain and thought about finding it next time she was near a perfume counter. Her favorite scents, she used to test when she was passing a perfume counter. A small spritz on her wrist that she would wander around smelling and remember memories or the women behind them.

"Alright, guys! Dinner has been served! Now let's dig in." Trisha clapped her hands together, ushering the two women into the dining room with her.

"Oh, my this chicken looks delicious. Did you cook it yourself?" Vienna asked as she sat down. The tasty aroma filled the dining room, making their mouths water.

"Oh, thank you. Yes, yes, I did. You see, for this recipe, I like to either buy thinly sliced chicken or slice regular chicken breasts in half from right to left, opening them like a book.." Trisha started explaining how she cooked the dish as Ashley looked at Vienna as if saying told you so. Vienna smiled at her and then focused her attention on Trisha, listening intently.

"So Vienna, Ash told me you have a double major. That's amazing."

"Yeah, I have a major in philosophy as well as art history, criticism, and conservation. I'm currently volunteering as an intern for the NYU Institute of Fine Arts."

"Wow. Beauty and brains, huh? Ashley sure landed the perfect person." Trisha winked, making Vienna laugh. "What do you get up to when you aren't studying and working?"

"I paint. I love to paint. Oil on canvas mostly." Vienna added.

"What do you paint?"

"Feelings, memories. I can paint anything, really, but often when I am overwhelmed with a feeling, I put it on canvas. Hard to explain, I guess, I would have to show you some of my pieces."

Ashley was intrigued. She enjoyed art. She had some beautiful pieces in her apartment. She was almost desperate to see what had spilled out of Vienna's lovely head onto a canvas.

"Oh, girl. That sounds deep and meaningful. I LOVE it." Trish almost danced a little in excitement.

"You two can come to my place sometime, and I'll show you." Vienna shocked herself by issuing an invite to her home. She never had anyone to her home. Never. What was she doing?

"I would definitely like that. Ash, wouldn't that be great?"

"Sure. I mean. I'd love to. Thanks."

The trio kept talking, and it seemed as if Vienna had always been a part of her life. Even though Trisha knew the arrangement and the casual dinner was out of Vienna's usual scope, it felt natural.

She enchanted Ashley. That was precisely Vienna's job, though, wasn't it? To be the best. To charm, to beguile, to intrigue.

"ALRIGHT, ladies, I think we should call it a night. I have a crucial meeting tomorrow." Ashley suggested.

"Noooooo. I thought we could have played spin the bottle!" Trisha quipped.

"Okay then, girls! Let me show you to your rooms for

the night." Trisha said to the women, getting up herself.

"Ash, you already know your room since you're an equal resident of this house." Trisha laughed.

Ashley rolled her eyes, smiling.

"Yeah, yeah. I know."

"Vienna, my dear. This is your room. And I don't just mean for tonight; you can visit anytime you like, and this room shall be yours from this day forth." Trisha told her with a grin on her face.

"Thank you so much, Trisha. This is really sweet." Vienna told her as she entered the room.

The room was much like the rest of the house with its simplicity and tidiness. It had a color scheme of beautiful lilac and white. There was a queen-sized bed in the middle of the room.

Trisha excused herself upon receiving a phone call from Kevin.

Vienna walked towards the windows, checking the view as Ashley stood in the doorway watching her.

"Alright, then. Uh.. have a good night. If you need anything, my room's just two doors away." Ashley told her, her eyes shamelessly roaming around Vienna's body.

Vienna, seemingly oblivious to Ashley's stare, smiled and nodded.

"Thank you." She said as Ashley walked off to her room.

LATER THAT NIGHT, Vienna went to the kitchen to grab a glass of water. Walking back to her room, she suddenly ran into someone.

"Oh, I'm so sorry," Vienna mumbled, rubbing her forehead.

"It's okay. Trisha has this habit of keeping the house completely dark at night. I've told her it's creepy, but she says she can't sleep otherwise."

A light above them flickered on as Vienna focused her gaze.

Ashley smiled at her, and her eyes took in the little silk spaghetti strap top that rose and fell with her high full breasts. Vienna's nipples prominent through silk. Little silk shorts showing her long tan legs. Her hair pulled up in a messy bun.

Vienna blushed under Ashley's penetrating stare. She was used to people looking at her. Used to eyes on her body. But this felt different. Ashley raised her hand to a strand of Vienna's hair and pushed it behind her ear, and Vienna looked up at her noticing her eyes darken. Ashley's hand came up to softly stroke Vienna's cheek. Immediately, Ashley snapped back to reality, and her eyes widened, and she dropped her hand.

"Uh, well. Goodnight then." She said to Vienna, hurrying to her room.

Vienna was still rooted to the spot. She brought her hand up to touch her cheek, where Ashley's hand had been. Forcing herself to move, she threw one last glance at Ashley's door and then went to her room.

Why am I behaving like a teenager? Maybe feelings are not just for seventeen-year-olds?

Vienna's voice and body echoed in her head as she went to sleep.

6

Vienna's doorbell rang as she was popping another popcorn in her mouth.

She was surprised to hear her door mid-afternoon, but paused the movie, and got up to answer it. Ashley walked in confidently and gave Vienna a brief hug.

"Hey, I hope this isn't a bad time. It's just, I thought it might be better to drop in and talk to you in person, for a change, rather than on the phone, if you were home obviously. Which it seems that you are." Ashley rambled on, scratching the back of her neck.

"You sure you weren't just missing my charm around you?" Vienna teased with a smile. This was probably the first time she had flirted genuinely with Ashley.

"Excuse my homeless look though, I wasn't expecting anyone," Vienna added, looking down at her casual shorts and tank top briefly before meeting Ashley's gaze again.

"No, it's alright. You look very beautiful. As always." Ashley complimented.

Vienna smiled, a hint of red covering her cheeks. Pulling herself together, she asked Ashley,

"What would you like to have? Coffee? Tea? Water? Beer? Wine? I have it all." She finished with a wink. It felt strange having Ashley, or anyone, in her home.

"A beer would do. Thank you." Ashley responded with a smile of her own.

They sat on the living room sofa, Ashley with a beer in hand and Vienna with a can of soda.

"So, what's up?" Vienna asked.

"There's a party tonight at The Beekman, that I've been invited to. It is all a bit last minute. It's just your everyday rich people's party, nothing special. What is special, however, is the people that are going to be there. These are very influential and important people. A great boost for the business, if scored. So, we'll have that charming personality of yours put to the test tonight." Ashley finished with a smile.

Ashley couldn't help but think that she found herself explaining everything to Vienna even though there was no need. All she needed to do was tell her what kind of a party it was, and the location and Vienna just had to do her job accordingly.

There was something new that Ashley couldn't quite describe, but she also couldn't deny that she kind of liked it.

"Oh, you'll be more than satisfied by tonight's end." Vienna winked.

Ashley couldn't help but look at her. Vienna. Her hair was up in a messy bun, and her face void of any makeup making her freckles stand out. She was flawless, Ashley thought.

"I'm sure I will be," Ashley replied, tucking a stray strand of hair behind Vienna's ear. This intimate act was becoming more of a habit now, and Ashley didn't want it to stop.

Ashley's phone started to ring. Vienna immediately tore her gaze and focused on the bowl of popcorn as if it was the most exciting thing to exist.

"Right so, uh... yeah. Tonight at 8, then. I'm certain you'll dress impeccably as always." Ashley told her after ending her phone call. Ashley's eyes burned through her clothes. Through her skin. As though to her very soul.

"Yeah. Alright." Vienna said as they both got up, walking to the door.

"See you tonight, then. Have a good day." Ashley told her, walking down the steps towards her car.

"See you tonight." Vienna breathed out.

Closing the door, Vienna set her back against it, heaving a sigh. She put a hand on her chest, feeling her rising heartbeat.

What was that about?

"It's so beautiful," Vienna whispered to Ashley, as they arrived at the venue, their fingers laced together.

"Fun fact: In the Victorian era, this building was called Temple Court and was home to law offices," Ashley told Vienna as they walked through the sea of people.

Vienna wore in a knee-length royal blue off-shoulder dress, and Ashley couldn't help letting her eyes drift over it. The lovely lines of Vienna's body. The way the blue set off her golden hair. The sparkling green of her eyes. The beautiful skin.

Ashley smiled at her, squeezing her hand. This woman had a presence that could make you smile anytime, anywhere. Steering her towards the person hosting the event, Ashley wrapped her hand around Vienna's waist.

"Ashley Davidson! I'm honored that you could attend tonight. My, my, you look so smart." Mr. Matthews called out, pulling Ashley in for a hug.

Elijah Mathews was the city's most influential businessman, owning up to 4 of the country's leading businesses as well as two top-tier media houses. Ashley's company had managed his son's wedding two years back, and the man had been in love with her work ever since. The man was 62, but it's as if he stopped aging after 40, looking as young as ever.

"It's good to see you, Elijah." Ashley pulled back and smiled at him, once again wrapping her hand around Vienna's waist.

Elijah hadn't been wrong, Ashley did look smart in a black silk button-down shirt and smart burgundy pants.

"And who is this lovely lady?" Elijah turned his attention to Vienna, taking her hand in his and kissing it.

"This is my girlfriend, Vienna," Ashley stated, proudly.

"Pleased to make your acquaintance, Mr. Mathews. I've heard a lot about you."

And sure enough, Vienna had heard about him. Ashley had spent a good hour briefing her on some of the prominent people that they would expect to see.

"Oh, please, call me Elijah." He offered with a warm smile.

"So will they all talk like this in a fake posh accent all night?" Vienna quipped into Ashley's ear, pretending to say something significant.

Ashley nodded, trying hard not to laugh as her whole

body quivered with Vienna's lips to her ear and her body close.

She always smells so good; I want more of that.

Stop it! What are you doing?

The voices in Ashley's head had a duel of their own. She shook her head and got back into the conversation.

Vienna was chatting to Elijah as though she had known him all of her life. Ashley just watched in awe of her.

"Ashley, I must say you are charming yourself, but this evening is now officially owned by your lady love." Elijah's voice reached Ashley's ears.

"Well, she is an art major, and I am kind of an artist myself, we were made for each other." Ashley had her reply ready. She was not the only one smitten by Vienna anymore.

"Speaking of art and the artist, I have investors coming from England soon, and you need to design the company dinner they attend, as well as the after-party. It should be one grand affair. I will email your secretary all the details." Elijah turned to Ashley.

"Don't worry, Mr. Mathews, everything shall be taken care of," Ashley said with the usual belief in her voice.

"But only if you bring Vienna with you. Otherwise, this project is not yours, and I am not even joking." Elijah continued with a sly smirk.

Ashley laughed, shaking her head, and then nodded.

"It would be a pleasure to attend Mr. Mathews. We will both there. Vienna is my lucky charm; I wouldn't come without her." Ashley said to the sneaky man.

"Good for the business and the heart. You are one lucky woman, Ashley. Now if you will excuse me, I have to greet the rest of the guests. You two ladies enjoy your evening." Elijah said while leaving the two alone.

Good for the business and the heart?

She looked up at Vienna and caught her looking back. A real look? Or an act? What was she thinking? What was she feeling?

The evening went by in a blur of mindless chatter with clients and the sound of champagne glasses clinking. It came with a lot of clients for Ashley, so she didn't complain. Vienna was, so far, absolutely acing the test her charming personality had been put through tonight. People looked at her in awe, and every single one wanted to spend more time with her. Nobody was immune to Vienna's charm.

Ashley looked at her beautiful 'girlfriend.' Vienna's smile dazzled back. Eyes bright, teeth straight and white. Ashley leaned over and kissed her on the cheek.

For the people watching? Or for herself?

ASHLEY PUT her car keys on the table beside the door as they entered her apartment. She could have dropped Vienna home, but she just didn't want the evening to end. They shrugged off their now slightly wet coats and put them on the coatrack. Vienna kicked off her heels and sat on the big sofa with her feet up and turned on the TV. Naturally. As though she had always lived there. Ashley brought them both some water, and they gulped it down.

"The heavy showers in New York City will be continuing through the night and throughout the week, at intervals. The citizens are requested to please remain indoors." the reporter announced in the news.

"Great," Vienna muttered.

"You could stay here tonight. I mean, I have more than enough room here. Besides, the rain doesn't seem like it's stopping any time soon." Ashley suggested, looking out the window at the heavy rain.

"If it's not bothersome to you." Vienna started.

"Not at all! I'd be glad to have you over." Ashley smiled at her.

"Thanks," Vienna replied with a smile of her own.

"Come on, let me show you to your room." Ashley got up with Vienna trailing behind her.

Walking up the few steps, she opened the door to the first bedroom in the corridor. The room was tidy and neat. The walls were painted blue and white. Queen sized bed, massive full-length mirror at the corner of the room with a table to the side. There was a bathroom off the bedroom.

"I'll get you some clothes for the night," Ashley said to her.

"I'm going to take a shower. I want to feel clean again."

"Sure. There are towels in there. Help yourself to anything you need."

The heat between them was palpable.

"I brought you some clothes." Ashley knocked as she walked into the bathroom, the water was running. Vienna was in the shower. She didn't look.

The cubicle door slid open, the steam and the heat from the water, and Vienna stepped out. Naked. Ethereal. Incredible.

Ashley's eyes to her body. Her breasts. Her hips. Her pubic hair. Her eyes. Those eyes.

"Do you have a towel?"

Ashley swallowed and grabbed a towel. Desire pooled in the pit of her stomach. "Er. Here." She passed the towel over. Looking. Trying not to look. "There's some clothes. I left them on the chair."

Hurriedly moving out of the room, Ashley rushed to the kitchen, gulping down a glass of cold water to calm her nerves. She had never felt this turned on. Ever.

ASHLEY LOOKED at her bedroom door, thinking she had heard something. Except for her own heart beating faster, there was no noise. She was moving restlessly on the bed. Her mind filled with images of Vienna's beautiful fragrant body, her long hair darker when it was wet, the perfectly toned hips that looked modeled from clay.

Ashley reached her hand between her legs. She was soaking—wet dreams of naked Vienna.

Why am I doing this?

Ashley made last attempts at self-control, tugging at her hair in frustration. She lay back, opening her legs.

Her fingers slipped and slid around her wet folds. She pushed inside herself.

Vienna's eyes. Her face. Her laugh. Her hair. Her body. Naked and wet.

She pulled her fingers out, and they slid around her clit. Teasing. Playing.

Vienna's full high breasts, the water running down them. Vienna's magazine perfect body.

She moved her fingers faster. Harder on her clit.

Vienna's dark blonde pubic hair.

Her fingers moved faster. Her back arched.

Vienna Vienna. Vienna.

She orgasmed hard against her fingers.

Sleep came quickly to her.

7

A shley was at the office with a coffee. She wanted to see Vienna, but there was nothing scheduled over the next couple of days.

"Ms. Davidson, you will be happy to know we are getting more clients than ever." Her secretary said politely.

"They have all been talking about Ms. Rhodes. She is as lucky for the company as she is for you." she continued.

It seems like everything these days revolves around Vienna.

Ashley thought to herself as she nodded and smiled at her secretary.

There was an idea. She could call Vienna, telling her she wanted to celebrate the company's recent successes. She was paying. Vienna had to do whatever she wanted.

VIENNA ARRIVED at the club and, for a moment, was stunned at how good the nightclub was. She smoothed down the short black leather skirt she was wearing.

She surveyed the crowd, and her eyes finally landed on Ashley sitting at the bar. Walking towards her, she had to blink a couple of times, Ashley in tight black jeans and a fitted tank top. Her small breasts and nipples were prominent. She confidently wore no bra. Her arms looked so defined. Vienna swallowed the lump in her throat and called out to Ashley over the loud music.

"This place is amazing!" she said to Ashley, taking a seat next to her.

"Yeah, it is. Trisha brought me here a couple of weeks ago. It's only recently opened." Ashley replied.

"Oh, wow. You really can't tell it's new." Vienna said as she took a look around.

"But I must say, I am a little surprised." Vienna continued.

"Why? Because I don't seem like someone who knows fun clubs?" Ashley replied, getting a little closer to Vienna, you could say the loud music made it necessary, but it was not just that.

"No, because you don't seem like someone who celebrates in fun clubs." Vienna retorted with her usual charm.

"You look amazing." Ashley kissed her on the cheek and smiled widely.

Vienna's eyes widened slightly, feeling Ashley's lips on her cheek for a brief second before she recovered to her usual calm self.

"You look stunning yourself. You suit a tank top and no bra." Vienna said with a laugh, her eyes twinkling.

Ashley smirked and ordered her a drink.

"Wanna dance?" Vienna asked Ashley, looking at the crowd on the dancefloor.

Not waiting for an answer, Vienna grabbed Ashley's

hand and dragged her to the dancefloor. Electricity ran between their fingers.

Vienna grabbed Ashley's waist and pulled her close and moved her hands up and down her body. Ashley's hands rested on Vienna's hips as she felt them sway. Vienna turned around in Ashley's arms, her back facing Ashley's front holding Ashley's hands against her hips. She absorbed herself in the music. Ashley felt close to exploding.

Vienna bent down slightly and pressed into Ashley, making her groan. Getting back up, she started to grind herself subtly against Ashley. Ashley's hands still on her hips. She was scared to move them and scared of what she might do if she moved her hands.

The heat between them was searing.

Ashley suddenly pulled back and whispered into Vienna's ear.

"Come to the bathroom with me." She grabbed Vienna's hand roughly and dragged her through the busy bar to the bathroom. It was empty and curiously quiet, the heavy beat of the music dulled.

They stared at each other, the tension in the room at its peak as Ashley grabbed Vienna, pushed her back against the sinks, and kissed her. Really kissed her. Like she had wanted to do since the first time she saw her.

Ashley's hand fisted in Vienna's hair, as Vienna's hands came to rest on Ashley's waist. Ashley's weight pressed into her, her right thigh pushing between Vienna's legs, tight against her as she leaned back on the sinks. Their tongues met Vienna's mouth and tongue insistent in response to Ashley. Every part of Ashley's body was on fire.

The door to the bathroom opened, and the two

women sprang apart, trying to look like they hadn't just been all over each other. A random girl walked in and stood in front of the mirror, touching up her makeup. Vienna stole glances at Ashley, who winked at her. Ashley felt alive for the first time in so many years.

The girl left, and Ashley took hold of Vienna and bundled her into one of the bathroom stalls. She locked the door before sitting down on the covered toilet seat, grabbing Vienna by the waist.

Vienna hitched her skirt up and straddled Ashley's hips. Ashley caught sight of red lace between her legs, pulled Vienna's face down to her and kissed her more. Her hands were roaming Vienna's body. She pulled Vienna's top down, spilling her breasts from the top of her bra.

Ashley took Vienna's nipple in her mouth. She was suckling her nipple, running her teeth across it, and up her breast. Ashley sucked her breast; it would mark later. Ashley wanted her. Wanted to mark her body. Wanted to take her in every way possible.

Ashley stood up, lifting Vienna with her, her hands on her ass.

She pushed Vienna up against the door, lifting her skirt. Her lips to Vienna's ear. "Is this okay?"

"Yes. Yes, I want you. Please. I need you inside me," Vienna breathed back. And she did. For once, she wasn't just saying what a client wanted to hear. She wasn't acting. "Fuck me. Fuck me, please."

Ashley didn't need asking twice. She pulled Vienna's red lace roughly to the side and felt her wet and ready. Ashley's strong fingers pushed into her. Vienna groaned as they entered her. Ashley looked deep into Vienna's eyes as her pupils widened. She lifted Vienna's ass slightly with her left hand as her right hand began to fuck her. Vienna's body was responsive. So responsive. Vienna moaned and gasped, her nipples rose, gooseflesh flooded her chest. Ashley added another finger, Vienna was so open to her. She was so wanting.

Ashley forced her back against the toilet door, releasing months of pent up passion on Vienna's body. Her lips to Vienna's ear.

"Is this what you wanted? All along? Is this what you have been begging for, all along? You need this, don't you? You need this like you need air? Don't you?"

"Yes." Vienna gasped. Ashley's dominance was making her heady with lust. Ashleys fucking was what she had dreamt about late at night in the quiet hours alone in her bed.

"You want more, don't you? Beg for it, if you do." Ashley took Vienna's earlobe in her mouth and sucked, and she pushed her tongue in Vienna's ear, her fingers still working hard between her legs.

"Please. Please. I need more. Please, Ash. I need to come." Vienna's words were broken and breathy. Her body was lost to the sensations. Ashley pushed a fourth finger inside Vienna's wetness and continued to thrust, her thumb slipping over Vienna's clit. Vienna's legs were barely holding her up, Ashley used her body weight to pin Vienna against the door.

"Come for me, come for me now. I want to feel your orgasm." Ashley's command firm in her ear.

The feeling inside Vienna filled up and spilled over. Vienna bucked and came, gushing and spilling over Ashley's hand and running down her naked legs. Her orgasm genuine for the first time she could remember.

She felt dizzy. Ashley kissed her neck. Still inside her. She opened her eyes slowly. Her wide green eyes fixed Ashley.

"That was just... wow. I can't even speak." Vienna said to her, breathlessly.

Ashley smiled at her, still holding her up, stroking her cheek before replying,

"I'd wanted to do that for quite some time now. You make it difficult not to kiss you with every word you speak, every look you give." Ashley said. "I know that is your job. So, I'm not sure what is going on here. But I know that I couldn't keep my hands off you a second longer."

Vienna blushed a deep red and leaned down to peck Ashley's lips. Ashley gently pulled her fingers out of Vienna and held her as she adjusted her underwear and skirt.

"God. I am soaked!"

Ashley laughed. "Leave it that way. Walk out proudly with your orgasm dripping down your legs like a slut who just got fucked in the bathroom. I like it. I won't be washing my hands."

Vienna laughed. "Ha. Okay, if that is a challenge, I'm not one to back down. It has got in my shoes too; I hope you know this?!"

"Also, a bathroom stall may be a weird place to have this conversation, but I still want to ask..."

"Yes?" Ashley motioned for her to continue.

"Why me? I mean, you are so sought after. Anyone that you wanted could be yours." Vienna asked.

"I have had a lot of women, but none of them excite me as you do. None of them make me laugh and make me feel things like you do. I don't know what is happening here. But, I want you badly, and I have for some time now. You do things to me. I'm sure you hear this from all your women. But, it is different with you."

"Yeah, but you know, you are grand and sophisticated, and you plan things so well. I am outlandish and um.. wild, although I do like driving sophisticated people wild... so maybe it will work." Vienna answered her question with a girlish charm.

"That is true. I have worked very hard to get here; every step of the way was planned and calculated. It's not easy, but even I am allowed to breathe and feel free. As you put it, feelings are for everyone." Ashley replied as if every word had both conviction and love in it.

They held each other's gaze for a moment. Each were envisioning what maybe could be. Each flashing back to the sex and the heat between them.

"Shall we go back to yours?" Vienna suggested.

"Absolutely," Ashley responded with a kiss to Vienna's lips.

TENSE IN THE ELEVATOR. Wanting. Needing. Ashley's eyes saw Vienna reflected over and over in the mirrored walls. Her golden hair. Her lovely face. Wait. Ashley. Wait.

Out of the elevator, into the penthouse apartment. Pulling her. Dragging her. Kissing her. Ashley's kisses all over Vienna's face. She was ripping her clothes from her.

Vienna, splayed on her front, bent over the white kitchen table, in her underwear. Red lace seductive. The scent of her sex was overwhelming.

"Stay there," Ashley commanded, knowing Vienna

wouldn't move, her cheek against the table, her hair everywhere.

Ashley quickly returned, wearing nothing but her favorite strap on. She loved the feel of the supple black leather over her hips—the feeling of the straps tight between her legs, pushing against her clit. The dildo was jutting out from her, phallic and proud.

She loved looking at Vienna's body, bent over in front of her. She hadn't moved because Ashley had commanded her to stay. Ashley pulled the red lace thong down to Vienna's mid-thigh. It was still so wet. She was soaked through from her earlier orgasm. She ran her fingers down Vienna's slick sex, and Vienna moaned, and her ass arched up towards Ashley. Vienna felt it. She really felt it. She had never been more into something. Someone. Confusion rushed through her head for a brief second, before she relaxed to it. Her body was acting of its own accord for once. Her body was wanting Ashley so badly.

Ashley's hands took hold of her hips, holding them tight. Her fingers were digging into flesh. She wanted to mark Vienna with her lust. The dildo pushed up to her wetness, then slowly pushing into her forcing Vienna's body to relinquish and let her in.

Vienna felt the big strap on pushing at her. Big, but she was so wet; it didn't hurt. She felt it opening her up; she knew her pupils would be dilating as it entered her. It felt incredible. She wanted Ashley to take her like this. She realized at that moment that she wanted Ashley to take her in every way possible.

"Use your hands, pull your ass cheeks apart," Ashley commanded her.

Vienna knew she would comply. Her hands reached

back and parted her cheeks, allowing Ashley better access to her burning core.

Ashley smiled smugly, watching Vienna's perfectly manicured neat and short red nails as she opened herself with her hands. Her nails matched her underwear. That was no accident.

"Push back onto me. I want you to fuck yourself on my dick."

Her words were so erotic to Vienna. She had never really known that this was something that she wanted— this level of capitulation. Funnily enough, given her job, although she had been asked to do many many things and nothing sexually shocked her, this was something new. This was something that sent thrills through her at the thought of exposing herself, opening herself up, and using Ashley's dick for her pleasure.

She raised herself slightly on bare feet onto her tiptoes to account for the slight height difference; her breasts and face still pushed against the tabletop. Her hands were working to pull her ass cheeks wider apart, and she pushed back on the big dildo, gasping slightly as it went all the way in. She felt it deep inside her. She felt pleasure course through her body.

She began to move backward and forwards. In and out. Feeling the pleasure herself and taking the pleasure for herself.

Ashley looked down at her and felt pure lust begin to pool deep inside her. She wanted to grab her and fuck her, but she could wait, watching this. Vienna spread open, doing as she was told. She was using the dildo for her pleasure, fucking herself on it slowly. Vienna groaned each time she pushed back on it.

Ashley took hold of the back of Vienna's red bra with

her hand, lightly pulling back as Vienna pushed back. The lines of her naked body were stunning. No surprises there, everything about Vienna was stunning. The roundness of her ass before the neat nip of her waist was beautiful. Ashley heard Vienna's wetness squelch and her moan. It was too much. She needed her.

"Do you want me to fuck you now? Say please, if you do."

"God. Yes. Please. More than anything." Vienna's voice was a whisper. Her desire was evident.

Ashley moved her hands to Vienna's hips, holding tight, pinned her against the table and fucked her. Hard. She fucked her with all the desire she had been building inside of her since the first time she had met her. Vienna gushed with the force of the dildo thrusting in and out of her, repeatedly hitting her G spot.

Vienna squealed as Ashley thrust. Nobody had ever taken her quite like this. Made her want it like this. Grabbed her and fucked her primally like this. Vienna usually was the professional leading, showing the way, taking them to their fantasies.

Not now, it was Ashley leading, showing Vienna fantasies she had never known that she had. Ashley's left hand grabbed a tangle of Vienna's hair.

Ashley felt the leather of her harness sliding against her wet clit. She saw the beauty of Vienna's ravaged body underneath her. She felt so close to orgasm.

"Come for me. Come for me, V, everywhere. I want to see it." she growled.

Ashley's words and the hand roughly pulling her hair back raised Vienna; she felt so taken, so absolutely owned. A sweet, hot heat rose through her and called out loudly as she came.

Feeling Vienna's whole body tense below her and more wet gushing down over the dildo, over Ashley's groin, Ashley came hard too against the black leather.

Vienna's red face mushed against the table, her hair a mess. She had never looked more beautiful. Ashley collapsed onto Vienna's back. Still, inside her, her breasts drenched with sweat as they pushed into Vienna's back.

They lay there for a few seconds, and Ashley held her. Then, Ashley pushed her lips to the back of Vienna's neck and shoulder. Light kisses. Light kisses that ran through Vienna's whole body like electricity. Who was this woman who could force orgasms from her ravaged body? Who was this woman, who could take her at will and make her feel things she didn't think possible?

Ashley's lips to her ear, gentle breath on her ear lobe. "Beautiful girl, you are incredible."

LATER THAT NIGHT, showered and clean, they lay next to each other in Ashley's big bed in the darkness. Neither of them sure what was happening or what might happen next.

"Vienna, would you go on a date with me? Like a real date? Not because I am paying you, but because you want to?"

"Yes. I think I would." Vienna smiled almost innocently.

Ashley smiled warmly.

"Hey, you! It's been a while. What have you been up to?" Vienna asked Chloe.

It had been quite some time since they last talked.

Chloe Martinez was Vienna's best friend. Perhaps her only friend. They had met when Vienna started at Black Label. Chloe was Spanish and looked like a model, and she had also started as a Black Label girl. As one of Meredith's girls. But unlike Vienna, she didn't enjoy the work and didn't stay.

Chloe was an up and coming fashion designer who had worked very hard to get to where she had. She was currently in Paris for the Paris Fashion Week, presenting her fashion house, Cloeque.

"Hey, I missed you too. Well, you know this stupid time zone difference messes everything up." Chloe rolled her eyes then resumed,

"How is everything? What's up with that new client you have been working on?"

"Well yeah, I have to tell you something about that. Ashley asked me out. Well, I don't know how to describe it, but she fucked me. In the bathroom at the club. And it didn't feel like work. Like, I don't think she meant it in an escort client way. I think she meant it in a relationship way." Vienna murmured in a softer voice.

"Wow. How was it? Well, do you like her like that?" Chloe asked.

"That's the thing, Chloe. I like her more than anything. She is just so... different and makes me feel alive. And, in the bathroom, it was like. Well, I came. Like actually came for the first time, since oh god knows. I am so used to faking it. But I just felt all hot and dizzy. And then I came."

"Eso es increíble! why do you sound worried then?" Chloe inquired, her Spanish accent seeping through.

"Anytime I want something or like it too much, everything gets messed up, I don't want this to happen this time." Vienna had her doubts.

"I know you are worried, but see, even talking about Ashley is making you happy, why not give this a shot? Besides, if she just wanted to have sex with you, she could simply pay you and do it. But if she's thinking about more than that, then this is special."

"I guess you're right. It's not easy for her, either. And yes, I want to see her as a regular person. You know, when there is no money involved, and I don't have to pretend to be some Barbie doll. Okay, you're right! I should give it a go, right?"

"Yay! That's my confident girl! Let me know how it goes." Chloe chirped.

"Yeah, but you get back here soon, too, okay. I am done seeing your blurry Skype face."

"Oh, don't you worry, I'll be back soon and be your wing-girl! But now I have to go. The tailor messed up a few of my dresses, and the show is in less than two weeks!" Chloe replied hurriedly.

"Don't worry! You'll do amazing, just as always. Good luck! I'll see you later. Love you!" Vienna called out as Chloe quickly replied,

"Thank you, and love you more! Rock that date, babe!" and then ended the call.

Vienna couldn't help but smile at the thought. She had an actual real date to attend.

Vienna arrived at Ashley's building and waited for her as she came downstairs. Climbing into the passenger seat, she leaned over and kissed Vienna. They had decided to take Vienna's car for the day, on her insistence, of course.

Vienna couldn't help herself as her eyes hungrily roamed over Ashley's body. She was casual in washed-out jeans and a tight white Tee shirt and Ray-Ban Aviators.

"You look so hot, Ashley." Vienna was almost a little awkward. She shouldn't be. She was the best in the world at going on dates. It was different when she had to bring her real self.

Ashley smiled. "Thank you. You, as usual, look incredible. You shouldn't wear these little dresses in front of me. They do things to me. How am I supposed to keep my hands off you?"

"Really? I put a lot less effort in seeing as I'm not being paid this time." Vienna commented with a laugh.

They started the drive to Sandy Hook. The atmosphere was light, and the silence was comfortable as the two exchanged few words, mostly admiring one another and the scenery they drove by.

"Can I ask you something?" Vienna started.

"Yeah, sure. Go ahead."

"Not seeming to be rude or anything, but why Sandy Hook? Is there something special here?" Vienna was surprised by the calm and eeriness of the location at this time of the year.

"Well, I used to come here all the time as a kid with my parents. They loved the silence here at the far side of the beach." Ashley had a story to tell.

"I'm sorry if you were looking forward to someplace else. It's just that I haven't been here in a long time, and I thought if I was ever to face the ghosts from my past, it might as well be with you by my side." Ashley completed, smiling at Vienna.

Vienna felt warm at Ashley's confession. But she felt the chill in the words.

"Things weren't ideal, were they?" she deduced.

"How did you know?"

"Well, this is the first time you've mentioned your parents. Doesn't exactly bode for an ideal childhood."

"You are right. This is the place where I used to stand alone." Ashley continued,

"As my parents and Stacey played and laughed in the background. Stacey is my elder sister. The perfect child, as people like to say. She is lovely and pretty and feminine. I was always this awkward tomboy girl. My mother kept trying to put me in dresses and then getting frustrated that it didn't look right. Stacey is a surgeon now. Her job is more impressive than anything I have done. Saving lives-you can't get close to that." Ashley was lost in thought.

"You'd think having an elder sister would be great, and you'd play together, be there for each other. It was nothing like that with Stacey. She never once acted like the bigger sister. She was always looking for ways to just stay on top. Ways to take me down. I mean there's always competition between siblings, But she was serious. She had to win at all costs. And my parents were proud of her. No matter what I did, I was never enough."

Vienna squeezed her hand as she drove, letting her know she wasn't alone. Ashley smiled at her sadly before looking out the window.

A memory flashed itself in Ashley's head.

"STACEY! GIVE THAT BACK!" *a 12-year-old Ashley yelled at her sister.*

She was running away from Ashley with Ashley's necklace

in hand. Her late grandmother had given it to her. The woman had loved Ashley while her parents had barely noticed she existed.

Stacey laughed as Ashley ran behind her, tears threatening to fall. The simple four leaf clover pendant necklace was something she loved more than anything.

Nearing to where their parents were, Stacey slowed down, looking back at Ashley, a glint in her eyes. Ashley tackled her to the ground, grabbing the necklace from her.

"Ashley Davidson! What is the meaning of this behavior?" her mother yelled, as elegantly as she could. She was all about appearances, after all. Her father trailed behind her with a disapproving look.

Stacey let out a fake cry and ran to her mother.

"I was just playing around with her and.. and look at what she did to me." She let a few tears roll down her cheeks, and the stage was set. Someone hand her a bloody Oscar, Ashley thought to herself.

"This is very disappointing, Ashley. She is your elder sister. You have to be respectful. People are starting to stare. Look at what you've done!" her mother scolded her before taking Stacey's hand.

"Come on, sweetheart, let's get you some ice cream." Lovely and feminine Stacey sniffed a few times and straightened her pretty dress before walking with her.

Ashley stood there, a few tears escaping her eyes as she watched her family neglect her. Her mother and father were showing genuine love and care to her sister. As for her, they had nothing but disappointment in their eyes.

She walked towards the seaside and let the water touch her feet. She looked at the necklace, a smile creeping on her face. Grandma had always managed to make her feel better. Even in death.

. . .

ASHLEY EYED the beach as it came into view and began,

"They weren't bad people, but they just did not get me. I just wanted to be with them and make them proud and feel loved."

Vienna had sensed sadness in her voice a few times. She felt honored that Ashley had opened up to her. She felt sure Ashley didn't often open up to anyone.

"Well, you are now the richest and one of the most successful women in the entire state. I am sure they must be proud now." Vienna said, holding her hand reassuringly.

"I stopped caring a long time ago."

Ashley continued, but the voice now had more calm.

"Sorry, this got too intense for a first date." She said with a warm smile.

"Are you kidding? Finally, someone who values me as more than an object. I know opening up is not that easy, but thank you. I like this date." Vienna told her, sincerely.

"But yeah, also pretty intense." She chuckled.

"You're impossible!"

Ashley burst into a hearty laugh.

"But yeah, probably I am too old for a regular dinner date." Ashley continued as she played with Vienna's fingers.

"If you are missing Trisha, you can tell me. I'll make the age jokes; yours aren't as good." Vienna teased as a smile spread across her lips.

"Oh speaking of Trish, I haven't told her yet. She'll be ecstatic." Ashley told her with a roll of her eyes.

"Besides, it was all her idea, to begin with." she continued.

"I am glad things happened how they did. But yeah, do tell her soon, I miss her slumber parties too." Vienna went on.

"Oh, you don't worry, she will dig everything out the moment she sees me." Ashley laughed.

8

"Hey Trish, I was thinking you and Kevin could meet me at Double Eagle Steakhouse. We could have dinner, and I also have a surprise for you." Ashley spoke softly over the phone.

"You are into surprises now? What world did I wake up into today?" Trisha teased,

"But alright, I will be there with Kevin."

"Okay, I am making an 8 pm reservation. See you guys, then!" Ashley hung up the phone.

VIENNA breezed into Ashley's penthouse as requested at 7 pm. She wore a short green dress. Her lovely legs perfect in heels. Her golden hair in loose waves and her make up minimal.

Ashley's eyes went straight to her. Every time she looked at Vienna, she was completely dismantled.

Her eyes were bright and vibrant, the same color as the dress.

"Ms. Vienna. Thank you for coming. We are double dating with Trish and Kevin tonight."

Vienna smiled widely.

"But, first. Come here." Ashley leaned casually against the back of the sofa in slacks and a button-down shirt.

"What are you up to?" Vienna asked almost shyly.

Ashley outstretched her hand, and Vienna took it. Ashley pulled her body close. "You smell incredible. Ashley buried her face in Vienna's breasts. She saw a small bruise on her left breast, which was probably from her mouth. She smiled to herself. She took her right hand and put it under Vienna's dress, pulling down her panties. Vienna raised each foot in turn as Ashley pulled them off her. Ashley put them to her nose and sniffed them. Vienna thought it was the most erotic thing she had ever seen. Ashley with Vienna's damp black lace thong in her hands.

"Fuck, you smell amazing."

She pushed her right hand back under Vienna's dress and slid her fingers lightly across Vienna's sex, making Vienna gasp.

"I want you. Now," she said.

Vienna nodded. There was something about Ashley's desire for her that made her speechless. As though her voice was only capable of saying, "Please. Please fuck me." and nothing else.

Their eyes locked. Vienna's whole body pulsed with excitement.

Ashley took her and led her out onto the roof terrace. They were so high up, the sound of the traffic was faint. The breeze was keen, and the sun was beginning to lower in the sky.

Ashley led Vienna to the edge and stood behind her.

Vienna looked down over the secure railings at the city below her. She leaned into Vienna's back, and her arms snaked around Vienna's body, pulling her breasts out of the top of her dress. They spilled over the top, and her nipples were instantly hard in the cool breeze. Vienna froze for a second, and her hands instinctively went to cover her breasts. All her confidence was suddenly nothing in Ashley's hands. She could see into offices, into other apartments. She could see the whole city from up here, and her breasts were suddenly completely exposed.

Ashley pulled Vienna's hands roughly down. "Leave your breasts open. Let the city see them. They deserve a treat. They deserve to see your beautiful body. They deserve to see you get fucked up here."

Her lips close to Vienna's ear again. Vienna felt scared and exhilarated all at once. Desire flooded through her body, feeling Ashley's hands rough on her wrists. What on earth was this? She had never imagined that rough sex would turn her on so much. She had never imagined that a client would turn her on this much.

Vienna's eyes nervously darted around the windows she could see. She daren't look down. Ashley's hands pushed the skirt of her dress up. The fingers of Ashley's right hand were between her legs, probing her wetness. Ashley's left hand wrapped around her breasts, grabbing them roughly, teasing her nipples.

Ashley leaned into her back, pinning her against the railings, Ashley's fingers were inside her and fucking her and Vienna forgot for a second how exposed she was. She loved the feeling of Ashley inside her. It felt like nothing else on earth. Those people in those offices. Were they far enough away? Surely they were far enough away that they wouldn't see her being fucked like a slut up here on the roof.

Ashley pulled her right hand out of Vienna and raised her fingers to Vienna's mouth. Vienna looked for a second at Ashley's fingers, slick with wetness from her arousal; she didn't hesitate, she took them in her mouth. She was licking, sucking, cleaning, suckling. She was tasting herself.

Ashley took her right hand back between Vienna's legs. Vienna was weak, unsteady. Ashley's right hand was persistent, thrusting, fucking. Her left hand moved to touch Vienna's clit.

Vienna came in seconds. Her climax was earth-shattering. Her world, as she knew it, entirely changed.

VIENNA AND ASHLEY entered the steakhouse and were hit by the smell of delicious steaks sizzling, waiting to be devoured.

Ashley took her hand and led her to their seats. Vienna still felt uncomfortably wet between her legs. Ashley had not let her put underwear back on, and knowing she was naked under her dress was a distracting turn on.

The waiter came and filled their glasses with wine as Ashley and Vienna talked and laughed.

Kevin and Trisha approached their table.

"Hey, you two! How are you? More importantly, how's the food here?" Trisha said once they settled down.

"Well, we.." Vienna pointed to herself and Ashley, "are good. And I hope so is the food."

"Hey Ash, what's the big surprise you told me about?" Trisha continued.

"Oh, I'll get there, but first check the décor ideas I sent you. I want your opinion." Ashley said, referring to an email.

"And also Kevin, leave some of your wife for me too. You have her annoying ass for life now," she said rather cheerfully to Kevin, who nodded with the smile of a teenager newly in love.

He brought Trisha's hand to his lips and kissed it tenderly, making Vienna squeal at the couple. Ashley put her hand on Vienna's naked thigh under the table and chuckled.

"Ash, you could have picked any one of them, you know my tastes," Trisha replied, her eyes still on her phone.

"No, it's your wedding. You should have something to blame yourself for too." Ashley answered as everyone broke into laugher.

"Excuse me, guys. I have a call to take. I'll be back." Kevin said, moving to a side, met by nods.

"TELL ME WHAT IS IT!" Trisha exclaimed curiously.

"I want you to meet my beautiful new girlfriend," she nodded towards Vienna.

"What? I know that already. I was the one who came up with.." Trisha stopped immediately and looked between the two before gasping loudly,

"Oh, you mean REAL girlfriend... OH MY GOD, THAT'S GREAT! Omigod, I can see it now. You two have just been fucking, haven't you? She's got that orgasmic glow all over her." Trisha yelled loudly as her expressions changed.

"Arghh. That bruise on her breast and her arms! ASHLEY! What have you done to the poor girl?!"

"Oh god, sorry I should have worn something else!" Vienna went to pull her dress up to hide the bruise. "I just... I like it. They are consensual." She looked at Ashley with puppy dog eyes and then to Trisha. "I like that she is leaving her mark on my body. Is that so wrong?" Vienna blushed.

"It is AMAZING. You are having great sex, right?!" Trisha winked.

"What's great?" Kevin's voice sounded surprised as he came back to the table.

"Um, Trisha was telling us how lucky she is to have you and how great everything is." Vienna chipped in, as she found words to complete the sentence.

"Oh, some beautiful wife I have. I am the lucky one." Kevin commented proudly.

The rest of the dinner went normally, Trisha dissected the food yet again while trying to get out as much information she could discretely about Ashley and Vienna.

Ashley's hand trailed up Vienna's thigh under the table.

Vienna felt herself melt with lust. She was amazed the others couldn't smell the sweet scent of her arousal.

THE TWO WOMEN arrived back at Ashley's penthouse, and Vienna took a seat on the plush sofa, making herself at home.

"Trisha was right; the night is beautiful," Vienna said as she gazed into the starry sky, and the city at night view, through the floor to ceiling windows. Ashley poured them both a glass of wine and sat down next to Vienna.

"I was wondering if you could tell me about your childhood. About life before Meredith Bowes and Black Label?" Ashley remembered Vienna's words the first time they met.

"It is not a happy story; it could ruin this romantic night." Vienna hesitated.

"There is nothing more romantic than opening up and pouring your heart to someone who cares." Ashley's voice had unusual warmth as she held Vienna's hand.

"Well, I never knew my father. I don't even know who he is, and I had an addict for a mother. She only cared for her drugs. Things regularly got bad. I was in and out of foster care. Many different homes. Many different foster parents. Some cared. Some didn't. I learned to be tough. I had to be. To survive." Vienna continued. Ashley didn't let go of her hand.

"But as much as I hate my mother for what a terrible parent she was, she gave me life. And she gave me this face and this body. I have had a lot of therapy, since joining Black Label. Meredith puts us all through weekly sessions with a therapist, so I have found ways to deal with it all. My face and my body have given me power. They gave me Meredith, and she gave me an education and a chance at life. I have the world at my feet now. Not a bad compensation, I'd say." Vienna continued, her wit and humor never leaving her, even during her pain.

"But I am happy now. Honestly."

"Don't worry; you have me," Ashley reassured her.

"That is what matters now," Vienna replied with a smile.

"I've been thinking, as well. The first time we had sex, I

was paying you for that date for your company. I just took you into the bathroom and had sex with you. I didn't ask you if you wanted to. I didn't clarify if it was a business arrangement or a separate thing. It was unfair and demeaning, and I am so very sorry about that. I didn't know where we stood. I didn't know what you wanted. I only knew I had to have you at that moment. " Ashley poured her heart out.

"I shall only accept the apology if you pay me back with more sex. Better sex!" The sparkle in Vienna's eyes was back.

"You know now, I've made it clear that our relationship is outside of our business arrangement, right? I know I am still paying your retainer and will still pay you to attend official functions with me, but outside of that, the time we spend, the dating and the sex, is entirely your choice?

Vienna nodded. "I know. I know." she laughed, musical. "I would like to say on record that I am choosing to have sex with you, even though you aren't even paying me."

"And the nature of the sex, you are happy with that? I know I can be a little rough. More so with you, because I want you so much. I see more and more bruises on your beautiful body from my hands and mouth."

"I like them." Vienna blushed. "I like the bruises. They make me feel owned. I like the sex—a lot. I never really had it this rough before, but it is a revelation. It makes me feel so alive and in the moment."

Vienna paused and then continued. "If I'm totally honest with you, I have always faked it. I always act in sex. Before you, it is very rare I have had genuine orgasms with partners. I always lead, usually. I've never been taken with the intensity that you take me. There is something about you, about how you treat me, devour me, and that turns me on so very much."

Ashley smiled at her softly and squeezed her hand. "I am so pleased about that. If you ever aren't happy, if it is ever too much, you just say, ok? You just say stop, and I will stop straight away."

Ashley smiled again, an idea popping up in her head. Grabbing a remote, she put on 'Versace on the floor' and then stood in front of Vienna, her hand extended.

Vienna looked at her, surprised before a huge smile graced her lips, and she took Ashley's hand.

Let's take our time tonight, girl

Above us, all the stars are watchin'

There's no place I'd rather be in this world

The song started as Ashley put her arms around Vienna's waist, and Vienna's came to rest on her shoulders.

Your eyes are where I'm lost in

Underneath the chandelier

We're dancin' all alone

Ashley looked into Vienna's eyes, leaning down slightly. Vienna's eyes fluttered shut, and she moved closer to Ashley.

There's no reason to hide

What we're feelin' inside

Right now

So baby let's just turn down the lights

And close the door

Ooh I love that dress

But you won't need it anymore

No, you won't need it no more

Let's just kiss 'til we're naked, baby

Versace on the floor

Ooh take it off for me, for me, for me, for me now, girl

Ashley's grip tightened on Vienna's waist, making Vienna open her eyes and gasp inaudibly at the emotions she saw swirling in Ashley's eyes.

Ashley's hand moved up and down Vienna's sides making her shudder and tighten her arms around Ashley's shoulders.

Ashley gingerly turned Vienna around in her arms so that her front faced Vienna's back, and her arms came to rest on her abdomen. Vienna blushed hard as Ashley put her head on Vienna's shoulder. The song continued as the two women swayed.

I unzip the back to watch it fall
While I kiss your neck and shoulders

As if on cue, Ashley placed a kiss at Vienna's exposed skin. Vienna tilted her head slightly, giving her more access as Ashley placed feather-light kisses to her skin.

"How are you so soft?" Ashley's voice whispered in Vienna's ear, making her smile. Ashley genuinely sounded curious.

So just turn down the lights (down the lights)
And close the door (close the door)
Ooh I love that dress
But you won't need it anymore
No, you won't need it no more
Let's just kiss 'til we're naked, baby
Versace on the floor
Ooh take it off for me, for me, for me, for me now, girl
Versace on the floor
Ooh take it off for me, for me, for me, for me now, girl

Vienna closed her eyes, leaning back, and put her head on Ashley's shoulder. Sighing, she let herself feel Ashley's body against her own. So blissful.

As the song neared its end, Ashley turned Vienna

around and pressed their lips together in a tender kiss. Vienna immediately responded, syncing their movements and pulled Ashley closer. Ashley poured her feelings into the kiss, and Vienna smiled, letting her know she felt the same.

Versace on the floor
Floor
Floor

The song ended, and the two women pulled back. Ashley tucked a strand of hair behind Vienna's ear and looked at her like she was the most precious thing in the world.

Grabbing her hand, she slowly lead Vienna up to her bedroom. The giant oak doors welcomed the two women as Ashley turned the knob and entered Vienna at her heel.

Ashley led Vienna to the bed and flicked on the side lamps illuminating the room with its soft yellow glow.

Ashley then let go of Vienna's hand and stared at her some more. Her already plump lips slightly swollen from the kiss. Her dress had moved a little, showing off her legs more. Her eyes twinkled with a feeling Ashley very much returned. Smiling, she moved closer and grabbed Vienna's waist.

"You are.. amazing. In every damn way." Ashley sighed. Vienna smiled at her and brought a hand to cup her cheek, gazing into her eyes lovingly. Vienna felt herself at a loss for words at this point. She couldn't believe it all; her feelings were almost too much. Her eyes welled up with tears, and she moved to kiss Ashley.

This time, the kiss was more frantic. Needy. Ashley pulled Vienna even closer, and Vienna put a hand behind Ashley's head, tilting it for a better angle. Vienna softly traced Ashley's lips with her tongue, and Ashley opened her mouth for the intrusion. Sparks flew everywhere as their tongues clashed.

Out of breath, they pulled back, and Ashley's lips immediately went to Vienna's neck, kissing the junction of her shoulder and neck. Ashley breathed in Vienna's scent and said,

"You don't know how long I've waited for this."

Vienna moaned softly as Ashley bit on her sensitive spot and then licked it.

Vienna's fingers dragged through Ashley's short hair, making her sigh into Vienna's neck.

"Ashley.." Vienna breathed out as Ashley continued to leave marks on her neck and shoulder, sucking her, biting her.

Ashley pulled back to look at her, all flustered and panting. Her hands moved behind Vienna and unzipped her dress, letting it pool at her feet.

Vienna's breathing quickened under Ashley's heated gaze. She was naked, having lost her underwear before they made it out for dinner.

"You're perfect." Ashley's eyes looked at her body, burning through her skin as if they could see into her very soul.

She unbuttoned Ashley's shirt and helped her out of her slacks and her underwear.

Ashley pulled Vienna to the bed and let her sink into the soft fabric. She looked exquisite, lying there with her golden hair sprawled across the pillows. Her breasts were lifting and falling with her breathing.

There was a peaceful intimacy to the night as Ashley lay on top of her, her right hand immediately exploring between Vienna's legs while she kissed her.

"A-Ashley.. please." Vienna moaned into Ashley's neck, biting down on the area as Ashley continued teasing her with her fingers.

Ashley groaned, feeling Vienna's teeth sink into her flesh and pushed her fingers inside Vienna. Vienna jolted and pulled Ashley even closer.

Ashley immediately pulled her hand back out and took the fingers dripping Vienna's juices into her mouth.

Vienna's eyes followed the movement, and she bit her lip.

"You're so wet, baby," Ashley told her as she bent down to kiss Vienna's neck.

"I know," Vienna whispered. "But, I was thinking... tonight might be different. I want to taste you."

Ashley drew back and looked into Vienna's insistent eyes, heady with lust. "I don't know. I don't usually.... I don't usually let women touch me."

"Please, Ash, please. I'll be so gentle. I'll be so nice. I could just use my mouth if you might like that." Vienna wriggled out from underneath Ashley as Ashley contemplated her request. Vienna pushed Ashley onto her back, her strong body open and almost vulnerable. Vienna above her, kissing her mouth, her face, her neck. "Please, Ash, please. I'll be so nice." Vienna was kissing down over her shoulders, running her tongue over Ashley's small breasts, her nipples that rose to meet Vienna's mouth. Ashley didn't resist. Vienna continued. "I'll be so gentle. My tongue is so warm and wet." Vienna kept kissing, down over Ashley's abs, trailing her tongue into her belly button, dragging it down to Ashley's thatch of dark pubic hair.

Vienna's kisses down Ashley's groin. Her inner thighs.

Vienna buried her face in Ashley's pubic hair and breathed warm breaths onto her clit.

Ashley groaned and relaxed into it, watching as Vienna pushed her leg's further apart, and her beautiful golden head made its way into her sticky heat.

Vienna ran her tongue down the folds of Ashley's vulva, which made her moan loudly.

"Oh V," Ashley breathed out, her eyes closing and her head tipping back.

Vienna lost herself in the taste of Ashley, enthusiastic as she licked and sucked, lost in the world of Ashley's sex. Tasting her wetness, feeling her body respond and react, hearing her groans. Ashley's hand fisting in Vienna's hair, Ashley was pulling her head closer while Vienna's mouth continued to work. Ashley's breathing quickened, and heat rushed through her body, and she climaxed loudly, pulling Vienna into her.

Ashley's hands tightened themselves in Vienna's hair, and she moved her hips to ride out her high.

Vienna stayed for a moment, smiling to herself between Ashley's legs, before moving up to kiss Ashley, letting her taste herself.

Ashley lay back, spent, gathering Vienna in her arms, and pulled the covers over them both.

Ashley kissed Vienna's head, and Vienna snuggled into her arms.

THE SUNLIGHT SEEPED through the gaps in the curtains, and Ashley's eyes flickered open. She tried to stretch but immediately found it impossible to do so.

Looking down at the person in her arms, Ashley

smiled as she looked at Vienna's sleeping body. They were clinging on to each other, legs entangled, and sheets a mess. Ashley brought her lips to Vienna's forehead, placing a chaste kiss that made Vienna smile in her sleep. Ashley's cellphone chimed, and she moved slightly to grab it from the side table while trying not to wake Vienna up.

I know what you are up to Ashley Davidson, you and the whore. Soon everyone else will too. You are ruined now, and I will make sure that happens soon.

Ashley's eyes widened. She frowned, not understanding the meaning of the text, but it soon dawned on her, and the expressions on her face changed rapidly from confusion to shock and then lastly, panic.

She looked down at Vienna and subconsciously pulled her closer to her body.

9

Who are you, and what do you want?

Ashley typed hurriedly. She was sitting in her immaculate kitchen now, having left Vienna safely in bed.

Who I am is not important. What I want is. If you want to keep your secret a secret, be nice to me, or all your clients will refer to you in the past tense. They will know you are a cheat and a liar.

A reply loaded with threats came back almost instantly.

After absorbing the initial shock, Ashley pulled herself together and looked toward the stairs, just as Vienna walked down half-asleep in a big T-shirt.

"Hey," she said lazily. "I want to say, 'oh God, I am late for work,' but you are my only client. So I am good." Vienna laughed as she hugged Ashley, planting a kiss to her lips.

Ashley immediately responded, wrapping her arms around Vienna's waist and pulling her close.

"I'll make us some coffee," Ashley said.

"Sure, can I get a shower before I head home?"

Ashley smiled and nodded. She watched Vienna. Beautiful, beautiful sleepy Vienna. Who was this mysterious texter threatening everything between them?

~

Ashley settled into her office and called her secretary, who came immediately.

"Yes, ma'am?" she said politely.

"Joanna, can you look into this number for me? I need its details to see if it's in the employee record. Or anywhere else for that matter?" Ashley stated.

"I'll send it to the HR guys right away and get back to you," Joanna replied determinedly.

Ashley nodded as she intertwined her fingers and put them on the desk in front of her.

"Everything okay, Miss Davidson?" Joanna inquired. She hadn't seen Ashley this tense and thoughtful before.

"Yes, just an old account to settle." Ashley was sure her unknown blackmailer was someone related to the company affairs.

"I will get back to you soon about the number," Joanna said, leaving the room.

Ashley stayed in the office reviewing some details for the events to come and approving some expenditures, she kept looking at the door. It had been a few hours, and she was expecting Joanna to come back with the details soon, or else she'd have to go down to HR herself.

Her patience was running thin. If this was actually a threat and not some bluff, as she had initially thought, this secret out in the open could ruin her reputation. How did this person know about Vienna?

A knock sounded on the door, bringing Ashley out of her thoughts, and Joanna walked in.

"I got the details you asked. It's someone named Paul Carter. He worked with us a few years back."

"Okay, thank you, Joanna. Good job." Ashley replied, dismissing Joanna.

She tried to remember anything she could about the name, but even after trying, it sounded like just another name. They had had so many employees over the years. It was a big company.

Ashley groaned loudly as she put her head back on the chair. She closed her eyes, and suddenly she remembered. His small piggy eyes and his greasy hair.

Paul Carter headed the IT department, and Ashley had fired him after a pretty bitter spat, following multiple harassment complaints.

I know it's you, Paul, drop it already. You cannot do me any harm.

She typed the text.

Her phone beeped.

Oh, well done! You are smart! Just another thing I love about you, Davidson. Speaking of harm, you ruined my career, so now I will destroy yours. Funny thing, though, you have a lot more on the line.

Ashley signed and typed back:

I did not ruin anything for you, it was your all your own fault. I am going to take this shit to the police and get my lawyers involved. So stop threatening me.

Her phone beeped again, immediately.

I don't need to teach you how the media works, Davidson. You take it to the lawyers or the police, and everything will be out in the media tomorrow. You and

your little paid whore! I have photos. Good luck with that.

Unless you behave and do what I tell you to do because this time around, I am the boss. Wait for my next text Davidson.

Ashley did not reply. She just sat for a while, thinking, then picked up her phone again.

Text to Trisha:

Meet me as soon as you are free. It's urgent.

ASHLEY WAITED at Maison Kayser for Trisha to show up. She sat at their usual table, picking at the skin on her fingers with anxiety.

The doorbell chimed and in walked Trisha, quickly moving to meet Ashley. Ashley enveloped her in a hug, and Trisha remained quiet, knowing instantly there was something up.

Pulling back, the two women settled in their seats as Trisha ordered coffee for them both. Ashley kept picking at the skin on her fingers and kept her eyes locked on the table.

The waiter set their coffee on the table, and Trisha waited for him to leave before she faced Ashley.

"I fucked up, Trish." Ashley started before Trisha had a chance to say anything.

"What happened? Did something happen with Vienna? You two were so good." Trisha asked, worriedly.

"No. No, it's not that. Things with Vienna are good, great in fact. She's everything I wanted, she's incredible, Trish." Ashley looked up at Trisha, unshed tears glistening in her eyes.

"And now it's all going to end because of some bastard!" she spat, her hands turning to fists.

Trisha only listened as Ashley poured her heart out, telling her about the best night of her life followed by that text and the conversation. She told her about Paul and his blackmail.

"Get your lawyers on him straight away," Trisha suggested

"It's a huge risk that he will just spill to the media before that, and then there is no going back. You know how the media gets onto me, I don't want all my clients to think I am a cheat and a liar. I don't want them to think our relationship isn't real either. Because it is now." Ashley had a valid point.

"I have built everything with years of hard work and patience, You know it, Trish, in business, particularly this one, reputation is everything. Once that is gone, everything is gone." She continued.

"You are right, Ash." Trish smiled sympathetically.

"You could come out with the truth, telling them you hired Vienna, but now you two really are in love and together, but I don't think that will work either. Unfortunately, people in my field only want scandals, and that's what they will focus on, and you cannot afford that. They will focus on her career as a whore and the fact you paid for sex." Trisha was making some good points.

"I didn't even have sex with her in the original arrangement. It wasn't about that."

"You know as well as I do, that the facts don't matter, sweetie." Trisha put her hand on Ashley's across the table. Her rich dark skin and long perfect nails calming Ashley's stressed finger picking.

Ashley nodded in agreement.

"He has photos too apparently. God knows what you can see in the photos."

"Oh, my darling. Have you told Vienna?" Trisha asked.

"No. I haven't. And I don't intend to. This will only upset her and.. and I don't know. Goddammit!" Ashley exclaimed.

"Don't you think you should tell her, Ashley? She deserves to know this too." Trisha whispered.

"I will tell her, but I don't think now is the right time, we just started the relationship, and she will think I got into all this trouble because of her." Ashley clarified.

"Alright, alright. I think you should meet this guy and do whatever he says until we figure something out. Don't worry, he doesn't sound too smart. I think he is just another regular thug looking for a shortcut to money. He is going to want you to pay him off." Trisha said, before continuing, "But we also cannot afford to underestimate him, so you should follow his instructions for now. I am here for you." Trisha consoled Ashley.

"I will let you know what he wants. He hasn't asked for anything specific yet." Ashley replied.

They talked for a while longer, and Trisha made Ashley promise that if things take a dangerous turn, she would contact the police as well as her. She assured Ashley that herself and Kevin would be standing beside her in whatever way was necessary. Ashley had hugged her tightly, tears beading in her eyes.

ASHLEY REACHED her office and sat on her leather sofa. Her thoughts drifted to Vienna and their relationship. She had been so caught up with Paul and his threats, she had completely forgotten about Vienna.

Ashley knew she had been detached from Vienna this morning, and she felt so guilty for it. Wanting to make it up to her, Ashley grabbed her phone and dialed Vienna's number. She wanted to hear her voice.

"Hello, you've reached Vienna. Please leave a message." The call went straight to voicemail, making Ashley sigh. She was probably busy at the art class.

"Hey V. I just wanted to apologize for this morning. I know we didn't get to spend much time together after last night and I had to hurry to work. So, I was thinking we could go out later. Let me know if you're free from classes, and then I'll come to pick you up. Okay then, bye. I miss you." Ashley hung up, staring at the ceiling of her office room.

When did it get this screwed up? She sighed to herself.

Her phone chimed, and she immediately picked it up, wanting to see Vienna's face pop up the text, and she was glad not to be disappointed.

It's a date ;)

The text read, making Ashley smile genuinely for the first time that day.

～

VIENNA PRACTICALLY RAN down the building stairs and jumped into Ashley's arms.

"I missed you," Vienna whispered as Ashley caught her.

Ashley smiled broadly at her and leaned in for a kiss. Vienna happily obliged, snaking her arms around Ashley's neck.

"Get a room!" someone yelled as they pulled back, laughing.

"I missed you too," Ashley replied to Vienna's earlier statement and then continued

"You look hot." Ashley was genuinely happy to see Vienna.

And sure enough, Vienna did look hot in her casual jeans and cropped T-shirt. Of course, Vienna looked incredible in anything. The tight jeans showed the lovely curve of her ass and hips.

Vienna laughed and thanked her.

"Ready to go?" Ashley asked as she opened the car door for Vienna.

Vienna nodded, smiling as the two settled in and drove off.

"Hey, you looked a little ruffled up this morning, everything alright?" Vienna's voice held concern.

"Um. You know how clients are, first, they call you to the office, mess up your schedule for just their appointment, and then when they get there, they'll be like it would be better if we talked over lunch." Ashley tried to cover up her absence as best as she could and followed it with a superficial laugh.

"But where are we going?" she said, diverting the subject.

"How about Piccolo Café?" Vienna replied

"Sure thing," Ashley said, looking at her briefly with a smile then concentrated on the road again. The two talked about their day as they sped towards the café, with Ashley omitting the details about Paul.

Arriving at the café, the women got out of the car and entered the place. It was a small space with vintage designs and had a very welcoming, cozy feel to it. The place was packed, but Vienna managed to secure them a table.

When they settled in and ordered their food, Ashley looked at her, surprised.

"I take it, you're quite familiar with this place?"

Vienna smiled broadly at her from across the table and said,

"I do, actually. Chloe and I used to come here a lot when she was in New York still. This was our meet up spot. We talked about all our drama here. I always love it." She laughed at the memories.

Ashley smiled warmly at her.

"Ah, I see. Trisha and I have a place like that too. You must've heard of it, Maison Kayser."

"Oh yeah! I have. It is the posh version of here to be sure! I'd love to go there someday." She told Ashley.

"Chloe is your best friend?" Ashley asked her as the waitress brought their food.

"Yeah, everything's been so sudden and all, I never got a chance to properly tell you. I met her when I started at Black Label. Meredith took Chloe on at a similar time. We went through our initial training together. But Chloe had so many other things she wanted to do. She left after Meredith put her through fashion school." Vienna laughed.

"Chloe is a famous designer now. She has her own fashion house, Chloeque. She's currently in Paris for the fashion week. It's been a while since I've seen her. Seeing you and Trisha together really reminds me of our own friendship. I really miss her. She is honestly the only person I am close to." Vienna told Ashley.

Ashley extended her hand towards Vienna's and put it on top of her, giving it a reassuring squeeze.

"We'll go see her one of these days. Together." Ashley promised as Vienna's eyes lit up.

"Speaking of seeing things, how about you see me tomorrow night? I have to sleep alone in my HUGE bed." Vienna's voice had a flirty tone to it, and it was like that on purpose.

"Only if you make me dinner first." Ashley smiled.

Vienna's face lit up. "Sure thing. I make a mean Carbonara."

Her eyes were bright, her hair was messy, there was a little coffee foam on her top lip.

Ashley was overwhelmed with emotion suddenly.

I think I love her.

∼

MEET ME AT LUCID CAFÉ. **No tricks, Davidson.**

10

Ashley arrived at the place as directed by Paul. It was a small café and one that promised privacy.

She entered the place and looked around to find Paul, as a hand raised from the crowd and called her over.

"Over here!" Paul called out, a smirk on his fat shiny face as Ashley settled down at the table. The waitress came to the table, and Paul ordered coffee for himself and Ashley.

All the while, Ashley kept her gaze firm on him, and her lips stayed in a thin, grim line.

"Didn't think I'd be seeing you again. I am honored." Paul spoke as he extended his big red hand for Ashley to shake, only to be met by silence.

He smirked as if he had expected Ashley's response. The words and the sentiment in his voice did not go together.

"Tell me what you want, and let's get this over with." Ashley said, noticing that Paul looked a mess.

He was wearing a pair of khaki pants with black

sneakers. His blonde hair combed back neatly. He kept pushing up the glasses on the bridge of his fat nose as the smirk never left his greasy face.

You'd have never guessed this man here was the reason for Ashley's torment, capable of blackmail.

"Oh sweetheart, you keep forgetting you aren't the boss here. This time, I'm in control. My decision decides your fate, your entire career. Ring any bells?" Paul's voice held bitterness.

"Look, it wasn't personal. You had to pay for your actions. You violated rules and suffered the consequences. Anybody would have been treated like that." Ashley spoke passively, trying to negotiate.

"The hell it wasn't personal! I was the best employee you had! The best! And you ruined it. You could have let it slide. You were the boss, you could have done anything! You chose not to. And now, you'll pay." Paul's elbows hit the table as his voice grew loud, which made some heads turn. His voice seething venom.

Noticing his outburst's attention, he calmed himself down, and a sly smirk spread on his face.

"Don't worry, folks, this is for a scene." he remarked as people returned to their chatter.

"I am not going to apologize for firing you, it's been years, let it go." Ashley told him sternly.

"No, no, no. I don't want an apology of any sort. Apologies are free. Some hard-earned, sweet cash, on the other hand, is not." Paul went on, revealing his terms to keep silent.

Ashley listened, not uttering a word.

"Since you were my boss, I'll be kind to start. A hundred thousand bucks in three days, and like the good nerd I am, I will keep my mouth shut. I'll make this easier for you, you don't even have to see my face again. Just transfer the money to the account details I send you." He continued.

"Why are you doing this? It won't end well for you." Ashley replied, trying to sound confident.

"Come on, Davidson, you made my life miserable. Now it's my turn to play. Haven't you heard of Karma? The tables have turned. And this isn't a great deal for a bigshot like you. Take it easy. You give me the money, and I keep my mouth shut. Easy peasy." He finished with a grin that scared Ashley.

"I don't believe you have photos," she said boldly.

"I thought you might say that." he produced a brown envelope from a file in his hands and pushed it across the table to her. She opened it and had a quick look inside. There she was with Vienna at a Charity dinner, Vienna smiling widely. She flicked to the next photo. It had been taken with a zoom lens from a nearby building. Vienna, on her roof terrace her breasts out of her dress and her eyes wild and scared. Ashley pushed up behind her against the railings fucking her. She had seen enough. She closed the envelope.

All Ashley could respond with was a blank stare. She wasn't used to feeling this helpless.

"Three days. Enjoy your coffee. You can pick up the tab." Paul said as he got up from the table and left.

THE NEXT DAY passed in a blur at the office, and Ashley was relieved to finally get to Vienna's place.

"Oh finally, you are here, and so is movie and

Carbonara night." an excited Vienna greeted Ashley in some little short Pyjamas.

"Sorry, I got a little late, but I picked up your favorite tiramisu." Ashley replied, smiling.

"Oh, you are SO welcome in my home, anytime if you bring me Tiramisu." Vienna smiled, kissing Ashley's cheek.

After dinner, the two settled in and found a chick flic on Netflix.

They ate popcorn, gulped down drinks, and cuddled close to each other.

Vienna laughed like a baby at the movie, and looking at her made Ashley realized how just being with her made everything better.

Her laugh could make her forget even the dreaded evening she had.

She deserves to know.

Trisha's voice played in her head. Pulling Vienna closer to her, Ashley decided Vienna really deserved to know and that she would tell her everything, first thing tomorrow morning.

It might upset her or she might leave, but I cannot base our relationship on lies, I am telling her everything.

Ashley nodded to herself, satisfied with her decision.

The film finished, and Vienna leaned into Ashley for a kiss. They made out on Vienna's sofa like horny teenagers.

"Why don't we take this upstairs." She suggested to Ashley.

"I don't like that look on your face. What are you planning?" Ashley asked her warily.

Vienna rolled her eyes at her, and they went upstairs to her bedroom.

Ashley immediately kissed her, pressing her against

the door as Vienna moaned into her mouth.

Ashley brought her hand to squeeze Vienna's breast as their tongues clashed, savoring the taste of one another.

Tearing her lips away from Vienna's, Ashley bit on the junction of her neck and sucked on the spot, leaving a mark. She threw Vienna back on the bed and stripped her shorts and tank top from her. Ashley's fingers quickly went to work inside her. She held Vienna and fucked her, and Vienna orgasmed for her strong fingers inside her and her thumb tight against Vienna's clit.

Vienna then wriggled out of Ashley's grasp and pushed her back onto the bed, pulling Ashley's clothes off.

Vienna got on top and straddled Ashley's hips, grinding against her. "Aah, yes." Vienna moaned. She spun around, so she was straddling Ashley's face. Ashley felt more and more excited. Vienna lowered herself onto Ashley, and she moaned as Ashley's mouth welcomed her wetness.

Vienna leaned forwards and buried her face between Ashley's legs, pushing them apart slightly, nuzzling between them, determined to taste her again.

They licked and sucked at each other lazily as though they had all the time in the world. Vienna's body hot and soft on top of Ashley's. Vienna's full breasts pressing into Ashley's hips. Vienna's pussy grinding into Ashley's mouth. Ashley came quickly, moaning and writhing under her. Vienna felt Ashley orgasm hard in her mouth her whole body writhing and her sex pulsing. Ashley's hands gripped Vienna tightly.

Vienna got off her and smiled languidly.

They took a minute, and a glass of water, and Ashley lay there smiling to herself. But, there was something else she really wanted to do.

"You blow my mind, V. Seriously. Thank you." Ashley smiled and sat up. "There's something I want to do. There's somewhere else I want to take you. If you are willing."

Vienna looked to her, confused as she tried to figure out Ashley's cryptic plans. "Sure. What is it?"

"Have you ever had a whole hand inside of you?"

"Fisting?" Vienna smiled. "No, I mean, I know that is hard to believe, given my line of work, but surprisingly, it isn't something that has come up. Well. Not never. I have done it to others, but I have never received it. I do have some lube, though. If you want it." Vienna leaned over to her bedside table and then passed a bottle of lube to Ashley.

Ashley smiled and rolled on top of her.

"Well. Tonight is when it happens. I think you are very ready for it. Open your legs."

Ashley settled herself between Vienna's legs, she poured the lube over her right hand and smeared it up and down Vienna's folds. She worked into her gradually until Vienna expanded to allow four fingers slipping in and out of her.

Ashley tucked her thumb in and made her fingers into a duck beak shape, still pushing in and out. Every time on the way in, pushing a little bit harder, twisting slightly, trying to find a way in for her knuckles, the fullest part of her hand. Vienna winced slightly, but Ashley expected it.

"It's okay, V, it's okay. It will just hurt when the knuckles go in, then it will be okay. Nothing worth having comes easy."

Ashley increased the pressure as she pushed into Vienna. Vienna opened slightly for her, and Ashley's hand slid right into her depths. Vienna cried out for a second. It felt too much, it felt too big. But then she took a deep breath and felt something else entirely. An intensity she couldn't find words for.

Ashley curled her fingers into a fist and settled her hand inside Vienna. Vienna's vulva tight around Ashley's wrist.

Vienna's pupils were wide as Ashley met her eyes and leaned over her.

"Are you okay?"

Vienna nodded speechlessly. "Are you in all the way?"

Ashley nodded and took Vienna's hand, reaching it down to feel.

"Omigod." Vienna felt Ashley's wrist. Her hand had disappeared entirely. "Wow. It feels. Amazing. Intense. Like nothing else on earth."

Ashley smiled at her and began to rock her hand deep inside Vienna. Her knuckles moved against Vienna's G sport. Ashley moved up Vienna's body, angling her wrist carefully and kissed her with her hand still inside. Tongue pushing into her mouth, intense in her kissing. Vienna felt full. Overwhelmingly full. It felt so intense. Feeling Ashley on top of her suddenly, the pressure of her weight brushing Vienna's clit, Ashley's tongue in Vienna's mouth, Ashley's whole hand moving inside her, Vienna came hard clamping Ashley's hand.

Her orgasm built deep inside her and radiated out. It was the most incredible orgasm of her life. Tears beaded in her eyes and rolled down her face onto the pillow.

"I love you." said Ashley, still inside her.

Vienna knew she loved Ashley, too, but it terrified her. She cried quietly in the dull light, and Ashley held her.

～

"Vienna, wake up."

Vienna stirred and opened her eyes, smiling lazily at Ashley.

"What time is it?"

Ashley looked at the clock resting above the fireplace and replied,

"8:30 in the morning."

"I'm going to go take a shower." Ashley told Vienna after a while.

"Want me to join in and help?" Vienna winked at her making Ashley laugh.

"I think I'll be okay." She said with a shake of her head. With one last kiss to Vienna's lips, Ashley went to Vienna's bedroom and hopped into the shower.

If only my reputation hadn't been at stake here. Oh, I would've shown that bastard.

Ashley thought to herself as she finished her shower only to realize, she had left the towel outside.

"Vienna!" she shouted loudly, poking her head out the bathroom door. Footsteps sounded off as Vienna entered the room.

"V, can you give me the towel." Ashley said to her as Vienna handed the towel.

Ashley's phone rang, and she turned to Vienna to check who it was. She had communicated with Paul solely through texts, so she knew it was safe to ask Vienna to see who was calling.

As Vienna moved to the bedside table, the phone stopped ringing.

"It was Trisha." She told Ashley.

Ashley nodded and got out of the bathroom in the towel, entering the walk-in closet.

Ashley's cellphone chimed, and Vienna turned back

again to see if it was Trisha, only to come face to face with a text from an unknown number.

Thanks for the dough, Davidson. Pleasure doing business with you, your secret whore shall stay safe.

Until next time, yours sincerely.

Vienna frowned as she read the text.

What's going on?

She thought to herself, curiosity got the better of her, and she unlocked Ashley's cellphone to further read the conversation.

Her eyes widened, and her breathing quickened as she read the exchange between Paul and Ashley.

"Hey V, how about we go that amusement park in the–.." Ashley came out, fully dressed, her eyes snapping to the cellphone in Vienna's trembling hands and then to her face.

What she saw broke Ashley's heart as Vienna's face was contorted into the most painful of expressions, her eyes full of tears.

"V.." Ashley started, cautiously making her way to Vienna's side. It didn't take a genius to figure out that Vienna had read the messages.

Vienna moved away from Ashley.

"What is this, Ashley?" she found her voice, locking her gaze with Ashley.

"I.. I was going to tell you. I just.. didn't find the right time to." Ashley said to her with a sigh and looked at the floor, unable to meet Vienna's eyes.

"Were you now? Okay. When exactly then? When were you planning to tell me that you had chosen your 'reputation'.." Vienna exclaimed, her fingers making a gesture,

".. over our relationship! Over me!" She finished, throwing Ashley's phone on the bed.

"Vienna, please. There's an explanation for this. It's not what you're thinking."

She tried to grab Vienna's arms only for Vienna to slap them away.

"Please let me explain Vienna" Ashley begged.

"Okay then. What's the explanation? Go ahead. I want to hear it." She urged Ashley with her hand, crossing her arms at her chest.

Ashley opened and closed her mouth several times before running a hand through her hair and looking away.

"I just didn't want to lose you or upset you. You're the best thing that has happened to me. I'm so happy when I am with you. I was just being protective." Ashley explained, her fists clenching at her sides.

Paul is going to pay for this.

"So you're saying, I am just for the fun and games, and you don't trust me with important things. I thought things were different with you. I really did." Vienna's voice broke in between as she choked.

"No, that's not true, you're the most precious thing I have." Ashley pleaded.

"Do you even feel anything for me, Ash? Or am I just a showpiece for your parties? And a hot body to fuck when you get home. Getting you more clients, because apparently, at the end of the day, this is the only thing that matters to you." Vienna was heartbroken. She knew their relationship had started off rocky, given their arrangement, but things had changed now. They actually wanted to be together.

Right?

"That's what it is. Your name, your brand, was more important than us. Than me. You couldn't come out and face the world about our relationship, so you chose the easy way out. How much did you think it would have damaged your reputation, Ashley? A relationship with a common whore? Definitely not as much as you'd like to think. The guy could have been in jail by now, and we could have openly declared our relationship. But no, you would much rather keep me as your dirty little secret." she said to Ashley, her voice rising with each word.

Ashley looked at her, distraught

"Vienna, I am so sorry. I just, I got terrified and–.." she began only to be interrupted by Vienna as she raised her hand to silence Ashley.

"Vienna, listen to me. I can fix this. I know I made a mistake, I–.." Ashley tried desperately as Vienna started to move out of the room.

"You know what was a mistake? This. I should have kept my heart out of this and just let work be work. But for once I thought, someone actually wanted to be with me with all their heart. That you were in love with actual me, not some false ideal of me. I thought maybe there was at least one person in this world to whom I was more than some sex object. But I was wrong. So foolish of me!" Vienna kept going, unable to contain her anger and disappointment.

She walked down the stairs towards the door, Ashley trailing behind her.

"Please. Vienna, please don't do this. Just wait. We can fix this." Ashley tried one last time as Vienna turned to face her.

"And to think I fell in love with you. A coward."

Vienna spat her confession and held the door open for Ashley.

"You can leave now." She told Ashley with a cold voice.

Ashley looked at Vienna, her eyes pleading, but when Vienna refused to even look at her, Ashley walked out of Vienna's house, her head hung low.

VIENNA WALKED TOWARDS THE DESK, greeted by a polite voice. Grabbing her ticket, she sat in the waiting lounge, her eyes on the massive 'arrival & departure' screens.

She ended her contract with Ashley and picked up another client, all the way in Paris. All she wanted was to get away as far as she could from anything that reminded her of her past.

"**Flight 253 to Paris is now boarding. All passengers are requested to please proceed to the check-in counter and receive your boarding passes.**"

A voice informed the people in the waiting lounge as people got up to board the plane.

Vienna grabbed her suitcases and walked towards the check-in counter. Getting her boarding pass, she went to the gate, and the attendant welcomed her to the plane, after giving her boarding pass a check.

Vienna sat down on her seat in first class and closed her eyes, taking a deep breath. A few tears escaped her eyes as the plane took off, and she looked out the window at the beautiful city.

Good bye, Ashley.

Vienna told herself as if she was repeating it again and again for her mind and heart to believe.

I just wanted to love you.

11

"Nous atterrissons bientôt à Paris. Merci d'avoir volé avec nous. Nous espérons que le voyage a été idéal."

Vienna was awoken by the sound of the pilot's voice, informing the passengers that they would be landing soon.

She groggily got up in a sitting position, straightening her seat and wiped the tears that had escaped her eyes while dreaming about Ashley and her fight.

She still couldn't wrap her head around what had happened. A disgruntled laugh escaped her as she recalled, finally opening her heart to someone, only for them to stomp on it.

Shaking her head, she prepared herself for the landing and looked out her window at the beautiful city coming into view.

I'm escaping from a screwed up relationship to the city of love—the irony.

Vienna thought to herself bitterly. But it was also a new beginning for her, now.

The plane landed, and Vienna went through the airport procedure and finally spotted her designated driver for the time she would be staying in Paris.

She greeted the driver with a nod, and he held the car door open for her as she sat down. Putting her luggage in the trunk, the driver started their journey towards the hotel.

Vienna stepped out of the car, and her driver followed her inside the building with her luggage.

"Bienvenue á Rio de Sicile – Rivoli, mademoiselle." A petite woman greeted Vienna at the check-in desk.

"Merci," Vienna replied politely. She dismissed her driver, and a bellboy came to carry her luggage for her to her room.

The hotel she was staying at for her time in Paris was exquisite with its beautiful designs and incredibly lavish styles.

Vienna went inside her room and gave a tip to the bellboy before closing her room door and admiring it.

Vienna walked out to the balcony and closed her eyes, breathing in. It reminded her of the roof terrace at Ashley's. She felt dizzy with the pain that swept over her.

Ashley. Ashley. Ashley

"COMING!" Chloe yelled, running to the door.

"Who is.. oh! Vienna! Hey! What... When did you come here?" Chloe fumbled with her words as Vienna invited herself into her apartment.

Her apartment was old Parisian style, with its old herringbone parquet floor, double windows that let in lots of light.

"I have been here for a couple of days. It was just another work contract, nothing special. The client was straightforward." Vienna didn't match her best friend's excitement.

"What? A freaking couple of days, and you didn't tell me?! I could have come to pick you up." Chloe gave her a stern look, filled with annoyance and disappointment.

"You look pretty tired. Come on, let's sit in the living room." She continued, walking towards the room.

"Uh, well, it's been a rather rough few days." Vienna crashed on the couch.

"Hey, you can go freshen up. I'll make you some coffee."

The sentence reminded Vienna of Ashley, but it was not her. She closed her eyes, wanting to drift away from her thoughts.

"So, how's everything back home? How are the art classes going?" Chloe asked a fresh and more relaxed looking Vienna. She knew something was up with Vienna but chose not to bombard her with questions and took a rather subtle approach.

"Well, the few last assignments, and I am done actually. Finally, I'll have my master's degree," she informed Chloe, Vienna's own voice sounding less happy than even she expected it to.

"Oh, that's great! And how's Ashley? Isn't she your only client at the moment? I thought you were dating too? What happened?" came a pretty obvious question from Chloe, and Vienna told her what had happened.

Chloe calmly listened to the whole story before she pulled Vienna in for a firm hug, knowing her friend needed it.

"Oh, come here, sweetheart."

"We can talk when you want to talk about it. I know you are hurt, this could have been handled better." Chloe's voice was pleasant and supportive.

"I guess love and relationships just aren't for me. When it comes down to it, I'm still just a whore. I'm always going to be a dirty little secret for someone like Ashley." Vienna started as she buried her face in Chloe's shoulder, tears escaping her eyes.

"From that difficult childhood up until now, I have made everything better, achieved things, earned so much money. I have a degree now, I travel places, but one thing that I've never had is a genuine relationship. A chance at love, you know. I thought, okay, this was it, my life is sorted, but I guess you can never have everything." Vienna went on, letting out all that she had been keeping inside.

"Maybe this is the rule this universe works on, no matter how much you try, one puzzle piece will always be missing. I have so much else in life. Maybe love is the one thing I am destined not to have." she ended with a sob.

"Look, what we feel is natural. It's just human, whenever someone leaves us, or things do not go to plan, we look at it and trace it back to our deepest insecurities. But relax, you have made your life on your own. And you'll get love too, you are amazing. And I have never met Ashley yet, I am sure she loves you as much as you love her. She may have messed up, but we all make mistakes, V. She won't have wanted to lose someone as incredible as you." Chloe told her, maturity and softness lacing her tone.

"Thank you. I am sorry, I should have come here earlier." Vienna's smiled at her and wiped her tears.

"Yeah, come on, if I say one more wise thing I'll turn into an owl." Chloe said as the two finally laughed.

"You stay here, and I'll get some bagels while we discuss more of our questionable life choices." Chloe remarked while going into the kitchen.

"You are an impossible asshole." Vienna exclaimed with a chuckle. She had missed this—her best friend.

"Or better known as your best friend in the whole world!" Chloe yelled back from the kitchen as Vienna smiled genuinely for the first time in days.

~

"YES, Mr. Mathews, it's all finished. The country club is ready to host your charity event. I've personally seen to all the preparations, and I assure you everything is in order." Ashley said over the phone as she checked the country club preparations once again.

It had been 4 days since she saw Vienna. She had tried to call her, only to be met by an electronic voice, telling her that the number was no longer in use.

She had gone over to Vienna's house and found it locked up and shut down. Even calling the escort company had been in vain as Vienna had canceled their contract, and the company refused to give out any personal information.

Ashley let out a sigh as she focused on the task at hand. Elijah Matthews' charity event was scheduled for today at noon, and she had to make sure everything was perfect.

After she was satisfied with how everything had been done, she drove to her penthouse and got ready for the event with Trisha accompanying her.

The party was held at the Paramount Country Club. It was a beautiful place with acres of lush green land. A golf course was situated a few kilometers near the main building, and there was a small lake with gorgeous swans next to the building.

The building itself was magnificent with it's grandeur style and rich history.

"Thank you for coming with me, Trish. I know you've had a lot on with the wedding in three days, but I just didn't feel like being here alone." Ashley said.

"Oh I should thank you. This is better than being with Kevin's parents again, as they boast about their Welsh ancestry for three hours, while I sit there, pretending to listen. Trust me, I love them, but it just gets a little too much sometimes. And well, yeah, I would have preferred a happy you and Vienna on my wedding day than any of the fancy and but perhaps that's how it is meant to be." Trisha replied with a sad smile.

"You do look stunning, Trish." Ashley told her for the umpteenth time as Trisha laughed.

She was dressed in a hunter green floor-length dress with a plunging neckline. Her black hair was straightened to within an inch of its life, and it shone in the light.

"Hey did you try reaching out to Vienna? Any luck?"

"No. I called and looked everywhere I could. I called Black Label too; they said she is not in the US and is busy with a client, but they refused to give any more information. She was pretty angry when she left, I don't think she wants to talk to me again." Ashley explained her attempts and getting to Vienna.

"Yeah I tried too; her number is disconnected.." Trisha trailed off as another person joined their conversation.

"Hello, Ms. Davidson. Ms. Peyton, how are you, ladies?"

Elijah came to stand with the two women and took

turns kissing their hands. The duo greeted him back as Elijah faced Ashley and started off,

"I am not happy with you, Ashley. You usually do such a great job, but you let me down this time." Elijah said solemnly.

"Oh I am sorry Elijah, is there anything wrong? You can me tell me, I'll get it fixed in a flash." Ashley babbled.

"No, no. Everything at the party is great. The guests are so happy. Well, both with the arrangements and the fact that they saw the sun after three months." Elijah chuckled at his own joke, the two responded with just polite smiles.

"But you broke a promise. You didn't bring the exquisite Vienna here." Elijah got to his actual complaint.

"Oh, I apologize, Elijah. She really wanted to be here, but she had to fly out for some art project. She did send her greetings."

"Oh what a lovely lady." Elijah responded,

"Enjoy your evening. I'll see you ladies around." He walked away from them.

ASHLEY WAS A SHELL OF HERSELF, desolate and distraught, and nothing Trisha said would help her.

Not being able to see her friend in pain like this, Trisha had an idea to learn about Vienna's whereabouts.

"Hi. This is Trisha Peyton from CNN." Trisha spoke on the phone as Ashley looked at her.

"Yes Miss Peyton. Good to talk to you again. How can I help you?" The women on the line spoke.

"Yes, I wanted to do a story about your employee Vienna Rhodes, regarding her paintings and art. Can you connect me to her?" Trisha spoke confidently as Ashley gave her a hopeful look.

"Oh, Ms. Peyton, I am afraid Vienna is in Paris for a job, and she intends to stay there for a while for personal reasons. I'll be sure to arrange a meeting whenever she is back here." The woman replied politely.

"Okay Thank you, I'll get back to you." Trisha said, hanging up, and turned to Ashley.

"So my spy told me, Vienna is in Paris." Trisha repeated the information to Ashley with a grin, as Ashley jumped to hug her.

"If she is staying in Paris, she must be with Chloe Martinez, her best friend." Ashley pulled back and frowned.

"Great. Do you have her number?" Trisha sounded like a detective with a newly found lead.

"No, but she does own Chloeque Fashion House." Ashley said.

"That will do!" Trisha exclaimed.

"THANK YOU, Madam. I will see you in Paris. Au revoir." Trisha hung up the phone, noting down an address- Apartment 12, 52a Boulevard Jourdan, 75014 Paris.

"This may not be the best time to brag, but after another imaginary interview booking, Trisha saves the day, here is your address." Trisha was chirpier than a kid.

"You have to fly to Paris tomorrow, go get your girl. And bring her back for my wedding." she all but ordered to a curious looking Ashley.

"But Trish, what if I don't find her? What if she refuses

to see me? She doesn't even want to see my face." Ashley argued.

"But what if you do Ash? I know you love this woman and she loves you. As they say, 'Better to try and fail, than never to try at all.' Or some such shit. Anyway, you cannot ruin my wedding." Trisha would have been even louder if they weren't at the party.

"Okay, okay. I will go. I need to see her. I need to try."

"Nous allons bientôt atterrir à **Paris. Veuillez boucler vos ceintures. Merci de voler avec nous.**"

The pilot's voice sounded as the plane landed in Paris.

Ashley couldn't contain her excitement on seeing Vienna again, as well as the fear that she would reject her. But she had to take a chance.

Ashley was met by her driver for her stay in Paris, who took her straight to the address she had given him. She couldn't wait until tomorrow or even later in the day. She to see Vienna now.

Arriving at Chloe's apartment, she took a deep breath and rang the bell.

12

Vienna opened the door and was surprised, to say the least, to find Ashley in front of her.

"Oh, Ashley, what.. What are you doing here?" She stuttered, unable to recover from her shock.

"I came to see you, V, I had to see you," Ashley replied.

"What do you want, Ash? Why are you making this more difficult than it already is?" Vienna began after she gathered herself, anger lacing her tone.

"And besides, won't being seen with a whore like me, damage you?" She continued.

"I came all this way just for you, Vienna. Can I please just come inside and talk to you? Just listen to me once. Please?" Ashley said softly.

Vienna looked at her for a few moments longer before letting out a sigh and inviting her in.

"Thank you so much, V," Ashley said to her.

"Don't. Don't call me that." Vienna turned to her, pain visible on her face.

"Who is it, V?" Chloe asked while walking towards the lounge.

"Hi. I am Ashley, Ashley Davidson. Vienna's gir-... um, client. Um. I don't know what." Ashley hurriedly spoke before Vienna could tell Chloe.

"Oh, hey. Vienna didn't tell me you were coming through. How are you? It's really good to finally meet you. Please come in, make yourself at home." Chloe greeted her cheerfully, making Vienna frown.

"Er. Thanks."

"Why don't you two talk and I'll see you in a while." Chloe moved away, sensing the situation but not before giving a reassuring hand on Vienna's back and a whisper in her ear,

"You'll be alright. Just hear her out. I have a feeling it'll be good in the end. She loves you. I can tell."

"Well, okay! If you guys need anything, I'm just a few meters away in the kitchen." Chloe told them one last time before disappearing.

"Do you not miss me?" Ashley asked Vienna as Chloe left.

"It is not relevant anymore." Vienna was still cold and hurt.

"You could have talked to Trisha, at least if not me. We've been really worried." Ashley told her softly.

"I just wanted to get away from anything that reminded me of you." Vienna's voice had more emotion as she looked ahead, trying not to meet Ashley's warm eyes. Because Vienna knew if she did, she'd melt.

"I am so sorry, V, I just freaked out. I should have told you myself." Ashley began,

"Please, come back home with me."

"And what after that? Wouldn't it ruin everything if you are seen with me again?" Vienna asked, her voice bitter.

"Yes, I acted selfishly earlier. I wanted to save everything I built, but I realized that there is no point in having all this if the only person I cherish more than anything, isn't there with me to share it." Ashley's voice filled with emotion as Vienna listened silently.

"I was worried about what would happen if all those people found out I was lying. But I don't care anymore, V. It doesn't matter if they think I am a cheat or a liar, but it does if you think so. I'll tell them all the story of how we met. I love you. I'm not ashamed of you. You are what I am most proud of." She finished with a sigh, running a hand through her, now mostly disheveled hair.

"I didn't want you to choose between your career and me. I value your hard work as much as you do. Besides, love is meant to lift up and empower, not ruin and destruct. But I just wanted you to share your heart with me, be honest with me." Vienna replied, calmer than before, as she looked at Ashley's defeated form.

"I know, I messed up, but I want to fix this." Ashley pleaded.

"I called Paul before coming here and told him, he could tell anyone what he liked, I don't care about what happens next. I never would judge you on your career. I am nothing but impressed by you. I don't need you to be a secret in any way. I want you, V, I need you by my side. God knows how I've spent this past week without you. I'm a wreck without you. I adore you, V. I love you more than anyone. More than anything. More than everything I have built." Ashley looked to Vienna, her eyes filled with tears.

"I liked your old haircut better." Vienna smiled at her. The two shared a hug, and needless to say, it was tight and long.

As they pulled back, Ashley cradled Vienna's face in her hands.

Vienna looked into her eyes, "I love you too. I'm scared, but I do love you."

Tears were now streaming down Vienna's face as she joined their lips in a sweet and tender kiss. The two stayed that way before Ashley pulled back to look at her.

"I'll look after you now. I've got you. We face everything together now." Ashley replied slowly, a smile forming on her face.

A cough resounded in the back, and the couple turned to face the culprit.

"Ahem, so the lovebirds are back together in the city of romance. Oh my. I swear you two make me miss love, sex, and all the drama." Chloe's voice filled the background, a warm smile on her face, but also a few tears in her eyes as she shook her head.

"Not as the warm as this moment, but would anyone like a coffee?"

"Doesn't she remind you of Trisha?" Ashley and Vienna both said at the same time, and the two laughed at a rather clueless Chloe and a coffee mug in her hand. Poor Chloe.

"Speaking of Trisha, she is kind of mad at both of us." Ashley said to Vienna after they introduced the concept of Trisha to Chloe.

"We did kind of ruin her wedding week. But when I go back, I am going to blame it all on you." Vienna announced with a childlike charm.

"Okay, okay. I kind of deserve that." Ashley replied with a smile.

"The wedding is in three days, and it isn't completely

ruined if we fly home tomorrow." Vienna exclaimed as she clapped her hands.

It's so good to have her back. Ashley thought to herself as she admired this exquisite creature she had come to love.

"I wish Chloe could come with us too." Ashley suggested, looking at Chloe, hopefully.

"Oh, listening to all these stories, I want to hop on that plane too. I'll be at your bloody wedding when you two get married. You two can leave without me tomorrow, but you are my guests tonight." Chloe said.

"Of course you will be in our wedding! Who else is going to be my bridesmaid and tell me to shut up and that my jokes are inappropriate?" Vienna looked to Chloe.

Chloe laughed with them both.

Ashley looked at Vienna, imagining her in a wedding dress. She would be the most stunning bride, of course she would.

I love you so much. I cannot believe I almost lost you.

THE DAY of Trisha's wedding arrived, and everyone was beyond excited. They had arrived at the hotel for the wedding.

Ashley was in charge of the wedding preparations, and even though she was the best woman, it still didn't mean she was let off her duties as a best friend.

The wedding was held in Sand Castle. A beautiful resort inspired by the Chateaux in Europe, it offered classical ambiance, service, and sophistication.

There were acres of landscaped gardens set with

outdoor benches and cocktail tables, as well as an outdoor marble top bar with a waterfall background.

Ashley ran through last-minute preparations.

"Joanna, I'd like you to go through the caterer's list again. Make sure the menu is not altered in any way. Oh, and make sure the security checks are back on all the workers for tonight."

Ashley ordered the utmost perfection for this day, and everyone did their best to deliver.

"How is my best friend doing. She ready yet?" Ashley asked as soon as she entered the dressing room.

"Are you kidding me! Of course, I'm not ready yet. I will be late. As usual! Oh, I hope I don't trip on my way to Kevin." Trisha rambled on.

"Hey, hey. Calm down. You'll be fine. It's normal to freak out like this before your wedding." Ashley put a hand on Trisha's shoulder, meeting her eyes through the mirror.

Trisha smiled at her while the make up artist worked on Trisha's face.

Ashley was wearing a three-piece suit and looked dapper, her hair in its new sleek shorter cut, looking dark and slicked back. Her wing tips shined to their maximum.

She looked around the room to find Vienna, at a dressing table, her hair being styled to beautiful waves with braids at the top. She looked like a mythical princess. The most stunning woman Ashley had ever seen.

Sensing someone looking at her, Vienna turned her head to look at Ashley and smiled, her perfect teeth gleaming. Ashley smiled back.

"You look incredible."

Trisha was finally ready. Gasps sounded throughout the room as Ashley's eyes filled with tears at the sight of her best friend, so beautiful in the big white dress with white lace around her collarbone. Her hair was pinned up in loose curls.

"You look amazing, Trish. So, so gorgeous." Ashley told her as Trisha's own eyes filled with tears. "Don't cry! This poor girl hasn't worked so hard on your eye makeup to have you cry it all off!"

Ashley then moved out of the room to oversee the preparations one more time before the music sounded off, and the wedding ceremony began.

Everyone moved to take their places as guests took their seats.

Trisha walked down the aisle with her father as Kevin smiled warmly at her from the altar. He was wearing a grey suit with lavender flowers tucked neatly into the front pocket of his jacket.

Ashley stood next to Vienna, who was striking in red silk. She held her hand as they watched the ceremony. The emotion of the wedding just made her want it all for herself and Vienna.

Trisha and Kevin sealed their wedding with a kiss, and the crowd erupted to cheers, celebrating the union.

Everyone moved towards the open yard where the rest of the party was to be continued, and Ashley and Vienna made their way towards Kevin and Trisha.

"Congratulations, you two!" Vienna and Ashley exclaimed together as they took their turns, hugging the bride and groom.

"Thank you so much. I am so glad you guys made it in time and together. This is all I needed." Trisha was as happy as she could be seeing her best friend and Vienna together again.

"Thank you for making me go and do it, but now your

maid-of-honor is back and at your service." Ashley said to her, mocking a salute to which they all laughed.

Ashley immediately snapped her attention to Joanna as she passed by, and told her to oversee the food again.

"Relax, now that you are here, everything will turn out just perfect." Trisha told her, smiling.

"Yeah, sorry I went away without telling you. But what's important is now we are back and ready to make this the best wedding ever." Vienna said, hugging Trisha as the two talked a while.

"But Ash, what about that blackmailer guy." Trisha asked curiously as Kevin asked the same.

"Don't worry, I have thought of something." Ashley replied confidently, her hand holding Vienna's.

Kevin nodded his head and said,

"Well, if there's anything you need help with, just let me know. You know we're here for you guys." Ashley and Vienna smiled at him as Trisha couldn't help but admire her husband.

"Thank you, Kev." They replied unanimously.

"You two look gorgeous, but my wife has stolen the show today, guys." He focused on Trisha, giving her a kiss, which she happily returned.

"She definitely has. And you treat her well, or she will run off to lesboland with us." Vienna chipped in as the four laughed heartily.

It was then time for the first dance, as Trisha and Kevin made their way to the center of the floor.

Have I told you lately by Rod Stewart, started as Kevin wrapped his arms around Trisha, and they danced.

Ashley stood next to Vienna, her hand loosely draped around Vienna's hip as they watched the couple staring at each other lovingly.

The song came to an end, and the crowd clapped as Trisha and Kevin moved to let the other couples join them on the floor.

Ashley took this as a cue, and the sound of a champagne glass clinking caught everyone's attention.

"Excuse me, If I could have everyone's attention, please. Before we all resume with the wedding party, there is something I need to say." Ashley announced as the chatter in the party gradually turned into silence.

"I want to tell everyone that Vienna was not my real girlfriend." hushed murmurs filled the place as Vienna's hand tightened around Ashley's, urging her on.

"I, in fact, hired her to pretend to be one, to attend all these events with me." She said as the murmurs died down, people eager to know more.

"She kept it professional, and I got away from all questions asking if I was single and lonely, so it worked for both us. But eventually, we fell in love." She paused, looking at Vienna with a small smile.

"We fell in love because she is the most amazing woman I have ever met. I apologize to all my clients because I lied to you. I know this may color your opinion of me, and make me lose a lot of work, but I felt it was easier to lie and hide my loneliness. I felt like people wouldn't care, or they won't understand. So, I took that shortcut too. I am human and full of flaws, but eventually, I have realized that truth is the best way out. Vienna wasn't my real girlfriend. But, she absolutely is now." She said with another pause, looking around at the people who surprisingly offered her smiles instead of disapproving looks.

"And now finally, not that I am jealous of you, Trisha, for getting married before me despite being a good three years younger, but I want to make this day even more special." Ashley turned to Trisha as Trisha laughed at her calculations of their age.

She then turned to Vienna and moved to stand in front of her,

"Vienna Rhodes.. lovely, beautiful, incredible, funny, Vienna." Ashley began as she pulled out a blue velvet box, she had been hiding in her pocket and opened it to reveal the most beautiful diamond ring.

Vienna gasped as she stared between the ring and Ashley, tears threatening to fall,

"Will you do me the honor of marrying me?" Ashley finished, her heart beating loudly as Vienna finally nodded and then let out a sob,

"Yes. Yes! Yes! Yes! Oh my God, yes! I will. You are the only one I want to spend the rest of my life with. Of course, I'll marry you!" Vienna said, as she let Ashley slip the ring on her finger and then jumped to hug her, the people clapping in the background.

"The gap is five years, by the way." Trisha yelled as everyone laughed.

VIENNA SAT across from Meredith Bowes in the Black Label NYC offices.

"My darling," began Meredith, fine lines on her face beginning to tell her age. "Nothing good lasts forever. You have been my best girl for some time now. I doubt I will ever have a girl like you again. But, now, you must go. I'm so happy to see you happy and in love. Love is the most valuable thing we have, you know. I have loved you since you were a screwed up teenager, rough around the edges, but so beautiful, even then. You just needed an opportunity to make something of yourself, and you grasped it with both hands." Meredith reached across the table and squeezed Vienna's hand. Her hands were aged too, Vienna thought. She wondered again how old Meredith was.

"Meredith, I will always be grateful to you. I cannot tell you how grateful I am for the opportunities you have given me. You saved me from the gutter and gave me a life and a future. But, it is time for a new chapter in my life- with Ashley. I want to do more art. I want to exhibit. I want to sell my paintings. I've had the opportunity with Black Label to make a lot of money. I want to use some of that money to help underprivileged young people. I want to set up a charity and do what I can to help troubled teenagers in the dark places I once was."

"My darling, you are a warm and giving soul, and the world is lucky to have you. Please, I will always be here for you. There will always be a home for you at Black Label. Do let me know if I can help you financially or otherwise with your charity." Her bright blue eyes burned intensely. "And, my darling, when I retire, I would like to offer you the opportunity to take over Black Label for me. There is no rush, you just think it over. But, Vienna, you are like a daughter to me. All the Black Label girls are my family, but you are my special one. Think about it, Vienna. Think about it, my darling."

EPILOGUE

"I cannot believe we are getting married today," Ashley said to Vienna as the two had a rare moment alone, amongst all the hustle and bustle of the wedding morning. "I absolutely adore you. I always have since I first met you. You are an incredible woman, and watching your success in taking over Black Label from Meredith has made me so proud. I can't wait to be your wife."

"Yeah, it kind of all happened gorgeous, didn't it." Vienna's voice was dipped in sweet nostalgia as she put a hand on Ashley's cheek.

"Maybe all that blackmailing and things that happened were actually good. They acted as a catalyst, and now here we are." She continued.

"Well, at my age, I can't afford to waste any time!" Ashley chuckled as she bent down slightly to put her forehead against Vienna's.

"Ash, honey, I love how you proposed to me and the grand romantic gesture, but the age jokes are still bad, once again, leave them to Trisha." Vienna shot back as both laughed.

"Where is Trisha anyway?" Ashley inquired.

"Yeah, I don't see Chloe, either," Vienna added, equally clueless about her best woman.

The momentary silence was broken as a cheerful voice called out to the two,

"Congratulations, ladies!"

"Shweta! It's so good to see you. I'm so glad you made it." Vienna let go of Ashley and hugged the older Indian woman.

She was dressed in a beautiful baby pink sari, her shining hair resting on her shoulders.

"Of course! I wouldn't miss your wedding for the world." Shweta said to Vienna as she turned to greet Ashley.

"You must be Ashley. I have heard so much about you." Ashley shook Shweta's hand as Vienna jumped in to explain,

"Ash, this is Shweta. A friend, former client. Remember, I told you about her, she fought her family and came out of the closet and left her husband about six months ago. Now she is here with her girlfriend." Vienna introduced Shweta as Ashley smiled, finally understanding.

"All because of your amazing fiancé." Shweta pointed to Vienna.

"It's great to meet you, Shweta. That's very brave of you to do what you did. It's not easy to break shackles, especially when they get old." Ashley said as the trio talked for a while.

"Oh, Vienna, I thought I'd never see you again." This time a male voice greeted the two and a rather chirpy one–It was Elijah.

"Oh, hey, Mr. Matthews, good to see you again too."
Vienna said rather awkwardly.

"I am so very sorry I couldn't make it to your party, I had an emergency work thing." She explained, pre-empting what he was about to ask.

"Well, we definitely missed you, but glad that you are finally back. You two look beautiful. Congratulations on the wedding once again.

I'm looking forward to a fantastic party, but I won't even credit you, Ashley, because that's basically your entire life." He continued with a loud chuckle as the two ladies smiled.

"I am glad you are enjoying yourself, Elijah," Ashley replied politely as he left.

"He probably missed me more than you did." Vienna chipped, looking at Ashley as the two did not laugh, but their eyes did.

~

"Oh, here are the lovebirds, glued together." the two recognized it was Chloe's voice without even turning back.

"Hey Chloe, have you seen Trisha? I have been looking for her." Ashley was asked with a frown as she looked around the area.

"No, I haven't seen her for a while, either. I thought she was with you." Chloe replied as she looked around, searching for Trisha.

"How are you, ladies!" Trisha exclaimed, walking towards them with a big smile on her face.

"Hey, Trish. Where have you been?" Ashley asked her.

"Uh, sorry, I had something very important to taken care of. But hey, no time for the story, we are running pretty late, and there are tons of things to do." Trisha replied hurriedly.

"Yeah, you two need to separate for now and shall see each other at the wedding vows!" She continued dragging Ashley away from Vienna.

"Yeah don't worry; you don't have to fly to Paris to get her this time," Chloe spoke, making everyone laugh. She dragged Vienna to her separate dressing room and got to work

THE WEDDING WAS HELD at Wave Hill.

Being the most peaceful place in the city, Vienna and Ashley had been more than thrilled to announce it as their wedding venue as it made a breathtaking spot to exchange vows.

The regal, vine-covered pergola, overlooking the Hudson River, practically begged to become an altar.

Ashley and Vienna walked down the aisle together, hand in hand as the music sounded off.

Guests sat on either side of them and looked at the couple with warm smiles.

Ashley wore a smart white three-piece suit and was dapper as ever with a pink rose in her lapel.

Ashley couldn't tear her eyes away from Vienna. She looked exquisite in her lace sleeved tulle wedding gown with a deep lace-covered neckline. It was backless. Her hair was in braids and waves, small pink roses braided into her hair.

She looked perfect, and Ashley's eyes filled with tears when she saw her.

The priest began the vows, and Ashley and Vienna held each other's hands, never tearing their eyes apart.

"I now pronounce you partners in life."

They kissed. Their mouths meeting, wanting, knowing how right this was.

Chloe and Trisha, the two best women, stood by the happy couple's side as the ceremony ended and then immediately tackled them for hugs.

They moved to the area where the rest of the arrangements were made, and the newly married couple cut their wedding cake as everyone cheered.

Following the cake, it was time for the dance. Ashley turned to Vienna

"Would you join me for a dance, Mrs. Davidson?" she lovingly asked Vienna, making her grin and place her hand in Ashley's.

"I would love to, Mrs. Davidson," Vienna answered.

The two ladies walked towards the floor and began to dance as Elvis Presley's voice came through the speakers.

Wise men say,

Only fools rush in.

But I can't help,

Falling in love with you...

"I love this song!" Vienna squealed as she heard it play.

Ashley let out a chuckle and kissed her nose.

"I know. That's why I chose it." She told Vienna, gazing into her eyes lovingly.

"I love you," Vienna told her as she pulled Ashley in for a kiss.

"I love you too," Ashley replied after they pulled back and resumed their dance.

The Next Day

"Where are we going?" Ashley was puzzled.

"Doesn't it feel like we are seventeen again? Sneaking out to get alcohol." Vienna was in a zone as Ashley rolled her eyes.

"You know this place very well. Relax!" She continued, looking at Ashley as the engine revved.

And she was right, the road lead to the beach house she used to come to as a kid and owned now.

"Doesn't it feel great! We are finally married." Vienna sighed, dreamily as they stood by Ashley's favorite spot with a wide smile on Ashley's face.

"You know, what's the best way to let go of bad memories connected to a place? Replace it with amazing memories at the same place." Vienna told Ashley, grabbing her hand.

"Thank you for everything. Thank you for just being in my life. You make everything so much better, V." Ashley's sentence was interrupted by a phone call.

"Why is Joanna calling?" She wondered aloud as she picked the phone.

"Hello, ma'am. Sorry to disturb you, but there is news about Paul Carter. He has been caught by the police for fraud and blackmail. You had an ongoing deal with him. The police have taken from him some photos and deleted them from his hard drive. They said, would you like the photos, or would you like them destroyed? Is it sorted, or should I involve our lawyers?" Joanna said on the line.

"Oh, I see. No, Joanna, my deal with him is sorted. Inform the police to destroy the photos. You don't have to worry. I'll see you when I am back at the office. Thank you for informing me." Ashley tried to hide the pleasant shock she got from the news.

"Okay, ma'am. Have a great honeymoon." Joanna replied politely, and the phone hung up.

Ashley told Vienna the news, and they kissed each other against the setting sun.

"You came here as a child. Want to make some adult memories this time?" Vienna's eyes shone as she held her partner's hand.

Ashley's phone beeped again. Text from Trisha:

Not to brag, but yet again, Trisha saves the day.

Ashley smiled widely.

You are such a sneaky witch

Ashley replied as Vienna scooted closer to join in on the conversation.

Sneaky witch says you're welcome!

CAME the reply as Ashley and Vienna laughed.

Thank you, Trish. We love you ❤

ASHLEY REPLIED and put her phone away, pouncing on her wife, kissing under the setting sun.

THE END

ELIZABETH'S ARTIST

A LESBIAN AGE GAP ROMANCE

1

"Five more minutes, everyone! Once you have completed the quiz, you may leave." Ella Ryan observed the lowered heads of her students, who were focusing on their test papers. It was an early Thursday evening in late September, and as the sun was beginning to set, the rays cast a golden hue across the classroom.

Tonight marked Ella's fourth week as an art teacher at the Chatsworth Community College, located in Chelsea, Manhattan. She landed the position in early August after spending the summer applying for jobs. Every Tuesday and Thursday evening, she taught an intermediate painting class to a small class of students who varied in age and purpose. Some of the pupils took the course as an additional credit towards a diploma, whereas a few people in the group merely wanted to learn more about techniques and principles.

Ella was grateful to have found employment in her field, although teaching a part-time evening course at a community college was not exactly her dream. At twenty-eight years old, Ella had received a Master's Degree in Art, specializing in Photography and Acrylic Painting from the Waterford Art Institute. She had aspirations of exhibiting her creations at the respected galleries in New York, preferably on the Upper West Side. In particular, she had her sights set on showing at the prestigious Amira Alder Gallery.

As ELLA'S class was coming to an end, she noticed a text buzz through her phone from her peripheral vision. While keeping one eye on her students, Ella quickly checked the message. *Hi sweetie, it's Mom. Thinking of you. I hope you can come to Queens for dinner soon.*

Ella groaned on the inside. The last thing she wanted to do was spend another evening with her bickering, stressed-out parents. There was no doubt that Ella loved her family but moving out had strengthened her independence. Besides, she knew that she would be walking into an environment of disapproval, fueled by her father's Irish temper.

Ella had spent the majority of her poverty-stricken childhood walking on eggshells at home. Being the youngest of four kids, it wasn't too difficult to slip through the cracks. Whenever Ella needed an escape, she would hide in her room and submerge herself into artistic creations. Her imagination and creativity blossomed in the middle of a war zone. And while nine-year-old Ella didn't know it at the time, her tiny bedroom that she shared with her sister Ciara was the beginning of a journey that would lead her towards a full scholarship to the Waterford Institute.

Ella could still recall the explosive fight that she had with her parents when she found out she had been accepted into Arts College. During her last year in high school, her high school art teacher, Mrs. Healy, encouraged Ella to apply for a grant towards the Waterford Art Institute. Knowing that her parents did not have the money to send her to the institute, let alone the inclination, Ella applied to receive the subsidy.

"Your mother and I worked our fingers to the bone so that you could spend your days *drawing* on a *piece of paper*? What type of work are you going to get with an art degree anyhow?" her father yelled furiously as a whiskey-scented vapor expelled from his breath.

"Your father is right, Ella. Painting is for lazy women who have rich husbands to take care of them. I mean, you have never even had a *boyfriend!* Why don't you become a nurse like your cousin Siobhan?" Her mother, Catherine, teared up. "Why do you have to be so *different?* You don't see your brothers and sisters fooling around with paints. They are attending college to get real jobs!"

Ella begged, "But Mom, this is my dream! I have a full scholarship, so you and Dad don't need to worry about money. Just wait and see; my art will hang in the most beautiful galleries in New York. Besides, I don't want a life like yours; I want to create my own way."

Ella's mother slapped her across the face. "What's wrong with our life? We worked hard so that you could have a future. Now you want to waste your time with a bunch of...art *freaks?* My god, Ella. That school is probably full of homosexuals too."

Ella cringed on the inside. *Um, little do you know, Mom, but I'm also gay!* However, Ella dare not say anything about her sexual orientation. She knew that coming out to her family was a battle she wouldn't survive. She barely had the energy to fight for her choice of college. There was no way that her conservative Catholic upbringing would support her being a lesbian.

Her father bellowed, "If you want to attend an arts college, then you can move out! I am not going to support a child who is making foolish choices in life. You want to make your own in the world? There is the door, Ella!" With that, her father retired to the bedroom, slamming it shut.

"Ella, please, we just want you to consider your options carefully." Her mother's voice grew gentler. "You are a smart and beautiful woman. There are so many careers that you could have. Why art, honey? Can't that just be a hobby?"

Ella sighed, "Because Mom, this is what I love. There are lots of positions available in the arts." Ella reached out to grab her mother's hands. "Mommy, can't you understand? I don't need a lot to survive, but art is what makes me happy, and I promise that if you let me go, I will get good grades and make you both proud. You'll see!"

Ella's mother shook her head. "I'm sorry, Ella, but I must respect your father. I understand your decision, but I disagree with it." Her mother's face sagged with sorrow as she whispered, "You can't live here, but I'll put a little bit of money in your bank account to help with dorm expenses. Just don't tell your father."

Ella hugged her mother tightly. "Thanks, Mom. I know that you don't understand now, but one day, I am going to make you both so proud of me."

Not one for overt forms of affection, Catherine patted Ella's shoulders begrudgingly. "Well, you just make sure that you work hard and get good grades. And if you want to make your father and me proud, then find a nice Catholic man and settle down with a family."

Ella smiled weakly while her stomach twisted into knots, but she managed to muster something agreeable. "I promise to do my best, Mom. I love you and Dad."

To this day, Ella credits the instructor who believed in her talent and encouraged Ella to chase after her dreams. Her teacher allowed Ella to remain after school, and Ella had found salvation, sitting alone in Mrs. Healy's class, poised in front of an easel. She wasn't sure if Mrs. Healy pitied her. Still, she was grateful to have a serene place to develop her acrylic technique, with a plethora of paints, brushes, and canvases at her disposal.

Something was soothing about running a soft-bristled brush across a stark, white surface, coating it with vibrant colors. In those moments, Ella began to understand the meaning of sensuality, and as a young woman, a curious arousal bubbled beneath the surface. Ella can still recall the scent of Mrs. Healy's perfume as she would lean over Ella's shoulder, inspecting her latest creation.

"Mmmm, very nice, Ella," Mrs. Healy would purr. "If I were you, I might think about adding just a *touch* of blue in this corner, right here." The teacher extended a glossy, manicured nail and hovered just above Ella's painting's surface, her gold bracelets jingling from her delicate wrist. Ella could feel a warmth emanate from Mrs. Healy, and it made her insides churn in a way that both delighted and intimidated Ella.

Sometimes Ella fantasized about wanting Mrs. Healy to touch her with a brush like she would a canvas. Ella imagined stories of her and Mrs. Healy visiting galleries together, examining great works of art, talking in hushed voices about highlights and uses of space. Ella knew these thoughts would never come to fruition, but it was still fun to think about; plus, her crush on Mrs. Healy was what fueled her creativity.

Once, Mrs. Healy asked, "I see you're working on a new piece, Ella. I love how you blend the tones right here. It's so ethereal. What inspired your use of red?" Ella's face blushed, and she looked down, chewing on her lip. "Oh, I-I don't know. I think I might like someone, but I am not sure how to express it. The red symbolizes love, I guess."

Mrs. Healy smiled knowingly. "Ah, yes! I have been there myself. I have had many crushes myself, and while some never amounted to anything, I knew I could always rely on art as a vehicle for expression." Ella felt a bond growing between her and her art teacher, so she decided to open up.

"Mrs. Healy, when I go away to Waterford, I really want to be, um, be *myself*, I guess. I find it so hard here, in high school. I want to feel as though someone like me belongs. Will it get easier in college?" Elizabeth asked. She tried to sound cryptic, but what Ella was asking was if she would ever be free to come out as a lesbian.

Mrs. Healy gave her an empathetic look, as though she could read Ella's mind. "My dear, you can *always* be yourself. You just need to be confident in who you are and what you want in life. But I know that high school can be tough. It will get easier, I promise."

Ella wanted to hug her teacher. While Ella couldn't wait to get to college, she knew that she would miss Mrs. Healy most of all.

During her education at the Waterford Institute, Ella's life changed considerably. In addition to mastering techniques in both acrylics and photography and discovering courses that gave her talents an edge in finding a career, Ella was finally free to come out.

She found empowerment in her femme identity, and soon, she experimented with her look. She got her first tattoo of a bird on her shoulder to signify strength and freedom. And then she got another, then another. Tattoos for Ella were as addictive as slapping colorful paint on a canvas, and soon, her body was as decorated as a mixed-media collage. Unlike the other dykes she knew, Ella decided to keep her long fiery-red locks, but she asked her roommate Michelle to shave the sides of her hair one night.

"Oh, come on, please? Don't worry, I promise that you will not fuck it up," Ella begged, but Michelle looked hesitant. "Girl, are you *sure?* I mean, it would look hot and everything, but damn, it's going to be bitch to grow out."

Ella shrugged. "Who says I will want to grow it out? Maybe I will keep it like this forever." Michelle shrugged and threw up her hands in exasperation. "Well, okay then! You asked for it." Michelle then added slyly while untangling her clippers, "Is this for your date tonight?"

Ella smirked and replied, "One of them. I am hanging out with Kali for dinner. But *later* tonight, I'm sleeping over at Renee's, you know, for *dessert.*" Ella winked as she and Michelle shared a wicked laugh. Ella added, "Renee mentioned how hot I would look with shaved sides, and I want to try it out." Ella turned to pout at her reflection, lifting strands of her hair away from her ears.

Ella settled into her seat, and as Michelle carefully dragged the clippers up the sides of Ella's scalp, she remarked, "You know, I thought it was a myth that art girls were slutty, but honey, you are living proof!" Ella laughed and playfully swatted Michelle, refusing to take herself too seriously.

With a full-time school schedule, Ella found that she did not have time for a serious relationship. However, in between assignments, projects, and personal creations, she made time to date casually. But Ella was focused on hustling her talents to take her to the top. Pussy and play would be the icing on the cake, but a girlfriend could not pay the bills or get her into the Amira Alder Gallery.

Eight years and countless paintings and resumes later, Ella found herself yearning for something more meaningful. She had followed the path that was supposed to lead to opportunities, and here she was, stuck in a drab classroom.

Once the last student had left, Ella gathered her belongings and prepared to go home. *At least I have my evening bartending shifts to add some spice and money in my life.* Still, Ella felt stuck and depressed. She needed a purpose—something that would inspire a great piece of art.

2

C*lick-clack.* *Click-clack.* Elizabeth Diamond's patent leather Louboutins pounded the pavement as she hurried towards the Amira Alder Gallery. It was a sunny Friday morning on the Upper West, and Elizabeth was on her way to meet with a promising new artist, along with the gallery's art handler, Samantha Fox. As she raced past the other New Yorkers on the street, her phone rang.

She carefully balanced her coffee in one hand while holding her cellphone to her ear.

"Hello, Elizabeth Diamond, here," Elizabeth greeted the caller in a rushed tone.

"Hello, dear! I haven't heard from you in over a week. Why haven't you called?" Elizabeth's mother, Hannah, replied in her signature nasal accent.

Elizabeth groaned and rolled her eyes. "Mom, I'm sorry. I've had a hectic couple of days." Impatiently, she checked her Breitling watch. "Actually, this isn't a great time. I'm just on my way to work right now. Can I call you later?"

Hannah seemed unfazed. "Oh, that's nice! Anything new happening at the gallery? I had *such* a nice time at the Oppenheim exhibit opening. And I loved meeting Rebecca."

"Mom, Rebecca and I broke up two months ago, remember? Anyway, yes, we have a new artist showing soon. I'm going to be late if I don't get to the gallery soon." Elizabeth dropped a hint.

"Well, okay, dear. But don't forget about Shabbat dinner tonight! And I hope you ate a good breakfast this morning. You looked so *thin* the last time I saw you."

Elizabeth bobbed her head while answering her mother. "Yes, Mom. Don't worry, I ate, and I *promise* that I will see you tonight, okay?"

"Ah, you are such a good girl. Your father would be so proud of you, bless his soul." Hannah's voice trailed off wistfully.

"Bye, Mom. I love you!" Elizabeth ended the call. Standing at the corner, she ran across the street towards the square brick building. The Amira Alder Gallery was a prestigious space, showcasing the finest (and often famous) artistic talent. It was also a cultural hub for well-heeled art lovers on the Upper West Side. One did not merely go to see art; the point was also to be *seen*. In addition to rotating quarterly exhibits, the gallery hosted private events along with bi-annual black-tie affairs.

Elizabeth Diamond was coming up on her tenth year as the head director. She had been appointed the position on her thirty-second birthday. Amira Alder was her grandfather's sister on her father's side. Haim Diamond had been a prominent and wealthy man who was celebrated in the Jewish community. He had passed when

Elizabeth was twelve years old, and after his death, Amira and Elizabeth's mother, Hannah, became very close.

Amira and her husband Caleb owned the gallery for close to forty years until they passed away. In Caleb's will, the gallery was passed on to Eli Schwartz, a businessman and immediate family friend.

Elizabeth could still recall her mother pulling her aside on the eve of her thirty-second birthday. They were attending a lavish birthday party for Elizabeth at the gallery.

"My Elizabeth, I am so proud of the woman you've become, and I *think* you will be getting quite a surprise tonight." Hannah's eyes twinkled. "I don't want to reveal anything, but remember: family is everything, and we must stick together, bubeleh." Elizabeth felt the tight grip of her mother's papery soft skin.

Later that night, Eli gathered all of the party guests into the front foyer of the gallery. With his champagne glass raised, he motioned Elizabeth to come forward.

"It is with great honor that I officially offer Miss Elizabeth Diamond a position as the artistic director of the Amira Alder Art Gallery. I know it would have been Amira and Caleb's wish to involve a family member in the business. With her MA and MBA, I know she will be a perfect fit for the job." Elizabeth was surprised but elated as friends and family congratulated her.

For Elizabeth, it was the role of a lifetime and very well-suited to her education. Ten years later, Elizabeth was living a privileged life with a well-respected career. The Amira Alder Gallery was the nucleus of the arts and culture scene of the Upper West Side.

While much of Elizabeth's life seemed glamourous from the outside, the truth was that Elizabeth was painfully lonely. Like many of those in high-powered positions, Elizabeth was a workaholic, and when she wasn't at the gallery, she was spending time with her mother. After Elizabeth's father passed away, Elizabeth felt guilty knowing that her mother was now alone in her Central Park West condo.

Hannah could often be demanding of her daughter's time. But on the flipside, Elizabeth was grateful that her mother had become more accepting of her sexual orientation. In an effort to be closer, Hannah began to take an interest in Elizabeth's personal life, even pushing Elizabeth to settle down with a *nice Jewish girl*.

"Don't you miss her? Do you ever think that the two of you will make up? She was such a *nice* girl with a good job. She was a good woman to you, Elizabeth. *And* she was Jewish. If you need to be with women, Elizabeth, I would prefer that over you dating a *Shiksa!*" Hannah wrinkled her nose in disgust.

"Mom, I already told you. Rebecca broke up with *me*. But no matter, the chemistry just wasn't there anymore. And her job was boring. Aside from the sex, we barely had anything in common. It had fizzled out long before we actually broke up." Secretly, Elizabeth was glad that she was no longer with Rebecca, but her mother seemed in denial.

"I don't know, Elizabeth. I just don't understand why you can't just settle down. You work too much, and you are getting too thin." Hannah shook her head, disapprovingly. "You are so beautiful, my bubeleh. Such gorgeous features and nice hair. You remind me of the goddess Ashera." Hannah stroked Elizabeth's thick dark hair and peered into her light blue eyes. "I won't be here forever, and I don't want you to be all alone."

Elizabeth laid her head on her mother's shoulder. "I know, Mamaleh. Don't worry; I am sure I will meet someone soon. I just love the work at the gallery, and for now, that is where my focus is."

However, deep down, Elizabeth yearned for a romantic love similar to what her parents had. She was less upset over losing Rebecca than she was over losing the prospect of a future with someone. But Elizabeth was not one to settle; she truly believed that the right woman would eventually come along and when she did, Elizabeth vowed that she would treat her like a queen. Until then, Elizabeth set her sights on the success of the gallery.

She swung open the large glass door and was immediately greeted by Zoe, the receptionist at the front desk.

"Good morning, Ms. Diamond." Zoe smiled cheerfully at Elizabeth.

"Good morning, Zoe. Has Samantha already arrived?" Elizabeth asked. Zoe nodded her head. "Yes, Ms. Diamond. Samantha and another person are waiting for you in the boardroom."

"Excellent, thank you." Elizabeth quickened her step and rushed down the small corridor towards the office space. *Crap! How did they get here before I did? I hate being late.*

From the doorframe, Elizabeth noticed Samantha sitting with a skinny, young-looking gentleman. *God, he looks like a teenager! Is this the new artist she was talking about?*

Elizabeth strode into the room and laid her belongings on the large, square table. "Hello everyone, my apologies for being late." Samantha stood to greet Elizabeth. "Hi Elizabeth, no problem. We just arrived about five minutes before you." Samantha then motioned towards the stranger.

"I would like to introduce you to Brent. This is the artist I was telling you about." Samantha grinned with excitement.

Brent remained seated. Unsmiling, he said, "Hey," offering a small wave. A leather-bound portfolio was in front of him. Brent appeared scruffy and moody, and Elizabeth was less than impressed with his attitude.

"Hello, Brent, nice to meet you and welcome to the Amira Alder Gallery. I understand that you are interested in showing some work here?"

Brent cleared his throat and sighed. "Yup. Samantha here was telling me that you were looking for new artists. She said that I might be able to score an exhibition?"

Elizabeth was slightly taken aback by Brent's bluntness. "Um, well, it's true. We are always looking for new talent. Of course, I would need to look at your portfolio and then discuss it with my group."

"Cool, check it out." Brent then pushed his portfolio across the table towards Elizabeth. "I work mainly in oil pastels, and most of my canvas are at least a few feet square."

Brent then leaned back in his chair and crossed his arms. Always the consummate professional, Elizabeth maintained a tight smile and placed her hands on top of Brent's portfolio. "I see, that's very interesting." She then glanced at Samantha and then back at Brent. "How do you two know each other?"

Samantha looked at Brent, and Brent smirked. Stammering slightly, Samantha replied, "Um, we met at a party in Soho last weekend and became...friends."

Elizabeth nodded. "Okay, I see." *Whatever, you two are*

totally fucking. But I will entertain this regardless. If the boy has talent, it might be worth this painful meeting. Elizabeth smiled politely at Brent. "Let's take a look." Elizabeth then unzipped the leather-bound case, turning to the first page. She remained silent as she flipped through the translucent inserts.

Hmmm, not bad, but not on par with the quality of work at the gallery, she thought. Brent certainly possessed skill and had technique down, but Elizabeth felt something was lacking in his art. As she continued to peruse the sheets, she wondering how to approach her rejection.

Finally, Elizabeth closed the portfolio and looked up at both Samantha and Brent, who looked eager for a reaction. Taking a breath, Elizabeth began. "Brent, you are quite talented in your medium. I love the vibrancy of colors and your use of space and shapes. How long have you been creating with oils?"

Brent grunted. "Almost two years. But I worked in mixed-media collage before that." His body language reeked of defiance.

"I think your work definitely deserves some kind of exposure, maybe an exhibition, but at this stage in your craft, I don't feel it is right for the Amira Alder Gallery." Elizabeth watched as Brent's expression grew dark.

Elizabeth's role was to maintain a high standard of work at the gallery, but she was never one to purposely hurt someone's feelings. She may have even considered showing one piece had Brent's attitude been more positive. Not only did the art need to align with the values of the gallery, but the artists themselves needed to be approachable enough to socialize with the esteemed patrons. Brent was simply too rude, and his work was not

yet polished enough for Elizabeth to overlook his personality flaws.

Impatiently, Brent stood up. "What do you mean it's
not right for your gallery? Why, am I not rich enough for
you or something?"

Elizabeth remained calm. She had dealt with artist
temperaments for many years, and Brent was not going to
be the one to throw her off her game.

"Listen, Brent, if you like, I can try and connect you
with other spaces. I have many connections in the art
scene. I am sure there is a space that may want to show
your work," Elizabeth generously offered.

"No way, man, I don't need your charity." Brent then
turned to Samantha and snarled, "You said this was a sure
thing!"

Samantha panicked. "No, no, Brent. I never said that. I
said that Elizabeth would be happy to look at your work
and that I would put in a good word for you."

"Liar. You thought that promising a show would help
you get laid! Well, see if I answer your 3am phone calls
again, bitch." Brent grabbed his portfolio. "I am fucking
out of here." Brent stormed out of the office.

Samantha turned to Elizabeth, her face red with
embarrassment. "Oh my god, Elizabeth, I am so sorry
about that! I mean, I could tell he had a bit of a temper,
but I just thought that was his passionate, artistic side. Oy,
what a mess!" Samantha covered her face with her hands.

Elizabeth sighed. "Yes, it certainly is. What were you
thinking? Did you promise him a show here?"

Samantha shook her head, tears forming in her eyes.
"No, not exactly. It was just like I said. I thought *maybe* it
could be a fit but that he would need to meet you first."

Samantha ran her fingers through her hair and looked

up at the ceiling. "Yes, we *did* sleep together, *but* I saw that as a separate thing, you know? I really had no idea he would behave this way."

Elizabeth remained silent. She had worked with Samantha for over five years, and while the woman could be a bit of a man-eater, she was also excellent at her job. Elizabeth decided to show some mercy towards her mortified coworker.

"Listen, it's not a big deal. I know you didn't mean any harm to the business. But I am disappointed because I *really* want to showcase some new work and create some excitement. The last few years have seemed kind of...stale, in terms of the energy and the openings. I want to freshen up our offerings. New York has so much budding talent that it seems like a shame not to take advantage." Elizabeth leaned back in her chair and shook her head.

Samantha was silent for a moment. "Maybe we need to start looking in less obvious places?"

Elizabeth gave her a look. "By *other places* do you mean parties in Soho?"

Samantha chuckled self-consciously. "No, no. Trust me, I learned my lesson with that one! I mean, like, get out of our immediate circle, you know? I feel like we've hit a wall because we are constantly around the same kind of people."

Elizabeth nodded. "Interesting, yes. I think you may be right." She looked out the window, observing how the fall leaves danced away from the branches before cascading to the ground. *Fall. Autumn. September. School. Yes, that's it!*

Elizabeth slammed her hands down on the office table. "I've got it! School, classrooms! That's what we need to do; scout out more students and maybe even teachers."

Samantha perked up. "Oh, cool! That's a great idea, Elizabeth. But do you mean, like, high school prodigies or something? Are you considering private boarding schools? I mean, obviously, we want the best of the best and preferably talent with a proper upbringing."

Elizabeth shook her head. "No, that is where we are going wrong. Sam, you and I are becoming big-time snobs. The reason everything is becoming stale is because we're not brave enough to move outside our own privilege."

Samantha looked to the ground and chewed her lip. "Yeah, okay. I see what you mean. But this is the Amira Alder Gallery! Are we really going to find such gilded talent at like, a *community college*?"

Elizabeth replied sternly, "You do realize that Amira was my grandfather's sister and that she survived the holocaust. Given what she had to go through and the sacrifices she made to create a beautiful space of creativity, I'll bet she would be ashamed of the direction we have taken. Do you seriously think you are better than someone else because you went to a private women's college?"

Elizabeth continued, clapping her hands together. "Yes, we want quality work, but we need to be much more *inclusive* in our thinking. We need to provide *opportunities* and to extend our reach. That is what Amira would have wanted."

Samantha put her hands up, "Okay, okay. You're the boss; I can't argue with that. But where should we explore?"

Elizabeth stood up, feeling empowered and decisive with her shift in perception. "You know what? I am going to take this on myself. I think I know exactly where I want to start looking." Elizabeth watched as Samantha's face became alarmed.

"Don't worry; you will still be involved in the process as usual," she consoled her coworker. "But, Sam, I'm craving some inspiration myself, and I think I want to take on the task of finding a new artist to exhibit here. I think this will be good for me, as the director, and also good for the gallery."

Nervously, Samantha conceded, "Well, fine. Just let me know if you need anything."

Soothingly, Elizabeth replied, "Of course I will. I'll keep you posted on what happens." Inside, Elizabeth knew that she was taking a bit of a risk deviating from her usual channels and social circles. Still, in remembering Amira, she knew that this was the right decision.

3

I t was an early Tuesday evening when Ella approached the front doors of Chatsworth. She arrived at the school a bit early in hopes of sorting out some administration tasks before her class began. As she strolled down the hall, past the main reception desk, Ella heard a voice calling out from behind her.

"Ella! I have someone I would like to introduce to you." Ella turned to find her supervisor, Mrs. Smith, standing beside a tall, attractive woman with long dark hair.

"Oh, hello! Yes, of course." Ella walked towards the pair with a friendly smile.

Mrs. Smith made the introductions. "Ella, I would like you to meet Elizabeth Diamond. Elizabeth is the director of the Amira Alder Gallery."

The statuesque brunette gracefully extended her hand. "Hello, Ella, it's a pleasure to meet you. Mrs. Smith has told me so much about you."

Ella was shocked! Due to its exclusivity, she had only been to the gallery a few times and had never attended a private function. But since it was her dream to exhibit there, she was blown away to be meeting the director. She wondered to herself, *Why is she visiting a community college? What's going on?*

Ella tried to keep her cool while shaking Elizabeth's hand firmly. "Um, wow! It's a real honor to meet you, Mrs. Diamond. I am a big fan of the Amira Alder Gallery." Ella felt a swarm of butterflies flutter inside her tummy.

Elizabeth chuckled softly. "Oh, it's *Ms.* Diamond. I'm, well, I am not married." Elizabeth squared her shoulders. "How wonderful to hear that you enjoy the Gallery! I understand you're a teacher here at the college?"

Ella felt breathless. *Oh my god, this is like meeting a celebrity!* "Oh, I am so sorry! Um, yes. Yes, I am." Ella stammered while she cleared her throat. "I teach an intermediate acrylics painting class. It's pretty cool, you know? My students are great. Really creative!" Ella was so nervous that she felt at a loss for words, and she so badly wanted to make a good impression. But inside, she was screaming. *I want to show at your gallery!*

Curious, Elizabeth asked, "Did you happen to catch the Carson exhibit last month? Her acrylic collection is so rich and vibrant!"

Ella looked down and tucked a piece of red hair behind her head. "No, I didn't catch that, actually. I *wanted* to but, I-I think it was an exclusive show, right?" Gathering up her nerve at the last minute, she quickly added, "I paint in acrylics too."

Elizabeth nodded. "Is that so? Very interesting. You're right; it was a private show, but you make a good point. I'm looking to diversify the Gallery and make it a more inclusive space."

Mrs. Smith interjected. "That's actually why Ms.

Diamond is here." Turning to face Elizabeth, the college supervisor added, "Elizabeth would like to sit in on a few classes here, and I thought that your class, Ella, might be of interest to her."

Ella was both flattered and excited. "Oh, really? Wow, that's great. I would love to welcome you and to introduce you to my students." *Holy cow, I can't believe my luck! Elizabeth Diamond is going to be sitting in on my class!*

"That's right! I saw the class listed in the curriculum, and I thought it would be great to attend." Elizabeth checked her watch. "Is it starting soon?"

Ella replied, "We still have an hour, but I was going to prepare some notes while I waited. Would you like me to walk you down to the classroom now, and you can check out the space?"

Elizabeth looked pleased. "Why yes, that would be lovely, thank you."

As Ella's nerves settled down, she began to notice Elizabeth more closely. *Gosh, she is so attractive. Her blue eyes are so pale against her creamy skin. She looks like she could be a model.* "Cool, so the classroom is right this way. Do you need a coffee or anything before we start? There is a cafeteria on the bottom floor."

"Oh, I'm fine for now, but thanks so much," Elizabeth replied graciously. The two women strolled down the hallway, which Ella noted was becoming empty as the evening stretched on. Ella felt both special and small in the presence of such a prolific art figure. *Mmmm, she smells like that expensive perfume I like. What is it again? Oh yeah, Chanel Chance. How divine!*

Elizabeth spoke up, bringing Ella to attention. "So when did you begin teaching here?"

Ella turned to look at Elizabeth, who was probably five

inches taller than her. "When I finally graduated with my MA from Waterford, I spent the summer looking for a job and landed this part-time position. So I am still fairly new; it's only been a little over a month."

Elizabeth asked, "Do you like it? Do you see yourself exploring more teaching positions or something full-time?"

Ella shrugged her shoulders. She didn't want to come off as ungrateful for her community college job, but teaching was not her passion. However, since Elizabeth had already been in contact with Mrs. Smith, Ella didn't want to speak badly about her opportunity. Still, she tried to take advantage of the fact that she was in the presence of a representative from the gallery of her dreams. *Hmmm, how should I approach this?*

"Well, to be honest, I do love teaching this class, and the students are wonderful. And I know how lucky I am to have landed a job so quickly, especially in this economy." Elizabeth nodded her head with empathy. Ella paused before continuing, "But, actually, my real dream is to be a professional artist. I want to work and sell my art and, well, I am a little hesitant to say this, but..." Ella scrunched up her face, suddenly feeling shy.

Elizabeth grinned at her. "What? What is it?"

Ella kept her eyes on the ground while she felt her face flush red. "Um, it's always been my dream to exhibit at the Amira Alder Gallery." Ella then shook her head, feeling as though she should backtrack. "I know, I know. You probably get that all of the time. I mean, it's just a dream, you know?"

Elizabeth replied, "Well, Ella, we should always have our dreams. Dreams and goals are what keep us living and helps us to thrive. And while I can't make any promises, the gallery is always looking to showcase new talent, as many galleries are."

Ella asked, "How did you become involved as the director?"

Elizabeth smiled mischievously. "Well, if you want to know the truth, it was a combination of education and nepotism. I have an MBA and an MFA, and I have been around fine art my entire life. My great aunt is Amira Alder; she was my grandfather's sister."

Ella was surprised. She hadn't thought to connect the prestigious Alder name to Ms. Diamond. But now, it all made sense to Ella. Oh boy! She must be loaded!

"Wow, that's so interesting. I didn't realize that!" Ella kept her eyes on the numbered classroom doors as well as the turns down the corridor. "We just need to turn here, and it's number 205."

Elizabeth followed Ella's lead. "Yes, it's true. That is why I'm such a believer in aspirations. Amira was a Holocaust survivor, and I believe that it was her dreams and her visions that not only helped to keep her alive, but it's also what kept her strong when she came to the United States."

Ella bobbed her head. Elizabeth's story was giving her goosebumps. "That is so incredible! I can't imagine how proud you must be to represent the gallery."

Elizabeth put a delicate and manicured hand to her heart. "I truly am. I mean, sure, art galleries are a business, and one needs to have a mind for commerce, but at the same time, the gallery is part of my family history, and it's also where my passion lies."

Ella was fascinated by Elizabeth. Not only was she beautiful and successful, but she also seemed to have a creative and empathetic side. As someone who did not come from money, Ella had always assumed that wealthy businesswomen like Elizabeth were cold and snobby, but Elizabeth didn't seem to fit that archetype. Ella wished she could keep chatting with the art director, but they had now reached Ella's classroom.

Swinging the door open, Ella said, "Here we go, this where the acrylic painting magic happens."

Elizabeth followed behind Ella, glancing around the room. "Is there anywhere in particular that I should sit?"

Ella shrugged. "Not really; you can take a seat anywhere. Oh, and feel free to check out the paintings around the room. They belong to the students; many of them are works in progress." Ella approached her desk and put her jacket on the back of the chair. "Make yourself comfortable."

Elizabeth continued to investigate, circling the room's circumference, taking in the colorful canvases on display. "Mm, hmm. Yes, I see." While Ella prepared her notes for the class, she continued to observe Elizabeth from the corner of her eye. She was captivated by how gracefully Elizabeth moved, almost like a dancer. She looked like she could be a life drawing model.

As much as Elizabeth entranced Ella, she wanted to understand more about this mysterious and rather spontaneous visit. Ella couldn't shake the feeling that Elizabeth was brought into her classroom for a reason. Still, it wasn't as if Elizabeth sought out Ella specifically as a potential artist to exhibit at the gallery. Ella wanted to find out more.

As Ella settled into her chair at the same time that Elizabeth found a seat, she began, "So, I hope you don't mind me wondering, but like, is there anything in particular that you wanted to get from observing the class? Do you have a particular person in mind or...?"

Elizabeth replied, "My apologies. You're right; I didn't make myself too clear. So, I'm on the hunt for some... inspiration, shall we say." Elizabeth then brought her index fingers together, pointing up towards her face.

Elizabeth looked up towards the ceiling and added, "I feel like the gallery has become too...limited in its scope, and if I want to bring in new faces and continue to generate interest, I need to look beyond my comfort zone. So I thought I would explore what else is out there, in terms of emerging artists and maybe in spaces I haven't yet considered."

Ella furrowed her brow and gave Elizabeth a wry smile. In her lightest tone, Ella replied, "Oh, I see. So you're, like, slumming it a bit at a community college?" She punctuated her comment with a soft laugh so as not to offend the art director.

Elizabeth laughed out loud. "Well, I haven't thought to word it that way, but I don't know, maybe you're right? I can understand how that may have come off wrong. But the Amira Alder Gallery has been known to be a bit stuffy, and I want to breathe new life into it."

Immediately, Ella felt bad. "No, no. I'm sorry, I was just kidding. Honestly, I think it's great that you're here. As I said before, exhibiting at the Gallery was...well, it *is* my dream as I'm sure it's a dream for so many others. So we are delighted to have you here, Ms. Diamond," Ella said with sincerity.

Suddenly, a few students started entering the class-room as Ella looked at the large clock on the wall. "Oh, right on time!" As bodies began to assume their seats, Ella announced, "Good evening, everyone. I am excited to introduce a special guest who will be observing our class. Please say hello to Ms. Diamond, the art director for the Amira Alder Gallery."

Elizabeth stood up, and the students addressed her with welcoming smiles and a few salutations. Ella tried to keep her mindset professional, but she couldn't stop looking at Elizabeth.

4

Elizabeth noticed the time and found herself feeling disappointed that Ella's classes were almost over. Over the past two hours, Elizabeth found herself mesmerized by Ella's ability to explain technique and color theory to her students. While Elizabeth's primary intention in visiting the college was to discover emerging art talent by students, her gaze seemed to rest on Ella's own painting demonstrations. Elizabeth had to keep reminding herself to keep an open mind and to shift her perspective. But in her heart, she knew what truly caught her eye; Ella had all of her attention.

Elizabeth was intrigued to find out more about Ella; how she began her artistic journey, her education, and what inspired her. When they had first started talking in the hallway on the way to class, Elizabeth could tell that Ella was eager to show at the Amira Alder Gallery, and Elizabeth didn't want to give a false sense of hope or make empty promises; she needed to keep her tone light and noncommittal for the sake of professionalism. But in being in Ella's presence and witnessing Ella's strength as an instructor and her command of the acrylic medium had inspired a spark within Elizabeth. She craved to learn more.

"Before I hand back your test results from the other night, I wanted to ask Ms. Diamond if she wanted to address the class or offer any information about the wonderful and well-known Amira Alder Gallery. Care to share a few words, Ms. Diamond?"

Elizabeth was broken out of her reverie upon hearing her name. She was not often caught off guard, but she couldn't help being distracted by Ella's wild red hair with the shaved sides. *How interesting*, she thought. *So very bohemian chic—punk meets Picasso! I can't only imagine what Mamelah would say if I shaved my hair like that! Gosh, I wish I had the nerve to be so bold!*

Elizabeth snapped back to reality and smiled brightly. "Oh, well, thank you so much, Ms. Ryan, for allowing me to sit in tonight." Elizabeth stood and looked around the room, addressing each of the faces in the classroom.

"So, as you know, I am the director of the Amira Alder Gallery, and I am so proud to announce that as we approach a new year, it is my hope to welcome new faces and new works of art to grace our walls." Elizabeth pointed to Ella. "It was such a pleasure to be welcomed by Ms. Ryan and Mrs. Smith tonight, and over the next few weeks, I will be observing different classes and hopefully speaking to some of you."

Ella clapped her hands together excitedly and addressed the room. "Very exciting news! Ms. Diamond, we look forward to having you grace our class. If you have any hand-outs about the gallery, feel free to leave them on my desk."

Elizabeth observed Ella as she sashayed throughout

the room; her fiery red locks trailing like flames as she returned marked test papers to her students. "For the most part, everyone has done very well on the test! When you receive your test, I'd recommend that you review my comments and if you have any questions, let me know."

The restless students murmured as each one received their test paper. Ella then looked up at the clock and announced, "Cool! It looks like you are free to go for the night. Again, let's give a big thanks to our special guest, Ms. Diamond."

The seated bodies stood up and waved to Elizabeth as they filed out. Elizabeth pulled out some pamphlets and some business cards and handed out a few marketing materials to interested students. As the last person filed out of the classroom, Ella approached Elizabeth.

"Hey, thanks so much for sitting in and for sharing information about the gallery." Ella looked at the stack of pamphlets. "Could I have one of those?"

Elizabeth grinned. "Yes, of course! And you are welcome; I thought that you were a bright and lively teacher." Elizabeth gave Ella a sideways look. "You obviously know your stuff."

Ella appeared to blush slightly, which Elizabeth found quite endearing. "You really think so? Wow, I appreciate the compliment."

Elizabeth nodded emphatically. "Oh, yes, absolutely. I would love to learn more about you and your journey; what your education was like, how you developed your technique." Elizabeth then added, "There is obviously a lot of talent found in this classroom, and I am sure, within the entire college as well."

Ella's green eyes grew wide with excitement. "Oh my goddess, it would be an honor to chat more with you! I'm very interested in learning more about you as well and like, what the gallery is looking for. I think this could be a great prospect for my students."

Elizabeth thought, *It could be an excellent opportunity for you as well, Ella. We shall see!* But she only replied, "Yes, absolutely." As Elizabeth packed her purse with the remaining materials, she had an idea. "Would you like to get together for a coffee or a drink sometime soon and chat?"

Ella looked up as she struggled into her faux leather jacket. Beaming, she replied, "Sure that would be great! Um, what is your schedule generally like? I'm assuming that you're usually pretty busy, huh?"

Elizabeth shrugged and smiled. "Most of my weekday evenings are free, except for Friday evenings when I have Shabbat dinner with my mother. What nights do you teach again?"

Ella replied, "I teach here on Tuesdays and Thursdays. I also have a part-time job bartending, usually on Wednesdays and Sunday nights. Sometimes other nights, too, if I can pick up an extra shift here and there."

The women gathered their belongings and headed towards the exit. Elizabeth asked, "Oh, really? Where do you bartend?"

Ella gave Elizabeth a sideways grin and raised an eyebrow. "Have you heard of La Crème? It's in the West Village."

A slow smile crept across Elizabeth's face. She certainly knew of La Crème. It was a well-known lesbian bar that had been a mainstay in the Village for close to thirty-five years. Before life had gotten serious and her career at the gallery took off, Elizabeth had spent many an evening seducing (and being seduced!) at La Crème. Still, she wasn't sure how much she should reveal to this prospective connection.

Aside from close friends within her inner circle, Elizabeth was still a bit conservative regarding her sexual orientation. Being a part of the wealthy Upper West Side arts scene had its privileges. Still, it also had its drawbacks, namely overly judgmental behavior and vicious gossip by influential people who had the power to make or break social status.

Still, as she looked at Ella and the lovely curve of her lips, Elizabeth knew she wanted to speak openly.

"Yes, I know of La Crème," Elizabeth chuckled. "That used to be one of my favorite hangouts, in fact. But that was many, many years ago."

Ella allowed Elizabeth to pass through the doorframe while she shut off the nights in the classroom. Locking the door behind her, Ella turned to look at Elizabeth with surprise. "*Really?* You used to hang out at La Crème?"

Elizabeth laughed out loud. "Don't be so shocked! Sure, I might look like a stuffy and old, but trust me, I *do* know how to have a good time!" Her intense blue eyes fixed on Ella's. She began to fasten the buttons on her coat. "Well, at least I did in my twenties and early thirties. But that was a long time ago."

Ella stopped to shake her head, holding up her hands. "Okay, my apologies if this is too personal, but how old are you now. You don't look at all like your early thirties were a long time ago?"

Elizabeth grinned proudly. "I don't mind your curiosity at all, in fact, it is refreshing. The world I live in, nobody would ever ask my age. I'm forty-two, and I am not one bit sad about it. Trust me; life truly begins at forty."

Ella dropped her jaw. "Wow! I would never have

guessed. You look...I mean, I-I *never* would have guessed that you were in your forties." Ella looked perplexed. "And you are also...a *lesbian?* I mean, I am as well. I'm just asking because you are obviously familiar with Le Crème, and that is no place for straight girls!"

Elizabeth smiled at Ella's forwardness. Ella was indeed refreshing. "Yes, yes, I am. It's not exactly public knowledge as far as the gallery is concerned, but you are correct." Elizabeth surprised herself with her openness, but at the same time, it was rather thrilling to share parts of her personal life with Ella.

Ella nodded as she processed this information. "Well, okay! So you, the famous *Ms.* Diamond of the Amira Alder Gallery, are actually this wild, cougar lesbian. I have to say, I am pretty impressed. I would never have thought!"

Elizabeth laughed loudly, "Wild cougar lesbian?" Now that is something I have never been called before. What makes you think I have a thing for younger women?" Elizabeth said as her gaze trailed over Ella's body.

Ella's face went bright red... "Oh god, I didn't mean..."

Elizabeth continued teasing, "Are high femme gallery directors not allowed to be wild cougar lesbians? All lesbians are supposed to look like you, with a shaved head and a bunch of tattoos? Do you have something against a tailored coat and a Burberry scarf?"

Ella chuckled and ran a hand through her hair, rubbing the shaved sides. "Okay, you got me. I guess I thought that, you know, coming from such a privileged background, that you might be kind of, I don't know...." Ella's voice trailed off.

Elizabeth waved her hand, playfully. "I'm just teasing, Ella. Don't worry, I know what you mean, and you know

what? You aren't entirely wrong. There is a lot of judgment and protocol in my world, so it's easier to fly under
the radar sometimes."

Ella shrugged. "Sure, that makes sense. There's been a
lot of judgment in my life, too."

Elizabeth nodded. "I'm sure there has. So do you enjoy
bartending? I'm sure the crowd at La Crème must be a lot
of fun, yes."

Ella replied, "Yeah, it's a lot of fun, for the most part. I
mean, it's not exactly where I want to spend the rest of my
life, but it pays the bills. And you're right; the scenery is
pretty fun. Lots of eye candy!" Ella nudged Elizabeth
playfully.

"Sounds like nothing has changed since the '90s. Well,
except for the haircuts, right?" Elizabeth played along.

"You have a point there!" Ella guided Elizabeth
towards the central doorway of the college. The women
stopped to face one another. "So here we are. Where are
you heading now?" Ella asked.

Elizabeth hemmed and hawed. She didn't have any
plans following the class, but she knew she wanted to
enjoy the rest of the evening. It was slowly becoming
dusk, but the early fall weather was still balmy. Whenever
she had the chance, she always enjoyed a good stroll
through the city.

Elizabeth checked her watch. "Well, it's only 9:30 pm,
and I think I want to get some fresh air, so I was going to
walk for a bit before catching a cab. What are you up to?"

Ella looked towards the door before answering. "Um,
well, I didn't have any definite plans, probably just head
home." Ella glanced at Elizabeth and bit her lip before
asking, "Do you...do you think I could maybe walk with

you for a bit? Maybe...maybe we could grab a quick drink somewhere? Like you said, it *is* early."

Elizabeth smiled. "That sounds lovely. Sure, let's do it!"

Ella grinned mischievously. "Cool! Well, if you are game, I know the perfect place. It's only about a thirty-minute walk from here."

Elizabeth bowed graciously. "I trust you, the artist bartender, to show me the coolest spot, Ella. Lead the way!"

Ella could not believe her luck! Here she was, strolling under the New York City sky with Elizabeth Diamond, a gorgeous, intelligent, and powerful woman who also happened to be a lesbian! She tried her best to play it cool, but she felt like jumping out of her body with excitement. She wanted desperately to get a chance to exhibit at the gallery, but the more time she spent with Elizabeth and looked at her exquisite face, the more she realised that Elizabeth did things to her. Desire pooled low in her stomach.

There was something so fascinating about Elizabeth; her grace, wisdom, and beauty was so enchanting.

Thus far, Ella was able to compartmentalize her attractions in order to attain her goals. She knew where she wanted to be, as far as her career, and in the past, Ella had not let fleeting romantic interludes cloud her vision. Ella sometimes wondered how she could be so calculating, but she chalked it up to living in a fast-paced city where *everyone* had a dream. *Eat or be eaten, Ella; that's* what she used to tell herself. But now, as she found herself standing at the crossroads of a potentially huge opportunity, she felt conflicted in a way that she couldn't understand.

As Ella and Elizabeth walked briskly down the street, a slight breeze was stirring around them. Ella shivered slightly as she dug her bare hands into her thin jacket. Her hair whipped around her face as she struggled to catch the flyaway strands.

"Wow, the wind is sure picking up. Summer is definitely coming to an end," Ella remarked. "But don't worry, the place I wanted to take you isn't too much further from here."

Elizabeth replied cheerfully as she brought the lapels of her coat closer to her face. "Oh, I don't mind too much. Honestly, I love being outside, walking around the city. When I was a little girl, I loved watching the people scurry around the street like ants, on their way to work or wherever they were headed." She turned to Ella, "I always told myself that one day, I would be a woman with places to go; I wanted to be part of that energy."

Ella chuckled, "Well, you definitely add to the energy of the city, especially the way you support the arts community. And look at us now, two little ants running from class to a nearby bar!" Ella noticed a left turn coming up. "Oh, the place is just right down here. Come on."

Ella guided Elizabeth down a quiet side street towards a large, grey building. The flashing retro neon sign read *Shakers*. This was Ella's favorite dive bar. While it was sad to see so many independent businesses be bought and sold in exchange for more polished-looking franchises, Shakers maintained its gritty sense of cool. It wasn't fancy, and the service left something to be desired, but to Ella, this bar felt like a place where she could decompress and release the day's stressors. She had even become chummy with some of the regulars.

If fancy Elizabeth can hang here, then she is definitely more than meets the eye. Still, in the back of her mind, she was concerned that Elizabeth might turn up her nose. *I guess we shall see!*

Ella pulled back the door handle as a small set of chimes signaled their entrance. Ella always thought that the door chimes were funny to have at a bar instead of a retail shop. But she had heard a rumor that, way back in the day, Shakers used to be a drop off spot for drugs and other illegal activities, run by the mob. Apparently, the chimes were a way to make the previous owner aware of when bodies were entering the establishment.

Ella never knew if that was actually true, and if so, it was long before her time. Still, it was fun to think about. In Ella's opinion, it gave the place character.

Ella led the way, and the floor seemed to creak below them as they approached the near-empty bar. At the far end, Ella noticed a gentleman slumped over in his chair. It appeared as though he was asleep, but Ella knew he was probably passed out on alcohol. While this was not an uncommon sight at Shakers, Ella glanced at Elizabeth, trying to read her face. But Elizabeth kept a neutral expression.

Ella bit her lip and cringed. "I know it's not the nicest place. If La Crème was closer, we could have gone there. It's probably not what you are accustomed to, right?" Suddenly feeling self-conscious, Ella asked, "I mean, do you want to go somewhere else? It's not too late to take a cab to the West Village."

Following Ella, Elizabeth grabbed a barstool and plunked herself down. She shook her head, "No, no. This is *fine*, Ella! Oh, my goddess, please don't worry. I know I look like an over privileged princess but trust me, I am no shrinking violet. I can handle sitting in a regular bar."

Ella smiled, "Honestly, I am not even sure exactly why I like it here so much. I think it's because it's completely void of pretense. The surroundings help my mind to unravel."

Elizabeth bobbed her head in agreement just as a burly bartender approached the seated women. "Hey, ladies. What'll it be?" he asked in a gruff voice.

Ella replied, "Jameson, neat." She turned to Elizabeth. "What do you want?"

Elizabeth answered, "I'll have whatever she is having. In fact, make mine a double."

Ella was impressed. Not only was Elizabeth cool enough to hang at a dive bar, but she could also drink. *Well, okay then!* Not to be outdone, Ella piped up, "Actually, I'll have a double too."

The bartender gave a short nod and pulled out two rock glasses. The women watched as he free poured a generous amount of liquor into each glass. It was obvious that the amount was a bit more than just two shots. Ella grinned and whispered to Elizabeth, "That's the *other* reason I like this place!"

The bartender slammed the drinks on the bar top. Ella watched as Elizabeth began to open her purse and stopped her. "No, no. Please, I've got this."

Elizabeth asked, "Are you sure? Well, if we get there, I'll get the next round."

Ella looked shocked. "Whoa, you are feeling brave! But okay, sure. Deal."

Elizabeth laughed. "Well, not necessarily. I'm just

enjoying the company, and I'm not really in a rush to be anywhere." Elizabeth clinked Ella's glass, "L'chaim!"

"Sláinte!" Ella replied back, thinking of how her father would toast to drinks when she was a little girl.

"So you're Irish, yes?" Elizabeth asked, taking a sip of the amber-colored liquid.

"Does the red hair give it away?" Ella asked.

Elizabeth ran her fingers lightly through Ella's wild red hair. A heated shiver ran through Ella.

"You definitely have the look of a wild irish girl. I could imagine you in the grassy hills of ireland bareback on a wild horse."

"Yup, both of my parents are Irish. They live in Queens," Ella replied, savoring the warmth of the alcohol as it coated her throat. "I moved away to attend the Waterford Institute, and honestly, I never really looked back. I mean, I *do* visit on holidays and stuff, but we aren't close, and they definitely disapprove of me being gay."

Elizabeth looked empathic. "Sure, I can understand. My parents were very hush-hush about the whole thing until my father passed away." Elizabeth swirled the whiskey in her glass while Ella rested her gaze on Elizabeth's delicate hands. Ella's mind began to wander. *Her fingers are so lovely, and her nails are so perfect. I wonder what it would feel like to be touched by them?*

Elizabeth continued, "But now that's it just my mother and I, we have become closer." She laughed and rolled her eyes as she untied her ponytail, letting her hair cascade around her face. "In fact, she is bugging me to settle down with a 'nice Jewish girl,'" Elizabeth said, making air quotes with her hands.

"Oh, so you're single?" Ella asked surprisingly, taking

another gulp of her drink. Her body began to tingle, and she felt her shoulders start to relax.

"Yup, I sure am!" Elizabeth tilted her head and knocked back the remainder of the whiskey. "I am such a workaholic that it's hard to find time to date. I mean, I'd love to be in a relationship, but it needs to be with the right woman. What about you? Are you single?"

Ella positioned her body so that she could face Elizabeth head-on. "Yeah, me too. My schedule isn't so hectic that I can't date, but my focus is on my art. I want to channel all of my desire and energy into my pieces." Ella followed suit and finished her drink. Turning to Elizabeth, she said, "Are we doing another round?"

Elizabeth grinned. "Sure, let's!" She motioned towards the bartender, who lumbered over. "Another round, same as before, please." The bartender answered, "Okay, lady. Coming up."

Ella took a small stretch in her chair, loosening up. She was secretly glad that Elizabeth wanted another drink. She was enjoying her time so much, and she didn't want the night to end yet.

As the bartender placed two more glasses in front of them, Elizabeth peered into Ella's eyes. She put a hand confidently on Ella's thigh. "So tell me, what inspires you, Ella?"

Ella felt electrified by Elizabeth's touch. *Is this really happening right now?* She felt both relaxed and excited, being so close to Elizabeth. Ella wanted to touch Elizabeth too. "Um, well, I am inspired by the elements that make us human. Moments of pure bliss, loss, grief, anger, *lust...*" Ella trailed off suggestively. She felt herself starting to flirt. Fortified by liquid courage, Ella placed her hand on the outer part of Elizabeth's thigh.

"Mm, hmm, I see." Elizabeth smiled and looked down coyly. Ella couldn't tell if Elizabeth was shy or if she was plotting something else. Either way, Ella didn't care. There was a heat building between them that felt so natural and fluid, and Ella was curious to see where that would go.

Suddenly, there was an awkward silence as the women realized that they had become closer in their chairs and were touching each other. To break the moment, both of them turned to their drinks, taking a healthy sip.

While staring straight ahead, Elizabeth said softly, "Um, I should go. It-it *is* getting late. I'll settle up here."

Disappointment clouded over Ella. The night was only getting started! Still, she didn't want to pout. Above all, Ella wanted to leave a good impression on Elizabeth. In a faux chipper voice, she replied, "Yeah, sure! No worries, let's go."

Elizabeth paid for the last round, and the women gathered their jackets. The bartender called out, "Bye, ladies, thanks!"

Ella called over her shoulder, "Thanks, man!" She followed Elizabeth out the door.

Outside, the women faced another under the night air, both seeming uncertain of what to do next. Ella broke the tension. "I'll wait with you until you catch a cab. But we should probably walk to the main street."

Elizabeth asked, "Do you want to share a ride with me?"

Yes, I do! Ella's subconscious screamed. Casually, she replied, "Oh, it's fine. I'm only a twenty-minute walk from here. I just want to make sure that you get into a cab safely."

Elizabeth grinned. "That's sweet of you, Ella, thank you." The pair headed towards the busy street in search of a passing taxi. Standing on the sidewalk, Elizabeth turned to face Ella.

"I had a lot of fun tonight, more than I thought I would, actually." Elizabeth tucked a piece of dark hair behind her ear and suddenly looked shy. "Um, I'm sorry about...about *back there.* I-I wanted to be professional, you know? I came to the college for a reason, and I, well, I guess I wasn't expecting to find someone as interesting as you."

Elizabeth looked up and bit her lip. "You seem like a remarkable woman, Ella. I am interested to learn more about you." She added cautiously, "Would that be okay?"

Ella felt a thrill surge through her body. *Oh my god? Are you kidding me? Is Elizabeth Diamond hitting on me?* Surprised yet elated, Ella replied, "Yes, it's absolutely okay. I think you are pretty remarkable too."

Elizabeth beamed. "Really? You don't think I crossed any lines back there? Like, at the bar?"

Ella shook her head, vehemently. "Not at all. I didn't want to leave just yet." Feeling confident and brave, Ella decided to put herself out there. "Elizabeth, can I kiss you?"

Wordlessly, Elizabeth gave an affirmative nod. She bent over to meet Ella's mouth. Ella melted against the warm softness of Elizabeth's lips. They kissed as hot breath formed between them as Elizabeth cupped her hands around Ella's small face. Ella did not want the kiss to end; she felt weightless, standing on the street corner, as though she was levitating mid-air.

As they kissed, cabs drove by, almost splashing filthy water on their legs. Gently, Elizabeth broke away and proceeded to flag a cab. "We should do this again sometime. Can I have your number?" A taxi pulled up to the side of the street.

"Sure," Ella replied as she watched Elizabeth begin to bend her body into the back of the cab. Suddenly, she could not resist her impulse to be with Elizabeth. "Why don't I get into the cab and give it to you?" Ella asked with a naughty twinkle in her eye.

Elizabeth looked shocked but pleased. She scooted over in her seat to make room for Ella. Ella climbed in as Elizabeth directed the driver. "Central Park; Hudson Condo Building. We are only making one stop."

6

—————

Elizabeth found herself emerging out of a dream where she was soaring like a bird across a Van Gogh vanilla-colored sky. As her body caught up with her mind, she felt the material from bedsheets that had twisted around her naked body during her slumber. Even behind her closed eyes, Elizabeth knew it was light outside, although she had no idea what time it was. Elizabeth fluttered her lashes, and a smattering of memories formed in her head like a collage. The reality of the morning was setting in, and she thought to herself as she came to life, *Oh boy, what happened last night?*

Taking a deep inhale, she stretched her body like a cat and rolled over. *Mmm, oh, wow! How long have I been asleep?* To her surprise, she found Ella perched over her, with a small sketchbook in hand.

"Good morning!" Ella greeted her, wearing a lovely open smile and nothing more. The only coverings on her body were an extensive collection of intricate and beautifully drawn tattoos. "Do you know how lovely you look when you are sleeping?"

Elizabeth laughed and put a hand to her temple. She was still shaking the cobwebs from her head and piecing together the events from the night before. The taxi had whisked Elizabeth and Ella away, as they kissed passionately in the back seat, throwing caution to the wind. Laughing, they had entered Elizabeth's condo, hand in hand, and rode to the 50th floor.

The women took advantage of the fact that they were alone in the elevator, pressing their bodies together in lustful heat. Elizabeth remembered a whirlwind of hands seeking warm flesh underneath clothing and legs scissoring together. That is, until the door dinged open. Elizabeth was aware that the luxury building was constantly being monitored, so with a finger poised to her lips, Elizabeth and Ella snuck quietly into Elizabeth's condo.

Once inside, the twosome settled in, and Elizabeth poured both her and Ella a nightcap of her favorite brandy. Elizabeth figured why not? They were enjoying such a nice whiskey buzz, which seemed to melt their edges as they continued to caress and kiss. While this seemed like a great idea, more alcohol consumption actually had the opposite effect, putting them both into a sleepy haze. After a short tour around Elizabeth's place, the women retired to the oversize couch, allowing their limbs to drape languidly over one another.

Elizabeth briefly recalled Ella talking about her family, the struggles, and the criticism she faced about wanting to study at the Waterford Institute. And while Elizabeth knew that they came from different economic backgrounds, they shared the fundamental similarity of feeling judged and dismissed for embracing their sexual orientation.

As she continued to sip her brandy, Elizabeth listened intently to Ella's art school tales and her Sapphic conquests. Elizabeth felt both turned on but also slightly cautious. She was also quite aware of how drunk she was starting to feel and how late it was becoming. It was quite out of character for Elizabeth to allow herself to become this out of control, this careless about time, but she chalked it up to the fact that both the alcohol and Ella were so intoxicating. Besides, she told herself, when was the last time you just let yourself go enough to enjoy the moment; you earned this!

But as soon as Elizabeth noticed the time on the microwave, she knew it was time for them to crash. "Ella, it's after 2:00 am. You are welcome to sleep here if you want," Elizabeth offered. She wanted more time with Ella, more chances to explore their sensuality and their desire for one another but not like this. Her days of messy, late-night hook-ups were over, and she had too much respect for Ella (and her gallery project) to become intimate at this very moment.

Elizabeth believed in savoring time with lovers, enjoying the tease and the slow burn of a passionate build-up. She knew that she wanted Ella, but she was willing to wait until they were both more present in their bodies.

ELIZABETH CLEARED her throat and wiped the sleep from her eyes. "How long have you been awake?"

Ella replied, "Oh, I don't know, maybe a few hours?" She put her pen down. "I awoke feeling restless and couldn't get back to sleep, so I decided to stay up."

Elizabeth gasped. "Oh, I hope I didn't snore or anything!"

Ella giggled. "No, you were fine. I didn't hear a thing. You were pretty tipsy last night, and I figured you must have just passed right out." Ella handed Elizabeth the sketchbook. "Do you wanna see? I keep a sketchbook on me at all times. Whenever I feel inspired, and I get the chance, I draw."

Elizabeth sat up and brushed the long dark hair out of her face. She took the book from Ella and looked at the drawing. Her eyes widened with surprise. "Oh, Ella! This is beautiful. Your lines and shading are stunning. It's a lovely sketch." Elizabeth beamed. "I feel so flattered. No one has ever drawn me before."

Ella leaned in closer to Elizabeth and said softly, "No, it's beautiful because it's you. The lines of your face and your body are so inspiring to me." Ella ran her hand lightly down Elizabeth's cheek, over her collarbone, softly brushing her breast and down over her stomach. "You have never had someone draw you before? Really?"

"Why do you say that?" Elizabeth asked.

"Well, I mean, you're the head of a fancy gallery, so I just assumed that you must have hooked up with many artists. You are so beautiful. All I want to do is capture that in every way." Ella exclaimed.

Elizabeth took Ella's hand and looked deep into her eyes. "Listen, Ella. Um, I am honestly not the type of woman to get drunk and take advantage of artists for my personal use. I meant every word I said about how much I want to diversify the content at the gallery. And I was also serious about you having an incredible talent."

Elizabeth let out a deep sigh, scrunching the bedsheets with her hands. "There is something really...

remarkable about you, and I may have gotten a little carried away last night. But I am a consummate professional, and I take my reputation and the gallery's reputation very seriously. I don't want you to assume that I do this kind of thing often."

Elizabeth waved her hands helplessly around the room. Sheepishly, with a small smile, she added, "And just so you know, my last girlfriend was an accountant, not an artist."

Ella tilted her head and looked amused. "It sounds like you're feeling guilty for having a night out. Is that what it is? Worried that someone in your inner circle is going to call you out for having some fun?" Ella teased Elizabeth. "I mean, if that's what being in your forties is all about, then I plan to never grow up!"

Elizabeth wacked Ella gently with a soft, down pillow. "Oh, stop! Listen, I know you're only in your twenties, but just you wait. You don't know everything!" Elizabeth playfully retorted.

"I'm actually nearly twenty-eight," Ella said, in a faux-haughty voice, to which Elizabeth chortled. Ella's tone became gentler. "I didn't think that you were trying to take advantage of me or anything. I'm a big girl, and I get that business is business. I just think that we have a hot connection, so why can't we just explore it without needing to make it into a big deal?"

Elizabeth thoughtfully bit her lip. She knew that Ella had a point. Regardless of the reason that brought them together, they did share an undeniable attraction to one another. As an older woman in a power position, Elizabeth needed to consider the power imbalance and the potential repercussions. In fact, she had just chastised Samantha for doing the same thing! Here she was chasing some hot young thing and using her position and power to her advantage. But she was curious to explore things with Ella, just as she wanted to learn more about Ella's artistic gift. Ella was right; why couldn't these two factors co-exist parallel to one another?

"I think I am more cautious at this age than I was at yours. But I still want to live, and last night I felt the most free than I had in a while. It was so nice just to spend time, you know?" Elizabeth grinned at Ella.

Ella looked down at Elizabeth and rested her hands on either side of Elizabeth's shoulders. Elizabeth felt Ella's soft strands of hair tickle her collarbone. Ella paused to look into Elizabeth's eyes; Elizabeth shivered with delight as she held Ella's emerald gaze. Wordlessly, Ella leaned in closer and kissed Elizabeth softy, letting her lips linger.

"Is this okay?" Ella asked. Elizabeth nodded. Ella kissed Elizabeth again, and this time, Elizabeth did not hold back. As the morning sun shone through her bedroom window, Elizabeth felt an intense fire burn from within her body. The clock on her nightstand read 10:07 am. *Okay, that's not so bad. I don't have a meeting until two this afternoon. I need Ella. I want her.*

Elizabeth pulled Ella's tiny frame closer so that she could feel the weight of Ella's warm, naked body against her own. As they continued to kiss, their tongues seeking out one another's, Elizabeth ran her fingers down Ella's back, tracing down the sides of her bony spine. Elizabeth heard Ella hum softly against her as she planted soft kisses against Ella's neck and the tips of her shoulders.

Ella whispered into Elizabeth's ear, "Open your legs," as Ella ran her hands inside the edges of Elizabeth's thighs. Elizabeth stretched out on her back and obeyed, allowing Ella to slide herself lower down until Ella's face was nestled between Elizabeth's legs. Through lowered eyelids, she watched as Ella traced her fingers along the outside of Elizabeth's labia. Elizabeth bit her lip and sighed, she couldn't remember the last time she was this turned on.

Ella coyly looked up as she brought a finger to her lips, licking the tip with her tongue. "I love to see your wetness glisten as I play with you. If I could, I'd paint a picture, using your juices."

Elizabeth laughed. "Now that, I would love to see." Throwing her head back with abandon, she urged, "Please don't stop."

Ella grinned in response as she moved back into position. Elizabeth closed her eyes and felt Ella's tongue graze the tip of her clit in small, soft licks. The sensations sent waves of pleasure throughout Elizabeth's body, reaching towards the ends of her limbs. As Ella lapped at her pussy, Elizabeth's breath quickened, and her body started to move to the rhythm of Ella's strokes. Subconsciously, Elizabeth gripped Ella's head with her hands and ground her pelvis harder against Ella's mouth.

"Cum for me," Ella grunted in a muffled voice as Elizabeth began to moan, her muscles becoming tighter and tenser as an erotic release began to build. As she continued to rock her body in time with the friction, a flash of ecstasy burst inside of Elizabeth like a volcano.

"Oh my god, oh my god! Ella, Ella!" Elizabeth cried out. For a split second, Elizabeth froze as her body flushed red with an intense orgasm. Then, she melted against the softness of the sheets. Elizabeth's mind was reeling. *Wow, it's been a long time since someone made me feel like that!*

Elizabeth caught her breath as strands of hair stuck to her sweaty face. Ella popped her head up and brushed her own hair out of the way. "God, you are so hot. And you taste so good!"

Elizabeth laughed. "Yeah, it's been a while!" Ella looked intrigued. "Oh, really?"

Elizabeth hemmed and hawed, "Maybe a few months?" Ella shook her head with surprise. "Wow, I don't think I could ever hold out for that long."

Elizabeth propped herself on her shoulder as Ella moved to lay beside Elizabeth. "Why, when was the last time you were with someone?" Ella tilted her head, thoughtfully. "Um, maybe three weeks ago? It was just a casual encounter with someone I had met after my shift at La Crème."

Elizabeth wasn't sure why, but for some reason, that information made her bristle a bit. She didn't want her mind to go there, but Elizabeth hoped that this free-spirited nymph wasn't using her. Not wanting to ruin the moment, Elizabeth dismissed the thought from her brain. Instead, she remarked, "Oh, to be young and wild! I remember many exciting moments there myself—especially in the bathrooms!"

Ella replied excitedly, "Right? They have the nicest bathrooms. I swear, they were created exclusively for dyking out."

"Speaking of which...," Elizabeth said seductively, as she turned towards Ella, mounting her. Ella remained on her back, allowing Elizabeth to take control. "I'm sure you know how much we fancy businesswomen like to be in control."

Ella purred, "So I have heard! Don't let me stand in your way."

Elizabeth moved on top of Ella and gently parted her legs so that she could move in between Ella's thighs. Ella kept eye contact while Elizabeth ran her fingers down Ella's naked torso. Elizabeth delighted in seeing Ella's nipples harden at Elizabeth's touch, budding like tiny berries. She bent over and gave each nipple a soft suck. Ella giggled and moaned, "Hmmm, I like that. My nipples are so sensitive!"

Elizabeth was captivated by Ella's beauty and her gorgeous tattoos. She noticed goosebumps form on the surface of Ella's creamy skin as she continued to caress her. Elizabeth gazed upon the tuft of strawberry blond fuzz that decorated Ella's pubic bone. Elizabeth stroked the trimmed bush, feeling the fine and silky texture between her fingers.

"I like that you have a bit of hair here. It's so cute and pretty," Elizabeth remarked.

"I'm so glad that you didn't say how well *the curtains match the carpet*. That is my absolute pet peeve!" Ella said, rolling her eyes in jest.

Elizabeth asked with a laugh. "Has a woman actually said that to you before?"

Ella nodded her head against the pillow. "Oh, it's happened alright! I think it is the red thing. Like red pubic hair is some kind of total novelty"

Elizabeth smiled and looked down. "Well, trust me, I would never use such corny lines." She continued to caress Ella, planting kisses where her deft fingers trailed off. She parted Ella's legs and began to stroke Ella's clit, very gently. She kept looking up towards Ella to gauge her reaction. Upon hearing Ella's sigh and feeling a twitch in her body, Elizabeth applied more pressure, noticing how Ella's vulva began to moisten with desire.

Ella moaned and her back arched. Elizabeth inserted two fingers inside Ella's pussy, feeling the tight warmth encase around her digits. Ella moaned with delight, "Mmmm, yeah. I love this." Her breathing quickened. "Fuck me harder. Please." Ella's eyes were glazed.

Elizabeth began to thrust in and out of Ella. As Ella started to buck against Elizabeth's hand, waiting more, Elizabeth pushed deeper and faster, taking cues from Ella's expressions of pleasure. Elizabeth added a third finger, curling her hand into a cup-like shape with her thumb moving against Ella's clit. In and out, Elizabeth continued to fuck Ella until suddenly, Elizabeth felt a tightness around her hand, followed by a bellow from Ella.

"Oh yeah, oh yeah...yes, yes, YES!" Ella cried out with ecstasy, cumming hard against Elizabeth's hand. Elizabeth felt the pressure of Ella's explosive orgasm, followed by a relaxing of the muscles. She carefully slid her fingers out of Ella, loving how they dripped with Ella's wetness.

Ella sat up and moved forward to kiss Elizabeth passionately. Their mouths melted against one another in post-coitus bliss. Ella whispered as she moved away from Elizabeth's lips, "You are so sexy, Ms. Diamond."

"And so are you, you little artist minx! I love how your body reacts to my touch." Elizabeth dotted Ella's neck with a few more kisses before the two parted.

Ella looked around the bedroom. "I need to start getting ready. I have some errands to do today, and then I am bartending tonight. I'm just going to look around for my stuff, okay?"

Elizabeth replied, "No problem. I should too; I have a meeting at the gallery at 2:00 pm." Elizabeth laid back down watching Ella's lovely nude body and the beautiful tattoos as shuffled around her condo. She had never met anyone quite like Ella. She had certainly never bedded anyone like Ella. She felt like she wanted to say something, to keep Ella at her place a bit longer. But she knew there wasn't much more to say and that the two of them needed to focus on their mutual responsibilities. Elizabeth only hoped that she would be able to see Ella again soon.

Ella called out from the living room, "Hey, are you coming back to my class? I mean, you are totally welcome to."

Elizabeth answered, "Yes, I'd like to. I enjoyed the class, and I would love to learn more about the students and their work." Biting her lip, she then added, "And of course, I want to see more of your work too, Ella. I'm still gathering ideas and potential contacts to exhibit."

"That's awesome. Yeah, sure, anytime. I'd love to have you back." Ella winked as she threw her shirt over her small pert breasts. Her nipples were prominent through the thin material. She approached Elizabeth and gave her a quick kiss before grabbing her purse. "I have to go, but maybe I'll see you again on Thursday?"

7

I t was a busy Wednesday evening at La Crème, and Ella was behind the bar, shaking a martini order. Dozens of women crowded against the rail, waiting for drinks. Wednesday evenings featured a weekly drag show, which was always a huge hit. In between Celine Dion and Whitney Houston tracks, the MC announced acts, which were peppered with lewd jokes.

Ella's co-worker, Ryan, a young, soft butch bar-back, hustled behind her, picking up bins of dirty glasses and refilled Ella's ice station.

Ella turned around in mid-shake. "Thanks, Ryan! You are such an amazing help."

Ryan gave Ella a sly smile and replied, "Don't mention it, doll. We're all a team here!"

Ella returned the flirtation with a knowing grin. She could tell that Ryan liked her, but then again, Ryan liked everyone. And at La Crème, there was a lot of yummy eye candy in which to feast.

There was a lull in the line-up as the guests moved towards the stage for the next act. As the orders slowed down, Ella took the opportunity to clean some glasses and wipe down the counter before two women approached the bar.

"Hey, ladies! What will it be tonight?" Ella asked, leaning in closer.

The taller woman, who presented more masculine of the two, spoke up. "I'll get a Pabst Blue Ribbon and a double vodka soda on the rocks for my girl, here."

"Coming right up!" Ella turned her back to grab a cold beer from the fridge and returned to face the customers as she made the vodka cocktail. "How's your night going so far?"

The petite femme answered, "Oh, it was great! We just returned from a private art show at the Amira Alder Gallery." Her counterpart then added, "The artwork there is just exceptional. It's a little stuffy, but I guess that's the payoff for being in the presence of great art, right?"

Ella replied, "Oh! Oh wow, yes, that does sound wonderful!" Ella thought back to the delicious erotic encounter that she had enjoyed earlier this morning, trying to hide her wicked smile. *The art director is also exceptional, but I'm sure you don't need to hear that!* Ella handed over the drinks to her customers.

The tall butch took the beer and poured it into a glass, thanking Ella. She then turned to address the petite femme. "You know, maybe it's just me, but I could have sworn that the director was hitting on you. Did you notice that, Tracey?"

Taking a sip of her drink, Tracey nodded. "Yeah, I definitely felt a bit of flirty vibes, especially when I mentioned that I did some art myself. I mean, I know it's just a couple of silly watercolors, but I thought it was strange when she asked me to return soon and to bring pictures of my art to show her." Putting a hand on the taller woman, Tracey then asked, "Sorry, Paula, did that bother you?"

Paula shrugged. "Meh, not really. I thought it was kind of cute, actually. But I'm guessing that's how she collects art for her exhibits, right?" Paula and Tracey both laughed, utterly unaware of the fact that Ella was eavesdropping on the conversation.

Ella's heart began to beat quickly as irritation set in. Ella wasn't sure if she had heard the exchange correctly, but to her, it sounded like Elizabeth had treated this Tracey woman a lot like she had treated Ella herself. Her mind began to race as it tried to replay moments from the night before. Anger and confusion were building fast inside her, and she struggled to keep a calm and chipper demeanor for the sake of customer service and much-needed tips. Did Elizabeth just have a thing for young petite artists? Did she just get off on the power she held?

Clearing her throat, Ella spoke up. "Well, um, enjoy the night! The stage shows are great on a Wednesday." Paula and Tracey nodded in agreement and raised their drinks in response. After a few minutes of what seemed to be small talk, the women left the bar and headed into the audience.

Ella took a deep breath as she reeled from the information. *I-I don't understand. Was I just a...conquest? Is she even interested in my classes or my art? Is she like this with everyone? Who is this woman, anyway?* Ella felt her stomach drop, and it seemed as though the floor beneath her had given out. She blinked and shook her head, comparing the tender and intimate moments she had shared with Elizabeth to the wretched conversation she had overheard between Paula and Tracey.

Ella was still lost in her thoughts when Ryan tapped

her on the shoulder. "Sorry, hun, but you have a few customers in front of you." Ella jumped and came back to earth. "Oh my goodness, I'm so sorry!" Becoming more present, Ella assumed her role and continued to take orders and to make drinks. But in the back of her mind, she was hurt and confused. *I thought that we had something kind of special. I mean, sure, I want to exhibit at that gallery more than anything but wanting Elizabeth sexually was separate from that. I didn't sleep with her to secure an exhibition, but I hope she didn't fuck me only to exclude me from that opportunity.*

Ella continued to perform at work to the best of her ability, but when the club finally closed and the doors shut for the night, Ella's mask crumbled. As she and Ryan proceeded to tidy up the bar area, Ella's face grew long and sad.

"Why so glum, chum?" Ryan asked.

Ella kept her eyes on the surface she was wiping down. Shrugging, she replied, "Mm, oh, I don't know. I just feel kind of stupid about something."

Ryan remarked, "Yeah, I noticed that you seemed a bit off later in the night. Did something happen with a customer?"

Ella sighed and rolled her eyes towards the sky. She took another deep inhale and exhale, unsure of what to say. Wringing a bar cloth in her hand, she paused briefly before revealing the source of her disappointment.

Leaning against the ledge of the bar, Ella asked, "Do you remember when I told you that I'm a painter and a photographer and that it was my dream to exhibit at some galleries in Upper West?"

Ryan stood, facing Ella with a mop in her hand. "Yup. And I think that would be so cool! I would definitely come to see your exhibition." Ella couldn't help but be charmed by Ryan's enthusiasm, although she was not in the mood for a cheerful exchange.

Ella impatiently shook her head to get to the point of her story. "I overheard some customers talking about a woman that I slept with. This woman also happens to be the director of a gallery where I desperately want to exhibit."

Ryan grinned as her eyes grew wide. "Oooh, the plot thickens! When did this happen?"

Ella looked at Ryan sheepishly. "Earlier today."

Ryan laughed out loud. "Seriously? Good for you, girl! Are you seeing her? Like, is it serious?"

"Honestly, I have no idea what is going on with us. We went out for drinks last night, and I ended up at her place. I like her a lot," Ella said earnestly. "She is gorgeous and successful, and she seems really kind. But the fact that we slept together might have complicated things a bit because we met under the pretense of business."

Ryan furrowed her brow. "What do you mean by *business*? She isn't like your boss or anything?" Ryan's voice trailed off. "Although, wow, that would be so hot…"

Ella sighed impatiently, steering Ryan back to the point of her story. "No, no. Apparently, she is looking for some new art or a new artist to exhibit at her gallery. The one *I* want to exhibit at! I met her at the college where I teach painting classes. I guess she is sitting in on a few classes to see if she can discover new talent or something. She came to my class last night, and we totally hit it off. I mean, we *really* hit it off!"

Ryan looked down to resume her cleaning, replying as she mopped. "Well, it sounds like some kind of crazy fate that you met one another. But what's the problem, exactly? You like her, and she is a possible lead for you to show at her gallery. That sounds pretty awesome to me so far!"

"Well, first of all, I actually don't know if she likes my art enough to want to exhibit. She has called me talented and has seen some of my technique in class, but she hasn't pitched any kind of proposal so far."

Ella followed Ryan's lead and started to dry off some clean, wet glasses. "The other part is that I am not sure if I fucked up my chances by having sex with her this morning. I mean, what if she was only using me for a good time? What if she doesn't see me as a serious artist but instead just as some kid who is an easy lay?"

Ryan asked gently, "Do you like *her*? Like, *genuinely*?" Ryan paused as she appeared to gather her choice of words. "Just to play devil's advocate, maybe she thinks you might be using her too?"

Ella tilted her head and narrowed her eyes. Ryan's comment caught Ella off guard, although it wasn't totally farfetched. Ella had not really thought about it like that, but she could see how Elizabeth could misinterpret Ella's advances upon consideration.

"That's an interesting point. I hadn't thought about it that way. But Ryan, I *do* like her. And the sex was pretty hot this morning. And I *also* want to show at her gallery. Can't I want both without seeming like an evil opportunist?" Ella questioned Ryan.

Ryan bobbed her head in agreement. "Yes, in theory, you definitely can, but I think you need to be clear about your intentions. Because I can see how this situation could get messy."

Ella went on to continue her story. "Well, trust me. It just got a little messy tonight. Two customers came up to the bar to order drinks, and I overheard them talking about a private exhibit at the Amira Alder Gallery. While I was serving them, one of the women mentioned to her friend that Elizabeth was *flirting* with her at the gallery! The *same woman* that I had *just slept with!*"

Ryan's jaw dropped. "Oh, snap! That's why you were so upset! Okay, I get it now. I'm so sorry, Ella."

Ella turned to the glass cabinet behind the bar and began placing the glassware on the shelf. "I mean, we aren't a couple or anything. Obviously, she can flirt with whoever she wants, and so can I." Ella huffed impatiently and slammed her bar cloth on the counter. "But that's why I'm questioning what happened between us and what Elizabeth's intentions were. Do you see what I mean?"

Ryan looked sympathetic. "Yes, I understand. It's complicated for sure. But I think you just need to have an honest conversation about what you want with your art *and* with her."

Ella ran her hands through her hair, exposing the shaved sides. "That's the problem, though. I know what I want for my art. I've always known where I wanted to go with my talent. I just don't know about having a relationship, though. She and I don't really know each other yet, and I don't even know if she wants a relationship at all, let alone with a starving artist who is practically twenty years younger!" Frustrated and tired, Ella rubbed her face.

Ryan had been emptying out the garbage when she dropped a trashcan. The metal base clanged to the floor, which made Ella jump. "Holy shit! You didn't tell me she was *that* much older! Girl, it sounds like you have gotten yourself into quite the predicament. Like, how much more complicated is this going to get!"

Ella gave Ryan a wry smile. "What kind of lesbian

are you, Ryan? When is being with women *not* compli-cated? But seriously, you're right. It's starting to get a bit weird, and I'm not sure what to do. Like I said, I *like* Elizabeth. Yes, we are completely different people, but there is chemistry between us. She also happens to have a fair amount of power and influence over my art career, so I want to tread lightly. But I would *never* want her to think that I am using her. I'm not that kind of person, Ryan." Ella frowned, almost offended at the idea.

Ryan lumbered over, carrying a garbage bag in each hand. "Okay, so, I have a thought. Even though you like her, you aren't sure about a relationship right now, and you said that neither is she, right? So instead, why you don't focus on what you *do* want, which is to exhibit your paintings."

Ella squinted at Ryan. "I'm not sure if I follow?"

Ryan continued, "Why don't you talk to her and be honest about your goals? It doesn't have to come off opportunistic, especially if you are being honest—just be clear about your passion. It might mean that you can't be intimate with her right now. But as an art director, I am sure she would understand. She has her own goals for the gallery too."

Ryan suddenly perked up. "Wait! I have an idea. Why don't you *show* her your pieces? Do you have a studio or anything like that?"

Ella shook her head. "No. Most of my recent work is either in the classroom at the college or home." Ella looked dismayed. "And she's already seen the work in the classroom. She said she liked it, but the conversation never went further than that."

"So, take it a step further and show her work that she

hasn't seen yet. I'm telling you, Ella! Invite her over to your place for a private showing," Ryan insisted.

Ella thought for a moment. *Hmmm, actually, that isn't a bad idea.* "I like how you think, Ryan. That's a great suggestion. You're right; I just need to go for it—show her what I've got!"

Ryan then gave Ella a sideways glance. "The question is, do you think you can...*behave?* Like, keep it restricted to just business? I mean, as fun as this all sounds, you *know* that fucking her is only going to complicate things, right?"

Ella laughed softly and bit the corner of her lip. An image of a naked Elizabeth flashed before her, and Ella could even recall the scent of her body. Ella found Elizabeth positively intoxicating. Ryan brought up a good point. Ella and Elizabeth had blurred some lines, and it was up to Ella to set more explicit boundaries if she was going to achieve her goals. But could she do it?

"Yeah, I'm aware of that. You're right, Ryan; I need to keep things clear between us. But she is just so hot!" Ella playfully whined.

Ryan joined her in laughter. "Trust me; I get it. But at the same time, you said yourself that you have always had aspirations about your art. Are you seriously going to let lust get in the way? This is *New York*, Ella. Everyone has to hustle. You need to stay focused, babe."

Ella groaned, "Alright, alright. You win. Honestly, thanks for listening and giving me some good advice. I feel much better now." Ella gave Ryan a kind smile.

8

E lizabeth sat across from Samantha in the boardroom at the Amira Alder Gallery. It was 2:15 pm on Wednesday afternoon, and the pair had sat down to discuss a vision of new work at the gallery. Since visiting Chatsworth Community College, Elizabeth had been inspired by what she had seen in Ella's class, and in particular, she was moved by Ella's acrylic paintings.

Elizabeth wanted to see more work from Ella, and while they had gotten sidetracked with an intimate (and alcohol-fueled) tryst, she tried to get back on course. The future of the gallery's success was mainly dependent on Elizabeth, and she had a lot of pressure riding on her shoulders. A small part of her regretted moving so quickly with Ella as it took her focus away from the larger picture, although there was no denying their attraction. Ella was a million miles away from Elizabeth's usual type but she couldn't shake the thought of her and the image of her beautiful nude body. Still, Elizabeth knew she needed to bring her attention back to business matters, and she was grateful to formulate a plan with her art handler, Samantha.

"I think what we need, Sam, is a clearer path in which to achieve our concept. The other day, I was exposed to some wonderful talent that could be a great fit for the gallery. But before I pursue this further, let's discuss what is actually needed here in order to bring in new customers, obtain more gallery memberships, and what would actually *sell* as a great show."

Samantha nodded earnestly. "Yes, I think you're right. Let's leave abstract thinking to the artists while we focus on business decisions."

"So based on your communications with clients and guest feedback, what do you feel the gallery is lacking, and how can a new artist fill that void?" Elizabeth pressed.

Samantha brought a pen to her mouth while she pondered the question. "Well, to start, I think people are hungry for change. I think you made an excellent point the other day about the gallery needing to become more accessible. Let's face it; nowadays, exclusivity doesn't cut it, especially with all of these grave, economic shifts."

She took a sip of her coffee and continued, "I feel like we need more color and vibrancy; an artist with lived experience. I think it should be someone who really represents the youthful vibe of New York. Someone that the common patron can relate to. Honestly, that is what's going to sell, in my opinion."

The wheels in Elizabeth's mind were turning. "Hm, mmm. Yes, I understand, and I agree with you. And I feel that is what Amira would want for the future as well." With any significant gallery decision, Elizabeth always defaulted back to her family.

Samantha then added, "And I think it should be a

woman. It's not like we've never featured female artists before, but I think it's been, what, at least a few months since our last showcase was by a female artist."

Elizabeth beamed, glad to hear that she and Samantha were on the same page. While these were thoughts that Elizabeth herself possessed, it was nice to hear them echoed by her business partner as well. She wanted to ensure that she was thinking clearly before she pitched her preference to Samantha, which had already appeared to tick off all of the boxes. And while Elizabeth possessed authority to make important decisions, she always wanted to collaborate with her team, especially with Samantha, who was essentially her right-hand woman.

Taking a deep breath, Elizabeth began, "Well, it seems as though you and I are thinking the same thing; a young, female artist who represents the grittiness of New York. Also, it should be someone who is on the verge of greatness but who just needs a gentle push and promotion from an esteemed gallery." Elizabeth's eyes twinkled as she crossed her fingers in front of her face. "I think the Amira Alder Gallery must act as the starting point for this artist's success because if we let such a talent slip from our fingers, another space will nab her up."

Samantha nodded intently. "Yes, yes, I absolutely agree. I know that we are one of the most respected galleries on the Upper West Side, but we're not the only one. Once we find our talent, we cannot let this opportunity go to waste."

Elizabeth leaned back in her chair and folded her hands in her lap. "So, I do have someone in mind. I met her at the Chatsworth Community College. She teaches an intermediate painting class. I sat in on the session the other night, and I was quite impressed."

Samantha looked pleasantly surprised. "Oh, really? Wow, that's great! Is it one of the students?"

Elizabeth answered, "No, it is the instructor herself. Her name is Ella Ryan, and she is a phenomenal acrylic painter. Quite honestly, she is too good to be teaching there, in my opinion, but that's neither here nor there. The point is; I think she is exactly who we are looking for. And the best part is that she has wanted to exhibit here for years. I believe that Fate brought me to her," Elizabeth sucked in a breath before continuing, "Sorry, I meant it was Fate that our paths crossed at the school." Elizabeth felt her face redden a bit, and she hoped that Samantha didn't notice.

Samantha looked intrigued. "Okay! Well, let's look at her website. Do you know what it is?"

Elizabeth blanked. During the course of their evening, they had not discussed Ella's site, which now, looking back, was a careless error on Elizabeth's part. *Obviously, I must have been distracted. That was so silly of me. If only Ella weren't so beautiful, so captivating, I would have*—Samantha interrupted her internal dialogue.

"Elizabeth? Do you know the site?" Elizabeth snapped out of her daydream and replied, "Oh, no, I am sorry. I don't have her business card on me."

Shit! How unprofessional. Recovering, Elizabeth added, "Her name is Ella Ryan, and she's a painter in New York. Let's just Google her; I'm sure we will find more of her work online."

Samantha opened her MacBook and moved closer to Elizabeth so they could share the screen. Samantha typed in *Ella Ryan, New York, artist, painter, teacher, Chatsworth*

Community College in the Google search engine. The screen was then filled with high-ranking links about art in New York plus a few ads targeting community colleges. As Samantha scrolled down, she found an article about Ella Ryan. "Oh, let's look at this."

Clicking on the link, the colleagues discovered an article entitled "Young Artist from Queens Gets Full Scholarship to Waterford Institute." The piece outlined Ella's journey as a young girl who came from a low-income home. She had discovered her passion for art when she was a child, and through the support of an art teacher in high school, Ella was able to hone her talent, going on to win multiple awards in high school.

As Elizabeth and Samantha continued to scroll, they came across a quote from a seventeen-year-old Ella. "I feel so lucky to have gotten a scholarship. My parents couldn't afford to send me to Waterford, so this will help so much. I also want to thank Mrs. Healy for encouraging me and giving me art free supplies to use." The article then went on to note Ella's ambitions and hopes for a new school year. Elizabeth and Samantha looked at one another, both obviously impressed.

While Elizabeth was already sold on the idea of exhibiting Ella's paintings, Samantha's curiosity seemed to grow. She clicked on Google images to peruse examples of Ella's work. "Oh, these *are* marvelous! You were right, Elizabeth. The woman is so talented. Gosh, this painting right here..." Samantha pointed to the image on the screen that read *Abyss*.

The painting was of a woman who had jumped into a body of water, wearing a flimsy white nightgown. The image was created from an underwater perspective. Swirls of oceanic blues and greens were dotted with pearly

iridescence to give off the impression of water splashes
and sea foam. The woman's expression was that of peace,
not fear, and it possessed a moving, ethereal quality. Elizabeth noted that the female subject also had red hair and
looked a lot like Ella herself, and she wondered if that was
a type of self-portrait by Ella. Elizabeth made a mental
note to ask Ella about it the next time she saw her.

"*This* is incredible! The painting would look perfect
over by the north wall, by the east entrance. Oh, and this
one," Samantha pointed to a vibrant, neon-pink acrylic
painting of a woman whose mouth was slightly open. It
suggested erotic rapture to Elizabeth, and she could not
help herself from thinking about Ella's intense orgasm
earlier this morning. She felt a restless urge growing
inside of her and a desire to taste Ella again.

Samantha leaned back and crossed her arms in her
chair. "I agree with you, Elizabeth. I think Ella Ryan
would make a fantastic addition to the gallery; I can
already envision her exhibition. And she has such a
marketable backstory. Like, the whole poverty-stricken
child who rises up in the art world is *such* a great hook."
Elizabeth observed Samantha's expression; she looked
like a cat who had just eaten a canary. "Oh, I can see the
promotional material now, and you are right, Elizabeth.
This will be great PR for the gallery. Personally, I am sold."
Samantha looked content.

Elizabeth was glad to hear that Samantha was on
board with showing Ella's work. However, she wanted to
be careful with how Ella was marketed and promoted.
While Elizabeth could agree that Ella's roots and the
development of her talent were remarkable, Elizabeth
wanted to avoid any exploitive marketing tactics. In
getting to know Ella on a personal level, Elizabeth not

only had respect for her as an artist but also as a beautiful and intelligent woman that she was beginning to care about.

While Samantha's primary responsibility with the gallery was to procure and carefully handle artwork, Elizabeth extended some of Samantha's tasks to overlap with her own position. Sometimes, Samantha worked as a project leader with the marketing department. For the majority of their years working together, this arrangement worked well. The employees of the gallery were a tight-knit group, strung together by close familial ties. Unlike similar businesses, there was less of a hierarchical structure. Because Samantha had been a part of the gallery for years, she had been awarded more authority than most who held her position.

However, Elizabeth was also aware that Samantha could be a bit of a shark, and she sometimes lacked scruples when it came to business. Elizabeth hated to admit that, more often than not, Samantha's tactics could be helpful. But in this case, Elizabeth felt quite protective of Ella. And she was beginning to think she should have more of a hands-on role when exhibiting and marketing Ella's work.

Elizabeth smiled calmly, keeping her emotions measured. "Excellent, I am happy to hear that. I will be in touch with Ella, and once we secure the dates and the contract, we can start the promotions. I'll keep you up to date and let you know when I will need to discuss installations and the transportation of pieces."

Samantha offered, "In the meantime, would you like me to go ahead and contact marketing to discuss some promotional concepts? I mean, just to get a head start on the process?" Elizabeth paused, unsure of how to move forward. Gently, she responded. "Why don't you let me make the arrangements with Ella first, and then I will let you know when we can proceed."

Samantha closed her laptop and nodded. "Sure, sure, that sounds fine. I'm just excited to bring her pieces to the gallery. I am envisioning some wonderful ways that we can represent her, and I think this will really bring interest to our members, as well as hopefully secure new memberships." Samantha put her hand on Elizabeth's arm. "Like you, I also want what is best for the gallery. You have a great eye, Elizabeth. You always have. Amira would be so proud of you!" she said with admiration.

Elizabeth smiled in agreement as her thoughts churned. *Hm, I'm not sure how proud Amira would be if she knew I had slept with this potential artist first, but Samantha is right; Ella is so talented. She deserves to show here. So what if we've been intimate? That won't take away from the stunning pieces that she can bring to our walls.*

Standing up, Elizabeth thanked Samantha, and the women exited the boardroom. Elizabeth was buzzing with excitement over the news, and she couldn't wait to tell Ella.

Checking her watch, she remembered she had a private showing tonight, featuring a sculptur from Israel, who was flying into New York for the week. Eli had made the arrangements, and it was up to Elizabeth to charm the patrons. In particular, she had been told to speak to a watercolorist by the name of Tracey. Apparently, Tracey was a friend of the sculptur and was interested in becoming involved in the gallery.

Even though Elizabeth and Samantha had already decided to work with Ella, Elizabeth knew that she needed to be congenial and offer some positive encouragement. The private exhibit was to begin at 6:00 pm, and Elizabeth needed to rush home to prepare herself. She had also remembered that Ella was bartending tonight at La Crème. *I'll call Ella first thing tomorrow and make some plans to meet and discuss this opportunity. She is going to be so excited!* Deep within Elizabeth's subconscious, her own excitement extended beyond working with Ella; the idea of getting to see her again gave Elizabeth a thrill. She could hardly wait until the evening was through so that she could share the fantastic opportunity with her crush.

EARLY THURSDAY MORNING, Elizabeth sent a text to Ella. She knew that Ella would not yet be awake, but she was too excited to wait. Plus, she wanted Ella to rise to an exciting message, especially because Elizabeth remembered that Ella was teaching at the college this evening.

Good morning! I hope you slept well. I have some fantastic news to share with you. Please call me when you awake and we can discuss. xo.

Elizabeth lay her head back on her pillow. It had been quite a while since she had such amorous emotions. Her last relationship fizzled out, and the magic hadn't been there for months. In meeting Ella, Elizabeth felt a newfound sense of energy whip through her being. While Elizabeth often found inspiration and connection through her artist community and via the beautiful pieces that graced the gallery walls, she also felt somewhat removed in remaining in her professional role.

Elizabeth was excited to collaborate with Ella because not only did she admire her talent and creations, she also felt connected to Ella as a woman and as a lover. Maybe

Elizabeth was getting ahead of herself, but she thought a potential working relationship could blossom into something grand. She continued to allow herself a few more moments of daydreaming before she rose from her bed to make coffee.

Her phone buzzed from the bedroom in the middle of pouring hot, dark liquid into a mug. Elizabeth carried her coffee back into her bedroom to check her phone, discovering a reply from Ella.

Morning! I'm awake. Is it cool to call right now? Elizabeth replied, *yes.* Seconds later, Ella's number appeared, and Elizabeth answered it on the first ring.

"Good morning! How are you?" Elizabeth greeted Ella in a cheerful voice.

"Hey there, I'm alright. It was a late night at the bar. I can't believe I'm awake so early," Ella replied in a groggy voice.

"Oh, I hope my text didn't wake you!" Elizabeth cringed, slightly embarrassed about her enthusiasm to speak so early. But Ella was unfazed. "No, not at all. So what's the news? I'm dying of curiosity."

Elizabeth suddenly decided that she preferred to tell Ella in person; that way, she would also see Ella's expression. "Well, first of all, it's *great* news, and it involves you, but I was wondering if you wanted to meet in person to discuss it. Are you free after class tonight?"

Ella pouted playfully. "Oh, man! Are you serious? Are you going to make me wait? I can't even get a hint?"

Elizabeth bit her lip to keep from chuckling. She knew that making Ella wait would drive her crazy, but she knew it would be worth it. "Um, it's about art, and it's about you. That's all I can say."

Ella paused. "Well, that sure sounds interesting! And

actually, I wanted to talk to you as well about art, specifically *my art*. I am guessing you won't be sitting in my class tonight?"

Elizabeth answered, trying to remain cryptic. "No, no need, actually. I-I have everything I need from the last session. But sure, I can stop by tonight. Trust me, this is worth waiting for, Ella."

Elizabeth heard Ella sigh impatiently on the phone before giving her directions to her place in Chelsea. "Call me at 9:30 pm, just to make sure I'm home. See you tonight."

Elizabeth hung up and did a little dance in her bedroom; she couldn't wait until this evening. As she prepared for the day ahead, she remembered one of her favorite quotes. *"Art and love are the same thing: It's the process of seeing yourself in things that are not you."*

9

E lla locked up the classroom door behind her and proceeded down the dark hallway of Chatsworth College. She had just finished teaching and was eager to return home.

All day, Ella was on pins and needles, wondering what Elizabeth needed to reveal. She felt a combination of anticipation, nervousness, and even a twinge of annoyance. Ella was not a patient person, and she was a bit miffed that such pressing news couldn't be shared on the phone.

Still, she had to admit that she was excited to see Elizabeth again, but since overhearing Paula's and Tracey's conversation at the bar, she wasn't quite sure what to make of this fancy art director. She had also taken Ryan's advice and prepared a few of her favorite canvases to be on display for when Elizabeth came over. No matter what, Ella was going to hold her ground and stick to her goals.

While she was attracted to Elizabeth and wanted to explore their connection, she would not be underestimated as a serious artist or overlooked as someone worthy of opportunities. If Elizabeth wanted to see her again, she would have to see *all* of Ella, which meant in-your-face exposure to her artwork rather than her body.

Climbing the steps to the building, Ella's phone rang; it was Elizabeth. Ella answered, "Hi there! I am literally coming up to my apartment now. Are you on your way?"

Elizabeth replied, "Yes, I was about to jump into a cab, but I wanted to make sure you were home from class first."

Ella retorted, "Sure, come over anytime. It's apartment number 354." They ended the call as Ella unlocked her front door.

Ella's bachelor pad was cute and relatively clean, but it was tiny, under 400 square feet. Like many artists, Ella's living space also doubled as her art studio. However, the size didn't matter much to her. She was living a vibrant and independent life, away from her troubled parents. Economically, she was considered low income, but somehow, Ella felt richer than she had, being trapped in Queens. Still, with someone as fancy as Elizabeth coming by, Ella couldn't help but wonder if she would be judged.

She made a few last adjustments to her canvases, aligning them so that they surrounded the solo couch in a half-circle, which served as Ella's living room. Feeling anxious, Ella bit her nails (a terrible habit that she developed as a child) while waiting for Elizabeth to arrive. Within ten minutes, she heard a knock. With her heart beating quickly, she answered the door.

"Hi, Ella! Thank you so much for having me over," Elizabeth said warmly. Ella replied in kind, with her arms outstretched, offering a welcoming embrace. Elizabeth's scent overwhelmed her senses. As Elizabeth stepped inside, Ella added, feeling somewhat embarrassed, "I know it's small, but it's home. I feel most free to create here."

Elizabeth looked around appreciatively. "It's lovely, Ella. Please don't apologize for the room. Oh, I can't wait to see more of your paintings!"

Ella led Elizabeth over to the small couch so they could face the series of canvases. Ella couldn't wait another moment. "Can you please, *please* tell me what is going on? I have been on edge all day, dying to know."

Elizabeth faced Ella with a huge grin. "I'm so sorry that I made you wait like that. I just wanted to share this with you face to face. Plus, I can't deny that I wanted to see you again in person."

Ella smiled and bit her lip, feeling both charmed and a bit shy. "Yeah, me too. I'm happy to see you again, Elizabeth."

Without further hesitation, Elizabeth began, "So, Ella, we have decided to exhibit a series of your paintings at the Amira Alder Gallery."

Ella's eyes widened, and her mouth dropped open. She felt as though time had frozen. For a moment, she thought she had misheard. "Sorry, what did you say? Are you serious?"

Elizabeth laughed gleefully, clapping her hands together. Elizabeth was enjoying Ella's shock. Elizabeth scooted closer to Ella and grabbed Ella's hands. "Yes, Ella, I am *serious*. I had a meeting yesterday with my partner and art handler, and we decided that we want to represent *you* at the gallery."

Ella was still having a hard time processing the information. It was all she had ever hoped for, but at the same time, the offer didn't seem real. *Is this a dream?* Ella ran her hands through her hair and shook her head in disbelief.

"So, like, how did this come about? I thought you were still on the hunt for more talent at the school?"

Ella searched Elizabeth's face for answers. "I'm surprised because I had no idea that I was even up for consideration. And you hadn't seen much of my work, except for in the classroom." Ella pointed to the paintings in front of her. "This is why I decided to display my work for you tonight because I wanted you to see the originals instead of any images online."

Elizabeth looked up at Ella's artwork, gasping slightly as she put a finger to her lips. Taking a deep sigh, she exclaimed, "Oh Ella, these are stunning! I'm so glad you've displayed these for me to look at. I absolutely love the *Abyss* painting. We were talking about it during our meeting, in fact!"

Elizabeth turned back to Ella to further explain. "I understand that this may come as a surprise, but my colleague Samantha and I did some thinking about what we feel would work best as far as an exhibition and the type of artist that would best meet our vision. I was very impressed upon meeting you and seeing your technique and samples in the classroom. Plus, you as a person would be a fascinating addition."

Elizabeth continued, "The gallery has its own goals too, like securing new memberships and renewing old ones. The Amira Alder Gallery wants to remain on the leading edge of art and design in the city, and upon looking at your work online and based on my interactions with you, we feel that you are the best fit." Elizabeth then motioned towards the original acrylics. "And in seeing these pieces in person only confirms my decision. What do you say, Ella? Do you want the gallery to represent you and to host an exhibition of your collection?"

With tears of joy in her eyes, Ella burst out, "Oh my god, yes! Yes, Elizabeth, that is a dream come true for me." Ella leaped from her seat on the couch to hug Elizabeth tightly. She breathed in Elizabeth's signature Chanel perfume, relishing how soft her cashmere sweater felt against her face. Ella felt overwhelmed with emotions; her insides swirled with a mixture of elation and desire. Elizabeth held her tightly; neither woman wanted to let go. Ella felt Elizabeth stroke her hair and rub her back, squeezing her close.

Pulling away, Elizabeth said, "Congratulations! I will draw up a contract, and we will have you come into the gallery to sign it. I also want you to meet Samantha as well, along with some of the other important employees." Elizabeth stared earnestly into Ella's eyes. "This is going to be a big break for you, Ella. Just wait and see. The gallery is going to put you on the map as one of the hottest artists to watch for, and you will be rubbing elbows with some important and influential collectors."

Ella couldn't resist. She cupped Elizabeth's face in her hands and drew her in for a passionate kiss. Ella noted how Elizabeth tasted like strawberries; her lips were soft as pillows. "I don't know what else to say but thank you. Thank you for believing in my talent and for bringing me into your world. I want to do something to show my appreciation for you."

Elizabeth looked at the original painting of *Abyss*. She rose from the couch and studied the work of art. Turning to Ella, she exclaimed, "We definitely want to include this as a featured piece. Perhaps something we can use towards our marketing and promotions."

Ella felt indebted to Elizabeth for this incredible opportunity, and she wanted to express her gratitude in the one way she knew how—through her art. Suddenly, she had an idea. Ella wanted, no *needed*, an outlet to show her appreciation towards Elizabeth, and she desired to pitch a thought that could serve as a gift to the gallery as well.

Ella stood behind as Elizabeth admired *Abyss*. Wrapping her arms around Elizabeth's waist, Ella murmured, "What if I painted a portrait of you and we used that towards the marketing of my exhibition instead? I want so desperately to paint you."

Elizabeth turned around to face Ella. "What do you mean? You want to paint *me*?" Ella smiled and bobbed her head. Reaching out to stroke her hair lovingly, Ella replied, "Yes, I do. You are so beautiful, and you have gifted me with an opportunity that has made my dreams come true." Ella pointed to the underwater-themed design. "I love this painting, and I am happy to include it in the exhibition, but I want to produce something new, something *magnificent*. Elizabeth, I want you to be my muse. And I would very much like for that painting to be the feature. What do you think?"

Elizabeth opened her mouth in surprise and smiled. "I would love to pose for you." Ella then noticed a small frown cross Elizabeth's forehead. "I think my only concern is that it might not be ready in time for when we print the materials. And there is a lot to arrange before the opening." Elizabeth wore a pained expression of worry and wanting.

Elizabeth stood while grabbing hold of Ella's hands. "If I say yes, can you have the painting completed by this weekend? I know that's a lot to ask, but we must stick to a timeline. I was hoping to have you come into the gallery on Monday to sign the papers so that we can get started."

Ella gave Elizabeth a sly smile. "Well, if you don't have anywhere to be right now, we could start tonight. I'll bet that I can have an outline of your gorgeous body on a 55" x 71" canvas by morning. In fact, hold on a minute!" Ella raced to the corner of her tiny kitchen and checked the side of her fridge. "Ah, there is it!" Ella exclaimed, vertically sliding out a blank white canvas. Turning to look back at Elizabeth, she explained, "This is where I keep my spares because there's nowhere else to keep them safe."

Ella presented the surface to Elizabeth. "I've got the canvas, the easel, and I've got the paint. Now, all I need is for you to disrobe and take a seat on this couch. I *promise* that I can have this completed by Monday. Besides a bartending shift tomorrow night, my weekend is free." Ella pleaded, "Please, Elizabeth. I want to do this so much. Your face and your body and you, well you inspire me so much. I want so badly to do you justice on canvas."

Elizabeth stared at Ella for a moment, holding a passionate gaze. Finally, she nodded. "Okay, Ella. Sure, let's go for it." Elizabeth closed her eyes and squealed, "Oh my god, I can't believe I am doing this!"

Elizabeth and Ella kissed again before Ella grabbed a soft blanket off her bed, placed directly across from the couch. She laid it on the sofa as a protective cover. Coyly, Ella said, "There you go. Now, as I set up my easel and paints, I want you to strip...and make sure you do it slowly. I want you to tease me and seduce me with your beauty."

Wordlessly, Elizabeth moved to the couch while Ella watched, as a playful grin spread across her face.

10

E lizabeth kept her gaze on Ella as she slowly stepped back towards the sofa. She felt a thrill shoot through her body like a bolt of electricity. Elizabeth had never allowed herself to be so candid, so vulnerable. Yet, in the presence of Ella, she felt like she could let her guard down; she wanted Ella to see her truly. And she was curious to see how this vision would be translated onto canvas. While many people saw Elizabeth in a powerful position within the New York art world, at this very moment, Elizabeth was the one who felt honored to have been asked to pose for someone as talented as Ella.

Elizabeth looked down at the belt that looped around her designer denim dress. Following Ella's orders, she slowly pulled the tie free, revealing a series of interlocking fasteners that kept the dress together. Raising her eyes to meet Ella's, Elizabeth began to unsnap the buttons, one at a time, starting from the top. Ella watched Elizabeth while she steadied a new, blank canvas upon the ledge of the easel.

"Mmm, I like that," Ella murmured. "I could watch you unbutton your clothes all day."

Elizabeth grinned as she slid her fingers down the middle of the dress, opening it up like a robe. Playfully, she teased Ella, partially exposing a matching black lace bra and panty set. With a coquettish smile, she asked, "Do you want to see more?"

Ella nodded. "Yes, I want to see it all. Take off your lingerie and show me your beautiful body." Elizabeth was delighted by Ella's assertiveness; it was exciting to be told what to do. Typically, Elizabeth was the one who remained in control, but in this very moment, she was at the mercy of Ella, and it greatly aroused her.

Elizabeth wrapped her hands around her back to unhook her bra without looking away, exposing her breasts and tiny pink nipples. She tossed the lingerie to the side and then bent over to slide off her panties. Elizabeth stood before Ella, in all of her nude glory. Ella smiled and seductively bit her lip. "Wow, you are truly incredible. You look like a goddess!"

Elizabeth felt herself blush as she looked over her shoulder and then back again at Ella. "Um, do you want me to sit or to lay down?"

Ella thought for a second. "Um, you can lay on your side in a comfortable position, with your head and body facing me like you are casually reclining."

Elizabeth settled into position as she draped one arm over her belly and cocked a hip, creating an enhanced curve from her waist. She touched her head, feeling the knotted bun at the top. "What should I do with my hair?"

Ella replied, "Let it down; I'd love to see it fall freely." Just before Ella turned her eyes back to the canvas, she added, "I love seeing *you* loose and free."

Elizabeth grinned as she loosened the knot, allowing her long dark locks to cascade around her face. She pushed her hair to one side so that it felt over one shoulder. "How's this?"

"Oh, that is perfect! Stay like that, and try not to move too much." Ella settled in front of her canvas, which was facing Elizabeth. Although she couldn't tell what Ella was doing per se, her long, sweeping motions seemed to indicate that she was creating an outline of Elizabeth's body.

She took a deep inhale and exhale, allowing herself to relax enough to sink into the couch. "Okay, I feel ready and still."

Elizabeth kept her eyes on the canvas, catching quick glimpses of Ella's face, as she peeked over to study Elizabeth's frame. Elizabeth felt like a prized possession, a special artifact on display. She could feel Ella's eyes flutter over her body like a butterfly as the artist diverted her attention between Elizabeth and the canvas. The feeling of being examined under Ella's watch was intoxicating; it felt as though Ella was caressing Elizabeth's bare skin with the end of the pencil. She felt goosebumps form over her limbs as she tingled with delight.

After about fifteen minutes had passed, Ella poked her head over the side of the canvas. "How are you feeling? Getting antsy yet? If you need to, you can take a stretch."

Elizabeth leaned back, arching her body, and rolled her neck from side to side. "I'm fine. It's pretty relaxing to lay here and watch you as you draw." The truth was that Elizabeth was becoming more and more turned on.

Remaining posed while nude only made Elizabeth want to reach out and touch Ella, to be touched herself. Taking one more deep breath, she extended her arms, releasing some tension. Then, she returned her hands to her torso and caressed her own breasts in a subconscious arousal without realizing it.

"Oh, sorry. I didn't even realize I was doing that." Elizabeth scrunched her face with embarrassment. But Ella's face lit up. "No, it's fine. In fact, it's *great!* You had the *best* look on your face as you touched your body. Just go with it, do what you want to do. I love capturing you at this moment."

Elizabeth suddenly felt shy. "What do you mean? Do you want me to keep touching myself while you paint me?"

Ella's face glowed with a mischievous grin. "Yup, I do! I mean, only if you're feeling it. I want to paint you uninhibited, and it would be so cool to see such pleasure on your face."

Elizabeth felt herself grow warm as the suggestion was quite appealing. "Okay." As Ella turned back to the painting, Elizabeth continued to run her fingers over her breasts, feeling her nipples grow hard. She looked in the direction of Ella as she moved her hands slowly over her torso and across her hip.

From six feet away, she heard Ella remark, "Very nice, Elizabeth. You look so glorious on my sofa, like a queen." Elizabeth noticed Ella put down her pen in exchange for a long paintbrush, and she wondered what it would be like to feel the soft bristles against her flesh. She brought a hand to her neck, stroking her clavicle, imagining it was Ella caressing her instead. Ella's eyes darted between the painting and Elizabeth's pose, and Elizabeth caught a glimpse of Ella's amused expression.

"Why don't you move your hand lower, right in between your thighs." Ella coly suggested, and Elizabeth followed the direction. "Ah, yes, just like that. I love you in that pose." Ella gave Elizabeth a quick wink and returned her eyes to the canvas as the end of the paintbrush danced in the air.

Elizabeth could not deny that she wanted to move her hand even lower, and the longer she remained outstretched on Ella's couch, the more turned on she became. Very slowly, she allowed her fingers to tiptoe closer to her vulva. She wasn't sure if Ella could tell; part of her wanted Ella to watch, and part of her wanted to be sneaky in touching herself.

As Ella's eyes remained glued to the painting, Elizabeth began to stroke her velvet-soft lips, placing her index and middle finger in between the folds of her clit. She pressed lightly and bit her lip, enjoying the sensation of pressure against her sensitive pearl. She kept rubbing, and the pace of the massage began to quicken. Careful not to make too much noise, Elizabeth tried to keep her breathing even. She continued to curl her fingers against her clit, closing her eyes when Ella interrupted her moment.

"Well, well, what's going on here?" Ella asked slyly. Elizabeth opened her eyes and let a small laugh accentuated by a pleasurable sigh.

"Ella, I'm really turned on. Between watching you paint and laying here naked before you, I-I want you, right now," Elizabeth replied in a throaty voice, thick with desire.

Silently, Ella moved away from the canvas, her paintbrush still in hand. "You make such a beautiful muse. I could just devour you." Elizabeth remained seated while Ella crept towards her, pausing to kneel in front of Elizabeth.

"Open your legs for me," Ella whispered firmly. Elizabeth obeyed, spreading her knees wide. While exposed, Ella crouched down and ran her paintbrush along the soft flesh of Elizabeth's inner thighs, as a trail of light, black paint followed behind. Elizabeth giggled and shivered with delight.

Ella raised her eyes to meet Elizabeth's as she moved the brush slowly up towards Elizabeth's navel. "You know, when I was in high school, I had a crush on my art teacher, Mrs. Healy. I used to fantasize about her running her paintbrush against *my skin,* just like I am doing to you now." Ella's eyes moved back towards the direction of the brush. Elizabeth noticed that her skin was becoming covered with thin, black lines.

She looked down and joked, "Are you making me into some kind of map?" Ella smiled. "Yup! I'm creating places on your skin that I want to visit with my mouth." Elizabeth sighed with excitement. "Touch me, please. I want to feel your hands and lips on my skin."

While still crouched, Ella put the brush down and removed her shirt so that she was naked from the waist up. Ella's small breasts were braless again. She never seemed to wear underwear. She pulled herself closer and laid her lips upon Elizabeth's stomach, tracing her tongue across her navel. As Ella paused to kiss her belly, Elizabeth closed her eyes and arched her back. Ella moved her lips down towards Elizabeth's pubic bone and grabbed her ass from behind. She scooped Elizabeth's body in her hands so that she could bring her warm mound closer to her mouth.

"I am so hungry for you," Ella murmured as she dove into Elizabeth's wetness. Elizabeth gasped and grabbed tightly onto Ella's head as Ella sucked on her clit. A throbbing, pulsating feeling grew in the pit of Elizabeth's core.

Suddenly, she felt Ella's fingers enter her, and as soon as Ella hit her G-spot, Elizabeth cried out loud, "Oh my god, yes! Ella, fuck me hard with your fingers. Right there, right there!"

Ella thrust hard against Elizabeth, and Elizabeth felt herself tighten as an orgasm began to form. As her muscles clenched, Elizabeth inhaled and exhaled, allowing her breathing to relax her body. As soon as Ella inserted a fourth finger, cupping her hand in a curved shape, a powerful orgasm exploded inside of Elizabeth. She bellowed loudly, ripping Ella's hair against her scalp. "Holy shit! Fuck, oh my god!" Elizabeth went limp as her face flushed red.

Ella kept her fingers inside Elizabeth and waited as her orgasm subsided feeling her body pulsing around her fingers. Ella began to move her fingers slightly again and a shiver ran across Elizabeth's body.

Elizabeth felt so wet and open as she looked at Ella's lovely face intent in concentration.

Ella's fingers slipped out of Elizabeth momentarily and she ran her hand up and down Elizabeth's sodden vulva, coating it in wetness.

"What are you up to, Ella?"

Ella smiled, wickedly, "Taking you somewhere else." Ella's fingers pushed back inside Elizabeth. And her thumb. And she began to work her knuckles in. "I think you'll like it. Have you been there before?"

Elizabeth felt an incredible intensity building inside of her and tipped her head back lost in ecstacy. "Yes," she replied. "A long time ago. I think I'll like it too." Her breathing quickened as she felt a slight pain as Ella's whole hand pushed right inside of her. The pain was momentary and was replaced by an absolute flood of pleasure. Ella was right. She was taking her to another world. Elizabeth lost herself in the moment, she felt herself tightening around Ella's wrist as Ella's hand made tiny movements so deep inside her.

Elizabeth's body relaxed to the intrusion and Ella's hand began to slip around more easily. Time was lost to Elizabeth as she never ever wanted this feeling to end. Ella's fist began to fuck her so slowly and deeply, Elizabeth had never felt pleasure so exquisite and she never wanted it to end.

Ella took her time, loving watching Elizabeth so lost in the moment, in the other world that Ella had promised. Her body was so so very beautiful in rapture with the lines of Ella's paint across it. Ella lowered her mouth to Elizabeth and enveloped Elizabeth's clit with the hot wet heat of her mouth.

Elizabeth orgasmed within seconds of Ella's mouth taking her clit. She called out loudly, "Oh fuck, Ella, YES," and her body shook wildly, almost crushing Ella's hand. She took a minute to recover and laughed with her head tipped back. Ella slid her hand slowly and gently and finally out of Elizabeth.

"Jesus, that was incredible. It has been forever since I felt anything approaching that. I cannot remember the last time I let myself go like that. You turn me on so much." Elizabeth sighed deeply.

"Come here, you little red minx." Ella popped her head up, and Elizabeth grabbed her face and kissed her deeply, tasting her own juices against Ella's lips.

"See how good you taste?" Ella grinned. "I could eat you all day."

Elizabeth laughed. "You know, I was just thinking the

same thing. Why don't you hop on my face and grind yourself against my mouth?"

Without hesitation, Ella stood up and slipped off her pants. Unsurprisingly she was not wearing underwear. Elizabeth stretched herself out on her back, and Ella bent down to kiss Elizabeth before straddling her lower body over Elizabeth's face. Enthusiastically, Elizabeth grabbed Ella's hips and positioned her mouth so that she could lick and suck Ella's clit. As she reached her tongue upwards, Elizabeth felt the soft petals of Ella's vulva drape against her mouth.

Elizabeth continued to lick, and she could feel Ella's body respond as her hips and ass began to hump against Elizabeth's face. A warm wetness grew, quenching Elizabeth's thirst. She loved the feeling of being smothered by Ella's pussy, inhaling her musky scent. She held Ella's body close, rubbing her hard against her mouth. She heard Ella moaning loudly, in ecstasy, occasionally bumping against Elizabeth's nose as she bore down.

"Oh, oh, oh! Oh, god, yes, I'm going to cum!" Ella shouted, and Elizabeth held on tight, maintaining her oral rhythm. She felt Ella throw her body back while she let out a primal cry. Elizabeth's face was slicked with Ella's juices, but she didn't mind; she savored the taste of moist desire from her lover.

Slowly, Ella moved off of Elizabeth, turning to look at her. With a flushed expression, she exclaimed, "Holy cow, my legs are shaking! Fuck, you feel so good." Ella threw herself on top of Elizabeth so that the women could lay naked against each other, looking into each other's eyes.

Ella stroked Elizabeth's hair, caressing her cheek. "I can't believe how lovely you are. It's a dream to have you in my home. I had no idea that you would be such an incredible woman, and I feel grateful to have met you."

Elizabeth felt herself melt. "I feel the same way. I mean, it's kind of a crazy coincidence how we met, but business aside, I'd love to continue to see you both on a personal level but also as an artist that I want to see grow and succeed."

Ella gave Elizabeth a soft, lingering peck before replying, "I think we can make that happen. I know we are both as focused on our passions as much as we are one another. I think we could be a great team! We are both lovers of art *and* Sapphic seduction." Ella grinned.

Looking deep into Ella's eyes, Elizabeth said with sincerity, "Then let's do this, Ella. I want to support your talent, and I want to *be* with you. What do you say?"

Ella smiled widely and squealed. "Yes, yes! Okay, we are doing this. It is official, Ms. Diamond. I am your girlfriend, the starving artist from Queens. I am sure that will go over well in your circle!" Ella joked although Elizabeth suspected there was a bit of truth behind her words.

"Don't worry. I know how to handle my crowd, and trust me; I would never let anyone disrespect someone I care about." Elizabeth was serious. "I want you to believe that, Ella."

Ella bobbed her head. "Okay, I will. I mean, I do. I'm not going to worry about social circle bullshit. I trust you, and we are together, end of story." She punctuated her statement with a tone of finality.

Suddenly, Elizabeth thought about the time and how late it must be getting. She groaned, not wanting to leave. "Babe, I'm sorry, but I think I need to get going soon. I have an early appointment tomorrow. But can I see what you have done so far on the painting?"

Ella exclaimed, "Oh yeah, for sure! I'll show you the outline, but I promise that I will finish it in time for Monday." Ella looked back towards the canvas and rubbed her hands together with excitement. "This is going to be in honor of you, of *us*. And I really hope we can include it in the exhibition." The women rose off the couch, and Elizabeth stepped towards the easel, moving in front of the canvas.

"Oh wow, I can't believe how much you got done while I was sitting there!" Elizabeth was impressed to see the outline of her shape, noting her earlier pose. Ella had already started some basic shading before their passionate tryst. Ella watched Elizabeth's expression before she spoke. "I know it's just a start, but trust me, I know exactly what I am going to do with this painting. You will not be disappointed."

Elizabeth beamed, feeling as confident as Ella. "I can already see it coming along nicely. I am not worried at all." Elizabeth reached out her arms to embrace Ella. With her face pressed against Ella's cheek, she asked, "So you are good to meet on Monday to go over the contract? Can we say at noon?"

Ella squeezed Elizabeth tightly. "Yes, beautiful. That works perfectly, and I am so stoked!" Pulling away to face Elizabeth, Ella added, "I'm excited about *everything;* you, me, the exhibit. Tonight has been a dream come true in so many ways, and I am eternally grateful for your support and your belief in me."

The lovers kissed passionately as though their mouths couldn't bear to part with one another. Their tongues woven tightly like ribbons, hanging on until Elizabeth's departure. Finally breaking free out of necessity, Elizabeth turned to put on her coat while Ella stood, watching her.

"I'm looking forward to you meeting our team on Monday. I think we have some cool ideas on how to promote and market your exhibit. It's going to be great!" Elizabeth squealed with joy, and Ella echoed her enthusiasm. They hugged tightly one last time before saying goodnight.

Elizabeth exited Ella's building, racing down the steps into the night air. She felt as though a new chapter of her life was beginning. She knew that if Amira and her father were still alive, they would be so proud of the original work that she had secured for the gallery. And it gave her such a thrill to taste Ella on her lips still.

She thought about one of her favorite quotes by Elie Wiesel, "*In Jewish history there are no coincidences.*"

11

E lla wiped a splatter of paint from her cheek and hooked her fingers around the handle of her coffee mug. It was 6:30 am on Monday, and Ella was putting the finishing touches on the painting of Elizabeth. In an effort to complete the piece in time for the meeting at the Amira Alder Gallery, Ella had worked on the portrait throughout the weekend.

On Sunday evening, Ella was filled with nervous energy and excitement. She found herself tossing and turning in bed, unable to sleep. Her mind kept wandering towards the painting in progress and the collection of art that she wanted to exhibit. Oppressive thoughts of self-doubt and criticism overshadowed her sleep like a dark cloud.

While Ella was confident in her talent as an artist, she hoped that Elizabeth's portrait would be well-received. Elizabeth had presented her with a major opportunity, and to Ella, it was a dream come true. But as the moment of truth rose like the morning sun, Ella had become anxious to the point of questioning her abilities.

After staring at the ceiling for what felt like hours, she decided to get out of bed and give the portrait one last once-over. Ella wanted it to be perfect, particularly because the painting had such personal significance. As she dabbed the surface of the canvas, adding bold strokes of color, she thought back to Elizabeth posing for her on the couch. *God, she is so sexy! I can't believe how hot the sex was that night. For someone so polished and measured, Elizabeth certainly has her own passionate primal side.*

Ella continued to glide the brush over the outline of Elizabeth's form, imagining that she was caressing Elizabeth's body once again. Preserving Elizabeth's image on canvas was also a way for Ella to revisit their steamy encounter. She felt proud to have captured a memory that would also be on display for others to see. Most of all, Ella was thrilled to see where her relationship with Elizabeth would go, the adventures they could have together. Elizabeth was more than just a lover, she was a muse and a source of inspiration for Ella, and she wanted to explore more creative possibilities in the future.

Starting at the painting, Ella had finally reached the point of satisfaction. *Hmmm, if I add anything more to this, I think I might ruin it. Better stop while I'm ahead.* She squinted and tilted her head to the side, studying the completed piece. Now that she felt more assured, Ella went to snap a photo of the painting. Since the paint was not yet dry and because the canvas itself was quite large, Ella decided to present the artwork on her phone at the meeting.

Ella was not used to getting up so early, and she was feeling at a loss over how to kill time. She was too nervous to focus on creating any lesson plans for her college students, and she wanted to do something that would relax her nerves; it was essential to Ella to enter into the meeting with a clear head of confidence. She was also curious as to what Elizabeth might be doing. Ella knew that Elizabeth spent Friday evenings with her mother for Shabbat and had plans with family friends over the weekend. But now that it was Monday, she wanted to connect with her lover and possibly receive some kind words of encouragement.

While searching for something suitable to wear, her phone buzzed. She checked it and was pleasantly surprised to have received a text from Elizabeth! *Good morning beautiful! I wanted to wish you luck at the meeting today. Don't worry; everything will go smoothly, and everyone at the gallery is excited to meet you. See you at noon! Xo*

Ella breathed a sigh of relief. It was just what she needed to hear. Ella grinned ear to ear as she selected a pair of dress pants and a silky, printed blouse. It was a more formal look than what Ella would normally go for, but she also knew that she would be surrounded by a more conservative bunch. She thought back to what her mother had always told her. "Ella, for important functions, always dress nicer than you normally would. It's important to make a good impression."

Regardless of her low-income roots and sometimes chaotic upbringing, Ella valued much of the advice she had received from her mom. Ella knew that Catherine did not have it easy. Still, somehow, she managed to raise four healthy and stable children under less than desirable conditions, and Ella respected her mother greatly for that. With her mother's words now in mind, Ella decided to text Catherine to let her know the good news.

Hi Mom. Sorry for the late reply. I have some amazing news! I'm going to be exhibiting at the Amira Alder Gallery on

the Upper West Side. I have a meeting this morning to go over
the contract. I promise to call soon. Love you. Xo

Once dressed, Ella stared at herself in the mirror,
throwing her shoulders back. She addressed the reflection
with positive affirmations. "Okay, girl. This is the moment
you have been waiting for. You are talented, and your art
belongs at that gallery just as much as anyone else's."
Feeling centered and energized, Ella gathered her belongings, including her portfolio of artwork.

Just before she left the house, Ella decided to send
Elizabeth a quick message to see if she wanted to grab
lunch after the meeting. Ella was hoping to spend some
time connecting with Elizabeth on a personal level. She
sent a quick text and proceeded towards the elevator.
Ella's brain was swirling with emotions, and somewhere
in the recesses of her mind was the question as to how she
and Elizabeth would be able to have both a personal and
professional relationship. But for now, Ella could only
hope that she would be accepted as an equal within Elizabeth's elite circle.

ELLA SWUNG OPEN the heavy glass doors of the gallery and
was immediately greeted by a lovely receptionist. "Good
afternoon. My name is Ella, and I am here to meet with
Elizabeth Diamond."

"Great, grab a seat! Elizabeth and Samantha will be
right out." The receptionist pointed to a small leather
couch positioned in front of the brick wall. Ella sat down
and placed the portfolio on her lap. Within minutes, Elizabeth and another woman with shoulder-length blond
hair and glasses came strolling towards her. Upon laying

eyes on Elizabeth, Ella smiled warmly and stood to greet them.

"Hello! I'm so excited that you are here." Elizabeth leaned to give Ella a hug. Even though the embrace was more on the professional side, Ella noted that Elizabeth took a few extra seconds to hold Ella close. Pulling away, Elizabeth gave Ella a quick wink before the woman in the glasses introduced herself.

"Hi, I'm Samantha." Smiling, the blond confidently stuck out her hand, and Ella grabbed it, giving it a few firm pumps. "It's such a pleasure to meet you. Elizabeth has told me wonderful things about your acrylic paintings. It's great that you could come by to meet with us today."

Ella gushed, unable to hide her enthusiasm. "I have heard so much about you as well! Thank you so much for the opportunity to show here. It's honestly a dream come true for me."

Elizabeth added, turning to Samantha, "I told Ella about your role here at the gallery and that we would be working together on producing the exhibit. Ella, Samantha has been with us for five years, and she is incredible." Elizabeth then motioned down the hall. "Shall we head to the boardroom?" Ella nodded and followed Elizabeth and Samantha.

Elizabeth led Ella and Samantha into the empty office and flicked on the lights. "Please, grab a chair." As everyone found their seats around the table, Ella lifted her heavy, leather-bound portfolio and placed it on the table. "I know that you both have already seen a lot of my work online, but I wanted to bring prints of samples as well."

Samantha slid her designer frames to her nose with a

single finger. "Excellent! Elizabeth and I talked about a few specific pieces that we wanted to include in the exhibit. May I see?" Samantha pointed to the portfolio, and Ella obliged, sliding the case towards her. As Samantha unzipped the edges, Ella exchanged a questioning glance with Elizabeth and Elizabeth gave Ella a small nod.

"Um, yes, I understand that there were some paintings that you had your eyes on, which is great. I also wanted to show you both something that I had just finished over the weekend. It's not in the portfolio because I literally completed it this morning, so I took a photo of it with my phone, instead." Ella bit her lip nervously. "I was wondering if I could show you this too."

Ella noticed a twinkle in Elizabeth's eye as she replied in an even tone. "Yes, absolutely. Let's see." While Samantha was still flipping through the portfolio, Ella handed Elizabeth her phone so that she could see the photo of the portrait. Ella kept her gaze on Elizabeth, curious to see her expression.

Upon seeing the image, Elizabeth's professional demeanor seemed to soften as a broad, beaming smile spread across her face. Ella's heart soared with joy. *Ah! It looks as though she likes it!*

"Wow, this is really beautiful. And I'm not just saying this because it's me." Elizabeth gave a little laugh. "The interpretation is excellent, and the color palette is divine. But of course, I might be a bit biased." Elizabeth passed the phone to Samantha, who looked up from the portfolio. "Here, check this out. What do you think?"

Samantha took the phone from Elizabeth and turned to Ella. "You just finished this morning? Cool, let's see." Ella watched as Samantha examined the photo, her expression turning from one of amusement to one of initial surprise. Samantha gave a small gasp. "Oh my! This is...is this...is this *you*, Elizabeth?" Ella noted that even though the painting seemed to catch the partner off guard, Samantha was still smiling, so Ella took that as a positive sign.

Ella looked quickly at her lover, and Elizabeth replied, "Yes, it's me. Um, Ella had painted me the other night and was thinking about including this piece. I know it's a bit risqué compared to other pieces here, but I thought we should at least consider it."

Samantha kept her eyes on the phone and nodded slowly. "Hmmm, I mean, it's a *lovely* portrait, and you are right; the colors and textures are sumptuous." Samantha narrowed her eyes, appearing lost in thought, and Ella began to feel as though Samantha might be on the fence about including the portrait. After a few seconds, Samantha raised her eyes, looking at both Ella and Elizabeth. "I mean, there are *so* many options available here," she emphasized, tapping the portfolio. "And Ella, we absolutely loved *Abyss*. We definitely want to include that in the exhibition as well."

Elizabeth gave Ella an empathetic look and turned to Samantha. "Maybe you and I can talk more about it after the meeting?" Ella suddenly felt dejected. She was hoping to catch Elizabeth for a late lunch or spend a few moments chatting before she went on with the rest of her day.

Samantha nodded towards Elizabeth. "Yes, sure, of course. For now, why don't we decide on our top fifteen favs, and after that, we can discuss how the portrait might fit? Does that sound okay with you, Ella?" Samantha asked diplomatically.

Ella conceded and shrugged. "Sure, that's cool with me. So I guess you'll both decide what you want to include, and then let me know? Is that how it works?"

Elizabeth answered, "Yes, we can do it that way. Don't worry; we will let you know by mid-week. From there, Samantha will make arrangements for packaging and travel." Elizabeth gave Ella a reassuring smile, which made Ella feel a bit better.

Elizabeth continued, "But for now, I also wanted to decide on the exhibition dates as well as the night for the opening gala. Samantha, can you please pull up the scheduling software on your laptop?" Upon instruction, Samantha then lifted her MacBook and typed away on the keyboard. She appeared to be eyeing an online calendar. "Sure, okay, here we are."

Elizabeth took a deep breath. "Great! Our next available slot will be at the end of October, so I would like to get started as soon as possible. Samantha, once the pieces have been decided, we can then move ahead with our promotional strategy."

Ella followed along while Samantha made a suggestion. "Now, I have a bit of a crazy idea, but as you both know, I want to shake things up around here. What do you think of having the show opening on Thursday, October 31? I know we have never done that before, but I think we can do something really spectacular with that date, and obviously, we can play up Halloween in our marketing."

Elizabeth tilted her head in thought as her eyes darted around the room. Ella watched Elizabeth marinate on Samantha's idea as she grinned. "Wow, cool! Personally, I like that idea myself. I mean, I know you're in charge here, but if you wanted to have the opening on Halloween night, I could see about finding a substitute to teach my painting class," Ella offered.

Elizabeth tapped her fingertips together before deciding. "You know what? I like it! I mean, it makes sense, and our members are pretty devoted. I can definitely see them wanting to visit us on Halloween night if we have something festive and interesting to offer." She turned to Samantha. "Let's do it. And Ella, you can make that work with your schedule?"

A thrill shot through Ella. *Oh my god, this is actually happening!* "Oh, yes, absolutely!" Ella then addressed Samantha. "Were you thinking, like, a *costume* party?" Samantha looked at Elizabeth and shrugged. "Um, well, I guess I didn't consider people dressing up. I mean, our members are pretty conservative. But since the date *would be* on Halloween, maybe a *classy* theme with a suggested dress code?"

The three women remained silent for a moment before Elizabeth exclaimed, "Oh my goodness, I've got it! What about a masquerade-themed?" Ella hit the surface of the table with her hand, unable to quell her excitement. "Holy shit, I love it!" Samantha also echoed the response, "Yes, that's brilliant! That will be so perfect for our members."

The energy in the office became heightened as everyone agreed to the theme.

Elizabeth then restored order and focus to the boardroom. "Excellent, we have a plan. Samantha, I trust you will work with the others on production, correct?" Samantha nodded and turned to Ella.

"You know, I am so curious to know more about you. Like, how did you begin your journey as an artist?" Samantha peered into Ella's eyes. "Understanding you as a person will help towards any marketing and promotion ideas. And *that*, in turn, will help you to sell more art."

Ella looked quickly between Elizabeth and Samantha. She wasn't used to needing to sell *herself* in order to sell a painting, but then again, Ella had never been in a position where she was exhibiting at a well-known gallery. She decided to let Samantha move ahead with her process.

"Okay, well, I guess to start, I'm originally from Queens. I come from an Irish-Catholic family, and I have three brothers and sisters. At the end of high school, I received a full scholarship to study at the Waterford Institute of Art, and then, from there, I—"

Samantha interrupted Ella. "I'm sorry, I don't mean to cut you off. These are all great details, and they will go into your artist bio for the exhibition. But I am talking about *you,* Ella. What makes *you* tick? What was your life really like, and how did that inspire your creations? I'm looking for less factual stuff and more, like, *heart*, if that makes sense?" Samantha pressed.

Ella felt a little flustered, unsure of how to respond. She looked nervously at Elizabeth, who gently replied, "It's okay, Ella. I think what Samantha is asking for is just a bit of backstory so that the gallery can engage the patrons. It's easier to do that if they *care* about who you *are*."

Samantha cooed, putting a hand on Ella's arm. "Yes, exactly. For example, what was your childhood like?"

Ella wrung out her hands as her mind raced. *Ugh, this just feels weird, but alright, I guess I'll play the game.* "Um, well, to start, my family *was* pretty poor. We had the basics, like a roof over our head and electricity *most* of the time, but you know, my parents didn't have the money for extras like art supplies or even things like nice, trendy clothes." Ella focused mainly on Elizabeth as she spoke, feeling more comfortable to reveal herself. "And of course, like any family who is struggling, my parents were pretty stressed out. So for me, doing art started as a way to escape and to create a magical world for myself, where I didn't have to worry about money or hear my parents fighting."

Samantha studied Ella with intensity. "Good, good. Oh, this is great stuff, Ella! Please, go on."

Ella took a deep breath and continued. "So, like I said, I got a scholarship to Waterford, which was encouraged by my high school art teacher, Mrs. Healy. And boy, were my parents mad, especially my dad. They honestly didn't want me to go, and my mom, well, she thought that..." Ella trailed off, uncertain of what to say next.

Samantha clung to Ella's every word. "What? What did she think" Ella replied, chuckling softly "Well, she thought that art school would be full of gays, and little did she know at the time, that I already knew I was a lesbian, so..." Ella shrugged. Samantha exclaimed. "Oh, fascinating! So, you are also a lesbian. Oh, this is great" Samantha turned to her laptop and typed in a few notes.

Suddenly, Ella felt confused. "Well, yes, I am gay. I mean, didn't you...?" Ella looked at Elizabeth and then back to Samantha. "I mean, I-I guess I thought you knew that about me, already?" Ella looked hard at Elizabeth. *What the heck is going on here?*

Elizabeth took over in an effort to explain the situation to Samantha. "Yes, Sam, Ella is gay. And you know that I am gay too. Ella and I, well, we have been *seeing* one another. But, but that's *aside* from this meeting right now." Samantha nodded as she absorbed the information.

"*Oh, okay!* I see. Well, I mean, you are right, Elizabeth.

We don't need to get into the specifics of personal relationships, but now that you mention it, everything makes a bit more sense now. Especially the portrait." Samantha then waved her hands, dismissing the awkward tension in the room. "It's not important. So you are both lesbians, cool. Let's move on from here" Samantha checked her notes on the screen and then turned back to Ella.

"So would it be safe to say that you came from nothing and then built up your talent on your own, without much help," Samantha questioned. "Like, because what I am seeing here is a great rags-to-riches story of a young woman who struggled as a child to become the successful artist that she is today. And *that* would make a great marketing hook."

Ella slowly bobbed her head. "Sure, I guess so. Yeah, that seems accurate enough, I suppose." Samantha looked pleased and leaned back in her chair. "Super! If it's okay with you, Elizabeth, I want to run with this a bit. What do you think?"

Elizabeth pursed her lips, casting her eyes to the ground before providing what Ella perceived to be a measured answer. "I think you can begin to move in that direction, as long as that works for you, Ella? And of course, I want to approve any final copy, as always."

Samantha nodded her head in agreement. "Oh, definitely. I just needed some kind of foundation with which to begin. But of course, I'll run everything by you."

"Okay. Well, I guess the only thing left to discuss is the contract. Samantha, do you have that with you?" Samantha looked around and groaned audibly. "Oh, no! I left it in my office. Hold on, one second. I will run and grab it." Samantha stood up quickly and raced out the boardroom, leaving Ella alone with Elizabeth.

Elizabeth reached out her hand to touch Ella. "Are you okay? You seem a little stressed." Ella sighed, relishing the touch of Elizabeth. "Yeah, I'm fine. I'm just not used to all of this, like, these *procedures*. But I trust you."

Elizabeth said in a comforting voice, "Please trust me, babe. I know this might seem a bit foreign to you, but Samantha is excellent at her job, even if she comes off a bit intense. It will all be fine, I promise. You should be excited! Can you imagine? An art opening on Halloween night" Elizabeth's excitement was contagious, and it made Ella feel better.

"I miss you." Ella looked lovingly into Elizabeth's eyes. "Do you have time for a quick lunch after this? It would be great to spend some time if you are free," Ella asked in a hopeful voice.

Elizabeth checked her watch and replied, "Yes, I can spare about an hour. All we need to do next is get your contract signed and then we can leave. Wanna go up the street to Hackler's Deli? They make the *best* matzo ball soup."

Ella didn't care where they went; she just wanted to spend time with Elizabeth that didn't involve business. As excited as she was about the show, discussing production and promotion just wasn't her thing. "That sounds awesome. I just need a bit of your time, and maybe a few kisses from that sweet mouth," Ella said flirtatiously.

Elizabeth grinned and squeezed Ella's hand. They shared a sweet moment before Samantha rushed back into the room with the documents. "Sorry! Here we are!" Elizabeth replied, "Thanks. So let's go over the notes, and then we can break for lunch."

12

The chimes above the door rang as Elizabeth and Ella entered the bustling deli. Hackler's was Elizabeth's favorite lunch spot. She had many fond memories of her late father, Adam, bringing her there after taking in a musical or an art exhibit. After their lunch, he would sometimes surprise her by secretly ordering a fresh chocolate Rugelach pastry. Now, as an adult, anytime Elizabeth entered Hackler's, she was instantly transported back to her childhood. And she was excited to share this spot with Ella.

Elizabeth held the door open for Ella as she spotted an empty booth near the back of the restaurant. "Let's sit over there," she pointed. "Normally, I like sitting at the deli counter when I am by myself, but the booth is so much cozier, don't you think?"

Ella nodded, following Elizabeth's lead. As they settled into their seats, she asked Elizabeth. "So what is Rug-um, sorry, how do you say it again?" Ella laughed as she struggled to pronounce the decadent dessert.

Elizabeth faced Ella head-on and took Ella's hands in

her own. "Look at my lips. It's pronounced *rug-a-lach*. It's a delicious, soft pastry that is rolled up, kind of like a cinnamon roll, but it can come with different fillings. My favorite is chocolate, and they make it fresh from scratch here!"

Ella looked around cheerfully, and Elizabeth noted that Ella seemed a lot more relaxed than she did during the meeting. "What are you thinking?" Elizabeth asked, curious to hear Ella's honest thoughts about the exhibition and the gallery's plans.

Ella bit the corner of her lip and grinned coyly at Elizabeth. "Well, I am very happy to be here with you. I missed you." Ella then lowered her eyes, almost shyly. "I can't stop thinking about last Thursday night. I won't ever look at my couch the same."

The couple shared a discreet giggle as they toyed with each other's fingers across the table. A server then appeared to take their order. Elizabeth turned to Ella. "Do you want me to order for both of us? Have you ever tried matzo ball soup?"

Ella looked at Elizabeth and then at the server. "Yum, yeah, I have! Sure, I will take one of those as well." Elizabeth ordered, "Two soups, please, and oh, can we order a chocolate Rugelach for dessert?"

"Yes, of course, my sweet dear. Coming up!" Their waitress, Ruth, was an older woman who Elizabeth had recognized over a period of many visits. Elizabeth was always charmed by Ruth's gentle nature, like she was welcoming grandchildren into her home, as opposed to serving strangers in a deli.

Elizabeth turned back to Ella, eager to return to their conversation. "Seriously, you seemed pretty stressed in that meeting. Is everything okay?"

Ella looked down and toyed with her paper napkin. Slowly, she began, "I am very excited to have the opening show on Halloween, and I love the idea of a masquerade-themed party." Ella then paused. "I was really hoping to include the portrait of you in the exhibit. Do you think that can happen or...?"

Elizabeth took a deep breath. A few nights ago, she was open to the idea of including the portrait, but upon seeing the completed painting, Elizabeth suddenly felt uncomfortable. She struggled for a way to express this to Ella.

"Don't get me wrong. I *love* the painting; it is so beautiful! But it's also quite intimate, and I don't know," Elizabeth paused, trying to find the right words, "I think it's best to decide with my team so that I can have an unbiased decision. I think it's just too personal of an issue for me to decide on my own. Is that okay?" Elizabeth asked gently. "I don't want to disappoint you."

Ella nodded. "I know. I understand. I think I was just so excited about the opportunity that I wanted to express my gratitude in a grand artistic gesture." Ella waved her hands, dismissing the question with a weak smile. "Whatever your team decides is fine with me." Ella then asked, "So the more important question is, will you be my date for the masquerade opening?"

Elizabeth grinned. "Of course, I'd love to. I'm excited to show you off, and I think the theme is a killer idea!" Ella's smile widened. "Cool, that makes me feel better. And you know what? I was thinking about inviting my parents."

Elizabeth looked surprised. "Oh, really? I thought you were estranged from them or something?" Ella shook her head. "No, it's not like that. We often don't talk, and I only see them on holidays, but we *are* in contact. I am closer to my mom than my dad. But this is a pretty big deal for me, and I'd love for them to come out to support the show."

Elizabeth cooed, "Yes, of course. I think that would be great." But inside, she felt hesitant. From what Ella had revealed about her family, they seemed like a rowdy bunch, and it was important that the gallery maintained a proper sense of decorum. Carefully, she asked, "Has your family ever *been* to an art opening before?"

Ella replied casually, "Well, no. Honestly, art isn't really their thing, but if they are there to support me, then what's the difference?"

Elizabeth backtracked. "No, you are right. It would be wonderful if they wanted to come out to support you. We just, well, there is just a certain kind of *behavior* that we want the guests to—" Before Elizabeth could finish her thought, Ella interrupted Elizabeth, her voice tense. "What do you mean by *behavior*? You think my parents don't know how to behave in public or something?"

Elizabeth was taken aback by Ella's defensive attitude, but she did not want to cause a scene at the deli. Calmly, she replied, "Ella, I think you misunderstood. The gallery is a private, members-only space. I'm not going to lie, it can be a bit snotty at times, but this is a huge opportunity for you. I just don't want anything to come in between your success."

Elizabeth studied Ella's face. "Look, I'm sorry if what I said offended you. They are more than welcome to be there. I can't wait to meet them!"

Ella met Elizabeth's eyes and sighed, "Okay, thanks. Sorry, I didn't mean to get upset. I guess I just felt a little out of my element in the meeting. And all of the questions about my past threw me off."

Empathetically, Elizabeth grabbed Ella's hand. "I get

it. I know it's a lot, and Samantha can be intense. But leave it to us so that you can focus on your artwork. You need to *trust me*, okay?"

Ella relaxed in her seat, bobbing her head. "Yup, you're right. I do; I trust you. Just let me know which pieces you want to include, and I'll make sure they are ready for you this week." Just as Ella finished her statement, Ruth appeared and placed two hot soups in front of the women. Elizabeth bent over her steaming bowl and inhaled the broth. "Ah! That smells so good!" Ruth smiled, leaving the women to enjoy their lunch.

The pair hovered over their meals, eating every bite. After some time had passed, Elizabeth leaned back against the booth, feeling satiated. Within minutes, Ella had finished her bowl as well. Looking up at Elizabeth with a curious look, she began. "Can I ask you something else?"

Elizabeth dabbed a napkin to her mouth. "Of course, anything!" Ella inquired, "I'm just wondering, are we, like, an official couple? I guess I'm asking because I want to take you as my date to the opening, but I also don't want to jeopardize your position at the gallery."

Elizabeth clucked her tongue against the roof of her mouth. She felt terrible that Ella asked that question, but at the same time, she understood why. Looking into Ella's eyes, Elizabeth replied softly, "I'd like that. I *am* out as gay, and everyone in my inner circle knows this, but I'm a little more reserved because of my position. For example, I might not always be into PDA, especially when at the gallery, but yes, Ella. I consider us to be *official*. Do you?"

Ella grinned. "Yup, I do. Wow, that makes me happy. And don't worry, I get it. I know you have an image to protect. I guess it seemed a bit unclear to me in the meeting, so I just wanted to double-check."

Elizabeth bobbed her head. "I understand. I think it may have been excited nerves on both of our parts. And this *is* a new relationship. I'll be honest, I have never dated an artist who has exhibited at the gallery before, so I felt a little self-conscious too."

Suddenly, Ella gleamed at Elizabeth like a Cheshire cat. "Where's the bathroom?" Elizabeth smiled slowly. "Um, it's just back here," Elizabeth turned her neck and motioned towards the small hallway behind their booth. "Why?" Elizabeth smiled curiously. "What's that look on your face?"

Ella looked towards the hallway and then back at Elizabeth. Standing up, she held out her hand. "Come with me, just a second." Elizabeth laughed, feeling confused but intrigued. "Um, *why?* What's up your sleeve?" Without waiting for Ella's answer, Elizabeth rose just as Ruth was returning to the table with the chocolate pastry.

"Oh, sorry! We, um, we'll be right back," Elizabeth said apologetically. Ella then added, "Yeah, we are just going to the bathroom."

Ruth kindly shrugged and smiled, setting the cake down on the table. "Okay, okay, take your time. No rush, girls."

Elizabeth followed Ella into the ladies bathroom. "What has gotten into you?" Elizabeth laughed, just as Ella shut and locked the door behind them. Ella then approached Elizabeth, pressing her body close. "Well, I know you said that you want to be discreet, but I *really* need to kiss you right now. So I thought we could have a quick moment of privacy to ourselves."

Elizabeth was surprised but aroused at the same time.

"Oh my goddess, you are *so bad!*" Elizabeth closed her eyes as she felt Ella's soft lips on hers. Ella replied, "I know you love it, though. Just because you need to act like a saint in public doesn't mean that I do!"

Against her conservative nature, Elizabeth decided to embrace this passionate moment with Ella. She, too, had longed to feel Ella's body against hers, and she was grateful to Ella to have stolen some privacy for the both of them.

The women mashed their mouths hungrily against one another while intertwining their limbs together. With Ella's lips on Elizabeth's neck, Elizabeth reached down Ella's waist and tugged at her blouse, pulling it away from her pants. Elizabeth then ran her hands up Ella's torso and over her exposed nipples, squeezing them gently in her hand.

"Fuck, I want you so bad," Ella whispered as she pressed her body harder against Elizabeth. In a frenzy of desire, Elizabeth hiked up her dress, presenting a pair of bare thighs. Ella hooked herself against Elizabeth and rubbed her clothed crotch hard against Elizabeth's leg.

Elizabeth's panties became soaked between Ella's hot breath tickling her décolleté and the dry humping friction. She couldn't believe how turned on she was. *This is so wicked of me, in the bathroom of a Jewish deli no less!* No amount of guilt could steer Elizabeth back. She was aroused to the point of no return, and she desperately wanted Ella's fingers inside of her pussy.

"Ella, please, please fuck me! Fuck me with your fingers," Elizabeth demanded while still keeping her voice at a whisper. Ella obliged as two fingers found their way inside Elizabeth's panties. She gasped as Ella plunged inside of her; she could even hear the *sploshing* sound of her own wetness.

Cumming hard and fast, she dug her fingers hard into Ella as they moaned simultaneously in a hushed tone. Quickly, they covered their mouths in silence. Outside the bathroom, they heard the din of the lunchtime crowd— plates, cutlery, and the customers' voices as they chatted over their pastrami on rye sandwiches.

The couple collapsed into a fit of giggles, trying to calm down before smoothing their disheveled hair and clothes. "You exit first," Ella whispered tersely. "I'll follow behind after about ten seconds." Elizabeth nodded quickly, taking one last look in the mirror before creeping out of the bathroom.

As she walked back to her seat, she saw the chocolate cake sitting on the table, waiting patiently to be eaten. Elizabeth suddenly felt self-conscious, as though everyone knew what she had just been up to. But she also felt a thrill like no other. It was as though she had been sleeping for years, only to be awakened by her desire for Ella.

As she sat down, she saw Ella approaching their booth, wearing a guilty smile. Ella raised her right hand to her lips and seductively sucked the tips of her fingers. The two shared a secret giggle before Elizabeth reached out to get Ruth's attention.

"I'm so sorry, but I was wondering if we could get the bill? And she will take the cake to go." Elizabeth pointed to Ella. As Ella began to protest, Elizabeth said with a wink, "Trust me, Ella. You want to eat this. It will be the second-best experience of your afternoon!"

13

"Alright, everyone, thank you for handing in your projects! Remember that late submissions will be accepted, but you will be docked ten percent towards the final grade." A slew of groans could be heard around the classroom as Ella tried to maintain order.

Maria, a mature woman in her fifties, raised her hand. "Ms. Ryan, is that woman from the gallery returning to our classroom? I was curious to check out the space with my son and was hoping to get more information on upcoming shows."

Ella responded, although she was somewhat unsure of what to say. "No, I don't think so, Maria, but I can provide you with her contact info if you would like to learn more. Also, they should have upcoming shows listed on their website." She addressed the students more generally. "For those of you who remember, Ms. Diamond is from the Amira Alder Galley." Inside, Ella was struggling as to whether she should announce her own, upcoming exhibit, but she felt uncertain.

Ella was still having a hard time believing in this

incredible opportunity, and until she saw the actual public promotions, she wanted to manage her excitement. It was unlike Ella to feel so unsure about herself, but the meeting with Elizabeth and Samantha yesterday had made her realize that she was now in a different league, and she felt quite out of her comfort zone. *As soon as it's listed on the website, I will announce the exhibit in class.*

Ella closed her lesson plan as her students began to file out of the classroom. Ella noticed Mrs. Smith inch her way inside the room as the last pupil exited from the corner of the doorframe.

"Good evening, Ella. I was hoping to catch you after class. Do you have a minute?" Mrs. Smith asked.

Ella stopped in the middle of shoving her notes into her bag as she zipped up her portfolio. "Yeah, of course! How can I help you?"

Mrs. Smith replied, "Well, I was curious to know if you had any updates on Ms. Diamond from her visits to the college. I understand that she was doing some research into new talent or students that she could showcase at the gallery. Has she expressed any news?"

Ella had been so caught up in her romance with Elizabeth and the sudden opportunity to exhibit that she had completely forgotten to check in with her supervisor. Apologetically, Ella responded, "Yes, actually, I have, and I am so sorry that I have not kept you up to date." Enthusiastically, she continued, "So, I was actually given the opportunity to exhibit *my* acrylic painting collection. I just had a meeting with Eliza—I mean, Ms. Diamond, and her partner Samantha Fox to discuss the show." Ella gushed with remorse. "Again, I realize that I should have said something, but it all happened so fast. So, to be honest, I am not sure if she is returning to class after this. But I can find out!"

Mrs. Smith clapped her hands together with surprised delight. "Oh, that is *wonderful* news, Ella. Congratulations! What an exciting prospect. I'll definitely put an announcement in the online college magazine in support. We love to support and cheer on our Chatsworth team. When is the show, my dear?"

Ella hesitated before responding, knowing that she needed to give her supervisor a straight answer. Ella also realized that she would need the night off from teaching, as the show was a Thursday. "It's actually on Thursday, October 31; Halloween night. The show opening is going to have a masquerade theme!" Ella then paused. "Um, I was wondering if I might be able to have a substitute instructor take my place that night?"

Mrs. Smith smiled widely. "Of course, Ella. I will make arrangements on my end." She then leaned into Ella, lowering the volume of her voice. "Do you think that you could arrange some names for the guest list? I know that my husband and I would *love* to see your collection. And it might be nice for some of the other students to be able to attend as well. What do you think?"

Ella shrugged and replied brightly, "I'm sure I can make some arrangements. It would be wonderful to have you both there, and yeah, I would love to see some Chatsworth students as well. Let me check with Ms. Diamond to see what the gallery will allow, but I'm pretty sure that it won't be a problem."

"Wonderful! Well, I suppose that answers my question then." Mrs. Smith turned towards the door. Before she exited, Mrs. Smith turned back to Ella. "You know, I was so excited to hear that someone as well known in the arts world as Ms. Diamond wanted to check out the talent here at Chatsworth. And even though she chose an instructor over a student, I still feel like that is something for us to celebrate and be present for. I look forward to seeing you on opening night, Ella!" Mrs. Smith then exited the room, leaving Ella by herself.

Damn, she does make a good point. I guess I did kind of take a spot at the gallery that could have been reserved for a budding student. I had better make that guest list happen! Ella chided herself, feeling guilty. She hadn't thought about that fact until Mrs. Smith brought it up. Now, she was feeling a bit anxious. *I really hope that adding names to the guest list isn't a big deal. I'm sure Elizabeth will make it happen. She is my girlfriend, after all.* Deciding to push the worries out of her mind, Ella packed up and proceeded to leave the college for the night.

14

Elizabeth sat at her desk, reviewing some design plans, when she received a call from Samantha, directly to her extension. "Hi! I was wondering if you might be able to spare a few minutes? I've completed the draft of the promotional mock-up for Ella's upcoming show, and I wanted to show you."

Elizabeth replied, "Oh, that's great. Sure, I'd love to see it. You can come by my office now if you like." Samantha agreed, and within five minutes, she had arrived at Elizabeth's door with her laptop in hand.

"I'm excited for you to see what we came up with!" Samantha bubbled with anticipation as she lifted the screen. She grabbed a seat in front of the desk while Elizabeth moved to stand slightly behind Samantha, looking over her shoulder. A bold tagline appeared reading *Escape the Haunted House; A Masked Affair featuring original paintings by Ella Ryan*. The accompanying graphic was a stock image of a woman, mock screaming as though she was in a horror movie.

It took Elizabeth a few minutes to process the title.

She wasn't sure if this was supposed to be a joke or that Samantha may have been playing too heavily with the Halloween date and theme. She struggled with her words, finally remarking, "Um, I'm not sure I completely understand this, Samantha. It's, well, it's kind of *campy*, don't you think?"

Samantha seemed already prepared for constructive feedback and readily replied, "Listen, I know what you're thinking, but just let me explain. First, yes, I agree that there is a kitschy vibe happening with the 1950's stock image and the title font. But Elizabeth, you said yourself that you wanted something unique and less stuffy. And finally, meeting Ella, well, I totally get why that angle might work best for her, you know, *brand*."

Elizabeth was still not following, but she was eager to hear more of Samantha's explanation. "You're right; I *did* say that I wanted something bolder and more modern. But...I don't know," Elizabeth tilted her head as she examined the screen. "I'm just not sure that *this* is what we want. Or what *Ella* might want."

Undaunted, Samantha shook her head. "But don't you see the double entendre here? The reference to the haunted house is supposed to speak towards Ella's childhood, her upbringing." Samantha dramatically waved her hands around the room to emphasize her point. "Like imagine growing up in poverty, with parents who argue all of the time. Picture this little girl, planning her escape from her family's home so that she can find freedom and success in the outside world."

The volume of Samantha's voice rose as she tried to express her vision, using air quotes. "In essence, Ella is 'escaping her haunted house' with an exciting exhibit at the Amira Alder Art Gallery, *and* she is doing this on Halloween! I mean, it's brilliant, isn't it?"

Typically, Elizabeth was calm and reserved under pressure, but she began to feel a bit overwhelmed. She now understood the connection between Samantha's haunted house motif and Ella's personal background. And admittedly, the copy *did* tie in well with the date of the opening night. But still, she was worried about Ella's potential reaction.

Naturally, Elizabeth would prioritize a proper marketing campaign over hurting the feeling of an overly-sensitive artist. But Ella was not only a client; she was Elizabeth's girlfriend and lover. Elizabeth had been freed by Ella or lost herself in Ella, or both. She felt protective over Ella, and she wanted her experience as an exhibitor with the gallery to feel positive and supportive. Elizabeth was at a loss over how to move forward.

Samantha studied Elizabeth's expression as though she was reading her mind. "Listen, I know what you're thinking. You're concerned that Ella might think that we're mocking her, using her life and experiences to push sales, right? But Elizabeth, you *know* how all of this works. Ella receives a big percentage of any gallery sales, which, as we know, are the highest of any gallery in the Upper West Side. And using shock tactics to pique interest and gain attendees is what is best for the gallery."

Samantha shook her head in frustration. "If you absolutely hate it, I can start over. But both myself *and* our marketing team were merely following your instructions, that's it." She crossed her arms in front of her in defiance.

Elizabeth slowly nodded. Again, Samantha had hit on some key points. *Perhaps I'm too caught up in my personal feelings for Ella to argue with Samantha.* "I see what you are saying, and in general, you aren't wrong. But you met Ella, and she is a special artist. Also, her background doesn't define her, and she did say amazing things about her mother," Elizabeth replied weakly.

Samantha narrowed her eyes. "We have worked together for many years, and if you don't mind, I'll be frank. I feel that you are losing sight of how this exhibition is important to *the gallery*, as much as it is important to Ella herself." Samantha continued in a gentler tone. "I know you care about her, Samantha. I can see the connection between both of you. But please, don't let your emotions cloud your vision. You have *always* put business first, and you need to, again."

Elizabeth sighed. "Well, I suppose you are right. Maybe I am too attached to this situation on a personal level." Elizabeth strolled back to her seat to face Samantha. "What if I stayed out of the marketing decisions, but you relay this to Eli for final approval. How does that sound?" She waited, leaning back in her chair.

Samantha mashed her lips together and wiggled her fingers nervously. "Well, I already *did*, Ella." Before Elizabeth could get upset, Samantha added quickly, "He happened to have emailed me about the Carson show in January, and I thought it would be a good time just to *show* him the mock-up as well. And he loved it! Please don't be mad."

Elizabeth felt stunned on the inside, but she managed to remain calm. *How dare Samantha go over my head like that? Who does she think she is?* Still, Eli had the ultimate authority, even if he wasn't around very often. While Elizabeth usually had the final say over such decisions, she knew there wouldn't be any point in arguing with Eli. He was her employer, after all.

Elizabeth had no choice but to admit defeat. Wearily, she ran her hands through her hair. "Oh, is that so? Well, I guess it's done then. Whatever Eli says, goes." Elizabeth tried hard not to let the disappointment on her face show.

Samantha looked sympathetic. "I'm sorry. It was just a matter of poor timing. Next time, I *promise* that I will just go directly to you." She then shrugged. "I honestly don't want to upset you. Are we okay?"

Elizabeth waved her hands in a dismissive gesture. "Yeah, sure, we're fine. Business is business, right?" She then looked down at her hands, which she had been wringing nervously. "Let's just hope that Ella is okay with it!"

Samantha responded, "Oh, I am *sure* she will be just fine!" Elizabeth wanted to believe her, but inside, butterflies swarmed inside her stomach. *Gosh, for the sake of my relationship, let's hope so!*

15

Elizabeth sat nervously in the Uber's backseat as she rode to Ella's apartment in Chelsea to pick her up. As the vehicle drove through Times Square, Elizabeth noticed the various storefronts sporting Halloween decorations as fallen, autumn leaves blew along the sidewalk, like miniature tornados. The exhibit's opening night was only two days away, and at this point, Elizabeth couldn't wait for Halloween to be over. As much as the past month had stressed her out, she was looking forward to a romantic evening with Ella. She felt they could both use an evening of fun and escape from all exhibit arrangements. In particular, the last few weeks had started to take a toll on their relationship, and Elizabeth wanted desperately for her and Ella to reconnect as lovers.

The Uber driver pulled up to the apartment building's front entrance, and Elizabeth could see Ella waiting inside the foyer. Upon seeing the car drive up, Ella swung the door and came outside. Elizabeth noted to herself how cute Ella looked tonight, in her leather jacket and tight, black jeans.

"Hey babe, thanks for coming to get me." Unsmiling, Ella crawled into the backseat and plunked herself beside Elizabeth. Elizabeth was hoping for a kiss hello, but Ella busied herself with the seat belt.

"Of course! I'm really happy to see you," Elizabeth said brightly, placing a hand on Ella's leg, hoping for a warmer response, but Ella kept her gaze ahead, ignoring Elizabeth's affectionate gestures. They rode in silence for a few moments until Ella finally broke the ice. Avoiding eye contact, Ella asked, "So, how was your day?"

Elizabeth replied, taking a big sigh, "It was okay. Pretty busy, I guess. We are just putting the finishing touches on the, well, you know..." Elizabeth's voice trailed off. Ella nodded, keeping her eyes in her lap. "Hmmm, mmmm. Yeah, I know."

In trying to keep the mood light, Elizabeth changed the subject. "I hope you're hungry! I've never been to Nonna's before, but I heard it's incredible!"

Elizabeth wasn't actually a fan of Italian food, as much of it wasn't Kosher, and there were too many dishes that paired meat and milk together. Still, she had chosen the restaurant specifically for Ella. After all, she felt it was the least she could do, considering the circumstances.

Ella peeled her eyes away from the window long enough to give Elizabeth a grateful look. Placing her hand on top of Elizabeth, Ella softly said, "Thanks, I'm excited as well. I was actually surprised to hear that you wanted to go there, considering all of your food restrictions."

Elizabeth melted against the touch of Ella. "I wanted to go there for *you*, Ella. Considering how bad I feel about everything, I wanted to do something unselfish. Tonight is supposed to be about *us*."

Ella gently rested her head on Elizabeth's shoulder as the Uber neared its final destination. "Yeah, I know, babe. I'm glad we are going out too. It will be nice just to let go of all of the stress and relax." Ella then turned her head to look at Elizabeth. "Listen, I don't want all of this shit to affect our relationship. I care so much about you, but you understand why I was mad, right?"

Elizabeth studied Ella's face, stroking her cheek. "I do." The vehicle then pulled up in front of Nonna's, and the women exited the car. Turning to Ella, Elizabeth then added, "Let's talk more about it inside, okay?" Ella bobbed her head, and together, they entered the restaurant, hand in hand.

A hostess welcomed the couple, and Elizabeth told her about their reservations. The hostess then led them to a cozy table towards the back. The restaurant's rustic charm immediately enamored Elizabeth, and she was particularly grateful to have a more private table. She hoped that between the romantic atmosphere, good food, and their obvious love for one another, she and Ella could recover from this unfortunate incident.

Settling into their seat, they folded the linen napkins in their lap as a server greeted them. "Could we please start with a bottle of Chianti?" The server replied graciously in a heavy Italian accent, "Of course, ladies. I will give you some time with the menu, yes?"

After the waiter had turned his heel to leave, Ella nudged Elizabeth playfully. "Good call on the wine." Elizabeth gave her a wink and replied ruefully, "Yeah, I figured it would be a good idea." Within minutes, the server reappeared with a bottle and two glasses. He uncorked the wine and poured a small amount in Elizabeth's glass. She took a tiny sip and nodded in approval. The waiter then poured a more generous amount into both glasses before disappearing into the crowd.

The women raised their glasses and stared into each other's eyes. Elizabeth remained silent for a few seconds as she gathered her thoughts. Finally, she felt ready to speak. "Ella, I know that I owe you an apology. I feel really bad about what happened, and I want you to know that I never intended to upset you." Elizabeth looked down, overcome with guilt.

Ella chewed her lip and looked tenderly at Elizabeth, maintaining a soft gaze. Exhaling a deep breath, Ella replied, "I know. And I owe you an apology too. It was wrong of me to lash out the way I did. If anything, I should be grateful for this opportunity, and instead, I acted like a bit of a brat."

Ella leaned in closer to Elizabeth and held her hands across the table. "Ugh, its just that that ad was pretty brutal. I mean, it's funny and eye-catching to most people, but I just would have expected more from you and your team, especially because you *know me*. I told you all about my family history, and for the most part, none of it was like a haunted house. Maybe where you come from being poor is scary, but I didn't know anything else growing up, and a lot of the time, it was *fine*. The ad felt like a personal attack and a mockery of my roots."

Elizabeth nodded empathetically. "You are absolutely right, and yes, you *should* have expected something better from the marketing department." Elizabeth then added, "On the positive side, the promotions have certainly gained the kind of exposure we want for your show.

Tickets to the opening gala sold out on Monday! That's exciting, right?"

Ella bobbed her head in agreement. "Yeah, no, that's great to hear. I'm thrilled that so many people are attending." Ella then sighed and furrowed her brow. "But I don't appreciate being misrepresented like that, for the sake of sales. Yes, I understand that people are coming to see my art, but don't tell me that your little gallery didn't also benefit from that ridiculous ad. I don't care that most of the guests won't understand the meaning behind it; I know." Ella pointed to herself. "Like, I don't even know how to explain that image to my students and my parents," Ella shook her head with frustration and ran her fingers through her hair."

Elizabeth's heart sank. "Believe me, I feel responsible for what happened, even though I didn't get the final say. I should have been more protective. But you have to understand something. As much responsibility as I have with the gallery, I still answer to someone else. And actually, Samantha had never once gone over my head to get approval until that ad. So I did not see that coming, Ella. I really didn't. I will take accountability over my role in this, but please, you need to believe that I never intended to make a mockery out of your personal life just to sell some tickets to a show," Elizabeth said earnestly, practically begging.

She could tell that Ella was still fired up. *That's okay; let her speak and blow off some steam. It's best that we deal with this now before the show on Thursday so that we can put this behind us and move forward.* Ella looked impatient. "I *do* believe you. I know that you would never embarrass me on purpose. I trusted you, and I still do! But I don't trust the people on your team, especially that Samantha woman. God, what a bitch!" Ella snarled.

Elizabeth remained silent. She felt that Ella was completely justified in her anger towards Samantha, and truth be told, so was Elizabeth. Hell, she was angry at Eli too. But the show was coming up, and she needed to delegate with her team in order to get everything done. For now, Elizabeth's disappointment had to wait, but she wanted to hold space for her lover's emotions towards the situation.

"And like, what was up with the attitude I got from her about adding names to the guestlist for Thursday? I don't understand why I needed to go through Samantha for that. *You* could have helped me yourself." Ella pointed accusingly at Elizabeth. "God, I just *knew* she was going to give me a hard time about it. Honestly, I am the featured artist! Is it such a big deal to add the names of my friends and some family?" Ella took a big gulp of her wine and shook her head. "I mean, *thank you* for making that right, but at the same time, it was an added stress that was completely unnecessary."

Elizabeth nodded in agreement. Ella made a good point. When Ella had first approached Elizabeth for the guest list, she directed Ella to Samantha, assuming that she could handle the request. After all, Samantha was responsible for the event production. In the past, she had always honored such requests with generosity and grace. She was shocked to hear that Samantha had given Ella such a hard time, and once that was revealed, Elizabeth stepped in. But to say that Elizabeth had regretted putting Samantha in charge was a huge understatement.

Ella looked at Elizabeth with a sad and tired expression. "I really care about you, and this relationship makes me so happy. Aside from the stress of the show, this past month has been amazing. And I know it's been equally hard on you too. I feel like Samantha is purposely trying to fuck with me, and I am not trying to blame you for everything. This show means a lot to me, and so do you. Hopefully, everything will get easier once we are past the opening night."

Elizabeth clutched Ella's hand. "Oh, me too. I am absolutely crazy about you, and I hate to see you sad and stressed, my beautiful girl." She locked eyes with Ella. "Thursday is going to amazing, and I can't wait to see you finally receive the recognition that you deserve. Plus, I'm sure you will look so sexy in your mask!" Elizabeth's eyes twinkled. "I guess the one great thing is that the portrait you did will be included in the show."

Ella smiled wistfully. "Yes, that's true. I really love that painting of you, and every time I think about it, I remember, well, *you know!*" Ella coyly trailed off.

Elizabeth smiled knowingly. *Oh, she remembered alright!*

16

E lla stood in front of the mirror, eyeing herself as she adjusted her masquerade mask. Tonight was the moment she had been waiting for since she was a teenager, and her biggest ambition was about to come to life. Her heart was beating fast in her chest as she sipped a glass of wine to calm her nerves.

Initially, when she and the team discussed themes for the opening night, Ella *liked* the idea of a masquerade event, but at the same time, she was a bit overwhelmed with the process. But now that Thursday was finally here, she was grateful to be able to wear a mask. A touch of hidden identity made Ella feel safe and less anxious as if she was hiding behind a protective shield. Ruefully she thought, *Well, I guess you aren't a complete idiot, Samantha!* But just as Ella's mood was about to sour, she pushed Samantha out of her head. *No, I am not going to let my anger towards that woman spoil my night. This is my time to shine, and my beautiful woman will be right by my side.*

Ella looked down and smoothed her black lace dress over her petite frame. Normally Ella's style was more bohemian chic, but tonight, she decided to vamp up her look with a racy outfit that screamed femme fatale. She especially loved the way the black mask with its jaunty side feather paired so well. Upon final inspection, she felt like a character from a movie, and it gave her a sudden burst of confidence. *I mean, it is Halloween night, after all! Why not embody a mysterious persona?*

Satisfied with her look, she checked her phone. She noticed a text from her mom. *Hi sweetie! Your father and I are so excited about tonight. We will be there at 9:00 pm. Do we just ask for you? Also, do we need to wear a mask? Your father doesn't want to* 🙁 Chuckling to herself, Ella typed back a reply. *Hey Mom! Awesome. Your names are on the guest list; just tell the person at the front door. Also, it's cool if you don't want to wear a mask. Love you & see you later. Xo*

Ella's clock on her phone read 7:46 pm. She knew that Elizabeth would already be there, helping with preparation. Ella wanted to get there early before the doors opened, and in particular, she needed a kiss and a hug from Elizabeth. She finally felt ready enough to call an Uber and head to the Upper West Side, taking a few deep breaths.

ELLA TOOK a step inside the Amira Alder Gallery and was immediately awestruck by her exhibit. The opening party had not yet begun, and Ella was happy to arrive before the guests so that she could take it all in and steal a few moments with Elizabeth before the excitement began.

In total, the gallery had two separate display areas, and Ella had been given one, full space for her show. Her eyes danced wondrously over the acrylic paintings that hung on the wall. Enthralled by the moment, Ella twirled like a child in the middle of the room.

While admiring the hangings, she heard the click of heels behind her. She turned around to see Elizabeth decked out in a stunning Venetian-style mask. A long dress covered her body, hugging her curves like a pour of black ink. With outstretched arms, Elizabeth smiled, motioning around the room. "Well, what do you think?"

Ella gasped at the sight of her girlfriend, shaking her head in amazement. "I don't even know where to look first! I think that *you* look as stunning as this exhibit, and as far as the placement of everything, I love it so much!" Ella squealed and put her hands to her face. "Seriously, this looks *so good*, and you are so beautiful!" Ella and Elizabeth warmly embraced, sharing a passionate kiss.

"I was hoping to steal you for a quick moment before the show. Tonight will be busy, and you will be in demand, my dear." Elizabeth whispered as she lovingly touched Ella's cheek. "So I am glad that you arrived early."

Ella nuzzled against Elizabeth, inhaling the Chanel that she craved now. "Mmmm, me as well. I feel like I am in a dream!" Elizabeth then exclaimed, "Oh! Did you see it?" Ella looked at Elizabeth questioningly. "What do you mean?"

Elizabeth laughed. "The *portrait*, silly! It's right over here." Gently, Elizabeth took Ella's hand and guided her over to the south wall, near the exit. "See? Doesn't it look great?"

Ella beamed at the sight of her portrait of Elizabeth against the white gallery walls. While she was grateful that the picture was included in the exhibition, she was slightly miffed that it was so far off to the end of the room.

Still, she wanted to keep a positive exterior and chalked up her disappointment to being nervous about the show.

Ella replied lightly, "Oh wow, yeah, babe. It looks awesome. I mean, it's a portrait of *you*, so it couldn't look anything less than spectacular." Just as Elizabeth wrapped an arm around Ella's waist, she heard more voices inside the space.

"Hello! Welcome, Ella. I hope you like how everything is presented."

Samantha walked towards the couple, carrying a few flute glasses. Extending her arm, she offered, "Champagne?" Ella gave Samantha a tight smile. "Sure, thanks."

Elizabeth turned to Samantha. "Oh, this looks wonderful. You did a great job. Thanks so much for your help." Elizabeth gave Ella a quick nudge. Taking this as a cue, Ella remarked. "Yup, looks good. Thanks." Still, Ella couldn't help herself. Putting a finger to her lips, she turned to Samantha. "Actually, I am just curious as to why this painting is all of the way back here?" In an effort not to sound combative, Ella then added, "I mean, since you asked and everything."

Samantha cooed, "Mm, hmm. Yes, I see what you mean, and I'm sorry if that didn't meet your expectations. *We* just thought that a nude painting of the art director might be a little, well, *risqué*." Samantha then patted Ella's arm condescendingly. "I know how much you care about Elizabeth, and we didn't want to leave it out entirely, so we just made a slight compromise."

As though sensing the tension rise, Elizabeth quickly jumped in. "It's just *fine*, Samantha. Both Ella and I are happy with the placement." She gave Ella's hand a hard squeeze. "Besides, I don't think I mind having my nude body off to the side. I wouldn't want to scare off any guests!" Elizabeth gave a self-deprecating laugh, and Ella couldn't help but roll her eyes. *Oh my god! Seriously, what an ass-kisser.* Ella was becoming annoyed with this phony banter, and she needed to escape this situation fast.

Ella noticed some catering staff appear out of the corner of her eye, carrying silver platters of hors devours. Taking Elizabeth's elbow, Ella suggested, "Hey babe, let's go mingle. I'd love to try one of those appetizers over there." Ella motioned towards the other side of the room.

Elizabeth picked up on Ella's cue. "Yes, let's. I want to introduce you to some important gallery members as well." Ella was grateful to be steered away by Elizabeth from Samantha's smirk.

"What is *wrong* with that woman? Didn't you see the way that she talked to me back there?" Ella whispered tersely. Elizabeth kept a pleasant smile plastered to her face but replied through her teeth, "I know, I know. She is pretty difficult, and I don't know why. But just smile and walk away. Don't let her attitude ruin your night, Ella."

Ella knew that Elizabeth was right, but at the same time, she was frustrated. Ella was someone who always spoke her mind, and she wasn't accustomed to dealing with smarmy remarks. She felt her Irish temper began to rise as she struggled to keep it at bay.

Suddenly, Elizabeth gasped and pulled hard on Ella's arm. "Oh! There's Mr. and Mrs. Townshead. He is the editor-in-chief for *Spatter Magazine.* You know, *the* art magazine for New York collectors? We *must* talk to him. Come, I'll introduce you!"

Linking arms with Elizabeth, Ella glided over to the elderly couple. The gentleman spoke first. "Elizabeth, my dear! How *lovely* to see you! You remember my wife, Helen?"

Ella observed as Elizabeth laid the charm on thick. "Yes, *of course!* Good evening, Helen. It's such a pleasure to have you both here tonight." Elizabeth pointed to Ella. "Let me introduce to you, Ella Ryan, our featured artist. Her exhibit will be up until the end of December."

Mr. Townshead stuck out his hand, and Ella gripped it warmly. "Congratulations! It's a pleasure, Ella. My goodness, your paintings are absolutely marvelous." He then remarked softly, although loud enough for the trio to hear. "You know, I *really* do need a new article for the January issue." Putting a hand on Ella's arm, he added, "We're going to walk around, but Ella, we should definitely talk after the show, yes? It would be wonderful to feature such rising talent as yourself in an upcoming issue of *Spatter*."

Ella's jaw dropped as Elizabeth hugged her close. Stammering, she replied, "Oh my god, yeah for sure! I would love to talk to you. I've never been featured in a magazine before!" The couple twittered gently, obviously enjoying the effect their influence was having on Ella. While Ella could sense an air of superiority from the couple, she didn't care. *Wow! A magazine article. That would be incredible!* Elizabeth then added before the pair wandered off to check out the paintings, "Thank you again for coming, and I hope you enjoy the show!"

A server carrying a platter sauntered over to the women, and Ella reached out to grab a bite-size puffed pastry. With a full mouth, she muffled, "Holy cow, that's crazy! He wants to interview *me?*" Elizabeth looked around quickly, giving Ella a cue to close her mouth while eating. "It sure sounds like it! That would be incredible exposure for you."

Leaning in closer to Ella, Elizabeth then said, "Ella, you need to, like, *sell* yourself more. Go and schmooze; make new friends." Elizabeth then turned her head towards the entrance and noticed a queue of bodies beginning to file into the gallery. "It's really starting to pick up now. As the artist, it's important that you connect yourself with the *right* people."

Ella understood what Elizabeth was saying, but she wasn't used to making small talk with strangers, especially those she didn't seem to have anything in common with. Hobnobbing with art snobs wasn't Ella's scene, but she trusted Elizabeth and wanted to show her appreciation. Still, she could schmooze with people she already knew.

Pondering her next move, Ella toyed with her champagne glass stem when she saw a warm and familiar face approach her. Ella's face lit up. "Mrs. Smith! Oh my goodness, you made it!" She hugged the woman warmly, grateful to see a familiar face.

Mrs. Smith gushed, "Oh, I am so proud of you, Ella! This is incredible, and wow, there are so many people here tonight." Ella looked around the gallery and suddenly noticed the sea of bodies, many of whom were wearing masquerade masks. Mrs. Smith apologized, "My husband couldn't make it tonight, but look—I did bring a mask!" She pulled a small, plain black mask out of her purse, and Ella giggled with delight. "That's awesome! I am so glad that you decided to come in theme. Here, let me take you around. There is a portrait that I really want to show you as well."

Mrs. Smith nodded as she followed Ella. "Is Elizabeth Diamond here? I'd love to say hello to her." Ella searched the crowd and noticed Elizabeth chatting with Samantha and some masked patrons. "Sure, let's go over and say hi." Ella guided Mrs. Smith over to the circle of bodies.

"Hey, everyone. This is my supervisor, Mrs. Smith. She works at the Chatsworth Community College." Elizabeth immediately turned to greet the woman warmly. "So nice to see you! Thanks for coming tonight." Elizabeth gave Mrs. Smith a gentle hug. Samantha looked at Mrs. Smith and gave her a forced smile. "Hello, nice to meet you.

Samantha then directed her attention to Ella, steering her away from Mrs. Smith. "Ella, you *really* need to meet Clay and his partner Dale." She pointed towards two men of similar height and build, both wearing masquerade masks. "They *love* your paintings. Here, why don't the three of you chat?" Samantha then pushed Ella towards the gentlemen, moving her away from Mrs. Smith.

"B-but, I was just showing Mrs. Smith," Ella tried to explain that she was showing Mrs. Smith around when Samantha cut her off, replying lightly, "Oh, don't worry, I'll take care of your guest." Leaning into Ella, she then said under her breath, "Ella, you need to meet influential people that can *help* you to succeed, not your community college supervisor!" Samantha chuckled cruelly.

Ella felt like she was being pulled in all sorts of directions, and it was beginning to stress her out. She tried to catch Elizabeth's eye for help, but Elizabeth was engrossed in conversation. Apologetically, Ella turned to Mrs. Smith. "Um, I am so sorry, I should chat these guys up. But I hope you like the exhibit, and I appreciate you coming tonight, really!" Ella grasped for Mrs. Smith's hand, and the woman replied, "Of course, my dear. This is your night, and it's good to mingle. Don't worry; I am fine on my own."

Ella nodded, feeling terrible about how rude

Samantha had come across. Turning to the masked men, she began to engage in small talk while she answered questions about her influences and inspiration. The conversation was going smoothly when Ella felt a hand pull at her elbow. She turned to find Elizabeth standing behind her.

"Hey, babe!" She smiled at her girlfriend. "What's going on?" Elizabeth leaned in and whispered, "Eli Schwartz is here! My *boss!* He must be in visiting from Israel." Elizabeth looked both excited and nervous. "This is a big deal. We *have* to go and say hello. He needs to meet you."

Once again, Ella felt like she was in the middle of a tug-o-war. She allowed Elizabeth to drag her away from Clay and Dale. It was easier to accept an order from Elizabeth than Samantha, and Ella recognized how important it was to meet the Amira Alder Art Gallery owner.

Ella and Elizabeth walked over towards Eli, who was in the middle of removing his coat. The couple waited until he was settled enough to give him their attention when suddenly, Ella heard a pair of familiar voices in the line at the entrance.

"No, no. It should be under *Catherine Ryan.* Catherine with a *C.*" The woman sounded exasperated as the puzzled-looking person at the door continued to flip through the sheets of paper attached to their clipboard. A gruff male voice then interjected, "Jesus Christ, Catherine! I told ya that we should've come another night. Now we have to stand in line with a bunch of hipsters, like a couple of goddamn teenagers!"

Ella gasped, just as Elizabeth pulled her towards Eli. "Oh my god, my parents are here; they're in line. And, oh, it sounds like there is trouble!" Frozen, Ella felt like her two worlds were about to collide. *Oh no, this is going to get ugly!*

Eli spotted the women, approaching them with a wide grin. At the same time, Ella's parents finally struggled through the entrance after a near-argument with the host. "Ella! Hi sweetie. We finally made it!"

Ella was at a loss, and she looked to Elizabeth for help, but Elizabeth looked just as alarmed. Ella thought to herself; I *need another glass of champagne, stat!*

17

"Eli! How lovely to see you; I wasn't sure if you were going to make it, but I'm so glad you are here!" Elizabeth gushed as they air-kissed. Elizabeth was surprised to see her boss, as she was not aware that he would be in the city this week. Still, she was excited to introduce Ella, as meeting Eli Schwartz would be an excellent connection for any New York City artist.

"Ah, Elizabeth, so wonderful to see you as well," Eli replied, in a heavy Israeli accent. "I know that I should have given you notice about my arrival, but everything was..." he motioned his hands dramatically in the air, "so *last minute*. But I am here now. Samantha told me that you are showcasing an excellent acrylic painter, yes?"

Elizabeth clapped her hands together and beamed. "Yes, her name is Ella Ryan, and hold on, I'd love for you to meet her." Elizabeth scanned the crowd, finally spotting Ella, who was surrounded by who Elizabeth assumed to be Ella's parents.

Elizabeth couldn't quite tell, but it appeared as though the three of them were arguing. *Oh no, this is bad! Ella, your parents cannot be causing a scene here.*

Elizabeth gently guided Eli towards the direction of Ella as she carefully moved her way through the crowd. She kept a congenial smile plastered to her face while she inwardly cringed. Of everyone she knew in her exclusive social bubble, Eli was most concerned about outward appearances, and in particular, he did not appreciate public outbursts. If Eli noticed fighting among artists and guests, it would not look good for Ella, and it would certainly reflect poorly on Elizabeth as well.

"MOM, I *told you*, I *don't know*. I asked for you and Dad to be on the guest list, and I just assumed it would be fine." Elizabeth could overhear Ella explaining. A plump, ruddy-faced gentleman hiked up his pants and looked around the room. "Hey! Where can I can a drink? Is there a bar somewhere?"

Ella's mother, Catherine, responded to her husband. "Now, honey, I am sure there are waiters that will come around to us. Just be patient. This is a *fancy* party, right, Ella?" Catherine winked and nudged Ella, and Elizabeth and Eli crept towards the trio.

"Good evening, I'm Elizabeth Diamond, and this is the owner of the Amira Alder Gallery, Mr. Eli Schwartz." Ella and her parents turned as Ella reached out to shake Eli's hand. "Hello, Mr. Schwartz! It is such a pleasure to meet you. Thank you for hosting my exhibition." Ella then presented her guests. "These are my parents, Liam and Catherine Ryan."

Elizabeth stepped aside as Liam and Catherine shook Eli's hand, discreetly wrapping her arm around Ella's waist. Elizabeth wasn't sure how obvious she should be about their relationship, but if Ella's parents noticed any physical affection between the women, they certainly did not mention it.

Eli said graciously, "It's a pleasure to meet you, Mr. and Mrs. Ryan. I see that your daughter has an incredible talent. You should be proud!" Turning to Ella, Eli added, "We are excited to have you exhibit with us. This gallery has been the starting point for many great artists in New York."

Liam spoke up gruffly, "Yeah, this is a real nice place, Eli. Seems very, ya know, upper class. How much does the average artist make in sales at a place like this?" Elizabeth observed Eli bristle at the abrupt question. However, always the consummate host, Eli continued to smile graciously.

"Ah, yes. Isn't that always the question!" Eli chuckled. "Of course, it's hard to say because every situation is so unique. But I can assure you that our gallery attracts serious buyers and collectors and our members are quite influential." Eli patted Ella kindly on the shoulder. "A pleasure, my dear. Will you excuse me? I am going to check out the rest of the collection."

Elizabeth nodded. "Excellent. See you soon, Eli. We hope you enjoy the show." With Eli now gone, the four of them stood around awkwardly.

Ella piped up, "So Mom, Dad, this is Elizabeth. The art director for the gallery and um, also, she is my girlfriend." Elizabeth was surprised but pleased to hear Ella's introduction. She knew that Ella was often at odds with her parents over her sexual orientation, so she didn't want to make the first move. Proudly, she grinned and squeezed Ella closer to her.

"Huh, I see. Well, that's nice." Liam clearly looked displeased, although, in Elizabeth's opinion, Liam seemed like the type of man who would be grumpy over anything. Appearing flustered yet encouraging, Catherine remarked. "Oh! Okay, well, as long as you are happy, I guess." Catherine leaned in closer to Elizabeth and added, "You are so beautiful! I would never have taken you for you know, a *lesbian*."

Elizabeth smiled tightly and gave a soft laugh. While the comment was rude, Elizabeth could tell that Catherine was trying to come from a good place. Still, Elizabeth wanted Ella to continue to work the room. She couldn't tell if Eli liked Ella or not, but if Ella truly wanted a strong network within the New York art scene, she needed to care about Eli's approval as much Elizabeth did.

Samantha snuck up behind the foursome. "Hi! I'm Samantha Fox, the art handler and one of the partners at the gallery." Her tone came off as more of an announce-

ment than a friendly introduction. She barely acknowledged Liam and Catherine before turning to Ella. "I'm
sorry to interrupt, but we *really* should mingle. There are
a few collectors to meet, and Eli has some questions about
the portrait in the back." Samantha tried to maneuver Ella
away from her parents, but she protested.

"Can you give me a few minutes with my family? I'll be
there in a sec." Ella retorted while Elizabeth cringed. She
understood how important it was to network at the opening, but she also felt that Samantha was acting brash and
dismissive of Ella's parents. She tried her best to smooth
over the situation.

"Ella, why don't you walk with Samantha, and I will
stay and chat with your lovely family." Elizabeth's smiling
eyes were met with deadpan expressions. It was obvious
that Ella's parents were as interested in hanging out with
Elizabeth as Ella was with Samantha.

Ignoring Samantha, Ella stepped forward. "Can I talk
to you for a minute?" Elizabeth nodded quickly as Ella
pulled her aside. "I feel like I'm being pulled in a million
directions. Can you tell Samantha to back off? I'm trying
to enjoy *my* night, and I have people here who traveled
from other boroughs to see me," she said tersely.

"I understand, and you are right; Samantha is difficult.
But the opening night is a chance for you to meet important people that will help with your sales and exposure.
We are just trying to help you," Elizabeth replied, feeling
exasperated.

Ella shook her head, impatiently. "No, you are trying

to help with *your* sales. I know that the gallery gets a hefty cut; I remember the details of the contract. Too bad if Samantha doesn't think that *my guests* are worth spending time with, but they are important to *me*." Defensively, Ella crossed her arms in front of her chest and took a few steps away. "This *so* is not my scene. I appreciate everything that you have done for me, but please just let me meet people at my own pace, okay?"

Elizabeth felt bad seeing Ella so overwhelmed. "Yes, of course. No problem. You do your own thing, and I will try to distract Samantha." Ella smiled gratefully and gave her a quick kiss. "Thank you; I really appreciate that. I *promise* that I will join you in a bit."

"How about if I speak with Samantha and I speak to Eli about the portrait instead? Ella, you stay with your family. We'll be back shortly." Elizabeth motioned for Samantha to follow her and the two of them slinked off into the crowd.

Elizabeth spoke under her breath. "Sam, why are you being so hard on Ella? Your behavior is really unnecessary."

Samantha bit back. "Actually, *Liz,* your *girlfriend*, is acting like a brat. Sure, she is a talented painter, but she is an unknown and definitely not at the caliber of many of our past artists. And her attitude is unreal. Did you see the way she and her parents were carrying on? I mean, this isn't a zoo."

Elizabeth was shocked. In the five years that she had worked with Samantha, she had never spoken to Elizabeth this way. It was not only out of character to Elizabeth; it almost felt suspicious. *What is her problem?*

Just as Elizabeth was about to confront Samantha, a voice was heard behind the women. "Ah, Elizabeth. Good, I wanted to speak to you." She turned around to face Eli. "Sure! What is it? How are you enjoying the show?"

Eli motioned for Elizabeth and Samantha to follow him towards the back of the gallery, near the portrait. "I was looking at this, and I don't know," Eli put his hand to his mouth while he studied the painting. "I don't think this is appropriate for the gallery.

Could we please remove it from the wall?"

Samantha interjected, "Absolutely. I agree; I thought it was a bit risqué, especially since it's a *nude* painting of our art director. But Elizabeth *insisted* that it be included."

Elizabeth's jaw dropped, and she replied menacingly under her breath, "You know that is not true, Samantha. Ella requested to include the piece, and this gallery has always tried its best to design exhibitions that align with the artist's vision. And not to mention, *you* were the person responsible for dealing with Ella. *You* let this happen!"

Eli tried his best to calm the tension. "Ladies, ladies, please. Let's not fuss." Turning to Elizabeth, he said, "There is no denying that it is a gorgeous work of art, but Samantha is right; it's just not right for the AAG. Perhaps you can speak to Ella about switching it out for another piece?"

Elizabeth felt frustrated and confused. It was as if Samantha and Eli were turning against her, and she couldn't understand why. Still, Eli was her superior, so it was important that she followed his orders. "Sure, I suppose I can ask her. But I certainly do not want to do it tonight. Can it wait?"

Samantha addressed Eli. "Personally, I think Ella is stubborn and difficult to work with. And she is so young-this attitude will only get worse! But if anyone should be asking her, it should be Elizabeth. I feel that my patience has been worn thin."

Suddenly, a voice piped up. "Talk to me about *what?*" The three of them turned to see Ella standing, facing the trio with her arms crossed. "What's the problem *now?*"

Elizabeth began gently, "Ella, we—I need to talk to you, I—" Ella cut her off and replied angrily, "I heard everything she said," pointing at Samantha. "That I'm difficult and stubborn. Clearly, I don't seem to fit into this perfect little art world." Ella then turned to Elizabeth. "You know how much creating that portrait meant to me. I created it for *you*! And please don't deny how much you loved posing for me in front of your snooty friends because we *both know* that would be a lie."

Elizabeth felt her face grow red as a few guests began to look in their direction. Eli approached Ella. "My dear, this is no way to behave in an art gallery. We are pleased to show your work but kindly lower your voice." Elizabeth watched Samantha smirk in the background.

Ella shook her head. "No, in fact, I will do you all one better. I'm leaving. I may not have as much money or experience as all of you, but I'm a good person who is passionate about my creations. Art isn't a *scene* for me; it's my *life*. And if you can't appreciate that in your *talent,* there is no reason for me to stay." Before Elizabeth could say anything, Ella stormed out of the building as murmurs rippled through the gallery.

Elizabeth looked at Samantha and Eli in shock before exclaiming, "I need to go and find her!" Eli and Samantha tried to protest, but Elizabeth pushed her way through the crowd, hoping to catch Ella on the sidewalk.

As she burst through the doors, the cold night air hit her face like a slap. Her eyes caught a taxi drive by with a lone woman sitting in the backseat. *Shit, was that her? Did she get into a cab already?* Panicking, Elizabeth cried out, "Ella! Ella, please come back! Where did you go?"

She pounded the pavement to the end of one block, making her way around the building. There was no sign of Ella in sight. Elizabeth was devastated. She decided to go back to the front of the gallery to try and call Ella on her phone. Just as she made her way around the corner, she noticed two bodies entwined in an embrace.

Slowing down her pace, she gingerly crept closer. She saw a woman with her back turned, sporting a mess of blond hair. The woman was kissing a man in a suit. As Elizabeth's gaze moved forward towards the bodies, she instantly recognized them. It was Eli and Samantha!

Elizabeth put a hand to her mouth to hide her gasp. In addition to Eli being the boss, he was also a married man. *Oh my god! I can't believe what I am seeing.* Elizabeth thought back to Samantha's combative behavior and insubordinate. *Oh my god, everything makes sense now!*

18

E lla caught her breath in the back seat as the taxi sped away from the Amira Alder Gallery. Ella's mind was racing as she struggled to process what had just happened. One thing was for sure; never in her wildest dreams would she had thought she would be leaving her first major gallery show in tears, escaping from both potential buyers and a girlfriend.

"Where to, lady?" the driver said gruffly, turning to face Ella. She blanked for a few seconds, unsure of what she wanted to do next.

Putting her hands to her temples, she took a deep breath. *Oh shit! It's actually Halloween night. Okay, I'll go for a drink somewhere.* Suddenly, she decided. "La Crème, please, in the West Village."

The driver looked up the name in his GPS and then headed off in the direction of the club. Ella leaned back, feeling slightly calmer. Even though La Crème was her workplace, it was also a bar where she felt comfortable and familiar. Not to mention, she was already dressed up. The more she considered it, the more sense it made. *It would be nice to see some friends and coworkers in their costumes and blow off a little steam. God knows I could sure use it!*

As she continued to fume, Ella thought about Elizabeth, replaying the sound of her voice, calling after Ella. Her heart felt bruised as a deep sadness overwhelmed her. She hated running out like that and abandoning the one woman who had supported her career since Mrs. Healy. But what hurt Ella most was Elizabeth's apparent lack of loyalty during this whole process.

Ella felt justified assuming that her lover would have her back, *especially* someone as influential as Elizabeth appeared to be. *Maybe she doesn't have as much power as I thought she had? It was pretty clear that she needed to suck up to Eli during the show. Maybe this whole scenario wasn't exactly what I had thought?*

Regardless of how painful and embarrassing it was, Ella felt justified in her emotions, and she wanted to put the incident behind her. And as the taxi slowly approached the night club, Ella was excited at the prospect of being with her own people. Plus, while Ella would never cheat on Elizabeth, she didn't see the big deal in a night of dancing, drinking, and a little harmless flirting.

Ella dug into her wallet and pulled out a few crumpled bills. "Thanks, man. Happy Halloween!" Ella hopped out of the backseat and proceeded to the front doors of La

Crème. Outside, she saw a few patrons dressed up in costumes. One called to her, "Ella! Hey Ella!" She turned to look at the customer, who was dressed as a mummy. She didn't recognize the woman, but she waved back anyway. "Hey, girl! Love your costume."

"Thanks." The mummy flicked a cigarette on to the pavement. "Are you coming in to hang out? It's *packed* in there!"

Ella pulled the door, and the mummy followed her inside. Over her shoulder, Ella called, "Yeah, I am. Looking forward to a good party!" The mummy tapped her on the back before heading off towards the restrooms. "Well, honey, you found one!"

Inside, the music was thumping as EDM beats blared through the speakers. Hundreds of guests swarmed the dancefloor in an eclectic array of masks, fabrics, and odd accessories that one would only ever see en masse inside a nightclub on Halloween night.

Adjusting her own masquerade mask, Ella found her way to the bar and positioned herself in the line. Ella was aware that she could have pushed her way to the front as an employee, but she waited politely. She was also aware that she had previously asked another employee to cover her shift due to the art opening, so she didn't want to push her luck.

Once at the front of the line, she noticed Ryan, hustling at the bar. "Hey, Ella! I thought you had the night off." Ryan exclaimed, wiping down the surface before leaning in closer towards Ella. "How did the art opening go?"

Ella shouted above the din of the music. "Oh, wow, it was...it was *fine*. I'll tell you more about it when it's not so busy." Ryan nodded. "Cool, cool. Where's your girlfriend? Did you bring her tonight? I'd love to meet her."

Ella shook her head as her stomach sank. Another wave of sadness cascaded over her shoulders. Fighting back the tears, she said, "Um, no. Not tonight." Ella looked around, feeling at a loss for words. She was still processing the incident.

Ryan could tell that Ella was visibly upset. "Hey, you okay? Wanna shot on the house?" Ella shook her head, unable to speak. It was as if everything that had happened an hour before was suddenly crashing down on her. She put her hands to her face, knocking her mask askew. Frustrated, she ripped it off. "Here, you wanna wear this? I don't want it anymore."

Smiling, Ryan took the mask from Ella in exchange for two tequila shots. Ryan plunked down the small glasses and poured a third one for herself. "You gotta catch up to the rest of us!" Ryan gave her a wink and waited until Ella had taken the first shot of tequila before joining for shot number two.

As the strong, honey-colored liquid coated her insides, Ella took a deep breath of relief. The burning heat from the alcohol seemed to calm the storm in her gut, like a torrential downpour. Gratefully, she looked at Ryan.

"Thanks so much. I really needed that." Ryan smiled. "Don't mention it. Go, have fun. More shots to come!"

Feeling fortified, Ella squeezed her way through the crowd, enjoy the sensations of sweaty bodies pushing up against her. At this moment, Ella reconnected with her spirit on the dancefloor. She had no intentions outside of losing herself to the music, but suddenly, she felt a hand around her waist.

Startled, she turned around to see a tall, beautiful woman dressed as a mermaid. The person immediately reminded her of Elizabeth. For a split second, Ella's mouth opened as a flood of emotion overcame her. But then the mermaid smiled, and Ella knew for sure that it wasn't her girlfriend. Still, she was numb enough from the tequila to engage. Ella managed to muster a smile. "Sorry, did I bump into you?"

The mermaid shook her head. "No, not at all, but I'm not going to deny that I bumped into *you*." She stuck out her hand. "I'm Lindsay." Ella took the hand and shook it. "I'm Ella." Ella blinked, feeling overwhelmed by the heat and the noise. "Sorry to stare, but you look exactly like someone I know."

LINDSAY SMILED FLIRTATIOUSLY. "Oh yeah, is she hot?" Ella bit her lip. *Yeah, she is the most beautiful woman on the planet.* But instead, Ella replied, "I mean, you can't compare a mere human to a magical mermaid goddess, right?" Instantly, Ella felt terrible for saying something so absurd. She didn't even recognize herself at this moment. Unfortunately, Ella wasn't in the mood for soul searching. Her eyes traveled to the bar for immediate relief from herself.

Turning to Lindsay, she said, "Hey! Wanna grab a shot at the bar?" Lindsay replied brightly, "Sure, let's go. What's your poison?"

Ella responded devilishly, "Tonight it's tequila. What's yours, sweetheart?" With a wink, the mermaid bantered back. "I'll have whatever you are having. Trust me; I can keep up!" Ella grinned, as all reasoning left her mind. "You're on. Let's go."

Hand in hand, they walked back to the bar, and this time, Ella was more aggressive in getting to the front of the line. Leaning against the railing, she caught Ryan's eye. "Hey, Ryan!" The bartender turned around, and upon seeing Ella with another woman, looked surprised.

As soon as she was finished serving another customer, Ryan approached Ella and Lindsay. "Hey, what's up? Want another shot?"

Ella nodded. "Yeah, actually four, please. We would love two tequila shots each, please." Ella dug into her purse to pull out some money. "Here, let me pay this time." Lindsay smiled with delight. "Oh, cool! Thanks. I'll get the next round."

Ryan raised her eyebrows but didn't say anything. She lined up five shot glasses and poured equal parts of tequila into all of them.

The trio grabbed their glasses, knocking back the

liquid in unison. Lindsay turned to head back to the bar, and Ella was about to follow her when she felt a grab on her elbow.

Ella looked back. It was Ryan. "Pssst, hey. Come here for a sec." Ella froze for a moment and shouted towards Lindsay. "I'll be right there." Lindsay walked backward, teasing Ella with her body as she danced seductively to the music. "I'll be waiting for you!"

Ryan leaned in closer to Ella, "Is everything okay with you? You're drinking like a fish. And who is that? You do have a girlfriend, right?"

Ella brushed off Ryan's concern. Sure, Ella knew that she was acting a bit too flirtatious, but in her opinion, it was just all in fun. Besides, after the night she had, Ella felt justified in acting out. "Honestly, it's fine. I'm great! Just trying to have a good time with my new friend over there." Ryan gave her a pointed look, but Ella was nonplussed. "Seriously, I appreciate you looking out for me. But I promise I'll be okay, alright?" Ella was starting to feel a bit lightheaded and warm from the alcohol, so she decided to step away and shake off the dizziness on the dance floor.

Ryan then demanded, "Hold on, drink this first." Ryan turned her back, and for a moment, Ella excitedly thought that Ryan was about to pour her another shot. But Ryan turned around with a glass of water instead. Rolling her eyes, Ella took the water glass and was about to take a big gulp when Lindsay reappeared from the crowd. Before

Ella could wrap her mouth around the glass, Lindsay grabbed her arm and pulled her onto the dance floor.

This time, Ella did not resist. She shrugged at the disapproving look on Ryan's face. "Sorry, buddy! I'm getting pulled into the ocean by a mermaid, and I can't be saved!

Ella again found herself in a sea of sweaty bodies. Lights and colors swirled around her, and the more Ella danced with Lindsay, the blurrier the images became. But she didn't care at this point. Ella felt free and light, and she loved how completely lost she felt. Dizzy and disoriented, she accidentally fell backward. She heard herself laugh out loud, and the sound seemed to echo all around her. Then Ella saw a mermaid peer down at her with an outstretched hand. After that, everything went dark.

19

E lizabeth leaned over Ella, gently removing an auburn strand of hair from her face. She studied Ella's bone structure, noting the perfect symmetry of her eyes. Elizabeth moved closer and softly planted a kiss on Ella's bow-shaped lips. Even the stale smell of alcohol couldn't keep Elizabeth away from her lover, and she was relieved that she could come to Ella's rescue.

Elizabeth's eyes landed on the portrait that Ella had painted. It was now resting against a wall, and as she observed it, a flood of emotion overcame her. So much had happened in between the painting and the art opening at the gallery. But Elizabeth needed to leave that all in the past. The portrait that was now displayed in Elizabeth's home was a sign that everything had changed.

As she continued to cradle Ella, petting her hair, she heard her phone vibrate. She anticipated many calls today and wanted to keep her phone on silent as not to disturb Ella. Elizabeth also did not want to be disturbed. She knew what she had done and the consequences that would ensue. For now, she was more interested in caring for the woman who laid in her lap.

Ella made a soft noise, and her eyelids began to flutter. A cough escaped her mouth before she opened her eyes fully. Surprised, she asked, "Elizabeth, is that you? Oh my god, where am I?" Ella lifted her head as Elizabeth slid a pillow underneath her neck. Ella put her fingers to her temples. "Oh wow, I have the worst headache!"

Elizabeth smiled gently. "Yeah, I figured you might. You were pretty wasted last night. Do you remember anything at all?" Ella frowned as she took a few minutes to think. Suddenly a look of recollection came over her face, and her eyes flashed. "I remember running out of the gallery and going to La Crème." Ella then cringed. "Oh god, I had a lot of tequila shots...then I was dancing...." Ella trailed off, looking pale and sheepish.

"Do you remember me picking you up off the floor and carrying you out of the bar? Well, I can't take all of the credit; Ryan helped me out." Elizabeth mused, playfully teasing Ella. Ella sighed and shook her head. "Fuck. Are you serious? God, I am such a loser," she groaned. Elizabeth put an arm around her, bringing her in close. "No, you're not. I understand why you were so messed up. I blame myself."

Ella then looked at Elizabeth as a dark look crossed her face. "Yeah. That was...wow. I still can't believe how bad that was." Ella exhaled deeply, and Elizabeth could sense the anger rising in Ella. "Like, seriously. What the actual fuck happened? Why was everyone so mean?" Ella stuck out an accusing finger towards Elizabeth. "And why didn't you defend me? I trusted you. You are the director of the gallery, and you were my girlfriend! You should have had my back the entire time." Ella's face was flushed as tears of frustration welled in her eyes.

Shamefully, Elizabeth sighed and lowered her eyes. "Well, I *was* the gallery director. But you're right about everything else."

Ella glanced at Elizabeth with surprise. "What do you mean you were the gallery director? What happened after I left?"

"Lots of things happened, Ella," Elizabeth replied, shaking her head in disbelief. She, too, had an overwhelming evening, and while she was not intoxicated, Elizabeth was still piecing everything together herself.

Ella said ruefully, "I'd love to hear all about it."

"Well, for starters, I found out that Eli and Samantha are having an affair. So that would explain all of the weirdness with Samantha. I guess she figured that because she was fucking our boss that she could do whatever she wanted, including undermining my authority."

Ella grabbed Elizabeth's arm. "Oh my god, no way! Did you catch them in the act?"

Elizabeth replied, "When you stormed out, I ran after you, but I guess you had gotten into a cab already. I walked around the block to see if I could find you, and when I circled back, I caught Eli and Samantha making out. They didn't see me, though."

Ella was hanging on to Elizabeth's every word. "Holy shit! That's crazy. Huh! So do you think that's why Samantha was such a bitch? Because I thought she worked for you and last night, it certainly didn't seem like that." Ella moaned and looked around Elizabeth's room. "Ugh, my head is killing me. Wait! Isn't that...my painting?"

Elizabeth looked over in the direction of the portrait and nodded. "Yup! So basically, after I realized that something was going on with Eli and Sam, I marched back into the gallery and gave them a piece of my mind. Then, I took the portrait off the wall and left the gallery to try and find you."

Ella looked at Elizabeth incredulously. "What?! You're kidding."

Elizabeth held Ella's hands tightly and looked directly into her eyes. "No, I'm not. Honestly, Ella, that was the last straw for me. I was appalled at how Samantha was talking to you at the opening. And I was just as confused and disappointed about how the exhibit had been handled in the first place. I had never had such issues with Sam before, but yeah, I'm guessing that she and Eli had their own little plan about how things would go down."

Fury rose within Elizabeth. "I am angry with myself over how you were treated, and I am angry with Eli and Sam for their deception. I can't tell you how long all of this has been going on. But last night and even before the opening, it was clear that neither of them had any respect for either of us. And that is something I cannot accept. Amira would never have approved of that behavior."

Ella softened her look and squeezed Elizabeth's hand. "Wow, I can't believe you did that! You seriously walked out of the gallery with that painting? Like, in the middle of the party and everything? I am super impressed. You are more of a badass than I thought!"

Elizabeth ran her hands through her hair and exhaled, "Yeah, I really did. And now, I am pretty sure that I don't have a job there any longer. It was almost as intense as when you walked out!" The pair shared a chuckle.

Elizabeth looked down at her phone, which continued to vibrate. She took it and tossed it onto the floor. "Ugh, I don't want to deal with this today. Sam has called me ten times since last night, and Eli has called twice. Once I'm ready, I'm going to give my resignation unless I've already fired. Either way, I cannot work in or support such a toxic space."

Ella gave Elizabeth a sympathetic look. "I'm so sorry. I know how much the gallery meant to you."

"But you mean more! As soon as you ran out, I needed to find you and make things right, Ella. What happened at the opening party was not okay." Elizabeth continued, "On a hunch, I decided to check out La Crème, and that's when Ryan helped me find you. Seeing you all drunk and slumped over like a rag doll broke my heart. I knew that I was responsible, and I needed to get you out of there." Ella handed her a tissue as Elizabeth wiped the tears from her eyes.

"Thank you for coming to get me. I hate that you had to see me like that. I was just so...so angry and hurt." Ella mashed her lips together and covered her eyes. "I feel so embarrassed." Elizabeth patted Ella's shoulder. "Well, that makes two of us, babe! Guess I'm a rebel, just like you."

Ella sat up and turned to embrace Elizabeth tightly. "I love you. Thank you for standing up for me like that. I had no idea. I can't imagine how hard a decision that must have been. The gallery was your life."

Elizabeth closed her eyes and hugged Ella back. "No, it's okay. I'll be fine. I was more worried about losing you. And besides, it's in everyone's best interest to let me walk away quietly from the gallery. I'll figure it out." Elizabeth looked at Ella. "I love you too. We are better than all of this."

The couple continued to hold one another tightly, caressing each other's skin. Their bodies began to intertwine as their kisses deepened. Passion rose between them as they sought comfort in each other's flesh. Elizabeth flipped herself on top of Ella and covered her tiny frame in pecks as soft as rose petals. Ella dug her fingers into Elizabeth's skin, and Elizabeth's mouth traveled down, in between Ella's legs. She inhaled the musky scent of Ella's arousal.

She continued to tease Ella's vulva, tracing her tongue around Ella's lips. She then found Ella's clit, and as her mouth danced, stimulating the sensitive nerve, she heard Ella gasp with pleasure. Holding on to Ella's hips and ass, she hungrily devoured Ella, relishing in the wetness.

"Oh, god, please. Yes," Ella cried out, and Elizabeth sucked harder against Ella's thrusting hips. Ella orgasmed hard for Elizabeth's mouth. Elizabeth thought to herself, *Ella, your body feels like home. It is within your body that I find the most divine spirit. I am yours completely.*

Together, they lay quietly, catching their breath. The spontaneous sex seemed to have quelled their emotions as they basked in a glow of healing and intimacy. Elizabeth still felt unsure about her situation and her future, but there was no uncertainty about her feelings for Ella. They were meant to be, and Elizabeth would make sure that she and Ella had a strong future together.

As they cuddled in bed together, Ella asked, "So what are you going to do now?" Elizabeth looked up at the ceiling, pondering her fate. "Well, I'm not sure what the rest of the year will hold, but tonight, I am going to Mom's for Shabbat dinner." Rolling over on her side, Elizabeth then asked, "Do you want to come? I'd really like to introduce you to my mom. What do you say?"

Ella beamed. "Really? Oh, that's so sweet. Yes, I'd love to!" Cheekily, Ella added, "She won't mind that I am a Shiksa?"

Elizabeth playfully lobbed her with a pillow and laughed. "Well, I can't promise that she won't mind, but my mom wants me to be happy, and you, Ella Ryan, make me so happy. Hannah will just have to get used to it. Unless you want to convert, that is!"

Ella shook her head. "I'm not sure about converting but, actually...!" Ella's eyes lit up. Excitedly, she grabbed Elizabeth. "Oh my god! What if we converted a space and started our own gallery? You have the know-how, and I have experience as both an artist and as a teacher. Together, we could create our space and run it the way we want." Ella paused before adding. "No, sorry, the way that Amira would have wanted."

Elizabeth's eyes grew wide as a smile crossed her face. "Wow, now that is a good idea! Oh, can you imagine? Working together and pairing our talents and knowledge?" Elizabeth stood up and waved her hands. "Yes, Ella! We should seriously think about this. I'll tell Mom what happened between Eli and Sam, and maybe she will have some answers for us about how we can go about making this dream a reality."

Ella stood to join Elizabeth, wrapping her arms around her. The two jumped for joy as the portrait of Elizabeth gave a watchful eye in the background.

Tenderly, Ella said, "No matter what we do, I want us to be partners in each other's lives. I know that together, we can do anything. We are a team, Elizabeth."

Elizabeth raised her glass of water, which was resting on her nightstand. "L'Chaim to us!" The women passionately kissed again, in celebration of new beginnings and their future as a loving couple.

THE END

EPILOGUE

Thank you so much for reading. I really hope you enjoyed the book. I'd love for you to read the epilogue which shows you what Elizabeth and Ella get up to in the following year and includes a bonus hot sex scene.

You can get the epilogue by clicking on the following link or if you are reading in paperback then please type the text for the link into your web browser.

https://BookHip.com/LLWXRP

(NB the epilogue doesn't include anything crucial to the story- the story is complete without the epilogue. The epilogue is just a bonus scene set in the future so it is entirely up to you if you want to access it.)

I'm asking you to sign up to my mailing list in order to access the epilogue. I hope you can understand why I am doing this as an indie author really trying hard to make a living out of writing. I am really trying hard to build my fan base by keeping my mailing list updated with details of my world and special offers and new releases. You can unsubscribe at any time. If you have any hassle getting hold of the epilogue, please do email me emily-hayeswrites@hotmail.com and I will email you a copy of it.

Again, here is the link for the epilogue:

https://BookHip.com/LLWXRP

I hope you enjoy it. :) Lots of love, Emily x

HER SEDUCTION

1

Quinn looked out across the skyline from the rooftop of Lix, an exclusive women-only club located in the palm of West Hollywood.

The city lights below seemed to twinkle mischievously, and it reminded Quinn of a spark that she, too, once possessed. A spark that had since dimmed, smoldering slowly over the past few years.

She remembered fondly creating Lix within the old and unassuming building all those years ago. So much of the work done by her own strong hands to create an incredible space where women could explore every aspect of themselves. Somewhere that women could feel totally free. She had built this community of women who loved women, and she had always been so proud of it.

Needing a break from the sweaty mass of bodies on the main floor of the club, Quinn quietly escaped up a few flights of stairs while the pounding beats from the DJ resounded through the walls. Her long legs propelled her lean frame forward as she gripped the railing, guiding her upwards to a door that led to fresh air, silence, and a few moments of freedom.

She took a deep sigh of relief as she ran a hand through her stylishly short, blond hair that had become peppered with greying strands. At forty-eight years old, Quinn was the definition of a silver fox. Her statuesque body stood at 5'10, but her dominating presence made her seem taller than she was.

Her real name was Kelly Quinn, but she was so well known as just Quinn. She needed no other name- the gender-free name, 'Quinn,' suited her perfectly.

A long-distance runner her entire life, she was athletic and sinewy. Every part of her was toned; even her forearms rippled with strength. Her androgynous aesthetic embraced a handsome masculinity, infused with a hint of graceful femininity. She was a delicious blend of all things queer that evoked a curious desire in every woman she had met.

Quinn was quietly compelling and utterly captivating. She possessed a keen business sense, but her primary talents lay in the art of Sapphic seduction. Quinn was a player, a hunter of nubile flesh with a real love for the sweet and submissive.

For many years, she prided herself on being able to sample the fruits of her labor, playing with and enjoying many of the women who frequented Lix. And why not? She was the owner of the most sexually permissive club in L.A for women. She was the nucleus of the lesbian epicenter, and it only seemed appropriate to consensually charm the pants off her guests and indulge her every desire.

Lately, however, an uncomfortable feeling had started to gnaw at Quinn. It was a combination of fatigue and apathy, intensified by a mournful ache. Her passion for

Lix was beginning to wane. The club had been her entire world for over a decade; she had put her heart and soul into creating and maintaining it. The staff and even some of the regular guests felt like her family, the only family she had ever known.

Quinn knew that as a business owner, she was burning out. She was never one to take time off, and even on the rare occasion that she did, she was never away for longer than two days. She was a loner, and outside of the club, she reveled in solitude.

It's not as though Quinn lacked friends and lovers; she had plenty of either to choose from when the desire struck. But she kept her affairs superficial and her play-things at arm's length. It was rare for Quinn to take her dalliances outside of Lix's sensual cocoon. Quinn enjoyed the hunt and the chase that led to primal, sexual, and kink encounters.

She loved the power she had over younger, shyer women who wanted her to take the lead. Quinn led them alright; she took them to the heights of ecstasy, and then, when it was over, she disappeared into the crevices of Lix. For many years, this was Quinn's vice, her escape. The work vacations she never took manifested themselves into casual sexual encounters. And for a long time, this seemed to suit Quinn just fine.

This evening, as she stood in reflective silence on the rooftop above the city, an unfamiliar feeling washed over her.

She was lonely.

The revelation hit her with such alarm that she felt breathless.

She shook her head and covered her face with her hands. She said out loud to herself, "I have no time to be lonely. I have no time for heartache. Things need to stay as they are, this is what is best for me, and this is what best for Lix."

She spun around, squared her shoulders, and lifted her chin. Determined to shake off this ridiculous notion, she smoothed down her crisp white dress shirt and ran her hands down her tight leather trousers. A slow smiled curled across her lips as she narrowed her gaze. The cure for her pain was downstairs and was hers for the taking. Armed with irresistible magnetism and an inflated sense of confidence, Quinn proceeded down to the main bar. "I got this," she thought to herself.

But deep within Quinn's subconscious, the discontentment lingered. It had entrenched itself deep within her heart, and like a tree digging in its roots, the loneliness would only grow stronger.

2

L auren stared at her reflection in the mirror and took a deep breath. She hummed to herself.

Oh my god, I am actually doing this!

Her whole body was buzzing with excitement.

She tousled her long brown hair and patted her glossed lips together. Buzzing with a sense of nervousness and excitement, she added the finishing touches to her makeup and slinked into a black lace bodysuit. The sheer fabric formed around her breasts, hugging her hips and accentuating her firm, round bottom.

This look was not Lauren's typical style. But Lauren was also not accustomed to visiting somewhere like Lix, and the dress code on the flyer noted a 'Leather & Lingerie' theme.

As a strict vegan for many years, Lauren did not own any leather, but the thrill of attending Lix for the first time led her to Fredrick's of Hollywood on Sunset Strip. A store where she knew she would be able to get the kind of clothing she needed for a Leather and Lingerie night.

Upon leaving the store with her brand new purchase, she felt like the ultimate femme fatale.

Nobody who knew Lauren would have described her as a vixen, but they would describe her as a femme. A lipstick lesbian who came out at the tender age of fifteen, Lauren had always been well-adjusted in her identity and comfortable with her sexuality. She was classically beautiful. Her feminine chic attracted all genders though men were always disappointed to hear that she wasn't interested in them sexually.

Since she always presented as more conventional than queer, she was often mistaken for straight. But that never bothered Lauren; she was secure in her identity, and she had no trouble meeting other gay women. She had a large circle of friends from all orientations, and she felt that it kept her balanced and away from the lesbian-specific drama.

Lauren dated casually and enjoyed a healthy social life, but her main focus was her career. She worked for one of the top advertising agencies in Los Angeles. And while Lauren successfully held a mid-level position as a project manager, her goal was to become an Advertising Executive. She hoped that one day, with a promotion and a pay raise that she would be able to move out of her cheap but cheerful one-bedroom apartment in Encino and into a forever home in West Hollywood.

Lauren's life provided her with a stable sense of security, and her glowing positivity was infectious. People liked Lauren. By all accounts, she was a good girl, certainly not the type of woman who would be engaging in an all-female orgy within the Grand Ballroom of Lix.

But Lauren was so eager to discover something more. She couldn't put her finger on it until an ex-girlfriend (who had since become a platonic friend) presented her with a flyer from Lix.

"Lauren, I am telling you, you need to check out this place. It will literally change your life and will get you out of your shell. I mean, you were a good lover and all, but I always felt like you were holding back. I think this place could really inspire you to explore new things..." Tania playfully taunted her.

Lauren looked at the flyer. It seemed so exciting. It had a photo of two women in a sexy pose on it, and it ignited something within Lauren.

Lauren's curiosity got the better of her. "Ok, girl, you sold me. I will plan a girl's night out with the crew. Maybe I should ask Maria and Cassidy to join us..?"

Tania interrupted her. "Ah, no, honey. This is something you need to do on your own. You and I have already been down this road. The whole point of going to Lix is to explore all of the options available to you! You will not fully enjoy this experience if you cling to your ex and a bunch of your buddies all night!" Tania lovingly joked.

Lauren paused in hesitation. She had never been to an erotic club before; even her sex toy collection was limited. But being the eternal optimist with a sense of adventure, Lauren decided to take Tania's advice. She would wear lingerie and venture to Lix as a solo, single, ready to mingle.

∾

THE UBER PULLED up to the main entrance of Lix, and Lauren's pulse quickened. High beam spotlights criss-crossed in front of the white industrial building. The large black front door appeared sandwiched between two potted palm trees.

A stern-looking bouncer guarded the door, keeping one meaty hand on the hook of the stanchion. A long red carpet stretched about twenty five feet to the left, filing the guests in a row as they waited their turn to enter paradise.

Lauren stepped out of the Uber, taking her place behind the other patrons. She was still processing her brazen decision that she didn't realize how quickly the line had moved. All of a sudden, she was standing in front of the butch bouncer whose name tag read 'Mickey.'

Mickey fixed her steely eyes on Lauren and sensing her skittishness, gave her a wink quick. "This your first time, cutie? Don't worry; we only bite with consent." She laughed to herself. '$50 and your ID, please.' Lauren was slightly taken aback by the cost, but somehow she knew that the price of admission would be well worth the ride. Lauren settled up, and Mickey stamped the inside of her wrist. With a swing of the door, Lauren stepped inside.

UPON FIRST IMPRESSION, Lix appeared to be an expansive nightclub. Nestled in the center was the dance floor, which was illuminated by fuchsia-colored lighting. The bar stretched across the right side, while the left side served as a lounge space.

A massive video monitor was the focal point, serving as a backdrop to the DJ booth. The screen showed excerpts from The Crash Pad series, stimulating the audience with images of queer women's porn.

Colette, the lesbian DJ du jour spun tribal house music that vibrated through the speakers, permeating through the core of those dancing in the center. Next to the DJ booth, a cage set on the risers featured a sexy go-go dancer who gyrated her body to the beat.

At the end of the lounge was a second entrance that led down a corridor, lined with two themed rooms, one each side. One was a dungeon that hosted the kinkiest of affairs, and the other was the Grand Ballroom, a play space that had the biggest bed area Lauren had ever seen in the center of it.

Lauren gazed around open-mouthed.

She saw a sign saying **Pool** and wandered to the end of the corridor. She pushed open the heavy glass door at the end and walked into the warm night air.

The grounds were breathtaking, lush and green, and magically lit with flickering fairy lights. The foliage was a mix of palm and cedar trees, speckled with rose bushes. The big aqua pool held court in the center of the garden.

CLOTHES OPTIONAL the sign read. Lauren's eyes widened.

Chaise lounge chairs and high-top tables were situated around the patio. Women splashed about like mermaids some in swimwear or underwear, some completely nude. Lauren was absolutely fascinated. This area was so much more than just a pool. The outdoor patio provided a freedom that could not be found anywhere else in L.A. It was here that women could shed their inhibitions, embrace their bodies, and connect intimately with one another.

Lauren's senses were in overdrive. There was so much to take in that she felt frozen in her tracks.

I need a drink, she thought to herself and marched herself back inside to the crowded bar. As she waited for service, she could feel hungry eyes on her, which made her feel shy, yet strangely aroused.

She quickly scanned the crowd around her without making direct eye contact. Like any lesbian bar, there was an array of presentation styles. Some women appeared androgynous, and some were unmistakably butch. Others seemed to be very high femme, and some possessed that quintessential rock and roll edginess typically found in the city of angels.

This club was different, though. There was a brazen sexual energy in the air that made almost anything feel possible. The vibe was one of acceptance; shaming was not welcome here, and vanilla was not the only flavor that one could savor.

Lauren finally found herself at the front of the line and ordered a vodka cranberry cocktail from a cute, punk-rock bartender. She sipped and slinked away to find a seating area.

Don't be nervous, Lauren; you can just sit and watch the crowd for a bit.

She found a comfy settee and settled in. Her body began to relax as the effects of the alcohol kicked in. Almost subconsciously, she started to move to the music, bobbing her head and grooving in her chair. A joyful emotion came over her, the sweet feeling of empowerment. She felt like she had come home, and after a second cocktail, Lauren was ready to dance.

3

Quinn stood near the DJ booth after descending from the roof. She surveyed the crowd, running her eyes through the bodies on the dance floor. The strobe light captured stop motion images of hair, arms, hips, and facial expressions, like a camera snapping pictures.

Quinn was filled with a detached sense of desire. Her position as a business owner had left her to be more of an observer, witnessing guest interactions from within a kind of bubble. She needed to remain slightly removed in order to provide a fantastic customer experience. Quinn was an untouchable queen of the Los Angeles lesbian nightclub scene. But she also knew if she asked-nicely and flirtatiously -that she could most certainly touch.

Quinn moved through the periphery of the dance-floor, keeping enough distance so that she could see but also been seen. Almost everyone at Lix knew who Quinn was; at least, they knew of her. Some were lucky enough to experience Quinn in the flesh. Except for a few select employees, hardly anyone knew Quinn as a close friend. It was best for the business that it stayed that way.

The allure of Quinn was in her mystery, and the perceived success of owning a successful nightclub (especially in L.A.) definitely helped in gaining attention. As Quinn slowly prowled the outskirts with a whiskey in hand, heads turned. Some women even pointed and whispered to each other. Quinn was confident and slightly cocky. Quinn loved the adoration, and the ache that had filled her heart earlier in the night seemed to heal with a superficial glow.

She started to make her way through the circle of dancers. With a sexy swagger, she moved her hips and flowed effortlessly with the shuffling bodies. She smiled, raised her drink in the air, and nodded in recognition to a few familiar faces. She seemed to dance seductively with everyone, and yet, no one in particular.

All who crossed her path seemed entranced by her presence. She had that effect on people. She could make them feel like they were the only person in the room; for even a few moments. But tonight, was the Quinn show. If anyone was receiving any admiration this evening, it was going to be Quinn herself.

As she danced to DJ Colette, Quinn became so absorbed in her own world that she took a misstep backward and lost her footing. She then did something that she had never done within the fifteen years of owning a bar; she bumped into a woman behind her, causing the guest to spill her drink.

∿

LAUREN HAD FINALLY WORKED up the courage to hit the dancefloor. She freed herself of any nervousness and tension she had felt upon arriving at Lix. While she didn't know anyone at the club, she seemed to connect with the other women in the crowd. There was an unspoken sense of welcoming, a camaraderie of queerness. The sexual identity that separated these women from heteronormativity is what bonded them together at Lix. Lauren knew that she belonged there and held her own, as a newbie in the club.

Lauren moved in tandem with the crowd, riding a wave of collective energy when a tall figure fell slightly backward, bumping into her. Her (third) vodka cranberry spilled up against her chest, soaking the black lace fabric. The culprit spun around to face Lauren.

"Oh my god, I am so sorry! I must have tripped. Are you ok?" Quinn lightly touched Lauren's upper arms with a sense of concern. "Please, let me get you another one and a napkin for the spill."

"Oh, um, that's ok. I mean, it's no big deal," Lauren stammered. "Maybe I shouldn't have any more to drink. That's very sweet of you, though." Lauren was caught off guard by the handsome stranger and her intense eyes.

"Yea, you and me both." Quinn chuckled. "No, seriously, I apologize. I'm not normally such a klutz. What do you say to seltzer water with lemon instead? My treat?" Quinn's eyes glimmered.

Feeling charmed, Lauren smiled and joked. "Sure, why not. I hear this place makes a mean soda water. Besides, I could use a break from dancing anyway." She extended her hand and allowed Quinn to guide her off the dancefloor, towards the bar.

Instead of standing in line as Lauren assumed they

would, Quinn led her to the side of the bar, near the open-ing. "Hey Chelsea, could you throw us two soda waters with lemon? I owe this pretty guest a drink." Quinn nodded and winked in Lauren's direction. Punk rock Chelsea replied, "Sure, no problem, boss. Coming right up."

Boss? Lauren wondered to herself. *Who is this woman?*

Quinn presented the beverage to Lauren. "Here you go, gorgeous. Cheers to bumping into one another." They clinked glasses.

"So...are you a manager here or something?" Lauren asked. "It appears that I just met a badass boss, woman." She jokingly smiled.

"Wow, I didn't even introduce myself; my manners are atrocious tonight. I am the owner of Lix." Quinn extended a hand. "Kelly Quinn, but please, call me Quinn. Everyone does." Quinn narrowed her gaze on Lauren. "You must be new here," Quinn stated, rather than asked.

"It's my first time, actually. I saw one of your flyers and my ex-I mean, my friend- convinced me to check it out. The theme seemed really cool. It inspired me to buy this." Lauren rambled and pivoted her body so that Quinn could check out her outfit. "I've never seen anywhere like this place. It has this great feeling to it. I feel so free here."

As Lauren posed, Quinn checked out more than just the lace outfit. "That's great. Thank you for coming and checking out the place. Have you had a chance to see...all of it? There is more than meets the eye." Quinn smiled to herself. Lauren was lovely. Really lovely. "Would you like a tour? That is unless you are keeping anyone waiting?" Quinn looked over Lauren's shoulders.

"I came alone, actually. It was recommended that I should?" Lauren shrugged her shoulders in a questioning manner. "I mean, it's not like I don't have friends. I am single, but I just...I just thought I would treat myself to an adventure." Lauren felt giddy and clumsy.

God, this woman is hot, and I am coming off like a complete dork. Get it together, Lauren!

Quinn smiled cunningly. "It would be my absolute pleasure to show you around. You have not truly been to Lix until you have seen all that it has to offer. Let's take a walk down that corridor. I will show you the other rooms, and you absolutely must see the outdoor pool."

"I had a little look at the pool earlier, but I would be so keen to see it again. I had no idea there were other rooms? If I am going to come to Lix, I want to see it all. Man, I wish Tania had told me about the pool. I would have brought my bikini."

Oh, you will 'come' alright. I have plans for you, newbie. Quinn's heartbeat quickened. She couldn't believe her luck! "Oh, you don't need a bikini to swim at Lix. Skinny dipping is perfectly acceptable here. Of course, only if you want to. Our clothing-optional policy is completely at your comfort level." Quinn reassured her.

"Uh, wow. Um, I am not sure about that yet. But I will take you up on the tour. I mean, it is my first time and all. I'm just not really sure I'll ever feel comfortable taking my clothes off in public." Quinn laughed hard, mostly out of embarrassment.

Quinn extended her arm for Lauren to grab hold. Quinn's rolled-up sleeves of her dress shirt revealed a faded skull tattoo. "Shall we, newbie?"

Lauren scoffed. "My name is Lauren. I might be a newbie here, but I'm not that innocent. And, I'm not straight or anything either- people always assume because of how I look. I am very much a queer woman and very comfortable in my sexuality."

"Of course. Ms. Lauren." Quinn bowed her head. "I meant newbie here. I never assume."

Lauren smiled coyly and took Quinn's arm. "In that case, lead the way...boss."

Good to know, Lauren. Good to know. Quinn guided them both to the corridor. The hallway led down a path of pleasures that Lauren was undoubtedly unfamiliar with. Still, in time, her curious nature would get the best of her.

4

___

Lauren and Quinn strolled past the lounge seating towards the doorway that led down the corridor. Although they were arm in arm, Lauren knew that Quinn was in control, and she reveled in the thrill of walking alongside Lix's owner.

Tania will never believe this when I tell her!

Quinn stopped at the corridor entrance. "As a responsible and ethical owner, I do need to inform you that past this point, you will most likely see nudity, possible sexual activity, and maybe light BDSM play. Before we go any further, I just want to make sure that you are comfortable with that and consent to follow me down the hall."

Lauren was impressed with Quinn's professionalism and transparency. And while she was just as nervous as she was excited, Lauren just knew she had to see the hedonism of Lix for herself. *I mean, isn't that why I am here?* "I really appreciate you making sure I am comfortable. And yes, it's totally cool; I consent." Lauren gave Quinn a short curtsey.

The hallway was cream-colored and softly lit, a

contrast to the dark nightclub with its flashing colored lights. It felt almost serene, as though they were inside a spa. A few, towel-clad guests with wet hair padded past Lauren and Quinn, softly giggling to themselves. *They must be coming from the pool*, Lauren thought to herself. *I wonder if they swam naked?*

Quinn interrupted Lauren's thoughts. She pointed to a door on the left. "This room is called 'The Crossroad,' which is the fancy name for our dungeon space. Most of the guests who use it call it 'The Cross.' Let me show you the inside, and you will see what I mean."

Quinn swung the heavy door open. Inside was an empty space, the size of a large living room. The walls were painted a deep, blood-red with an elegant white trim. The main focal point was a large, X shaped cross. It stood 7x5 feet, complete with arm cuffs that dangled off the edges.

"This is a St. Angela Cross. I made it myself and named it after my first girlfriend." Quinn felt a twist in her stomach. "Angela had passed away, so it was in memory of her. Most people call this a St. Andrew's cross, but this is my way of reclaiming a women-centered space." Quinn grounded her emotions and stiffened up.

Lauren walked over the cross and fingered the cuffs, fascinated by the idea of being tied up. For a brief moment, she imagined herself spread eagle and bare naked upon this cross; upon Angela. She suddenly felt shy and vulnerable in Quinn's presence.

To the right of the room was a giant, leather sex swing which hung in mid-air from the ceiling by heavy chains. The apparatus was positioned slightly off the ground but seemed easy enough for someone to crawl into. Lauren had never seen anything like it. She was not a fan of the leather material, but the concept was positively intriguing.

"Go ahead, try it out." Quinn urged her. "Just slide into it like you would a regular swing and grab the chains with both of your hands." Awkwardly, Lauren positioned her body against the back of the seating. She felt into it, as she took hold of the chains on either side.

Lauren laughed. "I feel like a giant kid inside some twisted adult playground." She wriggled about. "So hypothetically, what would happen next?" She smiled coquettishly.

Quinn walked over to Lauren and stood over her; Lauren looked up at Quinn from her sex swing seat. Quinn positioned herself directly between Lauren's parted legs and very lightly touched her outer thighs. Electric desire ran right through Lauren's body.

"Well, I suppose what happens next all depends on what you want?" Quinn's voice lowered softly. "But hypothetically, if it was me, I'd start by handcuffing you to the chains to make sure you were...secure." A slow smile curled up the corner of Quinn's lips.

"Then, I would spread your legs right apart and wrap them around my waist. Of course, there would be other things too, but, well, you are new here, so I don't want to scare you off." Quinn looked Lauren squarely in the eye and gently chuckled.

Subconsciously, Lauren bit her bottom lip, something she always did when she was turned on. Her stomach fluttered, and she grounded her pelvis deep against the leather seating. Her mouth watered; she was entranced.

In typical Quinn fashion, she abruptly broke the spell that she knew she had cast. "Come on, there is more to see." She patted Lauren's legs and motioned for her to get up. "This room will be here waiting for you if and when you choose to return to Lix," Quinn said slyly, giving Lauren another wink. This time, the look was more direct.

"That sounded like a dare." Lauren challenged and shrugged. "Who knows what the future holds?"

Yeah, I am definitely coming back here.

Lauren hopped up and gave the dungeon one last, quick scan. Aside from the swing and the cross, there were a few other pieces of furniture strewn about. There was a desk, a long black couch, and a bench that looked like gymnastic equipment. Perplexed but fascinated, Lauren followed Quinn across the hall into room number two.

Quinn and Lauren entered the second room on the right; the Grand Ballroom. But unlike the The Crossroad, this room was not empty. Quinn and Lauren were treated to a threesome engaging in some light foreplay upon the large mattress situated in the center of the room.

'Oh pardon us, I was just giving this new customer a tour. Sorry to disturb you.' Quinn respectfully moved back into the hallway.

"That's ok, Quinn," one of the women from the trio joked. "You of all people already know that we like an audience." Another voice piped up. "Yea, Quinn, you already have an open invitation to join us anytime. This one looks like a good time, too," addressing her comment to Lauren.

"Absolutely, but another time, ladies. You know me, business first. But enjoy, don't let us ruin your good time." Quinn turned to Lauren and laughed. "Just another day at the office! Take a quick look, and then I have one more thing to show you. Trust me, it's absolutely worth checking out."

Lauren took in the Grand Ballroom while the trio of

naked bodies languished on the bed, legs, and arms wrapped around one another, hands and mouths exploring. In contrast to the dungeon, this room was painted a soft lavender; at least three of the walls were. One of the walls was actually a huge mirror, covering one entire wall of the room. There was not much furniture aside from two cozy armchairs, placed on opposite sides, a few nightstands, and a few soft lamps. While the décor was rather romantic, it was clear that this room was strictly for sex. Each nightstand held a box of Kleenex and a wicker basket, filled with latex gloves and small, shiny silver packets.

Lauren looked at Quinn in a quizzing manner. 'What's with the gloves and the packets?"

"The gloves are for safer sex. Let's just say that this room tends to get a lot of action." Quinn said knowingly. "When you have a lot of strangers mixing body parts and fluids, it can be safer to wrap up the digits." Quinn rubbed her fingers together in front of her. "The packets are lube and condoms. Condoms for the sharing of sex toys between different partners. We like to keep these items disposable, for better hygiene."

Lauren felt a sense of relief, knowing that Lix provided these types of items to the guests. She had never used such protection before. Lauren had always been a monogamous lover. She had never been with more than one woman at a time, but the thought intrigued her.

While the thought of a gloved finger (or multiple gloved fingers!) made it all feel quite medical, it was comforting to know that a barrier could be used by strange hands while exploring her body.

She started to tingle. *Wait, whoa. Multiple hands and bodies? Where is my mind going?* She halted her desire with alarm. *I don't want to be in an orgy...do I?* Lauren felt a bit dizzy.

"Wow, ok." Lauren's head shook, "Cool. This is a great room, but let's continue with the tour, shall we?" As Quinn took Lauren's hand to lead her out of the Grand Ballroom, Lauren looked back at the threesome, one last time. The entangled woman who had addressed her earlier stared straight back and nodded. "Have fun, you two. I am sure we will see you both again." The trio cackled, and Lauren turned her back.

Feeling overwhelmed, Lauren remained quiet as she and Quinn walked to the end of the corridor.

"Are you ok? Don't worry, Maria is just kidding around. She has been a regular of Lix for over five years, and sometimes, she becomes a bit entitled to her humor. It's all in fun." Quinn reassured Lauren.

Quinn did not like to see any of her customers feel uncomfortable, especially new guests visiting for the first time. Even though Quinn was a player and no angel, she felt protective over her customers, like they were guests in her own house. And Lix was Quinn's home. Still, if Lauren really wanted to hang, she would need to learn to loosen up a bit because Lix was no place for those who were uptight with their sexuality.

"I am fine, seriously." Lauren brushed off her discomfort. "I've just never seen anything like this before. Honestly, I love the openness, the sensuality of it all. I am just taking it all in, at my own pace."

Lauren looked up at Quinn and placed a hand on the small of Quinn's back. "I really appreciate you taking the time out of your night to show me around like this."

"The best is yet to come, sugar. Welcome to paradise."

Quinn flung open the glass door that led to the outdoor garden patio.

QUINN STOOD at the entranceway while Lauren stepped out into the gardens. Quinn wanted to watch as Lauren absorbed the sights. She always got great pleasure watching a first-time guest respond to the beauty of the garden area.

Lauren felt breathless. It indeed looked like a magical garden from a movie, complete with a bevy of Sapphic nymphs.

Women of all shapes and sizes frolicked, proudly flaunting their bodies. Some were completely nude, some were in bathing suits or club gear. There were circles of friends who sat together and twosomes coupled off. Most of the guests were situated around the pool on lounge seating, but a few were found in the pool, playfully splashing about like mermaids.

Lauren looked on, enchanted by such an unusual sight. *Everyone seems so free and so comfortable in their skin. I've just died and gone to lesbian heaven.* She quietly laughed to herself. She couldn't believe that she had never heard of this place before and even more so that she would feel so immediately at home.

Quinn stepped towards Lauren and stood behind her. Placing her hands lightly on her shoulder, she spoke. "How is the newbie, I mean, Ms. Lauren, enjoying my backyard playground?" Quinn had a cocky edge in her voice. "Are you going to tell all of your friends what you got to experience tonight?" This was as much of a question as it was a business strategy for Quinn. Lix was built on word of mouth and referrals.

Lauren turned around to face Quinn, the top of her head meeting Quinn's delicate collarbone. Lauren had always had a thing for tall women. Quinn gave off a strangely nurturing energy that was coupled with something more primal.

Lauren couldn't put her finger on it, but it was almost as though Quinn was a lioness who had the hunter's instinct but who was also a fierce protector. Quinn made Lauren feel safe and also excited in a way that she hadn't felt before.

However, as new as she was to a scene like this, Lauren was not naïve. She had lived in Los Angeles her entire life. She was familiar with the superficiality of the night club scene and the parasites that lurked in the shadows.

There was no shortage of opportunists and sociopathic behavior. Strangers were not exceptionally kind unless there was an ulterior motive.

Lauren was always polite and friendly-even flirtatious-but she also kept a careful distance. She did not know what to make of Quinn, although she couldn't help but admit that she was captivated.

"It's an incredible place, Quinn." Lauren looked around in slight disbelief. "I am so grateful that my friend told me about it. I mean, it's like another world. How long have you owned this for? How did you even get into this business?"

Softly Quinn spoke, "This July will be our sixteenth anniversary of Lix. It feels so much longer than that; the club is my entire world. It's strange to think about it in terms of years; it feels more like something that has evolved throughout lifetimes." Her voice suddenly shifted to a harder tone. "But the backstory is pretty complicated, and I have kept you to myself for long enough. You should go and explore; swim, dance, and meet more women." Quinn pulled back, appearing to dismiss Lauren.

Sensing an emotional wall from Quinn, Lauren became more brazen, although she couldn't understand why. Perhaps it was the sexual tension in the clear night air that inspired her. She wanted to tease the lion, play with her a bit. In Lauren's mind, Quinn was not relationship material, but she did seem hella fun.

I feel like this chance meeting may lead to something more than just a tour. And besides, what would be the point of going to Lix if I didn't push my own boundaries a bit?

"Oh, of course. Yes, I am sure you have other guests to tend to, to welcome so warmly as you welcomed me." Lauren paused and placed an index finger to her mouth. "One last question; where are the towels, like for the pool?"

"There are shelves along the side of the building. There you will find freshly laundered towels and a place to store any personal belongings." Quinn pointed in the direction of where they had entered the garden. On either side of the entrance were indeed shelving units built into the structure that contained white, folded towels. I thought you didn't bring a bathing suit, newbie." Quinn taunted her.

"Good memory!" Lauren returned the serve. "You are right, I didn't." Lauren took a few steps back away from Quinn while still continuing to face her. "It's a good thing for me that Lix allows skinny dipping."

Lauren then turned her back, permitting Quinn to admire her shapely hips and firm behind. She stripped out of her bodysuit and stood naked by the pool's edge.

That's what you get for underestimating me, boss. Feast your eyes on this. With a light jump, Lauren plunged nude into the pool.

The warm saltwater enveloped her, surrounding her in an aqua-colored womb. The temperature was kept at 90 degrees Fahrenheit; Lauren was floating in liquid bliss. She dunked her head again and swam underwater, feeling the viscosity caress her naked body. She had swum nude before in the ocean but never in a public pool, let alone in a women-only sex club! Her entire being was charged with an electric thrill.

She emerged to the surface, shaking her hair and wiping her wet face with her hands.

I can't believe I just did that. What a rush!

She came back to reality and remembered where she had left Quinn.

Assuming that Quinn was still watching her, she pushed against the water to turn herself. Facing the garden entrance, she pulled herself up against the edge of the pool and scourged the patio. Quinn was no longer in sight.

5

Quinn watched as Lauren turned her back and proceeded to the edge of the pool, attempting to tease Quinn with her hourglass shape. Quinn knew what was going to happen next. Owning an erotic club comes with its advantages, but over time, it's hardly unpredictable. Quinn knew that Lauren was intoxicated by the atmosphere and was breaking out of her shell.

She thought that Quinn would play along, but Quinn was too wise and seasoned to partake in a cutesy show. It's not that she was trying to be cruel, but Quinn liked to be in charge. If she needed to leave and tend to other affairs, that is what she was going to do.

Quinn did like Lauren and appreciated her sense of wonder and openness. Lauren was not really innocent per se, but she was vanilla. Lauren was undoubtedly attractive, and physically, Lauren was exactly Quinn's type. But she felt Lauren might be someone who could get attached after a causal romp, and Quinn did not have the patience for that. More so, she knew that she could accidentally hurt someone as sweet as Lauren, and she needed to be careful with her own, jaded power.

What Quinn needed was to step away and give herself some space while she pondered the situation. She also wanted Lauren to enjoy herself, to fully enjoy Lix as a guest without all eyes upon the two of them. Quinn had a rep, and while she was pretty sure that Lauren could see that, she felt that it may hinder her first-time experience.

If Lauren sticks around, well, maybe we could have some fun. But the girl needs space to process this world on her own.

Quinn turned to walk back down the corridor when she spotted a small, gold clutch purse near the pool's entrance. To keep it safe, she immediately grabbed it. She headed to the lost and found area, near the front area, to leave it with a host. While Lix was not responsible for lost or stolen items, Quinn did her best to make sure that any missing belongings were placed where a guest could locate them later.

WHEN LAUREN EMERGED from the pool, naked and dripping wet, she felt a slight pang of disappointment to have lost Quinn. She was also slightly embarrassed. All of a sudden, her newness to a place like Lix became painfully apparent. Lauren felt as though she stood out in the crowd as a solo person, alone among the small groups and couples of other women.

Even though Lauren was slightly hurt, she did not want to dwell on how Quinn had left her alone in the pool. Quinn had already been very generous with her time in showing Lauren around, and Lauren knew that Quinn did not owe her anything more than professional curtsey. She knew better than to have expectations from a night club owner. Still, a small part of her had wished they had more time together.

Lauren grabbed her heels and her lace bodysuit from the spot where she had dropped it on the concrete. She then padded over to the shelves to grab a fresh, clean towel. As she rubbed herself dry, she noticed a couple sitting on the patio, smiling her in direction. One of the women gave Lauren a small wave.

Curious, Lauren walked over to the round table. *Do I know them?*

"Hi, I'm Fran." The woman with short, dark hair and an olive complexion extended her hand. "This is my partner Terry." Terry was blond and had a tan that seemed to glow, even against the night sky. Perplexed but pleased to have met other guests, Lauren shook hands with both Fran and Terry.

Fran continued, "You probably don't recognize me, but I remember you from Cafe Fresh, the coffee shop. Almond milk latte, extra foam?" Fran smiled as though they shared a secret between them.

It took Lauren a few seconds to collect her thoughts. "Oh, right!" I am so sorry; my head was somewhere else. Yes, you are the manager at Cafe Fresh." Lauren nodded her head, talking as much to herself as she did to the couple. Lauren laughed. "That's my order, alright; I can't start my morning without a latte."

Lauren was still a bit stunned to have been recognized at Lix. "Um, this is my first time. I, uh, I came alone, just to see what it was like." Sheepishly, Lauren pulled her towel tighter around her torso.

"Oh, don't worry! Your secret is safe with us," Fran said lightly. "It's nice to see a familiar face, and I figured since I haven't seen you here before, that you must be new. We didn't mean to bother you. I just wanted to say hi." Terry piped in. "I remember our first time." She touched Fran's hand. "We were so nervous. I needed two dirty martinis in a row before I could even move to the dance floor."

Lauren immediately felt warm and welcomed by the couple. "Thanks so much for noticing me. I decided that I might get more out of the experience if I came by myself, but yeah, it's a bit weird to be alone in a place like this. It's pretty cool, though. I am glad that I came." Lauren motioned to Fran and Terry. "How long have you two been coming here?"

Fran looked questioning at Terry. "I think it's been about a year now, right, honey?" Terry nodded in agreement. "We decided to celebrate our fifth anniversary by doing something different and boy, was it an eye-opening experience! I guess you could say that we have been regulars ever since."

Fran interjected. "By regulars, Terry means once a month at the most. I wish we could afford to visit every night, but it's nice to keep this place as a special treat. You know, for when we want to add a little extra spice in our life." Fran and Terry exchanged knowing glances and shared a moment between them.

Lauren felt a slight twinge of envy. Even though Lauren was perfectly happy being single, she wished she could experience Lix on a more intimate level. Right now, she felt like an observer, and she hated to admit it- a bit of an outsider.

"That's awesome, good for you!" Lauren chirped. "I can see how this place could become addictive. It's just so big, and there are so many things to see."

Terry exclaimed naughtily, "And do." Fran patted Terry on the leg. "My little nympho." They both laughed.

Lauren looked around and shrugged her shoulders. "I could see myself coming back for sure. Next time though, I would want to bring a date. Maybe I could use my Ruby account and find someone fun on there." Lauren referred to the popular lesbian dating app. Ruby- the source that connected queer women for casual encounters.

Fran and Terry bobbed in agreement. "Yes, using Ruby to bring a date here is a great idea, but make sure it isn't anyone too jealous or possessive. Lix is not the place for anyone insecure in their relationship. It works for us because we have been together for six years, and we share the same values when it comes to sex and play." Fran said knowingly. "But if your honey is too clingy, it might back-fire in your face!"

Ok, good to know. Lauren thought to herself. Grateful for the company, she relaxed into her chair. *Maybe I will grab another drink and sit here for a while longer.* "I am heading to the bar. Can I get you, ladies, to drink while I am up?"

"That is so kind of you. But no, I think we will head into the Grand Ballroom for one last snuggle before we need to leave for the night." Fran smoothed a piece of blond hair away from Terry's face, while she beamed with delight. "But enjoy yourself, and it was awesome running into you. We hope to see you again soon."

"You can sit with us anytime, let's hang out again." Terry gave Lauren the thumbs up.

"It was so nice to see you, Fran, and lovely to meet you, Terry. Yes, I am sure we will see each other again soon." Hand in hand, Fran and Terry headed towards the Grand Ballroom to enjoy some intimacy.

What a great couple! One of these days, when my life is in order, I would love to be in a relationship like that. Lauren stood up to exit the garden patio. *One last drink and then I will call it a night.*

Lauren felt much better after having connected with Fran and Terry. She lost her sense of self-consciousness and seemed to ease much better into her surroundings. As she walked away from the patio table towards the entrance that led to the bar, she stopped. Something was missing. She paused, and suddenly she realized with great urgency.

My purse! I've lost my purse!

6

In a panic, Lauren spun around and around, scanning the patio area, but her mind was frazzled, and she couldn't see anything clearly. She dropped to the ground and scoured the pavement, looking underneath chairs and tables. Breathe, Lauren. Just take a moment and retrace your steps. Her heart was beating, and inwardly, she was wildly shaking. Lauren felt like she wanted to cry.

Other guests glanced at Lauren with curious expressions. What was wrong with this woman?

"Excuse me! I lost my purse. It was a gold clutch. Small, like this." Lauren made a shape with her hand that seemed to indicate the size of a football.

Lauren felt dizzy. Her senses were already on overdrive from all of the sights and sounds. She was having trouble processing her thoughts and remembering the last time she had her purse. *My god, it could be anywhere! What if someone stole it? My money, my ID...oh, my god, my credit cards!*

Feeling overwhelmed, Lauren burst into tears. *This isn't happening. I am crying in public at Lix, and I've lost my ENTIRE LIFE in that purse!*

A staff member in a tight, white tank top with a name tag reading **Lucky** came over to Lauren, to help this guest who was so obviously in distress.

"Hey, are you ok? What's wrong? Can I help you with anything?" Lucky peered at Lauren's tear-stained face.

"I...I lost...I lost my purse." Lauren had trouble getting the words out, breathing heavily through her tears. "Sorry for causing a scene. It's is my first time here, and I have been all over the place. I just...I have no idea where it could be."

Lucky soothed Lauren's back with her hand. "It's ok, love. Take a deep breath. We have a lost and found area. Maybe someone saw it and returned it over there? Most of our guests are good, trustworthy people. We rarely have any theft, unlike most of the clubs in this town." Lucky joked, trying to calm Lauren down. Lucky was gentle and kind, and Lauren felt herself starting to ease up.

"Would you like me to escort you over there? I know this place can seem like a maze. Please, let me take you." Lucky extended her arm towards Lauren. Lauren nodded, her shoulders relaxing.

"I didn't even realize I was still naked." Lauren sniffed and giggled. "Let me just slip this on again." In front of Lucky and without any shame, Lauren tossed aside the towel and slipped back into her bodysuit. She put on her heels and followed Lucky out of the patio.

Together, Lauren and Lucky walked back through the corridor, past the Grand Ballroom and The Crossroad. They came to the end of the hallway and reentered the central area. By this time of night, the dance floor was thinning out, and the crowd was sparse.

"Over here," Lucky guided Lauren over the front, where Lauren had first arrived. As they turned to the right, there was a small door that read Employees Only. "Our lost and found is here. Let's take a look." Lucky knocked lightly. She started to pull out a set of keys that hung from her belt buckle.

"It's not locked. We're here, come on in" A familiar voice rang out from inside the room.

"Oh, hey, boss!" Lucky exclaimed. "There is a customer here that said she lost her purse. Any chance they were found? Lucky turned to Lauren. "What does it look like, love?"

Lauren peered her head inside the room and immediately saw Quinn inside, leaning against a wall, as she chatted with another employee. Lauren's eyes widened, surprised to see Quinn again.

"Gold clutch, right?" Quinn smiled slowly at Lauren, catching her gaze. "Sorry, I had no idea it was yours. I saw it on the patio deck and brought it back here for safekeeping." She handed Lauren the purse. "If I had known it was yours, I would have delivered it myself, personally." As Quinn gave Lauren her clutch back, their fingers brushed together, sending a delightful shock through Lauren's body.

"Looks like my work here is done," Lucky chirped. She turned to Lauren and touched her arm. "I am so happy you found it."

"Thank you," Lauren looked at the employee's name tag again. "Lucky. Well, isn't that a coincidence. You sure are! I can't tell you how much I appreciated your help back there. I was freaking out!"

"Don't mention it, cutie. Just part of my job." Lucky flirtatiously sized up Lauren and gave her a friendly smirk. Lucky looked back at Quinn. "I am going back to tidy up the patio, ok, boss?"

"Go ahead, L. Good job tonight." Quinn looked at Lucky and motioned to the door. Lucky left the employee office, leaving Quinn and Lauren together, alone.

"Well, it looks like someone is having quite a night. Everything ok? Quinn looked down at Lauren with concern. Lauren nodded; another wave of embarrassment washed over her. She didn't know how to act in front of Quinn. The activity from the night seemed to leave her feeling too exhausted to flirt.

"I'm fine. I just made the silly mistake of leaving my purse behind. Thanks for finding it. I think it's time for me to go home. It's been quite the adventure!" Lauren shook off her feelings.

Quinn paused and looked deeply into Quinn's eyes. She held both of Lauren's shoulders in her hands. "Listen. I am sorry that I couldn't stick around by the pool. I really enjoyed meeting you and showing you around. It's hard to keep an eye on everything at once, and I did need to return inside." Quinn shrugged, and all of a sudden, she looked tired. "It is what it is. My attention is constantly being divided, and it's been that way for fifteen years."

Lauren held up her hand. "Please, no need to explain. You don't owe me an apology. You have been the most gracious host, and you were even my knight in shining amour when it came to this thing." Lauren held up her clutch. "I couldn't have asked for a better first experience as a new guest. I know you are important and busy. No worries!" Lauren said lightly.

Quinn stared and spoke clearly and directly. "Lauren, there is something about you that I am attracted to; that I would like to explore. I feel that you and I have exciting chemistry."

"Now, I'd like to say that I don't do this often, but the truth is that I do. You need to understand that my business comes first and that this is my playground. I do what I please, and I enjoy what is around me because I can. I want to be very honest with you so that there are no expectations." Quinn looked at Lauren's mouth and licked her own lips. "That said, I'd be interested in spending some time with you here at Lix. Time that is not just a tour. I want to show you things, things I think you would like."

Quinn continued. "If you ever plan on returning to Lix again, and if you want to spend time with me here, I will give you my personal number. As long as you understand the arrangement, it would be casual, with no strings attached." Quinn searched Lauren's face for a sign. "And of course, whatever we do here would be at your comfort level. I admit that I am a player, but I would never hurt anyone, and I would only ever play with you on a level that you were comfortable with and with your full consent at all times."

Lauren's head spun. *What was happening? Is Quinn propositioning me?* Lauren cleared her throat and took a breath.

"Quinn, I will definitely return to Lix. It is the most magical place for gay women in L.A. I have been to a lot of bars and clubs, but I am impressed beyond words. Not to mention that your staff are so friendly and helpful." Lauren touched Quinn's hand.

"I can't deny that there is electric energy between us. I want to explore that as well. What you don't know about me is that I am hyper-focused on my career as well. I enjoy dating casually, and my life is great, but I don't think I have the time for anything serious either. So we are on the same page." Lauren smiled up at Quinn. "But as far as playful fun, yea, I think that that would be something I would like to explore." Lauren started to feel a wetness between her legs, tingling with desire for Quinn.

"Ok, little one. We have a deal." Quinn said in a husky voice. She turned towards a small desk and pulled out a piece of scrap paper and a pen. Quickly, she scribbled her number down for Lauren.

"Here you go. Give me twenty-four hours' notice before you plan on coming to Lix so that I can clear some time for us. That way, I won't be distracted, and I can focus all on my attention on you. At least for a few hours, anyway." She looked Lauren up and down and seemed to stare right into her soul.

Trembling slightly, Lauren took the piece of paper from Quinn and inwardly squealed. She felt high, possessed with passion. Shyly, she looked away. "Ok, um, I am going to call an Uber now." Lauren was at a loss for words.

"Before you do, may I?" Quinn moved against Lauren and brought her face closer, her lips inches away from Lauren's. "I'd love to give you a kiss goodnight if you are willing?" Quinn paused and teased Lauren with warm, whiskey-scented breath.

Lauren's legs went weak. She closed her eyes and smiled, wordlessly giving her consent to a kiss. She raised her mouth to meet Quinn's.

Their lips softly touched, like two beings discovering each other for the first time. Lauren's entire body became covered in goosebumps. Quinn pressed more firmly, her tongue tracing and searching for more. Lauren's tongue found Quinn's, and their lips moved together in tandem, like a dance. The kiss became more urgent, in their hunger for one another.

What seemed like an infinite amount of time was only mere minutes. Lauren was in another world.

She felt weightless, floating inside the Employee Only office at Lix.

In typical fashion, Quinn was the first to break away. She knew how to tease just enough to keep women wanting more. To keep Lauren wanting more. *Lauren, the beautiful doll. Doll. Oh, that would be an excellent name for Lauren. Yes, I must use that more often.*

Quinn gently pulled back, a faint trail of saliva connecting them like a tiny spider web. "Mmmm, your lips are sweet, like candy. I can't wait to taste the rest of you." Quinn let Lauren go. "Listen, doll; let's get you safely into an Uber. It's late, and I need to finish up closing down the place."

As if she was in a trance, Lauren bobbed her head wordlessly. *Whatever you say, boss. Hmmm, I could get used to having Quinn boss me around.* She bit her lip, trying to hide the giant smile that was coming over her face.

Lauren and Quinn separated so that they could adjust themselves; Lauren got the Uber app up on her phone. Two minutes later, she got the notification that an Uber was on its way to Lix.

"Ok, I am leaving. My Uber will be here very shortly." Lauren looked down at the number Quinn had scribbled on the piece of paper. "I will call you." Her face hurt from smiling.

God, Lauren, just be cool and stop acting like a teenager.

"Text only, please." Quinn winked. "I am not really a phone call person. Nothing personal. It's just more efficient that way."

Lauren scoffed. "Ok then, I will text you, Ms. Quinn." She joked. "Any other orders before I leave for the night?"

Quinn matched Lauren's wit. "Don't worry; I will let you know." She laughed. "And don't forget your purse again. You wouldn't want Lucky to have to come to your rescue again. It might start to go to her head. Good night, beautiful doll. Until we meet again." Quinn opened the door for Lauren, and she stepped out.

"Good night, boss. Thanks for a memorable evening. I am sure there will be more to come." Lauren headed out the door and made her way to the exit of the club.

You have no idea, Lauren. I am nothing if not memorable. As Quinn's ego inflated, another part of her also burned with passion. She knew she would hear from Lauren again soon.

QUINN RETURNED HOME after a late-night closing up Lix. Her West Hollywood bungalow offered a cozy serenity in contrast to the boisterous energy of the club. Quinn lived alone; the success of Lix afforded her the luxury of privacy.

Her home was her sanctuary, a place she could breathe in without feeling the need to be 'on' in front of guests and staff members. Quinn had lived here for ten years, and within that time, she could count on one hand the number of visitors she had hosted.

Quinn kept her circle tight, and it mostly consisted of employees who had worked with Quinn for many years. In between modeling gigs and commercial auditions, bar staff and night club hosts come and go. But to get close enough to Quinn, one needed to prove their loyalty to the business. Always a consummate professional, Quinn was also stingy with her trust, and she had good reason to be.

As Quinn settled into her queen-size bed, she started to process the happenings from the night. *Lauren and her beautiful hair and body...where did she come from? What was her story, and why did the Universe introduce us. Was Lucky flirting with Lauren? Yea, probably. I wonder if she got home, ok? I bet she will text, they all do. I want her. I want to smell her skin and taste her.*

Quinn started to move her fingers down her belly to the warm spot between her legs, the soft skin of her inner thighs sandwiching her hand. She curled two fingers against her crotch, stroking the softness encased by her white cotton Calvin Klein's.

As she moved her fingers, she breathed softly and thought of Lauren; the silhouette of her naked frame as she gleamed against the night sky, plunging into the pool. Quinn quickened the pace of her fingers, the hand finally slipping inside her underwear. Quinn was wet and silky with desire. She rocked her pelvis against her fingers, and her breath quickened. She moaned softly.

She imagined Lauren on the sex swing, smiling with her legs spread open, inviting Quinn to enter her. Quinn rocked harder with two fingers deep inside, curling hard against her G-spot. She moaned louder, her toes curling.

Quinn's entire body tensed up, finally crying out as an explosion of white heat surged through her body.

Quinn let out a deep sigh as she completely relaxed into her mattress. A glow came over her, and she felt content. Her mind was quiet as the events from the night finally escaped her psyche, leaving Quinn to peacefully rest.

7

Quinn bolted upright in bed, covered in sweat. She squinted at the clock on her bedside table, the neon numbers indicating that it was 8:00 am. Quinn had only slept three hours, but her heart was pounding in her chest. A prickly feeling of fear spread across her limbs and up towards her throat. She had awoken from a nightmare, the same dream that had plagued her for years since she was thirty-two.

Quinn fell back on her pillow and put two fingers to her wrist, feeling her pulse. Quinn deeply inhaled and exhaled to calm herself. Night terror was not a new feeling, but it was one that she dreaded. It seemed to come out of nowhere, without rhyme or reason, and it shook Quinn to the core, every time.

She closed her eyes as the haunting images flooded her mind. Angela. St. Angela's Cross. Quinn rolled over on her side and tried to shut out the visions. But she could feel Angela's presence in the room. Angela had come to visit her, in the middle of the night, through the portal of Quinn's dreams.

Something crumbled deep inside Quinn's chest and a wave of sorrow as ferocious as the ocean cascaded over her body. *I'm sorry, Angela. I am so sorry, my love. Why didn't you hold on? I had you in my hands. I had you! Why did you let me go? Please don't blame me. Please forgive me.* Quinn dissolved into tears, deep sobs wracking her body. She shoved her face into her pillow, muffling the noises of grief.

After what seemed like hours, Quinn finally drifted off again, fatigued from crying. This time, she slept soundly, as still as a corpse. When her alarm clock finally buzzed angrily at 2:00 pm, Quinn rose out of bed. She felt rested but gutted, like something- or someone-had scooped out her insides, leaving the hole in her heart empty and raw.

Quinn brought her hands to her face and rubbed her puffy eyes, which were swollen from crying. She sighed deeply and creaked out of bed. It was time to start the day, to do it all over again. It was time to fill the hole with more superficialities; more money, more women, more drinking, more sex. Every day was the same, and the older Quinn got, the harder it was to tell the days apart. They seemed to bleed into one another, losing their shape and becoming less and less filled with meaning.

THE UBER PULLED up to Lauren's apartment, and she exited, her heels click-clacking towards her front door. She entered quietly as her cat Sammy came to greet her, his fluffy grey body purring against her legs.

"Hello, gorgeous creature. I missed you. I'll bet you are

hungry, huh?" Sammy mewed in agreement. Lauren went over to her kitchen cupboard and took out a can of cat food. Sam cried out in delight. Lauren filled the cat dish, and Sammy immediately started to munch.

As the Uber whisked her away from Lix, Lauren felt like she was floating. She couldn't remember the last time she felt so alive. The atmosphere at Lix and her time with Quinn had stimulated her senses and awakened her sexual appetite. She was craving more Sapphic adventures, and she hadn't even reached home yet!

Preparing for bed, the firm softness of Quinn's kiss remained on her lips. She could still smell the whiskey that lingered on her breath. Her belly flip-flopped as she remembered Quinn's piercing blue eyes. She felt like Quinn could see into her soul.

Then logic struck Lauren as she splashed water on her face to remove her makeup. *Of course, it felt like she knew me; Quinn knows all of the women who come to Lix. Lauren, don't think you are unique to Quinn, you are just new.* Her subconscious warned her. *Quinn likes shiny new objects. You were her treat for the night.*

Snuggling into her duvet, Lauren grappled with her opposing emotions. On the one hand, she knew that Lix was a hedonistic playground and that Quinn was the ringmaster. Whatever happened at the club remained there; it was a sexy escape from reality and nothing more. But on the other hand, she felt that there was something deeper beyond the surface.

Regardless if she was only a plaything to Quinn, there was a definite vibe between them. Sure, maybe it was only sexual energy, but it was a bond no less. And the best sex- even if it's only sex-is best served with a connection.

Besides, Lauren thought to her herself, *Quinn can be my*

plaything too. Two can play that game, and I have a lot that I want to explore. Quinn has the experience, and she can show me things. If that is all it is, I may as well enjoy the ride. Like Tania said, I could learn a few ideas for my future girlfriends. That is when I can actually have the time to find a partner.

The high inside Lauren calmed a bit. *Yes, Lauren, enjoy Quinn for the time being, but remember to protect your heart. You don't have the time for drama and heartache. You have an advertising empire to build!* Lauren cocooned herself into her covers and tried to fall asleep, but the night's buzz seemed to linger and continued to hum inside her head.

LAUREN FLOATED *down the corridor of Lix, a sheer white fabric draped over her naked body. She was barefoot, but she couldn't feel the ground beneath her. The hallway was lit with a soft purple, and steamy fog seemed to cover the ground.*

Not realizing how she got there, she found herself inside the Grand Ballroom, on top of the giant bed in the center of the room. She was alone, but there were noises around her; they sounded like soft moans and sighs. She didn't know where they were coming from, but she didn't seem to care.

Lauren scanned the room. From the foot of the bed, a head popped up. Quinn was crouching at the base, peering at her the way that her cat would sometimes stare at her. While maintaining her gaze without blinking, Quinn crawled towards her in slow motion. Lauren seemed to melt into the bed as she turned her head back, exposing her neck.

Lauren felt an extraordinary ecstasy overcome her. Quinn was close enough to lift the soft white fabric over Lauren's head, exposing her body. Quinn ran her hand's inches away from Lauren's skin, but Lauren could feel Quinn's touch regardless.

"Hi Doll," Quinn whispered softy in Lauren's ear. "Hi," Lauren said, although it seemed hard to get the words out of her mouth. Quinn asked, "Do you want to see Angela? She is on the cross." Lauren nodded yes, and suddenly she was inside the dungeon, tied to the cross.

"Where is Angela, Quinn, I don't see her." Lauren's voice seemed to echo. Quinn smiled wordlessly. "Why are we here?" Lauren asked.

"You are my Doll, Lauren. I want to play with you. Is that ok?" Quinn pleaded, sounding desperate. Lauren agreed. "Yes, boss. Please play with me. I want you to teach me how to please you."

Quinn ran her fingers down to Lauren's breasts, this time physically touching her skin. Quinn's touch was cold but soft. Lauren's skin prickled with delight, and her nipples hardened into ripe, pink berries.

"So beautiful." Quinn breathed her in and took a nipple in each hand, rubbing the berries between her fingers. She squeezed a bit harder, and Lauren became wet. She started to thrust her crotch towards Quinn as Quinn continued to rub Lauren's nipples.

"Angela...can you feel me?" Quinn said with eyes closed, as caressed Lauren's body.

"Quinn, I am not Angela. I'm Lauren. Remember? From the other night?" Lauren stopped gyrating to get Quinn's attention.

Quinn stopped and opened her eyes. She stared at Quinn, her face frozen. Out of nowhere, Fran and Terry appeared in The Crossroad. They stood together, hand in hand, slightly behind Quinn.

"We want to touch you. Can we touch you, Lauren?" They said in a spooky kind of unison. They stepped closed to Lauren.

Lauren started to kiss Fran, as Terry joined in. Lauren was aroused by the feeling of multiple lips kissing her face and her neck. When they stepped away, Quinn had disappeared.

"Quinn...Quinn!" *Lauren shouted. Lauren was in The Crossroad alone. She was still tied up.* "Quinn...where are you?"

Lauren awoke with a start. She gasped and noticed that her fingers were slicked with her juices. She turned her head to the left and the right, getting her bearings as she returned to reality.

She was trembling, both with fear and lust. Her mouth was dry, and so she arose to drink some water before returning to bed. As the cooling liquid trickled down her throat, she thought to herself:

Who is Angela?

8

Quinn glanced at her phone, and inwardly, she chastised herself. *You have a busy night ahead, focus on your work, Quinn. Women come and go; whatever happens, happens.*

It had been one week since her chance meeting with Lauren at Lix. Aside from a quick text that Lauren had sent, letting Quinn know that she enjoyed meeting her, Lauren had not yet returned to the club. In maintaining her position of power, Quinn wasn't going to ask Lauren when she might be coming back. And so, the waiting game ensued.

Quinn wasn't used to waiting for what she wanted, and it was making her anxious. She continued to keep herself preoccupied with errands and business matters. Under normal circumstances, she would have set up another play date with someone else, to distract herself. But for some reason, her head wasn't in it. She knew she wanted Lauren and settling for an alternative seemed dissatisfying.

Buzz buzz Quinn's phone vibrated. Her heart did a

little flip as she checked her messages. It was a text from Lauren:

Hi Boss! I was thinking about coming to Lix tomorrow night. I was curious if you wanted to spend some time together?

As excited as Lauren was to receive the text, her ego wanted to remain in control; Quinn decided to wait a few moments to respond, as not to appear too eager. She watched the clock until exactly fifteen minutes had passed. Then she waited another two minutes for extra measure.

Why, hello, Doll! Lovely to hear from you. Sure, I can spare some time for us. Come early, and I'll reserve the Grand Ballroom for us before it gets too busy. 9 pm. Your name will be on the guest list.

Bursting with excitement that she did not want to acknowledge, Quinn scribbled instructions for the hostesses, for tomorrow. Lauren was to be let in free of charge and that Quinn would busy for a few hours.

EVER SINCE HER first experience at Lix, Lauren could not get Quinn out of her mind. The thought of seeing her again made her feel nervous and excited. Still, she didn't want to come off too overzealous. Lauren was not into playing mind games, but she also felt that perhaps, she should hold back a bit, with Quinn.

A week went by, and Lauren finally got the courage to

text Quinn. As she waited for a response, she started to second guess herself. *What if Quinn was too busy or had already made plans with another woman? Maybe a week was too soon? Or perhaps I should have texted earlier, so she knows I am interested? That's silly, Lauren, she knows you are into her. What if I had...*

Ding ding; a sound interrupted Lauren's thoughts, and she looked at the new message she had received from Quinn. She grabbed her phone and squealed with delight. Lauren was returning to Lix tomorrow night, and she would have Quinn all to herself, at least for a few hours.

Now she pondered what to wear this time. She opened up a dresser drawer and began to rummage through bits of lacy lingerie, tossed in with bra and panty sets. She selected a few items, smiled to herself, and let the news's happiness carry her away for the rest of the day.

THIS TIME, when Lauren arrived at the front entrance of Lix, there was no queue. It was too early, but that suited Lauren perfectly. She knocked on the door, and Mickey, the security guard Lauren had met on her first night, opened the door.

"Hey, sugar. We ain't open yet. Come back at 10:30 pm, ok?" Mickey went to shut the door.

"No, wait! I was invited to come for 9 pm," Lauren stammered. "By Quinn."

Mickey smiled to herself and shook her head. She called out from behind her. "Hey! Anyone on the guest list tonight for 9 pm? For..." Mickey turned to her, "What's your name, sugar?"

Suddenly Quinn appeared in the door frame beside

Mickey. "Don't worry, Mickey. I got this. Hi, Lauren."
Quinn smiled. "Come in. Sorry, I forgot to tell you to text
me when you arrived because we aren't open yet."

She guided Lauren inside and put a hand on the small
of her back. "But you are here now, and that's all that
matters." Quinn took Lauren's coat and gave it to Mickey.
Lauren and Quinn walked away from the front entrance,
leaving Mickey and the hostess to exchange knowing
glances.

The club appeared bare and rather drab without the
flashing lights and the music. Chelsea was behind the bar,
setting up for the night. A few cleaning staff mopped their
way through the dance floor while another hostess reposi-
tioned the chaise lounges.

"You look incredible," Quinn surveyed Lauren's outfit
and smiled as they walked towards the corridor. Lauren
tugged and smoothed down her white lace teddy. It was
just respectable enough to pull off at a nightclub but scandalous enough to double as lingerie. "Very angelic, you
look like an innocent angel." Quinn toyed. "The white lace
suits you." Quinn smiled to herself. They both knew the
innocent look was something Quinn very much enjoyed.

Lauren bit her lip and glowed at the compliment. "You
look pretty handsome yourself." She gave Quinn the once
over, admiring her long, lean legs and slender hips
encased in leather pants; the same one's she saw Quinn
wearing the night they met. But instead of a white dress
shirt, Quinn was wearing a black tank top, and it showed
off an intricate tattoo sleeve, ending at the forearm, which
was punctuated by a skull.

"Very cool!" Lauren exclaimed, touching the tattoo.
"Did it hurt?"

Quinn shrugged, "Kind of, but in a good way. I like the

pain; it makes me feel alive." Quinn took Lauren's hands and pulled her towards the door of the Grand Ballroom. "Do you know what else makes me feel alive?"

Lauren giggled as Quinn entered the room backward, tugging Lauren inside. Quinn reached behind Lauren and shut the door. Lauren leaned against the door, and Quinn pressed against her body. Quinn looked down and fingered a piece of Lauren's hair, leaving a soft caress against her cheek.

"You are so beautiful," Quinn whispered, and Lauren felt a twinge of déjà vu. Her dream! Quinn leaned down to kiss Lauren, cupping her delicate chin with one hand. A tingling burst of warm breath and soft skin overcame her and sent shock waves down Lauren's body, to the pit of her stomach and beyond.

Their mouths found each other in a fury of passion, and their tongues twisted together, wrapping around like ribbons. Quinn slid her thigh between Lauren's legs, and Lauren bore down, grinding her pelvis against the leather material and the firmness of Quinn's muscle. Together, they kissed deeply and rocked their bodies in tandem, faster and rougher, in a state of arousal.

Lauren sighed as Quinn grunted. Quinn pressed her pubic bone harder into Lauren, stimulating the sensitive nerves, her underwear becoming soaked with ecstasy. Quinn grabbed Lauren's hair from the back and playfully bit her neck. Lauren cried out with pleasure, gasping for breath as she continued to rub herself against Quinn.

Red and flushed, Quinn pushed away from Lauren, taking both of her hands and leading her to the massive bed.

Quinn leaned back on the bed as Lauren straddled

her. Quinn looked to one of the walls that doubled as a mirror, admiring their reflections.

"Well, don't we look hot together?" Quinn mused. Lauren also glanced at the reflection, as she sat on top of Quinn, her hair tousled about with her lipstick slightly smeared. She felt like a wild nymph unleashing her primal energy. Lauren shook her mane and pouted sexily in the mirror. Then she looked down at Quinn and unrolled her teddy, revealing her bare breasts and hard, pink nipples.

Quinn smiled hungrily and reached her head up her mouth, finding Lauren's nipple and sucking. Lauren tilted her head back as waves of pleasure rolled over her. Quinn then slid her hand between Lauren's legs and pushed the wet white lace of her panties aside.

Lauren raised her hips slightly in excitement to allow Quinn's hand access. Quinn's fingers slipped straight into Lauren's wetness. Two fingers pushed hard inside her and began to fuck her.

"Oh fuck...Quinn. Fuck. Fuck me. Harder," Lauren gasped as she bounced against Quinn's hand, the fingers curving into her G-spot. Lauren kept one hand on Quinn's shoulder to steady herself while the other hand moved to her clit. She rubbed furiously while continuing to buck into Quinn's fingers, riding like a cowgirl. "Oh god... please...oh yes...Fuck.... "

Quinn loved the foul language from Lauren's beautiful lips. She kept her fingers moving hard inside Lauren and watched avidly as her big breasts bounced with every movement of her body

Lauren called out with pleasure as she orgasmed hard. Her body was covered with a thin layer of sweat. She fell onto Quinn in a mess of hair and warm skin. Quinn slid her hand out from under Lauren, it was covered in her juices.

Grinning like a Cheshire cat, Quinn offered her fingers to Lauren's mouth. "Clean my hand, doll." Quinn's voice was low and throaty. Although it was something she had never done, Lauren didn't hesitate, and her mouth opened to feel Quinn's strong fingers pushing inside. Lauren tasted her sex on them. Her tongue and mouth cleaned Quinn's hand. Quinn stroked Lauren's hair as Lauren's heartbeat returned to a regular pace.

She liked the weight of Lauren on top of her. Quinn moved her hands down Lauren's back and grabbed her ass cheeks.

"Mmm. Did you enjoy that ride, Doll?" Wordlessly, Lauren nodded against Quinn's shoulder, still sprawled out on top of her body.

Lauren arched herself up to look at Quinn. She kissed her deeply. Their energies seemed to melt into one entity. Lauren stopped and looked into Quinn's eyes. "I want to make you feel good too." Lauren started to move one hand down Quinn's leather pants, searching for a zipper, eager to get closer to Quinn's body.

Quinn placed her hand on Lauren's wrist as a motion to stop. With all of her strength, Quinn rolled Lauren underneath her so that Quinn was now pinning down Lauren. Lauren laughed and capitulated instantly, "Yes, you certainly are the boss!" Lauren wriggled underneath Quinn in delight.

Quinn moved another strand of hair away from Lauren's face and caressed her neck. She looked down at Lauren's pink mouth, slightly open in rapture. "You will get your chance, little one. Right now, tonight is all about you." Quinn leaned her body upwards so that she was now sitting on Lauren, staring down at her, like she had just captured her prey.

Lauren shrugged. "Ok, boss. Whatever you say." Quinn cooed, "Good girl, that is what I like to hear." Quinn then moved so that she was no longer touching Lauren's body. Lauren felt a pang of separation, after being so united by that deep kiss. She studied Quinn, noticing her body language.

Quinn stood up to smooth down her tank top and looked at her watch. Lauren sat up from the bed, adjusted her underwear, which was uncomfortably wet, and pulled her teddy back on. Lauren wasn't sure what to do next, but as usual, Quinn took the lead.

With a hand outstretched, Quinn reached for Lauren. "We still have some time before I need to focus on the club. What does my lovely Doll want to do next?" Quinn said with a devilish smile.

Suddenly feeling exposed and shy, Lauren shook her head. "Um, I am not sure. Maybe we could visit the room across the hall? The Crossroad?" Lauren shrugged her shoulders.

Quinn nodded in a business-like way. "Excellent idea. And if you are so keen on pleasing me, I can show you what I like."

It was a statement, more than a question. Quinn took Lauren's hand and helped her up. Her belly fluttered with a post-orgasm thrill. "Lead the way, boss," Quinn reassured Lauren, a slight edge of cockiness to her voice. "Doll, I always do."

9

Quinn led Lauren into the dungeon. This time, Lauren took her time to examine the room more closely. She ran a hand across the various objects and the curves of the furniture. The sex swing was front and center, welcoming Lauren's return. She hopped in and wrapped her hands around the chains, wriggling her bottom with joy, as though she was on a swing set.

"This looks fun." Lauren hinted, but Quinn had other plans. "All in good time, little one." Quinn teased. "I think I would prefer to have you here." Quinn gently guided Lauren over to the cross. Lauren bobbed her head with consent. "I love a woman who takes charge."

Wordlessly, Quinn strapped Lauren's wrists into the padded handcuffs that hung from the cross's sides. Lauren's arms were bound to the top half of the X shape of the giant wooden cross. Lauren felt vulnerable under the direction of Quinn but safe and protected. She willingly submitted to Quinn's dominance over her.

After connecting the last strap, Quinn then paused to

look at Lauren, to examine her features. Quinn reveled in Lauren's beauty, and something inside her started to melt.

She is so exquisite. Her face and the color of her hair, that laughter. Her willingness to trust me, her openness. God, she reminds me of...

Quinn, lost in a few seconds of thought, suddenly snapped back to reality. *No, Quinn, don't go there. Lauren is beautiful and fun but keep your head in check. Remember why you are here. You are Kelly Quinn, the owner of Lix, and you have no time to get caught up in silly emotions.* Quinn's subconscious chastised her.

Quinn took a sharp breath in and then looked at Lauren with a no-nonsense look. 'Do you want to know what I like, Lauren? I like it when pretty girls like you do what I say. Does that excite you?" Quinn ran her hands slowly down Lauren's body, feeling her waist, hips, and curves. She took in Lauren's essence, while her eyes wandered over Lauren's body. Lauren's body shivered in desire at Quinn's touch.

"Yes, Boss," Lauren whispered quietly, trying to catch Quinn's gaze, but Quinn did not look her in the eyes. "What can I do? I want so badly to make you feel good, to please you, Quinn." Lauren closed her eyes, high from all of the physical sensations.

"Spread your legs for me," Quinn ordered, and Lauren obliged. Quinn knelt and strapped Lauren's ankles into cuffs on the bottom of the St Andrew's cross, spreading her open. Quinn lightly ran her fingers up the soft flesh of Lauren's inner thighs. Lauren shivered and moaned. Quinn continued to tease Lauren with her feather-like touch, and Lauren began to moisten more. She desperately wanted to pull Quinn close, to feel her with her own hands. She felt so close to Quinn but also so far away.

Why wouldn't Quinn let her touch? She felt more excited than she ever had.

Quinn leaned into Lauren's ear to whisper. "Do you want to come again?" Lauren nodded, oh, how she did! But she wanted a piece of Quinn too. "I want you, Quinn. I want to touch you."

Quinn kept Lauren handcuffed, ignoring her wishes. "You are touching me, Lauren. You are touching me without even realizing it, and right now, that is all that my Doll gets to do because I am the Boss, and I am in charge. Ok?" Quinn spoke like a school teacher to a student.

Wide-eyed and dizzy with desire, Lauren nodded. "Ok, then please touch me again. Please make me come again." Lauren whispered, arching her pelvis forward. Quinn traced the thin soaking lace between Lauren's thighs with her fingers. The pace was driving Lauren mad with longing.

Seconds felt like minutes as Quinn finally plunged deep into Lauren once again, and Lauren's body instantly responded to the delicious feeling of rough penetration.

With her arms still tied, Lauren thrust her hips towards Quinn, aching for more with limited movement. "That's a good girl." Quinn encouraged. "Yea, come for me again. Come for the Boss." Quinn continued to coax Lauren, as she curled her fingers inside Lauren in a come-hither motion while her thumb rubbed against Lauren's swollen clit. "Mmmm, yes, you are doing such a good job," Quinn whispered, embodying her role as the aggressor.

"Oh god...Quinn!" Lauren cried out as the second orgasm escaped, leaving her body flushed with red, and she fell limp in the restraints. Her limbs' tautness during arousal seemed to dissipate into relaxation, as Lauren crumpled from the cross. She was breathing heavily, mouth agape.

Quinn once again brought her fingers to Lauren's mouth. "Suck." She ordered. Lauren did as she was told, licking the wetness from Quinn's fingers, cleaning them obediently. Quinn then removed her fingers, and Lauren looked deep into Quinn's eyes.

"Thank you. That was so incredible." Lauren smiled. She had experienced an orgasm that let her pulsating.

Pleased, Quinn smiled. Quinn could sometimes be as callous as she genuinely enjoyed bringing bliss to women. She loved how hot their bodies got, how they writhed and moaned with enjoyment. Quinn's heart may have a wall, but her fingers (and tongue) knew what to do. What she couldn't provide in emotions came out in sex.

It wasn't always that way for Quinn; once upon a time, Quinn had an open tenderness, a sensitive core of softness and light. Over the years, through times of trauma and tragedy, a protective shield formed around Quinn's heart that kept others from entering in. Quinn felt as though she lived in a bubble, unable to truly connect in fear of being hurt or worse, losing someone she loved again. No, Quinn could not go through that one more. Not ever.

Quinn smiled tenderly at Lauren and kissed her with a closed mouth, as a reward for following her instructions. She released her restraints one by one. She could tell that Lauren was searching for more from her, but she needed to maintain an emotional distance, if not a physical one.

Lauren's hands came back down to her sides, the blood rushing back to her fingertips. She collected herself after such an intense experience. She reached out for Quinn and grabbed the leather material with straight, outstretched hands. "Wow, just wow." Lauren shook her head in disbelief. "If you aren't careful, I just might get addicted to you." Lauren flirted.

Quinn brushed it off casually with a smile. "Well, that wouldn't be so bad, now would it?" She allowed Lauren to grab her hips and leaned in an A-shape towards Lauren so that her shoulders and the crown of her head were closer, but she still kept a small space away. It was a bit of a power move, near but still a bit far.

All of a sudden, Lauren gasped. "Oh, I forgot to tell you! I had a dream a few weeks ago, in this very room!" Lauren stepped away from the cross and looked around the room. "Yes, it was here, and I was on this cross. You were there too." Lauren immediately started to feel shy, like she had revealed something she shouldn't have. Quinn's eyes twinkled.

"Oh yea, is that so? Well, do tell, Doll." This time, Quinn took a step towards Lauren, eager to hear more. "Was it...a naughty dream?" Quinn slyly asked.

"Um, well, yea, it kind of was," Lauren stammered, her face blushing with a pink hue. "You and I were here but, we didn't start off in this room. First, we were in the room next door. That is where it started." Lauren searched the recesses of her memory to try and recollect the images from her dream.

Quinn laughed heartily. "Aren't you just the little fortune teller! Maybe it was a wishful dream, huh Doll," Quinn drawled. "Did your wish come true?" Feeling more than a little pleased with herself, Quinn joked while her confidence soared.

Lauren chuckled and looked down, allowing Quinn her moment of triumph. "Well, I definitely did tonight, but this dream...it was more than just a sexy dream. It was kind of eerie. There were definitely some weird parts to it too."

Quinn pulled Lauren closer and brought her over the desk in the dungeon. The furniture was used for kinky role play scenes, but this time, Quinn wanted to provide them with a surface to sit on while they chatted about Lauren's dream.

"It's getting more interesting by the minute." Quinn perched upon the surface of the desk, while Lauren stood, in between Quinn's legs. Quinn wrapped her arms around Lauren's waist and curled her legs around Lauren's body so that she could stay close to Quinn.

Well, that's more like it! Lauren thought to herself. *God, it's pretty hard to get close to this woman, but what a treat it is when she finally lets me in.* Lauren started to feel more secure in Quinn's presence.

"Ok, well, we were playing on the cross, in kind of the same way we just did tonight," Lauren started, playfully glancing up at Quinn, "you were touching my body, and it felt delicious." Quinn nodded, pleased with what she heard so far.

"But then...something weird happened. I mean, dreams are just like, right? Strange things happen all of the time." Lauren shrugged her shoulders and waved her hands in trying to explain herself.

"What happened, little one?" Quinn became curious as Lauren's voice seemed to change. "Did I grow a second head or something?" Quinn joked. "Or...even better, did I grow multiple hands?" Quinn smiled impishly, fluttering her fingers like she was about to tickle Lauren.

Lauren softly squealed and giggled. "No, silly," as she squirmed away. "You called me by another name. You started off by calling me doll-which I love, by the way-but then you called me something else."

"Oh, wow," Quinn exclaimed. "You know that I have been with many women, Lauren. But I can honestly say that I have never, in my life, ever called out another's woman's name during sex. I can assure you that would never happen." Quinn laughed in disbelief. "But this is great, please, keep going."

Lauren paused, unsure if she should continue. She closed her eyes and took a breath. "You called me... Angela." Lauren opened her eyes and carefully looked up at Quinn.

Quinn went white upon hearing that name. Angela. Something inside Quinn broke and also hardened at the same time. The pit of her stomach dropped out, and she felt like she was falling. She was at a loss for words. Quinn could not touch the ground beneath her. She felt a deep sadness wash over her, coupled with waves of anger.

"Quinn," Lauren started to speak, gently and softly, "It's not a big deal, I know Angela was special to you. St. Angela's cross, right?" She touched Quinn's shoulder and tried to look deeper inside her eyes, searching for what seemed like an unrecognizable emotion. "I mean, it makes sense. I was dreaming about this room, and you had told me about Angela and the cross and, like, it was..." Lauren trailed off.

Quinn coldly started at Lauren, immediately cutting her off. "You don't know anything about Angela. You never knew her. Hell, you don't even know me very well." Quinn laughed cruelly. "I mean, you literally showed up to Lix a week ago. What do you know about anything?"

Lauren felt as though she had just been slapped. She was stunned. She had never meant to upset Quinn with her recollection of the dream; Quinn asked her to share the details! What was going on?

"Quinn, listen, I am so sorry. You are right; I didn't know Angela. I mean, you asked...I just, I didn't mean to upset you. It's just...it's just a dream." Lauren stammered, trying to backtrack and console Quinn at the same time. *Good job, Lauren, way to mess up a perfectly good evening.* Lauren berated herself.

Quinn was trembling with furious grief and anger. She felt violated by Lauren's mention of Angela. She knew that Lauren didn't mean anything by it, but still, it felt as if Lauren was prying into Quinn's past, a past that had left her devastated by heartbreak. Angela was Quinn's first and only true love. To hear another woman speak Angela's name-especially someone so new to Quinn's life-felt like an invasion.

Still, Quinn knew that she had to keep some semblance of composure. After all, she was the owner of L.A's hottest women-only night club and erotic playground. Quinn had an image to protect and a reputation to maintain. She looked away from Lauren and took a deep breath to control her emotions.

"Lauren...," Quinn stared off and sighed, avoiding Lauren's gaze, "Look, I know you didn't mean to say anything upsetting. It's that you don't understand the situation and what happened. It's just very...painful for me to hear her name, especially from someone I just met."

Quinn stepped away from Lauren and looked down at the ground. She proceeded in a more controlled manner. "It feels like you are bringing up a ghost, a ghost that haunts my dreams. I guess I just wasn't expecting to hear her name come out of your lips."

Lauren felt awful. The last thing she had wanted to do

was upset Quinn. Approaching Quinn carefully, she took a small step forward, to try and console her.

"Quinn, I am so sorry. You are right; I don't know what it's like to lose someone you love. I didn't mean to catch you off guard like that." Lauren reached out to Quinn, trying to bring herself closer, but the best she could do was touch Quinn's bare elbows, from an arm's length distance.

"Do you want to talk about it?" Lauren cautiously inquired. Quinn shook her head and continued to look away from Lauren. "Ok, that's ok. I get it, we are still strangers, and I overstepped." Lauren conceded. "Should I get going, then? Maybe you need some space?"

Quinn looked at Lauren with a combination of sadness and icy coldness. "It's cool, Lauren. Look, it was a long time ago. I mean, the past is the past, right?" She shrugged. "I accept your apology, but it's not necessary. You didn't do anything wrong." Quinn struggled, trying to keep the tears in her eyes from spilling over. *Don't you dare fucking cry, Kelly Quinn. Not in front of this bombshell and never, ever, at work. Pull yourself together already.*

Quinn straightened her shoulders and lifted her chin, gaining more poise. A long exhalation escaped as she ran her fingers through her hair. She reached for Lauren and grabbed both of her hands.

"Look, Lauren. I like you. I do. You are sweet and fun, and sexy as hell. You are young, and you have your whole life ahead of you." She looked down at Lauren's soft hands, encased in Quinn's grasp. "I don't want to disappoint you, but you need to understand that there is a limit to what I give you." Quinn finally connected with Lauren's stare and bore into her soul. "You deserve more. I can offer a good time and some hot sex, but..." Quinn trailed off, leaving Lauren to fill in the blanks.

Lauren received Quinn's touch with tender sympathy. She so badly wanted to console Quinn, to give her a safe space to grieve in her arms. Her heart ached for Quinn; this strong, statuesque woman trying so hard to hold it together.

Quinn's vulnerability had touched Lauren, and she appreciated that Quinn was finally opening up to her, even if only by accident. She only wished it wasn't because of something so sad.

"Quinn, I understand. You told me what the deal was, between us, when we first met. I am a big girl and I know what I am signing myself up for. I like you too, but I can make my own choices." Lauren said with conviction. "I willingly chose to be with you tonight." Lauren searched Quinn's blue eyes, which were as expansive as the L.A. sky. "Because I want you. And regardless of however long this will last, I will take you and this situation as it is." Lauren paused and coyly smiled. "Besides, no one has ever made me come while I was tied to a cross, so that was new!"

Quinn couldn't help but laugh out loud. She was enjoying Lauren's sense of wit and her ability to be so easygoing. *Ok, as long as you know what you are getting yourself into, Lauren, we will get along just fine.* She relaxed a bit more, knowing that Lauren accepted her and her emotional walls. However, she still felt a bit pensive and protective of her own heart.

Quinn squared with Lauren's gaze. "Alright. Yea, you are right. You are an adult, and I've been nothing but honest with you. If you can respect my boundaries, then I also need to respect your choices." A playful look came over Quinn, and she interrupted herself. "I don't only respect your choices, Lauren; I will make them worth your while. Believe me."

Something in the tone of Quinn's voice sent shivers down Lauren's spine. Quinn's words sounded as much like an invitation as they did a warning. Lauren knew she was playing with fire, but she could not resist Quinn's charm and sexual prowess. She wanted to stick her hand in the flame and to feel the warmth of Quinn. Maybe soon-if not tonight-Quinn would let her.

Quinn needed to change the energy between them; it was getting too dramatic for her taste. This conversation seemed to inch towards territory that made Quinn feel uncomfortable. *Time to lighten up the mood, Quinn. We are in the goddamn dungeon, for crying out loud.* She thought to herself. *Fuck, I need a drink.*

Quinn returned to her usual, dominant self and quickly grabbed Lauren, pulling her into her, meeting pelvis to pelvis. She ran her mouth up Lauren's neck, her tongue teasing the edge of Lauren's right earlobe. She resisted the urge to nip at Lauren's neck and instead gave her a series of soft, butterfly kisses. *I will leave biting for another time, best not to leave any marks on this beauty for tonight.*

Lauren softened into Quinn, allowing herself to be seduced out of her own thoughts and embarrassment over the dream exchange. *It is what it is, Lauren. Just go with it but remember to keep your feet on the ground.* Lauren would need to listen to her own advice if she was ever going to see Quinn again.

Quinn whispered in Lauren's ear. "How about a drink, little one? Something tells me that we have both earned one tonight."

Quinn moved her face to Lauren's face and sensually examined her mouth as she spoke.

Instantly aroused and thrilled, she nodded enthusiastically. A cocktail would be the perfect antidote to soothe her untamed senses. "That is the second-best idea you have had tonight, Boss. I accept!"

Quinn toyed. "Oh, yea? What was the best idea of the evening?" Lauren countered. "Bringing me into the Grand Ballroom and kissing me against the door." Lauren bit her lip in lust while doing a little shimmy with her shoulders. "I feel like I could hit the dancefloor in a bit, too." She did a little dance, which greatly amused Quinn.

Good girl, Lauren. Yes, let's shake off the seriousness and the sadness of the night. I want you to enjoy all that Lix has to offer, and don't feel that you need to limit your interactions with me. Quinn felt relieved that Lauren was easing up, and as much as she wanted to continue to play with Lauren, tonight had taken a toll. Quinn started to feel cagey like she needed some space.

"Let's head to the bar. We can always return here again, another time." Quinn took the lead and led them both out of The Crossroad. They headed down the hall and towards the bar for drinks.

10

As much as Lauren desired Quinn, she too needed a breather from the night's events. *Perhaps I was coming on too strong.* She pondered. *Maybe some casual conversation and light flirting will help to get us both in a better headspace.* As much as Lauren hated to admit to herself, she was really into Quinn-maybe more than she should be. But Lauren felt confident that she could handle whatever came her way.

By this time in the night, the club was in full swing. The lights had been lowered, and there was a crowd of women, warming up on the dancefloor. It was a stark contrast to when Lauren had first arrived.

"Hey, you two!" Punk rock bartender Chelsea cheerfully greeted them as Quinn and Lauren approached the bar. Quinn, who had been holding Lauren's hand, quickly dropped it. "Hey, Chelsea. Looks like things are picking up nicely for tonight. How have the sales been so far?" Quinn readjusted into her owner role.

"Pretty good so far. The mojito special that I created seems to be popular with the ladies tonight. What can I get you two?" Chelsea's eyes bounced between Lauren and Quinn, a knowing smirk crossed her face. Chelsea, who had been working at Lix for close to eight years, could spot chemistry when she saw it, and she found the connection between Quinn and Lauren to be quite evident.

Quinn was annoyed that the staff seemed to think there was a relationship between her and Lauren. Quinn was very open with her dalliances; she was the owner and felt no need to be anyone else but her true self. But Quinn also needed to keep a safe distance from anything serious. How was she ever going to manage Lauren's expectations if the staff assumed that they were becoming a couple?

"Sounds lovely. Make this one a single mojito," Quinn gestured her neck in Lauren's direction without taking her eyes off Chelsea. "I will take a double, please."

"Coming right up!" Chelsea took the order and efficiently went to work, preparing the drinks.

As they waited on their beverages, Quinn continued to face the front, her eyes scanning the bar's length without turning to Lauren. While they were standing beside one another, Quinn seemed to grow a shell around her being.

Lauren glanced up at Quinn, who seemed to be in her own world. Lauren put a hand up to Quinn's shoulder and attempted to engage her in conversation.

"I love the DJ tonight! Is it the same person who was playing last week?"

"Mmm, hmm, yea, Collette is great; she has a residency here," Quinn said, somewhat absentmindedly. Chelsea brought over the cocktails, and Quinn grabbed hers right away, slipping fervently. Lauren had thought Quinn would have passed over her drink as well, but

Quinn continued to focus on her own alcohol consumption.

"Thanks, Chelsea," Lauren chirped, as she dug into her purse to leave Chelsea a tip. Quinn brushed her hand over Lauren. "Don't worry about it, Lauren. I will cover this. Why don't you go over to dance and enjoy yourself?"

"Do you want to join me?" Lauren asked, looking up at Quinn with flirtatious doe-eyes. "I think you and I could cause a sexy commotion out there," Lauren gestured to the dance floor and grabbed Quinn's hips in an attempt to move their bodies together.

Quinn wriggled away and smiled wanly. "No, I am good right here. You go ahead." Quinn continued to sip her drink. "Besides, it will be fun to watch you from afar," Quinn said, almost as if it was an afterthought.

"Um, ok," Lauren shrugged, mustering a smile. "Well, in that case, you are in for a treat because I have some serious dance moves," she joked. Quinn nodded and continued to stare at her cocktail glass. Quinn finished her drink, slurping hard to suck out the remnants of rum from the muddled pieces of mint and granulated sugar.

Lauren paused and looked at Quinn before heading off in the direction of the music. Something seemed off with her tonight. She felt as though Quinn was brushing her aside, like a pest. *How strange she thought. Maybe Quinn is just having a bad night? Is she still upset about the dream conversation?* Feeling uneasy, Lauren struggled with her thoughts. *Lauren, don't be clingy. Just go and enjoy the club and give Quinn some space.*

As Lauren walked away from the bar, she overheard Quinn bellow. "Chelsea, throw me another double, will you doll?" *Doll,* Lauren thought. *I thought 'doll' was my pet name.* Chelsea slid over to where Quinn was standing and started to prepare a second mojito. Quinn seemed to say something to Chelsea that made her hysterical. They laughed heartily in unison.

Lauren escaped, bobbing and weaving through the crowd in an attempt to shake off her feelings of hurt. She felt confused. Earlier that night, she and Quinn enjoyed a hot, intimate connection in the Grand Ballroom, and now, Quinn acting like she didn't want Lauren around her. Lauren played back the memories in her head of her conversation with Quinn in the dungeon. *Is this all in my head? Am I paranoid?*

Lauren spotted Fran and Terry on the dance floor in a twist of luck, the couple she had met the week before. They waved at her.

"Hi, Lauren; it's so good to see you again!" Fran went in for a hug, followed by Terry. Lauren returned the embrace, grateful to see some familiar faces. After feeling rejected by Quinn, she was starting to feel self-conscious, being at Lix. Running into Fran and Terry gave her a sense of footing.

"I didn't think I would see you both so soon! I thought you were only once-a-month regulars," Lauren playfully joked with Fran, tapping her on the arm in fun.

Fran shrugged, and Terry cuddled in close. "What can we say?" Fran threw her arms up by her sides. "We love the place, and DJ Collette is my favorite. Besides, it's Terry's birthday tonight, so we thought we would celebrate."

"What? Oh, that is great!" Lauren exclaimed. She hugged Terry again. "Happy birthday! How are you enjoying the night?"

Glowing with joy and squeezing Fran to her side, Terry gushed, "It has been the most amazing day. We spent the afternoon at the beach, and then Fran treated me to a romantic dinner at Trois Fourchette, which is my absolute favorite restaurant. But I definitely wanted to end my night with some drinks and dancing."

Fran interjected. "After dinner, I thought this place would be perfect for some dessert," Fran seductively turned to Terry, pulling her close. The couple shared an intimate kiss.

Lauren felt a pang of envy. Fran and Terry seemed so connected, and it was apparent that they were very much in love. She loved to see how affectionate they were, with one another, so proud to be in each other's company. Lauren didn't even think that she cared about having a partner at this stage in her life, but seeing Fran and Terry made her long for something more.

Fran turned to Lauren. "What about you? Did you come here alone again, or are you with someone?" Fran teased with a twinkle in her eye.

"Well, I was with someone earlier, but, um, I wanted to dance a bit so..." Lauren hesitated, unsure of how to proceed or what to say. She wasn't sure how much of her rendezvous with Quinn she should disclose. She didn't want to gossip or name drop, but part of her desperately wanted to tell someone, if only to relive the memory that seemed to be fading as the night went on.

Terry interjected, "Oh, do tell! Where is your date now?" Terry looked across the dancefloor. Lauren played with her hair, which was something she always did when she was nervous. She suddenly felt very on the spot, and it just hit her that perhaps, she and Quinn were supposed to be a secret.

"Oh, she just went to get a drink," Lauren said lightly, brushing off the question. "She will be back soon. I am just enjoying myself here for now." Lauren wanted to change the subject. "Have you been to the pool yet, tonight?"

Fran spoke, "Not yet. I think we are going to dance a bit first and work up a sweat before we take a dip," Fran turned to Terry, kissing her on the cheek. "Right, honey?"

Terry turned to her lover, "That sounds like a delicious idea." Terry brightened. "But first, we need more drinks!" Terry looked at Lauren. "Come to the bar with us. Let's do some shots."

The last place Lauren wanted to go right now was back to the bar. She didn't want Quinn to think that she was stalking her. But it was Terry's birthday, and the least Lauren could do was buy her a shot to celebrate. She liked this couple, and she was happy to spend time with people who appreciated her presence. "Sure, let's go. Drinks on me, ladies."

Lauren strategically led Fran and Terry to the other end of the bar, away from where she had been with Quinn. By this point in the night, the bar became packed with bodies, and Lauren felt safer, being able to hide in the crowd. Fran and Terry stood behind Lauren as she positioned herself at the front to order.

Lauren turned back to Terry. "What would you like, birthday girl?" Terry looked at Fran like she was a schoolgirl who was about to do something naughty. "Tequila shots!" Terry exclaimed while Fran laughed, putting her hand to her face. "Oh boy, this is going to be one hell of a night!" Fran said. "But it is my baby's birthday, so let's go for it!"

Lauren bobbed her head in agreement. "I can get down with some tequila. Let's do it!"

A different bartender who was working on the opposite side of the bar approached Lauren. She was a high femme blond with killer biceps who possessed the body of a personal trainer. "What can I get you?" She said in an impatient rush. The bar was bustling and this bartender was hustling as hard as she could.

"Three tequila shots, please." Lauren threw down a fifty- dollar bill. "Take one for yourself," she said, feeling generous and excited to treat her new friends.

The hot blond bartender gave Lauren a sexy smile. "You got it, cutie." The bartender slammed down four shot glasses, filling them quickly with gold-colored liqueur. She passed three of the shot glasses over to Lauren, who, in turn, handed two back to Fran and Terry. The foursome clinked and swallowed in unison.

"Happy birthday!" Lauren and Fran shouted to Terry over the loud music. Lauren, filled with mirth, felt comfortable in her surroundings. She no longer felt like a self-conscious outsider. In fact, she forgot about Quinn for a quick moment when her eyes grazed along the bar.

Suddenly, her eyes landed on Quinn, leaning over the bar, whispering something in Chelsea's ear. Quinn's posture seemed lax and languid as if the countertop was holding her up. She had seemed to lose her typical, controlled demeanor and was now appearing rather sloppy. Quinn was definitely drunk.

As Lauren continued to stare, Quinn picked up an empty glass in front of her and handed it to Chelsea, who then filled it with ice and a splash of liquid from an unidentifiable bottle. Quinn raised her glass to Chelsea, who laughed along, putting a hand on Quinn's arm from over the bar counter. Quinn downed the drink and slammed it in front of her. She put her hand on top of

Chelsea's grasp and leaned forward as if to tell Chelsea another secret.

Chelsea leaned in closer to Quinn, their faces almost touching. Quinn seemed to be mouthing something to Chelsea, and Chelsea nodded in agreement. Then, Quinn put her hand on the back of Chelsea's neck, pulling her close, kissing her on the cheek. Chelsea smiled, scrunching her face into Quinn's grip, nuzzling against it. As soon as Quinn had kissed Chelsea, she hazily glanced over the bar, catching Lauren's gaze.

Lauren was aghast, her mouth open. Quinn's eyes widened in surprise, caught in the act. Time froze for a few moments while Lauren processed the scene in front of her. She felt as though she had just been slapped. Lauren and Quinn were locked in a passionate embrace only hours ago, with Lauren reaching peaks of ecstasy that she had never known. They had gone from lovers in the Grand Ballroom to Quinn, quickly brushing her aside, at the bar. How did things between them decline so rapidly; it hadn't been a full twenty-four hours!

Fran and Terry noticed the look of alarm on Lauren's face. They looked at her and followed her gaze to where Quinn was standing, and then they glanced at one another.

"What's wrong, Lauren? Do you know those two, Kelly and Chelsea?" Fran peered into Lauren's crestfallen face. "Kelly is the owner of Lix. Everyone calls her Quinn. The bartender's name is Chelsea. The rumor is that they are seeing one another. But then again, Quinn gets around so, who really knows for sure?" Fran shrugged.

"Yea, it wouldn't surprise me if they were dating." Terry agreed with Fran's sentiment. "But I don't think that Quinn ever serious about anyone, so maybe it's just a fling." Terry turned to Lauren to speak in her ear over the loud music. "What do you care, Lauren? Are you into Chelsea or something?" Terry then turned to Fran. "All of my love feelings aside, if I had to choose, Quinn would be more my type physically, but I am not into the player game. Besides, I have the perfect woman right here." Terry exclaimed, giddy from her alcohol buzz, hugging Fran close to her.

"Oh my god, wait..!" Fran gasped and grabbed Lauren by the shoulders. "Lauren, is Quinn, the woman that you were spending time with earlier? Was that supposed to be your date tonight?" Fran looked wide-eyed at Lauren. "Oh my god, this makes so much sense now!" Fran turned to Terry.

Lauren, still in a state of shock, shook her ahead in both agreement and disbelief. "Quinn and I had met last week, the same night I had met both of you. She encouraged me to come back to Lix to spend time with her."

Lauren put her hands to her temples. "I know that Quinn is not looking for a relationship, but I don't know..." Lauren trailed off. "I thought we had a connection. I mean, we were just, you know, with one another a few hours ago."

Fran and Terry looked at each other and then back at Lauren with sympathy. Fran consoled Lauren. "Oh, honey, I am so sorry. I didn't realize that Quinn was the person you were talking about earlier." She put her arm around Lauren. "Look, I am not sure about Quinn and Chelsea. It's just one of those Lix rumors. You know how people like to start drama."

"Yea, Lauren, no one knows for sure. But Quinn is a night club owner; she likes the chase." Terry chimed in.

"She seems like she would be a lot of fun for a night; I don't think that she is girlfriend material."

She then directed her comments to both Fran and Lauren, bringing a hand to her chest. "I mean, that is just my opinion. I have heard stories about Quinn was well, but who am I to start rumors." Terry loudly slurped the remainder of her drink. "Do you guys want to dance some more? I love this song!"

Fran put her arm around Terry and gave her a look, motioning towards Lauren. "Are you ok? What can we do to help you?" Fran seemed concerned, and Lauren was touched. "Do you want to come and dance with us?"

Terry reached over and hugged Lauren. "I know it sucks to see something like that, but there are so many hot women at Lix, and you are absolutely gorgeous, Lauren. Don't let it get to you, babe. You have known Quinn for how long? A week? The night is young; plenty of fish in the sea!"

Lauren was becoming overwhelmed with the conversation, as well as with tonight's scene at Lix. She needed to clear her head to fully wrap her head around the situation. One thing was for sure; she definitely needed to get away from Quinn.

"I need to get out of here. You two stay and have fun. I don't want to ruin your night." Lauren grabbed Terry in for one last hug. "Happy birthday." She turned to both Fran and Terry. "Seriously, I am ok, but I need some air. It was so nice to run into you again." Lauren wanted to escape as quickly as possible. "Maybe I will run into you both again soon." She hurried away.

Fran called out after her. "Come by Café Fresh. Almond milk latte, extra foam! I got you, Lauren!" Lauren turned around and gave Fran the thumbs up. "Café Fresh;

got it! Thanks, Fran." Lauren blew a friendly kiss to the couple and scurried out of Lix.

As she ran out of the front entrance, she paused to make sure that she had all of her belongings this time. With her gold clutch in hand, she angrily pounded the pavement for a few blocks before calling an Uber to pick her up.

11

Quinn woke up with a pounding headache. Her hair was in disarray; silver and gold strands were poking out from all directions. Her face felt swollen, and her eyes were puffy from lack of sleep and dehydration from the alcohol she drank the night before. Her alarm clocked buzz with an urgent warning. *Get up, get up, get up, get up.* To Quinn, it sounded like a flock of seagulls screaming in her face.

She sat up, feeling dizzy and slightly disoriented. The room looked fuzzy like it was still coming into focus. She knew she was at home in her bed, but how she got there was a mystery. With a jolt, she felt the covers around her and looked around in a panic. *Did I...? Is anyone else here...?* Upon realizing that she was alone, she sighed with relief. *Whew, okay. At least I didn't make that mistake again.*

Quinn sank back down into the covers to stop the room from spinning. She tried to collect her thoughts, which felt like they were spilling out of her head like a stack of loose papers. *Okay, Quinn, you have been here before. Backtrack.* Quinn remembered that she was at Lix. *I was at the bar...Chelsea...mojitos, oh my god, mojitos.* Quinn's stomach became queasy, and she tried to take a few deep breaths to calm her nausea.

Bar, Chelsea, music, dancing, oh yea, Collette's set was on fire last night, what else....oh fuck! Lauren! Quinn's nerves surged with electricity, and her heart jumped out of her chest. Quinn sat up quickly, and the entire room whirled around her. This time, she remained sitting upright. *Oh no, Lauren, Chelsea, the kiss, did Lauren see that...Fuck, I think she did!* Quinn felt frantic, collecting the pieces from the puzzle of her debaucherous evening.

A sickening pang of anxiety overcame her. This emotion was not unfamiliar to Quinn, although it has been quite some time since Quinn was this hungover. However, unlike previous times, this felt worse to Quinn. Her guilty conscience only intensified the brutal, physical symptoms.

It had also been a long time since Quinn felt so irresponsible. Usually, Quinn owned her choices- the good, the bad, and the ugly. But as the memories resurfaced, the look of pain on Lauren's face from across the bar imprinted itself into Quinn's mind; it was all she could see, and a deep hurt rose from her chest.

No! Quinn, you idiot. Why did you do that? Quinn remembered flirting with Chelsea and how they were touching one another.

Quinn remembered planting a kiss on Chelsea's cheek, a kiss Chelsea had consented to. Quinn breathed. *Yes, I remember asking Chelsea if I could kiss her on the cheek, and she said yes. Okay good. At least I didn't sexually harass her. My god, could you imagine?* Lauren's look of shock intervened itself again into Quinn's mind.

Okay, Quinn. Pull it together; you need to get ready for

work. Besides, what's the big deal? You are not exclusive to anyone, and Lauren knew the score. Chelsea has always known the score. You've been more than honest with everyone. So you are off the hook. It was nothing, just a tiny peck between friends! Quinn's alter ego argued with the guilty conscience.

But Quinn could not shake the feeling of having done something wrong, although she didn't understand where all of these conflicting emotions were coming from. The sense of guilt remained, burning into her psyche. Her ego started to bargain.

Look, Quinn, just text Lauren and apologize. I am sure it's okay; she probably doesn't even care. You and Chelsea are just close friends. Friends sometimes kiss, right? Besides, it's not any of Lauren's business what you do at your club. Lix is your home, your turf. You don't need to explain yourself to someone you have only known for a week. Come on, Quinn, toughen up!

Feeling shaky, Quinn stood up and got her bearings. She searched her bedroom, picking up bits of strewn clothing on the ground. She didn't remember taking her clothes off before collapsing into bed, but apparently, she had.

She scoured the ground, looking for her phone. *Oh god, where is my phone? What's this?* Quinn picked up a crumpled piece of paper. 310-555-7856: Sasha xo. Call me! Quinn put her hands to her head. *What's this? Sasha? Who is Sasha?* Another memory floated into Quinn's mind. She remembered dancing with a sexy, Russian redhead and asked for her number. *Did I also kiss Sasha?* Quinn filed through the images from last night, relieved that she did not actually kiss someone named Sasha; at least, she didn't remember doing so.

Finally, locating her phone, Quinn quickly checked

her text messages. There was one from Chelsea, making sure that Quinn got home safe. Quinn texted, apologizing for not returning the text sooner. She scrolled through; there was nothing from Lauren.

Disappointment sunk in and buried itself deep into Quinn's stomach. She wanted so badly to text Lauren herself. She wanted to run out of her house and go to Lauren, to say that she was sorry. Quinn struggled and finally lost the battle with her ego.

Quinn was devastated because she knew she had hurt someone; someone she shared a connection with. Someone, she realized all of a sudden, that she really cared about. There was no excuse, nowhere left to hide. Quinn had messed up.

Quinn began to prepare herself to leave the house and head back to Lix.

The nights were bleeding into the days, and every day felt the same as the last. Quinn felt like she was running on a hamster wheel. She was just going through the motions and living out a routine with no real sense of purpose.

She tried to remember when she felt genuine enthusiasm for the day ahead when it hit her. The last time she was genuinely excited about something was two days ago when Lauren had texted about wanting to visit her at Lix.

As she gathered herself together, she kept glancing at her phone. Quinn's mind knew that Lauren was not going to get in touch, but a part of her still clung to hope. Quinn started to punch in some letters to write a message to Lauren, but she stopped herself. Quinn did not know how to phrase her feelings or explain why she had acted the way she had; she just felt overcome with regret. Maybe it was best to leave things as they were.

Lauren did not deserve someone as clearly damaged as Quinn.

Feeling unworthy of forgiveness, Quinn dug herself into a hole made of self-pity. *I cannot face another moment of this day without a strong cup of coffee and some greasy food.*

She decided to escape the confines of her home to treat herself to coffee and a late afternoon lunch.

LAUREN AWOKE AFTER A SPORADIC SLEEP. Lauren had dreamt of strange occurrences; images of various faces floating into her subconscious; Quinn, Chelsea, Fran, the blond bodybuilder bartender from Lix. Upon recollection, nothing seemed coherent enough to form a narrative, but she still felt haunted, regardless.

She had returned from Lix late, taking some time to unwind and to think about the scene that she saw at the bar.

Her heart ached, and she felt like a fool. She remembered how excited and hopeful she felt on her way to see Quinn, how Quinn had passionately kissed her against the door in the Grand Ballroom, the waves of orgasmic bliss she felt as Quinn penetrated her core. *Was that all just a figment of my imagination? Was any of that even real?*

Her mind then wandered to The Crossroad, where Lauren shared her dream about Angela. It was at the very moment where Quinn's demeanor had transformed, right in front of Lauren's eyes. Quinn's grief was apparent; it was clear to Lauren that Quinn was still mourning the loss of Angela, although it seemed that Quinn was not self-aware enough to recognize her own pain. While Lauren was initially drawn to Quinn's self-confidence and swagger, it became evident to Lauren that Quinn was hiding real darkness within her.

Lauren felt conflicted, not only about her feelings towards Quinn but also concerning her own self-respect. Yes, Quinn had been honest with Lauren about wanting to play the field, and Lauren did agree with the arrangement to keep things open and light between the two of them.

On paper, everything seemed technically transparent. However, Lauren could not shake the sense of feeling disrespected by Quinn. How could someone show that much intensity and desire one minute and turn their back completely, only moments later? Regardless of their verbal arrangement, Lauren felt used.

The scene of Quinn kissing Chelsea resurfaced to her mind. Lauren felt an ache in the pit of her stomach as she remembered the rumors that Fran and Terry shared with her.

Lauren started a dialogue with herself. *I cannot believe Quinn was actually kissing the bartender at her own club. Quinn! How cliché is that?* Anger rose inside of Lauren. *Like, couldn't she have just waited until the end of the night, when I was gone? How fucking selfish of her!*

Tears of anger and humiliation swelled in Lauren's eyes. She was hot with indignation. She did not deserve to be treated that way; to be seen as disposable. She began to berate herself. *It's your own fault, Lauren. You knew what you were getting yourself into, and yet you choose to get involved with a troubled nightclub owner. What did you expect was going to happen?*

Lauren did a full body stretch before sitting up in bed. She needed to shake this off this feeling and ground herself. Lauren was not someone who lacked confidence, but this situation with Quinn was shaking her foundation.

She craved a supportive conversation with a trusted friend over coffee. As Lauren arose, her stomach grumbled. She forgot to eat with all of her tears and anger, and suddenly, a fierce hunger consumed her. She remembered Fran's words from the night before.

She gave herself a pep talk. *Yes, good idea; Café Fresh! Okay, Lauren, pull yourself together. Call up Tania and have her meet you. All you need is some good food, some laughs and a change of scenery. You are strong and beautiful and smart; you will get through this.*

Lauren bolted up and started to dress, as she texted Tania at the same time, to meet her for coffee and a late lunch. Tania, sensing a good gossip session, returned Lauren's message quickly, making herself available. Lauren started to feel lighter as she regained her footing.

While Tania and Lauren were once lovers, they had realized that they actually loved one another more as friends, and as such, a beautiful platonic bond had blossomed. Lauren felt lucky to have Tania in her corner, especially during a time like this. With a quick brush of her hair, she slung a colorful handbag over her shoulder and proceeded out the door.

12

A bell on the front door of Café Fresh jingled as Lauren came through the front entrance. The restaurant was calm and inviting, with sheer white curtains blowing softly against the air-conditioners breeze. Potted palm trees and other foliage lined the countertops and hanging vine plans draped across the ceiling.

Café Fresh was best known for its delicious vegan cuisine and ethically sourced coffee beans, ground in-house. The interior reminded Lauren of a botanical garden where one could be surrounded by lush greenery and feast on Mother Nature's colorful palette of fresh California fruits and vegetables.

Lauren was the first in her party to arrive, so she grabbed a table for two within the casual dining space. At this point in the day, the restaurant was half empty after finishing a busy lunch rush. Fran, who had been working in the kitchen, spotted Lauren right away and came out from behind the counter to greet her.

Before Lauren could even sit down, Fran rushed over to give her a big hug. Lauren welcomed Fran's warm embrace, relishing in the healing powers of Fran's caring energy. "Lauren, I am so glad you decided to stop by! Are you feeling a bit better after last night, my friend?" Fran carefully inquired. "I know that last night was a bit rough on you."

Lauren lightly brushed off Fran's concern. "Oh, I'm fine. I mean, it wasn't the best night of my life, but I will survive. I am hungry, though!" Lauren cheerfully reassured Fran. She wanted to change the subject. "How is Terry doing this morning? Lauren smiled knowingly. "She looked like she was having a blast!"

"Oh, Terry is definitely hurting today; the woman doesn't drink a lot, but when she decides to party, look out! She was still sleeping when I left the house."

Fran looked at the large clock on the wall. "Hmmm, maybe I will call her again while on my break to see how she feels."

"Well, I am happy to hear that she enjoyed her birthday and I am so glad that I ran into you." Lauren, noticing that Tania had just entered the restaurant, motioned her over to the table.

Fran looked in the direction of Tania and gave a small wave. "Let me get you both some menus, but first, I have one almond milk latte coming up on the house." Fran winked at Lauren.

As Fran turned away from the table, Tania came over and gave Lauren a big hug. Lauren immediately felt grateful and appreciative to receive such loving kindness from her friends. *See Lauren? This is all you need; close friends who support and care about you.*

"Hi, love, so nice to see you. Thanks for calling me to arrange a hangout. I feel like I haven't seen you in a month!" Tania exclaimed as she plunked down in her seat.

"Okay, before we talk about anything else, you have to tell me about your visit to Lix. What did you think?"

Lauren laughed softly under her breath and took a deep breath. "I have so much to tell you, but first, I want to thank you for introducing me to Lix. It's a gorgeous spot, and the vibe is so incredible. I have never experienced anything like it in my life."

Tania grabbed Lauren's hands in excitement and squealed. "Yay, I am so glad to hear that. Okay, tell me everything! What did you do there?" Tania's eyes narrowed slyly, grinning from ear to ear. "Who did do you?"

"Well, you are never going to believe this, but..." Lauren started from the beginning, recounting the details of her first visit to Lix with Tania. She told Tania about her skinny dip in the pool and meeting Fran and Terry.

Tania looked over towards the direction of the kitchen. "So, the woman who just served us was also at Lix with her partner; what a small world!" Tania exclaimed, "I love that our community is so small." Tania and Lauren shared a knowing laugh.

Lauren paused before revealing to Tania juicier details about her chance encounter with Quinn. That was the second course of their conversation.

Tania looked over, toward "Oh my god. You and the fucking the owner of Lix?!" Tania almost shouted, and Lauren hurriedly looked around the restaurant, motioning for Tania to lower her voice.

"Wait, Tania, there is more to the story. Later that night, when Quinn and I went to the bar..." Lauren ventured into the story about Quinn and Chelsea, as Tania's eyes widened in disbelief.

"No way!" Tania exclaimed, coming to the defense of

her friend. "I can't believe she did that to you right in front of your face! Well, I mean, I guess I can believe it because I have heard lots of stories about that woman, but..." Tania scrunched up her face, "no one treats my Lauren that way." Tania banged her fist on the table, and Lauren looked down, slightly embarrassed. However, as self-conscious as she felt, Lauren also loved how loyal Tania was.

"Listen, L, you are gorgeous and smart; you are a total catch. I would know." Tania peered at Lauren's face, which now seemed sad as she told Tania about Quinn had acted towards her. "I am not sure what Quinn's problem is, but you deserve so much better." She held Lauren's hands in hers, consoling her with reassurance.

Lauren nodded; she knew that Tania was right, but the scene from the night before seemed to haunt her. She felt confused about her feelings for Quinn. Even though she knew that Quinn had acted wasn't right, she still wanted her, and a part of her yearned to comfort Quinn; to take away her grief and show Quinn genuine care and affection.

Deep in her heart, Lauren knew that she wasn't quite over Quinn, although she had no idea what to do next. She also wasn't sure how Quinn felt about her. Their sexual chemistry was undeniable, but did Quinn care about Lauren as a person? Or was Lauren nothing but another conquest to Quinn?

The pair continued to catch up on lighter subjects, as they finished up their lunch and coffees. Tania brushed some crumbs off her hands and dabbed her face with her napkin.

"I should get going; I have some errands to run, but it was lovely to see you and catch up; I missed you." Tania stood up and came over to Lauren for one last hug. "I am sorry to hear about Quinn, but remember, she is just one woman in a sea of beautiful creatures. Don't let one bad experience turn you off from exploring other options at Lix."

Tania grabbed her purse and left money on the table towards the bill. "I really hope you go back there, at some point. I think it would be good for you. Besides, I love to see you come out of your shell. I think it's hot!" Tania patted Lauren on the bum, in a playful manner.

Lauren kissed Tania on the cheek and waved goodbye to her friend. She immediately felt better, like a weight of sadness had been lifted from her shoulders. The hole in her heart started to heal.

As Lauren gathered her belongings, preparing to leave, Fran came over with a small dessert plate. "Wait, Lauren. Before you go, I wanted to give you a sample of my new, house-made carob brownie. It's not yet on the menu. I want you to be my guinea pig." Fran presented the plate in front of Lauren. "Taste test it and let me know what you think. Then, you are free to leave." Fran bowed in front of her and floated away from the table.

"Fran, you are too good to me!" Lauren called out as Fran headed back to her kitchen station. Lauren looked down at the small, moist square in front of her. Lauren had a penchant for sweets and could never resist a tasty dessert. Picking up her fork, she carved out a small piece and brought it to her lips.

Just as she was about to take a bite, the front door chimed again. In walked a tall, lean figure wearing a white cotton t-shirt, fitted denim jeans, and mirrored sunglasses. Lauren's eyes rested on the person coming through the door and instantly recognized her.

Lauren's jaw dropped in surprise.

Quinn.

QUINN SAUNTERED INTO CAFÉ FRESH, looking cool as a cucumber, but inside, she was feeling like death; hungry and in desperate need of caffeine. The gentle chime of the front door clanged inside her head like a pair of symbols.

Quinn had been to Café Fresh on occasion; many of her Lix regulars raved about it. Quinn was not a strict vegan by any account, but like most L.A. women, she appreciated quality produced and healthy cuisine and excellent coffee, even if it meant the odd, deep-fried tofu dish.

As Quinn slinked in, a chipper server came over to greet her. "Welcome to Café Fresh; would you like a seat inside or outside?"

"Uh, inside is cool, thanks. Would you mind bringing me a coffee and a glass of water right away? I have a killer headache." Quinn removed her sunglasses and rubbed her temples.

"No problem," the server cooed. "Right this way." She led Quinn over to a table and placed a menu in front of her. "One coffee and one water, coming right up."

The server scurried off, leaving Quinn to peruse the menu. Quinn carefully laid her sunglasses on the table and rubbed her eyes once more. She sighed and looked around the restaurant. Picking up the menu, she scanned the selections.

From her peripheral vision, she saw her coffee and water, making its way over, as the server balanced the drinks on a tray. "All set to order?"

Quinn pointed to the menu. "Yes, I will have the jackfruit tacos with a plate of French fries, please." The server jotted down the order, giving Quinn a quick nod and a smile. "Excellent choice. And just let me know if you need any more coffee; refills are on the house."

Quinn looked gratefully at the server whose name tag read **Cassie**. "Thanks a bunch; cheers." Quinn raised her cup to the server, with a weak smile.

Suddenly, Quinn felt as though someone was staring at her. A tingle ran down the back of her spine. She looked to the left of her and saw Lauren.

Oh my god, no! Of all of the restaurants in West Hollywood, you had to pick this one. Quinn chided herself. Quinn felt frozen as she met Lauren's surprised stare. She wanted to disappear under the table.

Lauren didn't say anything, and Quinn knew that she would need to be the one to break the ice. *Maybe this is a sign from the Universe?* Quinn felt both nervous and nauseous.

Quinn gave Lauren a small smile and a meek wave. "Hi," she mouthed the words, although the sound was barely audible. Lauren, who continued to stare, did not respond.

Quinn let out a deep sigh, and her entire body sagged. Quinn felt gutted, knowing she had hurt Lauren. She recognized that this was her cue to apologize. She rounded up her courage and called out to Lauren from her seat. A bit louder, she said, "Could I come over to your table for a sec?"

Wordlessly, Lauren bobbed her head in agreement. Quinn slinked over to Lauren, which felt like the longest walk in her life, even though Lauren was only about 15 feet away.

Lauren continued to stare as Quinn pulled up a seat in

front of Lauren. Quinn got the eyes of the server who had taken her order and gave her the thumbs up. "I'll be back in my seat, just saying hi to a friend." Quinn faked a cheerful smile. The server returned the thumbs up with an okay symbol with her hand.

"Hi," Quinn said again, this time, looking directly at Lauren. Lauren looked down and started to fidget with her napkin. Quinn sighed nervously.

"Lauren, I...I don't know what to say, but I can start by saying how sorry I am for...for last night." Quinn began. "I acted like an asshole. I feel awful. I don't know why..." Quinn closed her eyes and rubbed her face. Shaking her head, she opened her eyes and continued. "The way I treated you last night wasn't right. I know we have a... complicated arrangement between us but still...you didn't deserve that." Quinn felt like her insides her breaking apart.

Lauren looked up at Quinn with a sad look of concern. Quinn thought to herself. *Well, at least she is looking at me. That's a good sign.*

"Lauren, I...I like you. I just don't know how...I have been in the night club business for a long time. Sometimes, I get a bit carried away with the lifestyle." Quinn trailed off, and Lauren finally spoke.

"You get carried away with using women and then dropping them when you get bored? Is that what you mean by the lifestyle?" Lauren asked in an icy tone.

Quinn shook her head, wanting to reach out to Lauren, to touch her. "No, no, Lauren. I mean, I know I hurt you. I never meant to. I'm just...kind of fucked up when it comes to showing emotions and getting attached. I think the whole dream conversation about Angela really affected me without realizing it, and I think I was just...

acting out. That doesn't make my behavior okay, but I think that is what happened." Quinn stumbled, trying to piece together her thoughts.

"Quinn, I can tell that you are grieving. I see the hurt all over your face." Lauren's tone softened. "I said I was sorry about bringing up Angela's name." Lauren looked away, slightly frustrated. "You asked me to talk about my dream! I had no idea it was going to upset you like that."

Lauren looked directly into Quinn's eyes. "It wasn't my fault. You had no right to treat me like that, especially after we were so intimate. I get that we have an arrangement or whatever you want to call it, but..." Lauren trailed off and looked away. Her voice broke. "I felt humiliated."

Quinn's heart broke at the sight of Lauren tearing up and the crack in her voice. "Lauren, please. I am sorry, really sorry." She reached out to take Lauren's hands. Lauren allowed it but refused to look directly at Quinn. She felt Quinn's strong rough hands on her own.

"Lauren, you have every right to be upset. I would understand if you never wanted to talk to me again. I just want you to know how horrible I feel. Please forgive me, Lauren." Quinn begged, shocked at her own vulnerability. "This is all new territory for me, ...liking someone as much as I like you. It's been such a long time. I don't even know what to do with myself." Quinn tried hard to look into Lauren's eyes.

Lauren squeezed Quinn's hands and finally met her gaze. Lauren took a breath. "Quinn, I appreciate the apology, and I like you too. I really do, maybe too much. It was just as much my fault for getting involved. You told me who you were from the beginning, and I should have listened." Lauren looked down; her words directed towards her lap. "I feel this deep, like, connection to you. I can't explain it, but I know it's too much for you to handle. I don't want to get in your way."

"Lauren, babe, you are not in my way. I had the best time with you last night...that is, until I...fucked it up." Quinn said sheepishly. "I'd really like to make it up to you. I am not perfect, and I am someone who needs my space, but at the same time, I know I can do better. You deserve better."

Lauren sighed, shaking her head. "Quinn, I accept your apology, okay? I can tell you feel awful and that you are sincere. I know you are not a bad person, but I feel, like, I need to be careful around you."

Lauren shrugged. "I don't really know what to do here. I am not looking for a serious relationship either, but I also feel that if you choose to be intimate with someone, there needs to be a level of respect. Right?" Lauren looked deeply into Quinn's eyes.

Quinn shook her head in affirmation. "Yes, absolutely. And I messed up yesterday. But it doesn't change the way I feel about you, the way you make me feel. You might be right to be careful around me, but...I'd really like for us to be cool." Quinn's hands moved up Lauren's arms, grabbing her elbows. "Could we at least be friends? Maybe start over?"

Suddenly, Fran appeared at the table, holding a plate of food. A consummate professional, Fran bit her tongue and pretended not to know anything about Quinn's and Lauren's scuffle. "Well, hello there! I have jackfruit tacos and a plate of fries. Would that be for...?" Fran looked at both of them, playing her part as the restaurant manager.

Quinn raised her hand. "Uh, over here." Fran slid the plate over to Quinn. "Wow, that looks delicious!" Quinn looked down at her plate and felt ravenous. Fran feigned a smile at Quinn, internally siding with Lauren. "Wonderful! I hope you enjoy it. I'll be back to check on you two...I mean, to check on you." Fran quickly corrected herself; Quinn seemed oblivious to the slip. Lauren shot Fran a sharp look, and Fran returned the expression with wide eyes.

As Fran walked away, Quinn began again. "Lauren, what do you say?" She extended a hand towards Lauren. "Can we just move forward with each other?" Lauren looked down at her lap and then looked up again at Quinn. She paused.

"Okay, Quinn. Okay, I forgive you, and yes, we can be friends." She took Quinn's hand, her arm becoming electrified by Quinn's warm and robust grasp. "Let's start over. No expectations; just mutual respect and kindness, okay?" Lauren said softly. "We can give each other some space and be cool. I am not sure what the future will hold, but just...just don't be an asshole to me again."

Quinn immediately felt better, a wave of relief shot through her hungover body. She wanted to cry out and lift Lauren into her arms. *Oh yay, she forgives me!* Quinn wanted to weep with happiness.

"Lauren, thank you. Thank you so much for being so sweet and understanding. I know this isn't easy... But I know that I can be a better person. If not just for you, for myself as well. You have no idea how much your forgiveness means to me." Quinn's entire energy transformed from lean and cool to warm and grateful.

A small smile came over Lauren's face. "No problem, Quinn. We are good." Lauren squeezed Quinn's hand. "Really, we are fine," Lauren said in a reassuring voice. "But..." Lauren started, with a tone of warning, "If you want your freedom, then you need to give me mine. Know what I mean?"

Quinn understood. Quinn needed to respect Lauren's right to engage and explore her desires at Lix, whether or not Quinn was involved. If they were to remain friends, there needed to be more balance, and Quinn could respect that.

"Yup, I get it. I am just happy that you still want to talk to me." Quinn smiled, a genuine look of gratitude spread across her face.

"Look, I need to get going, but it was good to see you, Quinn." Lauren stood up. Suddenly, Quinn didn't want her to leave. "Wait, um...let me at least walk you out." Quinn stood up with her.

"Don't you want to finish eating?" Lauren asked, puzzled? Quinn brushed off her hunger. "Come on; it's the least I can do. Allow me to be chivalrous for a second. I will come back to this."

Quinn waved to Fran, who was wiping down a counter in the back of the restaurant. "Could you hold this plate for me? I will be right back, just saying goodbye to this gorgeous creature."

Fran called out, "Sure, no problem. Just make sure you leave your wallet at the table, okay?" Fran's eyes twinkled. "Nothing personal, we just want to make you return to pay the bill." Quinn left her wallet near her plate. "No problem at all. I will be back in two minutes."

Fran shot Lauren a look from across the restaurant, and Lauren smiled, shrugging her shoulders. Fran smiled with a look of approval. Have fun! She mouthed the words to Lauren, without Quinn noticing.

Cling clang; the door chimes called out as Quinn and Lauren walked out the front door. They stood facing one another. Quinn held out her arms "Thanks for making my day. Can I hug you, Miss Lauren?"

Lauren looked up, mesmerized by Quinn's charming blue eyes. "Sure, Boss, I'd love that."

Quinn gathered Lauren up, and their bodies met in a warm embrace. She smelled the sweetness of Lauren's freshly washed hair, the soft scent of her perfume. She loved the feeling of Lauren's face against her chest. Quinn felt complete and at peace with Lauren in her arms.

They held each other for seconds that seemed to bleed into moments. Quinn stroked Lauren's hair as Lauren ran her fingers up Quinn's back, feeling the tiny bones along Quinn's spine against her thin white t-shirt. Sexual energy was starting to build, and this time, neither of them felt any reason to fight it.

Quinn looked down at Lauren; Lauren was peering up at her, as she ran her fingertips up Quinn's chest, feeling Quinn's nipples harden beneath the t-shirt.

"Lauren..." Quinn breathed, closing her eyes. "What are you doing to me?" Lauren continued to stroke Quinn's hard nipples, giving them a quick pinch, followed by a softer rub. Lauren stood her on her tiptoes, and Quinn looked down.

They softly kissed, tentative, as if to test the waters of their so-called new friendship. The chemistry between them heightened as the kisses became more intense, more urgent. Quinn grabbed Lauren's face, wanted to consume her mouth; her tongue collided with Lauren's. Their sighs melted together in hot breaths; they moaned in tandem.

Lauren grabbed Quinn by the waist, leading her towards the back exit of the restaurant. Lauren walked backward, pulling Quinn closer. Quinn followed but hesitated for a moment. "Wait, my food is inside!" Quinn laughed.

"I don't care," Lauren gasped. "You owe me." Quinn stopped struggling and conceded. Quinn allowed Lauren to take control, following Lauren's passionate lead. They stopped, and Lauren leaned against a white brick wall. She pulled Quinn even closer.

"Quinn, please...I want you. I want to touch you. Please let me." Lauren was breathless with desire, fiddling with Quinn's button and zipper fly. Quinn was slightly shocked at how assertive Lauren was being. This was new for Quinn; typically, she was the aggressor. She loved how Lauren claimed what she wanted. She was unbelievably turned on by this exciting twist of fate.

"Okay, little one. You can have me. But only because..." Quinn looked down at Lauren and spun her around so that Quinn's back was against the restaurant's wall. "Only because I do owe you. Take what you want from me."

Lauren pulled at Quinn's zipper, and suddenly, her hand was inside Quinn's jeans, feeling the soft material of Quinn's underwear and the coarse, bristling pubic hairs beneath. Quinn bucked her pelvis against Lauren's hand, badly wanting to be fucked. Quinn grunted and moaned. "Lauren, don't stop. I want you. Put your fingers inside of me. Please!" Quinn begged, which was a very un-Quinn thing to do. Quinn almost didn't recognize herself, but she suddenly needed this more than anything.

Lauren expertly slipped three fingers into Quinn's wetness, while rubbing Quinn's beady clit with her thumb. Quinn cried out and grabbed Lauren's hair in ecstasy. She could not believe that she was letting herself be finger fucked by this petite little femme! *What is happening to me?*

Lauren took her other hand and rubbed herself through her silk panties while continuing to finger Quinn. They smashed against the back wall of the restaurant in broad daylight, but neither of them seemed to care.

"Come for me, Quinn. I want to hear you come with my fingers deep inside you." Quinn released a loud moan as she climaxed, and Lauren's hand become flooded with Quinn's wetness. Lauren could feel the inside of Quinn's vagina, pulsating against her fingers. Quinn's face was red and slightly sweaty. She looked down at Lauren, who smiled, seeming very pleased with herself.

Quinn grabbed at Lauren, pulling her close for a deep and passionate kiss. She could hardly believe what had just happened as a rosy, post-orgasm glow filled her body. Lauren returned her kiss and stepped away from Quinn to take a breath. Quinn laughed out loud.

"Wow, Lauren. You certainly surprised me. I did not see that coming." Quinn continued to shake a little, waves of pleasure still pulsed through her core. Quinn was breathing hard and smiling, with surprise.

Lauren looked up at her and seductively smiled, knowing she was the victor. She sucked on her fingers, tasting Quinn. Quinn continued to shake her head, chuckling to herself.

"Friends, right?" Lauren squared with Quinn, looking her deep in the eye. She extended her hand. "Friends." Quinn shook Lauren's hand. "You little devil!" Quinn said with approval.

With that, Lauren turned to walk away from Quinn. "Your food is getting cold. Don't forget to pay your bill." Lauren called out over her shoulder.

13

It had been two weeks since Lauren's encounter with Quinn behind the restaurant of Café Fresh. Lauren had surprised herself for being so brazen, but there was something about Quinn's vulnerability that had both aroused and empowered her. Quinn's apology awakened something in Lauren; she felt validated, respected, and seen.

It gave her the power to act on what she wanted instead of sitting back, waiting to be taken.

Over the weeks, she had exchanged naughty texts with Quinn, but neither of them had made plans to play again in person. Lauren needed a break and some space to process her feelings, and she was grateful that Quinn respected that.

However, she did have a craving to return to Lix, and the club's annual fetish party "Bound" was happening tonight. Tania had mentioned it to Lauren and even offered to go with her in support.

"Lauren, we need to go to this party. It will be so fun. We can wear our wildest outfits. I think I am going to go as a sexy cop, complete with handcuffs!" Tania and Lauren chatted on the phone, as they planned their costumes.

Lauren was excited. She was new to the fetish scene, but she welcomed any reason to dress up. Her outfit choices were somewhat limited, so she decided upon a naughty school girl look, which included a scandalous skirt, knee-high socks, and a pair of faux eyeglass frames.

As she added the finishing touches to her outfit, she tried to keep her expectations of Quinn at bay. She decided not to text Quinn to let her know that she was coming. Part of her desperately wanted to see Quinn, but another part was fiercely protecting her heart. Lauren craved Quinn's skin and scent, but she did not want to put herself in a position to be hurt or embarrassed. Going to Lix with Tania seemed like a safe approach. At the very least, she was going to enjoy a night out with a good friend.

Whatever happens, happens. Maybe I will meet someone new? I should explore my options; there were so many hot women at Lix. Lauren thought to herself. Deep inside, she knew who she really wanted but was trying hard to convince herself otherwise.

Beep beep! Lauren heard the sound of Tania's car horn, beckoning her to come outside. She tucked her white blouse into her sexy kilted skirt and bounced out the door. She was ready for an adventure.

Tania waved at Lauren, wearing a fitted blue bodysuit, decorated with a fake badge, and other embellishments from the driver's seat. Tania rolled her mirrored sunglasses down to her face and called out, "Excuse me, miss. I may have to arrest you for looking so sexy; you know that's a crime in this state, right?"

"Officer, I am so sorry. Guilty as charged. Are you

going to handcuff me?" Lauren joked along. Tania slid her sunglasses back up to her face and nodded at Lauren with approval. "That's the spirit, girl! Tonight is all about us, taking back the night and getting into some trouble." She high-fived Lauren, and away they sped to Lix.

Lix was in full swing by the time Lauren and Tania had arrived. The line-up to get into the club was longer than usual, but it did provide a chance for the duo to gaze at the eye-candy, who wore all manner of fetish attire. Lauren was amazed at the incredible leather and latex outfits and the mysterious masks, headgear, and accessories that some of the guests had brought.

As Lauren and Tania headed towards the direction of the bar, they noticed that the large-scale video monitor behind the DJ booth screened images of fetish play between three latex-clad women; one of whom was wearing a collar and leash. Tania pointed up to the screen while Lauren shook her head in amazement.

"Isn't that wild, L? I would love to pour myself into an outfit like that and have my way with a gorgeous woman on a leash!" Tania laughed in delight and turned to Lauren. "How would you imagine yourself in a scene like that?"

Lauren shrugged, "I don't know. I have never done anything like that before. Maybe I'd be an extra, in the background?" Lauren joked, and Tania lightly tapped Lauren on the arm. The fetish scene was arousing yet unfamiliar to Lauren. She didn't quite know how to place herself, but she was curious about kinky forms of play.

The pair grabbed their drinks and scanned the club. The crowd was an eclectic mix of colorful costumes and lingerie; Dominants proudly displayed their submissive partners, and there was an edgy, primal energy in the air.

Tonight, the kinksters had come out to play. In Lauren's mind, she wondered where Quinn might be, but she dared not try and look.

"Let's check out the pool area and make our way around the playrooms." Tania suggested. "We can dance and drink at any club or any other time Lix is open. Tonight, I want to check out some hot, live-action." Tania licked her lips, a hungry look in her eye. Tania wanted to be naughty, and Lauren-not sure where to go-was grateful to follow Tania's lead.

They sauntered down the corridor that led to the outdoor patio. An array of red lights had been strung around the garden's circumference to create a more ominous environment. The aqua-colored pool was packed with nude bodies, laughing and splashing in the warm water.

Above water, other guests remained clothed, preening like peacocks in their assorted fashions. Clearly, they were looking to be noticed. Lauren noticed a small gathering of women, seated on lounge furniture, having their feet rubbed by other women, who knelt in front of them, wearing hooded masks. The seated women chatted and laughed with one another, occasionally snapping a finger or barking an order towards the person beneath them.

"Look Lauren; Femme Dommes." Tania motioned in the direction of the small, seated crowd. "I love how powerful they are. Imagining getting a foot rub in the middle of a party, just with a snap of your finger!" Tania exclaimed.

Lauren was more captivated by the devoted scene of servitude. There was something so loving and caring about the way the submissives tended to their Dommes.

While Lauren had never seen anything like that in person, there was something about the scene that intrigued her.

Tania and Lauren grabbed a seat by the pool and enjoyed the remainder of their cocktails. They indulged their voyeuristic side, observing a nude threesome in the pool who were obviously mischievous with their hands underwater. Every so often, one of them would gasp or cry out in ecstasy as the water splashed around them. Then, like mermaids, they would collide into each other in a mix of hair, lips, and bare breasts.

As soon as Lauren and Tania finished the last slurps of their drinks, they stood up, eager to explore more of the party. Tania smoothed her blue bodysuit to emphasize her curves, and Lauren adjusted her knee-high socks, twisting the front of her white blouse into a knot, just above her belly.

Tania grabbed Lauren's hand and pulled her towards the Grand Ballroom. "Let's look in here, L." Lauren followed Tania in hot pursuit. Lauren's stomach fluttered, both worried and hopeful that she might run into Quinn. *Lauren, you are not going to chase Quinn. Just go with the flow and enjoy the moment; whatever happens, happens.* Lauren lectured herself in an attempt to quiet her active mind.

They stepped into the Grand Ballroom and were greeted with a packed room. Unlike the other times that Lauren had been in this room, tonight there were pockets of guests talking to themselves, amidst erotic exhibitionism in the background.

The large bed welcomed an orgy of six bodies, with an odd couple, sitting at the foot of the mattress; both of them locked in an embrace. The couple seemed to be enjoying their own private moment, oblivious to the sounds and scents of sex happening behind them. Similarly, the orgy of women were in a bubble of pleasure. One of the participants was kneeling on the bed while wearing a strap-on harness. Two women lay flat on their stomach, taking turns stroking and sucking on the strap. The Top petted each women's hair in approval as they took the strap deep into their mouths.

Lauren was fascinated by it all.

Lauren noticed the bare back of a nude woman in the Ballroom corner, straddling someone underneath her. Two, black-gloved hands wrapped around the women's ass, lifting her up and down on their lap. Lauren turned her head slightly to get a closer look. The person sitting appeared to be a large, spiky-haired dyke wearing a leather vest and leather pants. She was completely clothed but wore a harness and cock above her pants, which the nude woman was riding. The dyke slammed the woman down hard on the cock, and the naked beauty shouted with joy, "Yes, Daddy."

'Wow, it's packed in here tonight." Tania spoke in Lauren's ear, in an attempt to be audible above the din. "I have never seen it so busy!" Tania looked around, taking in the sights. "What do you think? Is there anyone here that you might be interested in?"

Lauren was too overwhelmed by the mass of bodies to notice any one person in particular. Her senses were overloaded, and while she enjoyed the raw sexuality around her, she felt somewhat frozen in her role as an observer. She had never seen anything like it.

Lauren shrugged, unsure of her next move. "I am just enjoying watching. All of this is so hot, but I am not sure how to pick anyone up. Everyone seems pretty...busy." Lauren grabbed Tania by the elbow in support. At this exact moment, Lauren actually looked like a timid schoolgirl, seeking the protection of a sexy and more confident police officer.

Tania and Lauren stood together against a wall while they continued to survey the room. Suddenly a short and stocky older woman approached the twosome. The woman was cinched up in a deep purple-colored corset; her body encased shiny, tight black pants which were tucked into long, thigh-high black boots. A thick leather collar, centered with a silver heart, covered her chubby neck. She carried a flogger in her hand; multiple strands of leather swung from the handle by her hip.

"Hello ladies, I'm Jay. That's exactly as it sounds, like the letter." She stuck out a hand, and both Tania and Lauren shook it. "Is this your first time at Lix? You both look rather new." Jay gave them both the once-over, with a devilish grin.

Tania laughed. "No, neither of us is new. It's just our first time at this party. We were just checking things out, right Lauren?" Tania nudged Lauren in the side. "Yup, that's right," Lauren chirped. "I have been here a few times but, yea, never to a fetish party." Both of the friends felt as though Jay wanted to devour them.

Jay circled the duo. "I see, I see. Well, I am quite familiar with this world. I have been a professional Dominatrix for almost twenty years," Jay said as she slowly paced around Tania and Lauren. "Have either of you had a chance to visit The Crossroad yet?" Jay purred, swinging the flogger slowly in her hand.

"I wanted to check it out next. What about you, Lauren?" Tania spoke up. Tania was less interested in playing with Jay as she was having her friend experience the swift, sweet sting of the flogger. *I should give Lauren a little push in the right direction.* Tania thought to herself. *She is such a bottom; I know she would love it.*

"Uh, I mean, sure, we can check it out." Lauren shrugged with uncertainty, grabbing Tania's arm for added security. "I'm Lauren, by the way. This is Tania." She introduced herself to Jay. "We are just friends, by the way. I guess, in case you are wondering." Lauren blushed, unsure as to why she felt so shy, all of a sudden. And while Lauren was not exactly attracted to Jay, there was something about Jay's cagy and dominant energy that drew Lauren in. Deep in her subconscious, it reminded Lauren of someone.

"We are actually ex-lovers," Tania interjected. "But not friends with benefits; just two chicks who used to fuck but now who love each other like sisters." Tania threw an arm around Lauren's shoulder in playful jest. "Jay, did you want to show us the dungeon area?" Tania was pushing to get Lauren into the room so that she could enjoy some entertainment.

Jay positioned herself in between Tania and Lauren, linking both of their arms. "Follow me, ladies, right this way." Jay led them into the room across the wall.

Like the Grand Ballroom, The Crossroad was also packed, but the scenes appeared to be much kinkier. There was less nudity in this room, and more people dressed in fetish costumes. Small groups of guests were formed around the dungeon.

Lauren noticed a crowd of onlookers, surrounding a woman who was tied to the St. Angela Cross, her body covered in colorful splatters of hardened wax. One guest stood in front of the nude woman, holding a small candle and a flame. The guest lit the candle, and as the fire danced down the string's length, a pool of warm wax formed at the base of the candle. Then, the guest tipped the candle towards the nude body, dripping warm wax down over her breasts. The flow of the wax slowed as the material started to harden. The naked woman closed her eyes and breathed a sigh of pleasure as the wax dripped over her body.

Ouch? Lauren said to herself, feeling puzzled as to how this activity could bring someone pleasure. Still, she found it intriguing, and the wax drippings looked rather beautiful, like flecks of colored paint strewn across a canvas.

Jay leaned in close, whispering the Lauren. "Oh, hot wax. Yes, that is always fun." Jay hissed, stroking a single finger up Lauren's arm in a soft caress. "Have you ever tried something like that?" Lauren shook her head wordlessly. "No, not yet. It looks cool, but I am not sure how I feel about hot wax on my body." Lauren laughed nervously. Tania looked on, seeming to enjoy the sights in front of her.

"Mmmm, you smell so sweet, Lauren. Just like the scent of vanilla." Jay breathed in Lauren's skin. "You are so fresh and so new to everything. It would be a pleasure to um..show you the ropes." Jay slithered, inching closer to Lauren to seduce her. Jay fingered her flogger, undressing Lauren with her eyes.

Lauren was starting the feel nervous. She was heading into unfamiliar territory and was uncertain as to the intentions of this older woman. Jay possessed a certain charm, but at the same time, she also came off as a bit predatory. Lauren shot Tania a look. Help me!

At once, Tania wriggled in between Lauren and Jay, coming to the aid of her friend. She guided Lauren away from Jay with swift ease. "Lauren, do you want another drink? Let's head to the bar." Lauren enthusiastically bobbed her head in agreement. Tania turned to Jay and cooed, "Excuse us, we will be back in just a moment."

Lauren and Tania turned their head back toward Jay to say goodbye. As the twosome began to exit the Cross-road, a tall figure wearing a three-piece suit suddenly appeared at the entrance. The statuesque being leaned against the door frame, stretching out like a cat.

The pair nearly bumped right into the person who was standing in front of them. Lauren looked up, and her heart sank to her stomach. It was Quinn! Lauren's nails dug into Tania's arms; both of their eyes widened in surprise. They halted in their tracks.

Quinn looked down at them, catching their gaze and holding it in a razor-sharp focus. Quinn looked more amused than surprised. Tania almost laughed out loud in an attempt to cut the tension, as Lauren continued to dig into Tania's arm.

Without addressing Lauren and Tania directly, Quinn looked over their heads and focused her gaze on Jay. "Hey, Jay! Are you bothering these two? Don't you have your own submissive to play with?" Quinn's voice seemed to fill the room, and the din of the voices quieted down. Quinn flexed her powerful energy. "If you are wondering, I believe your girl Tricia is out by the pool. Maybe you should go and find her?" Quinn coyly suggested.

"Oh, thank you, Quinn. Yes, I was just looking for Tricia. I thought she might have been in here." Jay quickly recovered from the confrontation in an attempt to save face. Lauren and Tania moved out of the way as Jay lumbered out of the dungeon, meeting Quinn's dominant stare on the way out.

After Jay had exited the dungeon, the three of them-

Lauren, Tania, and Quinn-stood together in a few seconds of deafening silence. Tania looked at Lauren and Quinn, breaking the ice. "Well, I am going to head to the bar. Lauren, you are good here, right?" Tania stated, forming a sentence, rather than a question.

Lauren looked fast at Tania and then at Quinn. Her mouth was slightly open, and her legs felt like jelly. Quinn spoke for both of them. "Yea, we are good here. Your drink is on me, by the way; just let the bartender know. See you in a bit!" Quinn dismissed Tania. The crowd in the dungeon started to dissipate, and Lauren found herself in a quiet moment with Quinn.

14

Quinn looked down at Lauren, taking pleasure in watching Lauren squirm sheepishly. "Well, isn't this a surprise," Quinn said softly and evenly. "I didn't expect to see you here." Lauren couldn't help but blush and look down. "Yea, I uh, we...Tania and I..decided last minute to show up." Lauren laughed to herself, playing with her hair and biting her lip. She felt an intense combination of shyness and arousal.

"You look very nice, very innocent." Quinn toyed with her. "We both know that you are not, but it's a good effort regardless. You almost had me fooled." Quinn was enjoying herself. Lauren felt as though she had been caught doing something bad and was about to be punished in the most exquisite way. She was giddy from being surprised by Quinn and also with desire.

So, now that you found me here, what are you going to do with me?" Lauren batted her eyelashes, flirting sweetly with Quinn, leaning her on feminine charms.

Quinn took a step towards Lauren as Lauren took a

step backward. They seemed to be dancing themselves deeper into the dungeon with Quinn in pursuit. A few remaining guests who were playing in the room glanced over at the pair, entranced by the chemistry that they exuded.

Lauren stopped, and Quinn got even closer to Lauren. Quinn started to finger the buttons on Lauren's blouse, gripping the knot that Lauren had tied earlier. "You may have turned the tables a few weeks ago but make no mistake, Miss Lauren. I am always the one in charge when you visit Lix." Quinn stroked a strand of Lauren's hair, looking deeply into her eyes. "Is that understood?"

Lauren looked wide-eyed at Quinn, nodding yes while blushing from her collar. She bit her lip in an attempt to keep her arousal in check. "Yes, Boss, I understand. You are in charge."

"Good girl, that's more like it. I'll bet it was a sweet victory for you to have your way with me, right?" Quinn questioned Lauren in a way that made Lauren tingle with anticipation. "It's only fair that I return the favor," Quinn whispered to Lauren, her warm breath tickling Lauren's earlobe.

Lauren reached out and grabbed at Quinn's tie. "I like your suit, boss. You remind me of the professor I had in college." Lauren touched the lapels of Quinn's silky suit jacket. "Boy, I had such a crush on that professor; I almost failed her class. I could barely pay attention." Lauren started to walk backward again, backing up into the desk.

Quinn moved towards Lauren. "You are most certainly the naughtiest girl in my class, Miss Lauren." Quinn slid her hands up the sides of Lauren's thighs, pulling up the short skirt. "I think I am going to have to make you stay after class for detention." Quinn put her hands firmly on

Lauren's hips and spun her around so that Lauren faced the desk instead of Quinn. "What do you think about that?"

Lauren shook her head yes, her back to Quinn. "I think you are right, Boss. I deserve a punishment for not paying attention." Lauren stretched her arms and arched her back, bending over a bit so that that Quinn could have a better look at Lauren's ass in the short skirt.

The other guests in the dungeon began to stop what they were doing and watch Lauren and Quinn. Quinn loved to perform. She came alive for an audience.

"Sir," Quinn sternly demanded, "Right now, you will call me Sir. Got it?" Lauren sighed, passion rising up in her voice. "Yes, Sir. I understand, Sir."

Pleased with Lauren's agreement, Quinn grabbed a bunch of Lauren's hair, at the base of her neck. She pulled firmly but gently and yanked Lauren closer to her. "Bend over, Miss Lauren." Quinn jeered. "Lift up your skirt for me." Lauren's hands reached back towards her skirt, and she lifted it upon command. Then, she bent her body over the desk so that her black thong panties and ass were exposed for Quinn.

"Very nice, an A for effort." Quinn ran her hand slowly over Lauren's round behind. "Now, I am going to show you what happens to bad girls who don't pay attention while I am teaching. 'Blackboard' will be your safe word. If you say it, I will stop immediately. I suggest you use it if you need to; otherwise, I will continue to punish you." She grabbed another fist of Lauren's hair. "Are you listening carefully to me?" Lauren had never heard Quinn speak in such a menacing tone. She was thrilled to be back in the grasp of Quinn's power.

Slap! Lauren felt a hot sting on her behind, followed

by a tingle. Slap, slap! Lauren closed her eyes and sighed. Quinn was sending a message to Lauren, with every spank. This was the attention that Lauren had yearned for for so long before she had arrived at the club. The pain was sharp, but she soon realized that she was enjoying it.

Quinn's spanking paused, putting Lauren on high alert. Lauren stiffened; goosebumps covered her body. Quinn knew what she was doing by keeping Lauren on her toes. After a few moments of silence, Quinn spoke.

"Now, Miss Lauren, I am going to give you a lesson in sensory deprivation. Do you know what that means?" Lauren paused before answering. "Sir, I know what sensory deprivation means, but what does that mean for me now?"

"Excellent question! I love an inquiring mind," Quinn was enjoying herself, reclaiming her natural dominance. "In my hot little hand, I have a blindfold, which I brought especially for tonight's lesson. I would love it if you, my favorite student, wore this blindfold so that I could limit your sight." Quinn posed the question in the form of a statement, as to avoid any argument. Lauren consented. "Yes, Sir, I would be honored to wear the blindfold. Thank you for thinking of me."

Quinn was impressed with Lauren. *What natural!* Quinn slipped the blindfold from her suit jacket pocket and placed it around Lauren's face. She patted Lauren's hair as she continued to speak.

"As the teacher, it is my job to be the eyes of my student. And as we continue the lesson, I will describe exactly what I am going to do to you, so that there won't be any surprises." Quinn kept Lauren bent over the desk and gave the back of her hair another, gentle tug. "Do you understand?" Lauren nodded silently, thrilled beyond words. "You don't need your eyesight when you have Sir to tell you what is happening, right, Miss Lauren?" Lauren piped up, "Yes, Sir."

"Very good. Now, since you have been such a delightful student so far, Sir is going to give you a special treat. First, I am going to remove your panties because you certainly don't need to wear them in my classroom." As Lauren expressed her agreement, Quinn slowly slid down Lauren's panties so that her bare ass was exposed to Quinn. Lauren felt vulnerable and nervous but also safe in Quinn's presence. She wanted to give her all to Quinn, as much as Quinn desired.

"Such a beautiful ass,' Quinn's hand came down on one cheek. Slap. Lauren moaned. "Now it's time to inspect you very carefully. I am curious about how you taste." Quinn slid her fingers between Lauren's ass cheeks and dipped her head so that she was eye level with Lauren's behind.

Quinn ran a few fingers underneath, stroking Lauren between her legs while her tongue started to explore Lauren's crack. Lauren felt an unusual sensation, Quinn's hot wet insistent tongue on her and a shocking wave of pleasure washed over her. No one had ever licked her there. Quinn's tongue pushing at her anus.

Oh my god, what is happening? Lauren moaned and sighed. *This feels...illegal, but I love it!* Lauren pleaded with Quinn, "Sir, I love that; please don't stop."

"Lauren, I will stop whenever I feel like it." Quinn sharply stated, embodying her role. "But..." she said slyly, whispering into Lauren's ear. "I am so happy to hear that you are enjoying my tongue because I have more to give you." Quinn stiffened her stance, letting go of Lauren's hips. "Stand up, turn around and spread your legs for me, on the desk. Leave the blindfold on."

Obliging the order, Lauren turned around and faced Quinn. She leaned back on the desk and lifted her legs up and out. She actually felt like a rag doll, a doll that was becoming Quinn's plaything.

Enjoying the sight in front of her, Quinn lowered herself on her knees so that she could feast on Lauren's warm, wet lips. Quinn licked and sucked, stimulating the tiny pearl of Lauren's clit with her fast, sharp tongue. Her tongue moved lower, pushing inside her and then lower again, teasing the tight scrunch of her anus. Lauren writhed with pleasure, and she grabbed Quinn's hair with her hand. Quinn hummed and slurped, savoring every drop of Lauren's juices and inhaling her musky scent.

"God, you are so delicious. I could eat you for breakfast, lunch, and dinner." Quinn gasped as she came up for air. She ran her fingers down Lauren's belly and caressed the soft flesh between Lauren's thighs. "Time for the final lesson, Lauren. I need you to come for me, and when you do, you will say thank you, Sir.' Can you do that for me?"

"Blindfold off or on, Sir?" Lauren asked like the good little sub she was. Quinn shook her head in disbelief over Lauren's organic, submissive qualities. "Blindfold on. I like that you can't see anything, all you can do is feel."

Lauren laid back on the desk with her legs spread apart. Quinn reassumed licking and sucking Lauren as Lauren bucked her hips against Quinn's face. Quinn's neck moved furiously as she increased the pace and the force of her tongue.

Lauren was panting, getting closer and closer to her orgasm.

As she felt Lauren getting close, Quinn slid two fingers

deep into Lauren's ass, stretching her and curling upwards to push against Lauren's G-spot through her thin internal wall. Quinn felt Lauren seize up with a full-body contraction and then sploosh! Lauren exploded like a tsunami, soaking Quinn in the face, ejaculate spattering on Quinn's dress shirt. Her ass contracted hard and pulsed like electricity around Quinn's fingers. "Thank you, Sir!" Lauren loudly cried out. A smatter of soft applause surrounded her, as onlookers approved the scene.

Lauren sat up, dizzy, and disoriented. Her entire body was trembling as she removed her blindfold and looked dazed.

Breathless, Lauren looked at Quinn and then nervously around at the onlookers in amazement. It was the most intense orgasm she had ever had.

Quinn met Lauren's look and smiled as she wiped her face down. Quinn couldn't help but chuckle to herself. She was blown away by Lauren's commitment to their role play. Quinn was not often surprised, but Lauren had impressed her. Deep down, Quinn also felt incredibly grateful that Lauren had allowed such intense, kinky play in front of an audience. She felt as though Lauren trusted her, and it made Quinn beam with pride.

The two looked at each other and laughed out loud. Lauren looked around the room and gave a bow of her head towards the other guests in the room.

She didn't realize just how on display she was, and it made her feel like a rock star.

Quinn scooped up Lauren off the desk and into a warm and tight embrace. "That was beautiful, little one. You made me very proud." Quinn said softly, feeling the softness of Lauren's cheek against her own.

Lauren hugged Quinn back with all of her strength.

"Wow, I am still shaking!" Lauren's eyes were shining with joy. "That was such an incredible experience, Quinn. Thank you." Lauren's walls were down, and all bets were off. She was officially head over heels for this woman.

"Would you like to take a break and sit together outside by the pool? I think a bit of fresh air would be great, right about now." Quinn offered, extending her hand to Lauren.

Lauren accepted and grasped Quinn's hand firmly. "Yes, I would love to. Good idea!" Lauren felt as though she had been lit inside out by the sun. She beamed brightly, entirely captivated by Quinn's presence.

The pair headed outside to the patio and settled themselves into lounge chairs. They shared a moment of silence and gazed at the lights that reflected themselves off the crystal blue water. Quinn took a deep sigh and turned her head to the side to look at Lauren.

"You have an incredible gift inside you, Lauren. You are a natural submissive, and I don't mean for that to sound derogatory. You have this natural ability to understand the needs of someone like me, who is Dominant, who craves control. I felt so validated and accepted back there, in the dungeon." Quinn motioned towards the corridor entrance. "I have been with many women who know how to act the part but you..." Quinn looked into Lauren's eyes, "You are the part. Nothing about that scene was an act for you." Quinn continued. "I can tell that you are the real thing, and that is something I have been searching for a long time."

Lauren's insides melted. She understood what Quinn was saying. Their interaction was more than just a playful scene; it was a communion of two kinky souls who intrinsically knew what the other needed. And while the sex was incredibly hot, there was something deeper between the two of them.

Quinn continued, "Lauren, it's obvious that we have an intense connection, and I think you feel it too. You know that I have a hard time letting my walls down. I can't promise that will ever change, but I also can't ignore that I want you." Quinn reached over and took Lauren's hand. "I want to ask if you will be my exclusive play partner here at Lix. My submissive, my doll. I don't always understand conventional relationships, but this..." Quinn pointed around her, "this is what I understand. This is my world, and I would love for you to be a main part of it."

Quinn looked at Lauren with urgency. "What do you think? Do you want to be mine-all mine-within these walls of pleasure?"

Lauren felt her heart burst with joy while her head felt confused. She was thrilled at the idea of belonging to Quinn at Lix. She loved the idea of being closer to Quinn and being considered special and important in her life. But Lauren's world was bigger than Lix. *What happens to me when I leave for the night? What happens if I don't visit Lix every weekend or every night? Am I still important to you, then?*

Lauren remained quiet as she contemplated the question. Part of her wanted to accept Quinn's offer without hesitation. But another part of her felt pensive, curious if this arrangement could be mutually beneficial. *What if I want more from you, Quinn?*

Just as Lauren was about to speak, Tania came bounding towards them, slightly intoxicated. "Oh, there you are. Lauren, I was looking for you all night! What's going on, you two?" Tania plunked herself down on the concrete floor, between Lauren and Quinn.

Lauren and Quinn exchanged knowing glances and rolled their eyes playfully at Tania. "Quinn, I will text you once I get home safely. I should probably get this one home." She pointed at Tania, who had splayed herself out on the ground. Quinn nodded and smoothed herself down as she stood up. Quinn assumed her owner's role, once again.

"It looks like your friend needs an Uber. Let me arrange one now for both of you. It will be waiting at the front." Quinn mouthed to Lauren *Text me later.*

"Wait!" Tania cried out. "I have my car here!" Lauren looked sharply at Quinn and then at Tania.

"Tania, give me your car keys," Lauren asked. Tania handed them over, and Lauren put the keys in her handbag. "You are in no shape to drive."

"Don't worry, ladies," Quinn reassured them. "Your car should be safe. Why don't you leave it where you parked it and return in the morning?" Quinn suggested.

"Fine with me!" Tania threw her hands up in the air and laughed. Lauren rolled her eyes again in amusement and looked up at Quinn. "Thanks, Quinn, yes, I think that is the best idea."

Quinn headed back inside to call an Uber while Lauren helped Tania to stand up. Tania giggled to herself as Lauren held Tania tightly in her arms, to keep her upright. The two made their way to the front of the building and waited for their Uber to arrive. As they exited, Lauren looked around to see if she could find Quinn for a final goodbye, but Quinn was nowhere in sight.

15

———

I t was almost five o'clock in the morning by the time Quinn had closed the club. The Bound party had gone late into the night, and while the bar had stopped selling alcohol hours before, many of the guests were interested in staying late to indulge in hedonistic pleasures.

Quinn waved goodbye to Mickey and headed out the door. She found her car and plunked herself inside. It was a long night, and she should have been exhausted, but Quinn was still buzzing with energy as she recounted her scene with Lauren. In her head, Quinn replayed delicious scenes of Lauren's body, bent over the desk in the dungeon, and the way Lauren's face flushed with a glowing red as she orgasmed for Quinn.

Quinn rubbed her face and ran her hands through her hair. She sighed deeply. Quinn's entire life was Lix, but some days-particularly as of recently-Quinn felt like she only existed within the club's confines. As soon as she left, she felt deflated and empty.

Her heart ached with loneliness; she wished she could

snuggle up to Lauren's body and caress her soft curves. But therein existed an opposing force within Quinn that kept her trapped within an impermeable bubble. She wanted to break free from her pain and to break down the protective walls that she had created. But over the years, the wall had gotten so thick and strong that it had become an impossible feat.

When Quinn was acting as the owner of Lix, she was stoic and seductive, utterly untouchable. But as she drove home, she softened and allowed thoughts of Angela to pass through her mind. An incredible sadness washed over her, but it was ok. She could let herself feel these things, now that she was alone and outside of the club.

Quinn and Angela had met when they were seventeen years old. They had found one another as runaways, hanging out on the Sunset Strip. Both had come from traumatic upbringings. As a child, Quinn had bounced from foster home to foster home; she never felt like she belonged anywhere or to anyone who truly loved her.

By the time Quinn was 15, she had become self-sufficient. During the day, she scraped by with odd jobs, washed cars, cleaned homes in the neighborhood, and even ran a few casual errands for small-time crooks. Sometimes Quinn would pick up stacks of money for local drug dealers or act as a lookout during robberies. At night, she would drag her ratty sleeping bag in search of an empty bus stop or an alleyway so she could sleep in peace.

Quinn was rough and scrappy, but since she was also a young woman, the hustlers felt that they could use her as an accomplice without suspicion. Quinn didn't care who she worked with, as long as they paid her.

But even with these ominous influences in her life,

Quinn managed to stay on the periphery of danger. The L.A. streets were full of evil, but Quinn was a survivor at heart. And while she didn't exactly know what the future held for her, she knew that she would become someone one day.

One day, an acquaintance had introduced Quinn to Angela; apparently, they were going to do a job together because this particular robbery required two women to act as a distraction. The first time that Quinn laid eyes on Angela, she was completely infatuated. Angela was petite with long, dark brown hair and deep brown eyes.

Angela appeared years younger than her age; she liked to joke that she was sixteen but trapped in the body of a twelve-year-old with the soul of an older woman. Physically, Angela was the opposite of Quinn, who had grown tall and lanky. But when they had met, they instantly knew each other. Within a day, they were best friends, soul mates, and literally partners in crime.

Angela was more delicate than Quinn; she felt things deeply, and she was sensitive to her seedy surroundings. Where Quinn was tough and abrasive, Angela was soft and gentle. Their opposing energies balanced each other out. Angela's empathy brought warmth to Quinn's life, but she was also cloaked in deep-rooted sadness.

For the most part, Quinn's emotional state was consistent. Quinn rarely let her feelings dictate decisions; remaining rational and detached had become her survival mechanism. Emotionally, Angela was all over the place. Her highs were incredibly high, but her lows brought her to the depths of incomprehensible depression. Angela was mentally frail, and in the end, she was too fragile to survive the darkness of street life.

My sweet angel, I hope you are having a peaceful night. I

miss you so much. Quinn spoke to the spirits above her, images of Angela deeply embedded in her heart. For years after Angela's death, Quinn spoke to Angela through her thoughts and in her dreams. Recently, Quinn had become distracted with business, so the conversations had lessened.

But tonight, Quinn felt as though Angela was with her, accompanying her on the ride home. *Tonight was so much fun; you would have loved the party.* As soon as Quinn thought about Lauren and the scene in the dungeon, she felt instantly guilty. Quinn carried the responsibility of Angela's death on her shoulders like a giant weight. Subconsciously, she was blocking herself from having any real feelings of happiness, as though she did not deserve it.

She felt as though she would be betraying Angela, replacing her. Even though it had been seventeen years since Angela's suicide, Quinn couldn't bring herself to have another, committed relationship, something as profound and as powerful as she had once had.

Angela died one year before Quinn officially opened Lix, and when Angela passed, Quinn put her blood, sweat, and tears into the business. Lix was her distraction, and it also became a way for Quinn to channel her grief. Becoming a night club owner forced Quinn to direct her focus productively. This was especially true during the first few years of Lix; Quinn simply did not have time to grieve as she was busy building her clientele. It also didn't hurt that the club brought its own amusements; women, sex, and alcohol helped Quinn to cope on the days when her heart was dragging on the ground.

As Lix became more and more successful, Quinn's ego grew while her shell hardened. Whatever pain Quinn was feeling was being soothed by superficialities. It was only over the past two years that Quinn started to return to a place of sadness. She didn't know why, but suddenly, everything around her was beginning to lose its luster and meaning.

Her chance encounter with Lauren awakened something in Quinn, a desire and a longing to connect with another human being, that wasn't an employee or a one night stand.

Lauren and Quinn undoubtedly shared an intense sexual connection, but there was something more between them. Quinn was also terrified to admit that Lauren even looked a bit like Angela. As soon as the thought crossed her mind, Quinn felt her stomach sink in a sickening panic. She felt horrible comparing Lauren to Angela, but the physical similarities were there; it was undeniable.

Quinn thought about her offer to provide Lauren with the opportunity to be exclusive with her at Lix. While Quinn had never offered any of her previous paramours that kind of arrangement, she also knew deep in her heart that Lauren deserved more. Quinn's existence was limited to the night club, but Lauren's was not. Lauren seemed to have a deep and enriching life, diversified by friendships and a fulfilling career. She was so full of life.

Quinn desperately wanted to free herself from her shackles of mourning and escape from the guilt that consumed her, but a relationship outside of Lix seemed almost inconceivable. The idea of it felt foreign to Quinn. *What would I even do outside of the club? How would that work? Her head was spinning, and she felt overwhelmed. No, this was the only way. It needs to be within the walls of Lix or not at all.* Quinn argued with herself. *You are almost forty-*

nine years old, Quinn. This is the world you know, a world you built! Lix is where you feel comfortable. Lauren needs to come to you.

Quinn rolled into her driveway and unlocked her door. She felt weary, sad, and confused. She knew that she wanted Lauren more than she could comprehend. *Maybe she will go for it, being my girlfriend at Lix girlfriend. And if it goes well, perhaps it could grow into something more? One step at a time, Quinn.* She continued to bargain with her psyche.

But what would Angela think? Quinn, how could you turn your back on your first and only true love? Why didn't you pull harder? Why did you let Angela slip through your fingers, to her death? It's your fault, Quinn; it's all your fault! The demons in Quinn's mind shouted at her, berating her in anger.

Quinn's mind traveled to the last moment of Angela's life. Angela was standing on the ledge of a building, her back facing Quinn. In front of Angela, the L.A. skyline glistened, and the dark sky above them was sprinkled with stars. A light breeze was blowing through Angela's long, dark hair. Angela had her arms outstretched, greeting the winking lights below.

"Angela!" Quinn shouted. "What are you doing?!" Quinn rushed over to Angela in alarm. "Angela, please come down. It's going to be ok. Please, don't do this." Quinn pleaded with Angela, hysteria rising in her voice. "Angela, I know you don't want to die! Please come down, baby." Quinn had tears streaming down her eyes. She wanted to run and grab Angela with all of her strength, but she was also afraid to scare Angela. She carefully approached and continued to beg.

"Angela, honey. It's going to be ok; I am going to take care of us. I am going to keep us safe so that he can never hurt you again." Quinn took a few more tentative steps towards Angela, reaching out her hand. "Angela, please just grab my hand." Quinn started to sob in despair.

"Quinn, I'm tired. I just want to be in peace. I am not built for this life like you are. I don't belong here anymore." Angela's voice was haunted by misery.

"Angela, come down! Come down right now!" Quinn started to scream. She leaped towards Angela, grabbing one of her outstretched hands. At the same time, Angela jumped. Quinn was a fraction of a second too slow. She felt Angela's fingers slip through her palm, and the weight of gravity pulled Quinn forward, to the concrete pavement. Angela fell over the ledge, her body plummeted towards the ground, towards the greenery below, disappearing into the oak trees.

"No!" Quinn screamed. She continued to scream as she crumpled to the ground. As she cried out, a part of her soul floated from her body and sailed away, never to return.

16

"Oh my head," Tania sat up on the couch, her hair a tangled mess. She smacked her lips and looked around. Lauren was sitting in an armchair, sipping a coffee.

"Good morning, sunshine! Nice to see that you are finally awake." Lauren patted Tania's leg over a blanket. "You passed out like a corpse in my living room."

After leaving Lix, Lauren decided to have Tania over to crash for the night. Tania was quite inebriated and upon entering Lauren's apartment. Tania immediately sought refuge on Lauren's couch. Lauren found a blanket and covered Tania, letting her sleep off the night.

Tania rubbed her eyes. "So you never did tell me how your night went. I remember leaving you in the dungeon and going to the bar." Tania shook her head to clear her thoughts. "I can't remember what happened next. I think I was dancing...and I may have made out with a few hotties." Tania shrugged and then became alert. "Wait, I left you with Quinn! Oh my god, Lauren. What happened?"

Lauren chuckled. "Well, you did ask about my night while we were in an Uber on the way home. I am guessing you don't remember asking me." Tania looked blank and then gasped, "Where is my car?" Lauren comforted her. "We left it at Lix, remember? We can take another Uber down later and pick it up. Don't worry."

"I'm sorry, Lauren, I really don't remember anything that we talked about in the Uber." Tania looked apologetically at her friend. "So, what happened to you two?"

Lauren sighed with bliss and rolled her head back, closing her eyes. She had replayed the scene with Quinn in the dungeon over in her mind dozens of times. She could still feel Quinn's tongue between her ass cheeks, the pressure from Quinn's fingers inside of her. They felt electric. Goosebumps prickled over her arms as she recalled the smile on Quinn's face afterward. *Mmmm, god, that was so hot!* Lauren thought to herself, savoring the erotic memories.

"We had some kinky fun in the dungeon." Lauren smiled and looked down, biting her lip. "It was so sexy. Quinn had me bent over a desk, and people were watching and ...wow. Yea, it was pretty amazing."

"Girl, you are glowing! I mean, I had my concerns about this woman when we spoke at Café Fresh, but she seems to have a pretty positive effect on you." Tania thought for a moment. "Oh yea, now I remember seeing you both outside by the pool. You two certainly looked pretty cozy." Tania said, slyly.

"We did... I mean... she did... I mean... she gave me anal, and I came like never ever before. Also, I didn't know it was possible to gush everywhere from anal, but apparently, it is. It felt incredible."

"Anal? Wow, Lauren! Was that your first time?"

"Yep! I didn't even think twice about it. Honestly, I would have let her do ANYTHING she wanted to me. She has this effect on me. I never knew I wanted it until now. And now it is ALL I can think about!"

"You dirty dog! I LOVE how adventurous you are becoming!" Tania smiled wickedly! I remember trying to do you up the ass years ago, and you were having none of it!

"What can I say? Times change!"

Lauren's mind then traveled to the discussion that she had with Quinn and Quinn's puzzling offer. She still wasn't sure what to make of her proposition. Tentatively, Lauren began to tell Tania what Quinn had asked her; she had the opportunity to be with Quinn exclusively at Lix if she wanted.

"What do you think, Tania? Am I getting played here?" Lauren needed advice from her friend. She felt confused and torn. She wanted to be a part of Quinn's life but, was that all that there was to Quinn? *To only exist in a night club, like a vampire?*

"Hmmm, Lauren. I am not sure. That's a tough one." Tania pondered. "On the one hand, it would be pretty cool to say that you are Quinn's girlfriend when you go to Lix. Like, you would never have to stand in line or pay admission!"

"Tania, that's not the point." Lauren was slightly exasperated with her friend. "I don't want to date Quinn for status. You know that's not my style. And besides, I would only be Quinn's girlfriend within the club. What happens to me-to us-when I leave Lix? I mean, I don't live there." Lauren was becoming frustrated.

"Oh my god, do you think Quinn lives there? Wouldn't

that be wild?" Tania joked with Lauren. "No, I see your point, Lauren. On the one hand, it's an interesting offer, but on the other hand, you are right. It does seem a little limiting." Tania continued to think. "But...imagine the amazing sex you would have! Isn't it almost worth it, just for that reason alone?" Tania's eyes twinkled with mischief.

"God, Tania. Some help you are!" Lauren playfully whacked Tania with a throw pillow. "Look, I am serious. I really like Quinn. Yes, the sex is amazing, and Lix is an incredible place, but I need more from Quinn if I am going to consider her my girlfriend." Lauren shook her head while in critical thought. "I just feel like I am getting shortchanged, you know? That arrangement would work just fine for Quinn, but what about me?" Lauren exhaled a breath. "It just seems a bit...selfish, I guess."

"Lauren, honey," Tania spoke gently. "You know that I always want the best for you, and I would never want you to settle. I was more or less kidding about Lix. I know that you like Quinn, and I can tell she genuinely likes you too. I noticed the chemistry right away, when Quinn came up to us-no, you-in the dungeon." Tania leaned into Lauren with concern in her eyes. "If you feel that you deserve more from Quinn and I think you do, just talk to her about it." Tania patted Lauren on the leg. "Quinn may be the owner of L.A.'s hottest women-only club, but that doesn't make her God. You have every right to ask for what you feel you deserve." Tania readjusted herself on the couch. "I support whatever decision you make, but that would be my advice."

Lauren thankfully nodded at Tania, grateful for the kind words and sound advice. Tania was right; Quinn's offer was far more advantageous to herself than it was for Lauren. Causal sex was one thing, but if Quinn expected her to be exclusive, Quinn would need to up her game and step out of her comfort zone. Lauren may be in lust for Quinn, but she also had both of her feet planted firmly on the ground.

"Thanks, Tania. Everything you say makes perfect sense." Lauren looked around her living room, seeming to search for something that wasn't there. "I like Quinn a lot; I would love to be able to be with her, but I am no one's whore." Lauren pursed her lips and scrunched her face in thought. "I think Quinn and I should talk a bit more. We need to establish some middle ground if this is going to grow into anything serious."

"Good girl, I am proud of you." Tania squeezed Lauren's hand. "You have always had such a good head on your shoulders; I know you will make the right decision for yourself. I am always here for you." Tania jumped in her seat. "Oh, I just remembered something. I got someone's phone number!" Tania rummaged through her purse and pulled out a crumpled piece of paper. "Marley: 310-555-3234. I remember she had long blond hair and was built like a bodybuilder. Like, killer body." Tania thought back the moment. "Oh, I think she said that she actually worked at Lix, but it was her night off?" Tania looked questioningly at Lauren.

Lauren shrugged; she had no idea who Tania was referring to. She let her mind wander for a moment. Then it hit her; Tania had met the bartender that had served Lauren tequila shots at Lix on the night of Terry's birthday, the high femme blond with the impressive biceps.

"Well, look at you!" Lauren said while sipping her coffee. "Do you think you are going to call her?"

Tania shrugged. "I don't know, maybe. She was really cute and is obviously fit; I'll bet she could throw me around pretty well!" Tania laughed and winked at Lauren. Then, Tania grabbed Lauren's leg. "Lauren, I have the perfect idea. I will call up Marley, and you can date Quinn, and then the four of us can double date at Lix!" Tania and Lauren howled together. "Then we can all visit the Grand Ballroom for a post, double-date orgy!" Tania doubled over in laughter while Lauren covered her face with her hands. Of course, she knew that Tania was joking, but there was a lot of truth to the incestuous nature of the queer's women's community.

"Sure, that sounds like a great idea Tania," Lauren said sarcastically. "Why don't we invite our ex's on the date while we are at it," Tania screamed with glee. "Lauren..." Tania struggled to catch her breath; she was laughing so hard. "We," Tania pointed at herself and Lauren, "are each other's ex-girlfriends!" Lauren almost choked on her coffee, amused by the hilarity of the situation. She was so comfortable with Tania as her friend that she had forgotten for a moment that they used to be a couple.

The pair continued to chat casually in the living room, as Lauren started to feel more empowered. While she understood the risks of putting Quinn on the spot, she knew how she needed to move forward with Quinn. First, however, Tania needed to grab her car, and Lauren decided the accompany her.

"Let's get moving, T." Lauren pulled out a shiny set of keys and jingled them in front of Tania's face. "We need to pick up your vehicle before it gets towed." Tania's eyes widened as she started to gather her belongings strewn about the living room.

The two friends walked out the door, while Lauren picked up her phone to punch in the number of an Uber.

Good night my precious doll. Sweet dreams.

Lauren's heart jumped. It was a text from Quinn, from the night before.

17

The Uber took Lauren and Tania over to the large white building that was Lix, which appeared to be plainer in broad daylight. Tania's light blue Honda Civic was parked in the same spot that she had left it the night before. Tania was going to jump out while Lauren remained in the Uber so that Lauren could get back home.

"Thanks for an amazing night out, L." Tania leaned over to hug her friend and hopped out of the Uber. "Remember, don't settle for anything less!" Tania called out as she traveled in the direction of her parked car.

Lauren waved and blew a kiss to Tania. Settling back into the seat of her Uber, she looked at her phone once again. Lauren wanted to text Quinn back right away, share her blissful thoughts, and wish Quinn a good day. But she stopped herself and decided to wait until she returned home. Lauren contemplated her feelings about Quinn while her body reminisced over their erotic encounter. She craved Quinn's body, the smell of her skin and the gentle, yet firm way that Quinn kissed her. At the same time, her heart sagged with longing.

I just need to ask for what I want, and if I lose it all, then at least I put myself first. Lauren thought to herself. *If Quinn is really serious about me, then she will meet me in the middle. If not, then at least I know where I stand.* Lauren felt a twinge of worry. She hoped that Quinn cared enough about her to at least put more effort into something more serious. She braced herself for disappointment- it could go either way.

Upon returning home, Lauren got comfortable on the couch. Her cat Sammy jumped up and snuggled into her lap. She petted his fluffy grey fur in an attempt to comfort herself. Lauren's heart was beating in her chest; her hands clammy with sweat.

Hey Quinn, Lauren started to type. She stopped and erased the words. **Hello Sir, so lovely to hear from you!** Lauren shook her head. No, that wasn't right either. **Hi Quinn, thanks so much for a fantastic night.** Lauren paused for a moment before continuing. **I was hoping we could meet in person to chat more and discuss things?** Lauren sent the message and chewed on her lip, absent-mindedly. She searched for the words that would make the text message complete.

What are you doing later tonight? Today was Sunday, and even though the club opened later that night, Lauren knew that Quinn wasn't at the club on Sunday nights. This was Lauren's way of testing Quinn; to see if Quinn would make an effort to meet with Lauren outside of the club.

She sent the text, putting the phone face down beside her. *Let the waiting game begin.* Lauren thought to herself.

Lauren forced herself off the couch and forbade herself to pick up the phone for the next half hour.

QUINN'S PHONE buzzed as Lauren's text appeared. Quinn breathed a sigh a relief; she was happy to hear back from Lauren, and she was keen to continue their conversation, the conversation that had come to a halt last night at Lix. However, Quinn decided to play it cool. *Don't come off too eager, Quinn. Give it a few minutes and then text Lauren back.*

Quinn thought back to the image of Lauren; her body splayed upon the desk in the dungeon. Quinn became filled with desire. She could still taste the sweetness of Lauren. The thought of Lauren's bare ass in the air made her feel ravenous; she wanted to devour Lauren, consume her warm flesh, and bury her face in her. Quinn was overcome with passion and desire. She couldn't remember the last time she had felt this overwhelmed with lust for anyone.

Not being able to wait a second longer, Quinn texted her back. **Good morning doll!** Quinn backtracked and erased the text. By this time of day, it was the afternoon, not the morning. Quinn wanted her text response to sound just right. **Hello doll, glad to hear that you and Tania made it home safe and sound.** Quinn reread her message to ensure it came across in the perfect way; friendly and light but not over the top. She continued, pausing with uncertainty. It took her a couple of tries before she crafted the perfect response.

Sure, I can be free tonight; after 8 pm? Where should we meet? Quinn gave her text the once over before sending it. She nodded at the message in approval before sending it. Quinn became anxious. *Why am I so nervous? It's just a chat. Quinn, you got this, it's not a big deal.*

Quinn was beside herself. It was the first time in a very long time that Quinn felt less than confident about a woman she was pursuing. Usually, Quinn was in the driver's seat and could manipulate a dating situation to her advantage. But Lauren was different. She made Quinn feel as though she was on shaky ground, and perhaps that is what drew Quinn towards Lauren. Maybe, that's what she needed in her life. A woman who was both vulnerable and submissive to her yet, at the same time, secure and confident in herself. Lauren was most certainly both.

Quinn attempted to distract herself with menial tasks as she awaited Lauren's response. She felt like she was on the edge of her seat. She looked up at the clock; she had sent her text 15 minutes ago. Why wasn't Lauren answering? Maybe Lauren wasn't available any longer? Quinn started to panic. She picked up her phone again, wanting to send Lauren another message, but she stopped herself. She put the phone down and put her hands to her temples.

Finally, Quinn's phone dinged. A new message! Quinn jumped up in her seat and breathed a sigh of relief, excited to finally receive a response from Lauren. Cool!

How about 8:30 pm? My place?

Quinn felt butterflies in her stomach. Lauren's place! Quinn had never visited the homes of her lovers. They had always come to Quinn and, in fact, almost always had they come to Lix. Quinn felt as though she was entering unfamiliar territory. Quinn's hands were trembling as she texted back.

Ok. What is your address?

Quinn decided to take the plunge and meet Lauren on

her turf. She stood up and breathed deeply as her ego took over. *Head up and shoulders back, Kelly Quinn. You are the owner of Lix; you are successful and attractive, and women love you! Don't be nervous. Women come and go, just be cool.*

Even while she entertained these ridiculous thoughts, Quinn was anything but cool. Lauren was not just any woman. If Lauren left her life, she knew she would never see another one like her. There was something about her that she just felt comfortable with. Something about Lauren that made her want to be more, to be better. She struggled against her demons. Quinn wanted to run over to Lauren's house right now and swoop her up into her arms. But grief and guilt continued to poison Quinn's mind, creating a protective shield around her heart. Quinn would go to Lauren's house, but she would maintain her footing. Quinn was terrified to relinquish her control, but when it came to her feelings about Lauren, power was slowly starting to slip out of her grasp.

Quinn's phone buzzed again; Lauren had texted Quinn her address.

See you later, little one.

Quinn retyped. She originally included a few 'x's' and 'o's' but decided against it. She removed the kisses and hugs and sent a plain confirmation instead. Her ego piped up again. *You can take Quinn out of Lix, but you can't take the Lix out of Quinn. You go, girl!* The false sense of bravery that momentarily fortified Quinn left her again within a minute.

LAUREN SQUEALED WITH EXCITEMENT. Quinn was coming over to her house! She sighed deeply and started to relax.

Lauren felt that this was a positive sign, as it meant that Quinn was willing to make an effort to see her on her turf. She ran her hands through her hair to collect her thoughts. She had many hours to kill before Quinn came over.

Maybe I should tidy up a bit. Lauren looked around at her spotless surroundings. Aside from the wrinkled blanket and pillow that Lauren had left for Tania, she generally kept her apartment very tidy. Lauren's nerves were pushing her into overdrive. *No, the place looks fine, Lauren. But you should shower and wash your hair. And put on something nice, ...but not too nice!* Lauren's mind raced with excitement. She headed into her bathroom, soaring with happiness.

Lauren emerged from the shower and wrapped herself in a fluffy towel. She ran her hand across her bathroom sink mirror, cleaning off the steam to peer into her reflection. As Lauren examined her skin- plucking out a few eyebrow hairs-she felt fresh and dewy. In anticipation of Quinn's arrival, she thought about what to wear. She strolled into her bedroom and opened her closet. *I think I will go for a more casual look; don't try too hard, Lauren. Just be your natural, beautiful self.* She selected a white, billowy tank top and her favorite pair of jeans. As she slipped into the pants, she loved how the worn denim hugged her body. *Perfect,* she thought to herself, *not too tight but just the right fit.*

As Lauren brushed out her long, brown hair, her stomach started to grumble, a fierce hunger had hit her. Moving into the small kitchen, she threw a frozen dinner into the microwave. *Hmmm, I wonder if I should make up a few snack trays to offer Quinn when she comes over? Wait...do*

I have anything to drink? Maybe I will run out and grab a bottle of wine. Oh, and flowers too!

Lauren's mind buzzed with excitement as she started to make a small grocery list of items in anticipation of Quinn's arrival. *Cashew cheese spread, crackers, grapes, strawberries, wine,* Lauren squinted in concentration, tapping a pen to her mouth. *Oh yes, flowers...I wonder what kind of flowers Quinn would like? Wait, does she even like flowers?* She started to feel a bit frazzled. *Lauren, calm down. It's just a visit; it's not a date.* Lauren questioned herself. *Wait, maybe it is a date?* She took a few deep breaths to center her thoughts. *Remember to stand your ground, Lauren. Don't settle for anything less. Maybe it will go well, maybe it won't. No matter what happens, just stay true to yourself.*

Feeling grounded, Lauren gathered her belongings and headed out the door to complete her errands. She hummed to herself and allowed her mind to travel back in time to the night before. As her body recollected the feeling of intense orgasm, an image of Quinn's face swam in front of her. *God, that woman is so handsome. How did I ever get so lucky to meet someone as sexy and as charming as her?* As she headed to a nearby corner store, Lauren felt as though she was walking on a cloud.

18

A fter obtaining Lauren's address and firming up plans, Quinn had decided to take a quick nap. She was still exhausted from her night at Lix, and she wanted to feel well-rested for when she saw Lauren, later that evening. Quinn hadn't slept well upon her return home from Lix, thoughts of both Lauren and Angela plagued her subconscious. She found herself tossing and turning late into the morning. Years of night club life had turned Quinn into a night owl, and she usually slept in until the middle of the afternoon. Her text message exchange with Lauren seemed to calm her, and her body finally allowed fatigue to settle in. She set the alarm on her phone and crashed out hard on top of her bedcovers.

After what seemed like hours, Quinn awoke to the sound of her phone ringing. She shook her head and sat up, feeling disoriented. The phone chimed loudly. Reading the time, she noticed that she had only been asleep for two hours. *Wait, that is not my alarm!* Feeling fuzzy, Quinn turned over to her nightstand to grab her phone. It was Mickey calling, the bouncer from Lix.

Quinn answered the phone groggily, "Hello? Mickey? Quinn was still half asleep.

"Heya boss. Were you sleeping? Listen, I am so sorry to bother you at home." Mickey sounded urgent. "I am at Cedars-Sanai. Last night on my way home, I got into a fender bender. I broke my arm, and they are saying that I may have a mild concussion. I am just getting my cast set now."

Quinn was now fully awake and stood up in alarm. "Oh my god, Mickey! Are you ok? What happened?"

"Ah, this driver swerved in front of me and knocked my car into the side of the road. The entire left side of my ride is totaled. But don't worry, I am ok. Hell, I am lucky to be alive! I mean, it was the other driver's fault. I can't wait to get my hands on that insurance money." Mickey chuckled. "But boss, listen, I am sorry, but I can't come into work tonight. You understand, right?"

"Of course, Mickey. No problem, I am just relieved to hear that you are ok. I mean, I am sorry about your arm and all. That's horrible." Quinn consoled Mickey. "Take whatever time you need to heal up. Don't worry, I will figure something out for tonight."

"Oh gee, thanks so much, Quinn. I am sure I can be back at work later this week. The doctor says that I should take it easy for now, in case there are any complications with the concussion, but for the most part, I feel fine." Mickey reassured Quinn. "I got the most amazing painkillers, and you know I would have no problem working with a cast. I just need a day or two to rest up."

Quinn couldn't help but laugh a little. Mickey was a tough

cookie, a real badass with a heart of gold. She knew that Mickey would be back at work in no time, but she was also concerned for her employee. Concussions could be severe, and she wanted Mickey to heal before returning to Lix.

"It's no problem at all. I will handle covering your shift, you just relax, ok? Please call me tomorrow and let me know how you are feeling." Quinn soothed her oldest employee. Mickey had been with Quinn since the opening of Lix, and she was like family to Quinn.

"Alright, boss, you are the best. Talk to you tomorrow." After Mickey hung up, Quinn continued to stare at her phone. *Ok Quinn, think fast. Who can you call to cover Mickey's shift?* Quinn flipped through her phone in search of suitable contacts.

Quinn had many phone numbers of potential bartenders and servers, but replacing a bouncer was more difficult. Mickey had a strong presence and a no-nonsense attitude, which were essential qualities in a front door person. Her mind searched the periphery of acquaintances she might know. No one stood out to Quinn as someone who could replace that position.

Damn! I don't think I have any options other than to do this myself. Quinn bit her lip and shook her head. *We definitely need to have someone at the door; I can't leave this position empty. I guess I gotta step in and take one for the team.*

Sunday nights were generally Quinn's night off. In the earlier days of Lix, Quinn was there every night, and she taught herself every position in the club. She knew every inch of Lix. She had personally trained everyone so that all of the staff were operating to her standards. Quinn could easily handle the door position, and of everyone she knew, Quinn herself had the right personality. *Besides,* she thought to herself; *it might even be a treat for the guests to meet me as soon as they arrive.*

Quinn started to formulate her plan of action. *Sunday nights are slower than Fridays and Saturdays. I think we could get away with no bouncer after midnight. So I can step in from 9 pm until midnight, which should be enough to cover the shift. But remind yourself to start looking for back up bouncers.* Quinn made a mental note to herself.

As Quinn started to prepare herself for the night ahead, she suddenly remembered her plans with Lauren. In her hurry to solve the situation with Mickey, she had completely forgotten that she was supposed to arrive at Lauren's for 8:30 pm.

Shit, I forgot about Lauren! Oh no, I am going to look like such an asshole! Fuck! Quinn started to panic. She was in a bind. There was no way that she was going to leave Lix unattended, but at the same time, she didn't want to disappoint Lauren either.

Quinn didn't know what to do. She rarely found herself in this kind of position. For the most part, Quinn's staff were loyal, hard-working, and committed to their jobs. Quinn was lucky in that way, many other night clubs had to deal with theft and other issues, such as substance abuse and dysfunctional behavior from their staff. Quinn ran a tight and mighty ship, and because Lix had such a unique environment, choosing the right employee was important. Quinn hand-selected every staff member herself, and the lucky ones who got the job, knew that they were a part of something special. In particular, Mickey was a crucial part of Lix, and as the owner, Quinn knew it was her responsibility to support Mickey in this time of need.

Quinn shrugged her shoulders helplessly. The situation was an emergency and something that Quinn needed to fix herself. Her insides sank with disappointment and concern that Lauren would be upset. Consumed with dread, Quinn texted Lauren.

Hi, doll. Listen, I am so sorry, but something urgent came up at work.

Hunched over, Quinn continued to punch the characters into her phone.

Mickey, my front door person, got into an accident and I need to be at the club for a few hours.

Quinn stopped for a moment and looked at her message before she sent it. *Fuck!* She cursed herself. She hoped that Lauren would understand. It was one of the drawbacks to being a business owner, she was married to Lix, and in the case of an emergency, the business had to come first.

Quinn started a new message.

I can be out of there by midnight, and if you are still willing to see me, I could come by later?

Quinn paused and then added,

please let me know. I would really love to see you.

Quinn stopped, feeling overwhelmed. Soon, she would need to start getting ready, but until she heard back from Lauren, she felt frozen in her tracks. Quinn sat on the bed and looked off in space for a few minutes, trying to collect her thoughts.

Brrring, Brrring. Quinn's phone rang. She jumped with a start and looked at the caller ID. It was Lauren! "Hello? Quinn answered in a hurry.

"Hi, Quinn? It's Lauren." Lauren's voice sounded concerned. "Look, I am sorry to call you. I just got your message. What happened, are you ok?"

"Lauren! I am so sorry. I just got a call from Mickey. It

turns out that she was in an accident last night." Quinn heard Lauren gasp on the phone.

"She is ok, but she does have a broken arm and maybe a mild concussion," Quinn explained. "Hey, I am really sorry, but I need to be at the club for a few hours. I need to cover Mickey's position. This hardly ever happens, but it's important." Quinn continued. "If I can make it over to your place just after midnight, would you still want to see me?" Quinn asked, waiting in anticipation of Lauren's reply.

Lauren paused on the phone for a few seconds. "Um, I guess...I mean, sure. I think that would be ok. I do need to work in the morning, though." Lauren emphasized to Quinn.

Quinn breathed a hard sigh of relief. "Oh my god, Lauren. Thank you for being so understanding. I know I am the owner and all, but it's not all glamour and glitz. The whole place is ultimately my responsibility." Quinn tried to laugh in an attempt to lighten the mood. "Mickey is like family to me, and she has helped me out so many times. I totally owe her one."

Quinn continued. "It is only for a few hours, things die down pretty quickly at Lix on a Sunday night. I can be out of there by midnight, no problem."

Lauren paused again before speaking. "Ok, sure. That sounds ok. I was just hoping we could talk a bit, outside of the club, you know? I wanted to chat with you about... about last night." Lauren's voice faltered slightly.

"Yes, I know. I do, as well." Quinn felt horrible. She could sense the disappointment in Lauren's voice. "Thanks again for being so cool about everything. I promise I will text you as soon as I am on the way." Quinn said encouragingly.

Even though Lauren seemed patient on the phone, Quinn wasn't completely convinced.

"Ok, Quinn, well, thanks for letting me know, and I am sorry that you have to deal with this tonight. Just text me when you are on the way, and I will stay up and wait for you." Lauren said, in a smooth and even tone. "Have a good night and see you soon."

"See you soon, doll." Quinn got off the phone and moaned to herself. Man, I hope she is not pissed. The voice of Quinns' alter ego echoed.

Quinn, you know the club has to come first. If Lauren is upset, then it's too bad for her. She needs to understand that Lix is your life, and if she can't wrap her head around that, then it's her loss.

Quinn wanted to fight back against the voices in her head, the sounds that had robbed Quinn of genuine happiness and true love. These thoughts were what kept Quinn from having a life outside of the club, and she was at odds with herself.

As Quinn's own anger with herself grew, the more she desired something more with Lauren. Lauren was the missing puzzle piece to her life, and she was suddenly frustrated with the toll that Lix was taking on her personal life.

Ok, Quinn. You will fill in for Mickey tonight, but after this, you need to step it up and hire more security staff. You need to take a break from all of the nightclub chaos. If you ever want to have a chance at happiness, you need to make time for yourself. The club will always be there, you just need to learn how to take a step back.

Quinn started to calm herself. Yes, it was true. What was the point of the money and status if she could not enjoy it? Since she was a young girl, Quinn had worked her hard her entire life. At forty-eight years old, it was time for a change.

The chance at a new beginning was right in front of Quinn. The big question was whether Quinn was willing to escape her demons and embrace the opportunity.

As Quinn prepared to head down to Lix, she felt a lightness in her being. She felt ready for a new life, and the possibility to have love enter her life. Her heart soared at the thought of seeing Lauren later that night. As she pulled over to the side of the road and entered the building, she felt excited about the future for the first time in many years.

19

L   auren had returned home from her afternoon of
         groceries and errands. She had initially intended
         to pick up a few snack items for her and Quinn,
but midway, she decided upon cooking a full dinner
instead. In her mind, she tried to brush this off as a
casual act.

*Lauren, you need to eat a full dinner anyway, so you might
as well cook something. If Quinn wants to join you for dinner,
you can fix her a plate too. No big deal! It's not a dinner date.
You are already doing this for yourself, right?*

Lauren knew that she was getting ahead of herself, but
she couldn't contain her excitement. Deep down, she really
wanted to cook a meal for both her and Quinn. To have them
sit together and bask in each other's company. Even though
their physical encounters were intimate on a sexual level,
Lauren craved more quality time with Quinn. Lauren
continued to talk to herself. *And if Quinn can see what a
fantastic cook I am, maybe she will see me as more than just a fling!*

She burst through the door of her apartment, her

hands heavy with bags and a bouquet. The flowers were not specifically for Quinn, she wasn't sure Quinn was a flowers kind of girl, but Lauren wanted to have them displayed as a centerpiece on the table while they ate dinner together.

The more rational part of Lauren's brain knew that Quinn might be hesitant to get into something more serious. She was trying to remain realistic about the situation, but Lauren had a powerful inclination towards romance and the belief of soul mates.

This whimsical sensibility often made Lauren more susceptible to disappointment, but it was also a quality that she admired in herself. Lauren was not afraid of getting hurt. The way she saw it, it was better to have loved and lost than to have never experienced love.

Past lovers were drawn to Lauren's open heart, and she saw her ability to welcome love into her life as a strength and not a weakness.

Lauren had suffered from having her heart broken before, but she healed from failed relationships quickly. Part of what drew Lauren to Quinn was the fact that they were polar opposites in that way. Where Quinn seemed like a cagey tiger cat, Lauren was a playful puppy, filled with boundless mirth and energy. Lauren knew that she possessed the ability to love someone as guarded as Quinn. She wanted to try her very best to make tonight magical; she needed Quinn to see that she was authentic in her care and that she would never hurt Quinn or let her down.

Lauren got to work, unpacking her groceries, and gathering the ingredients. She pulled out a bottle of red wine, and after a few moments, she decided to uncork and poured herself a glass while she made preparations for the evening.

She wrapped the bouquet of flowers, snipped off the ends with a pair of sharp scissors, and plunked them into a large vase full of water. She placed the arrangement on her small kitchen table, and immediately a fresh floral scent filled the room. Lauren beamed at how the colorful flowers and lush petals brightened up the dining area.

Lauren started to wash some vegetables under the sink when her phone buzzed. She looked over, and it was a message from Quinn. Lauren smiled to herself and checked the text. Slowly, the smile had started to drain from her face.

Lauren's bursting heart felt like it just got popped with a balloon; she felt utterly deflated. *Are you serious right now, Quinn? Are you ditching me, or is there really an emergency?* Lauren scrunched her face with uncertainty, unsure if Quinn was pulling a fast one. *Fuck it; I am just going to call her. Screw this text nonsense; I want to know the truth.*

She called Quinn, thus receiving the news about the car crash. Quinn let her know that she needed to fill in at the club tonight. Lauren felt like crying, but she tried her best to remain cool and friendly. The last thing that Quinn needed was some woman going psycho on her for breaking plans, especially in this type of emergency. Lauren wanted to be understanding and supportive, but inside, she felt discouraged and slightly insecure. *Was this Quinn's way of brushing her off?*

Lauren, do not take this personally. You know that Quinn is a busy woman and a business owner. Just be patient and understanding. Lauren tried to pull herself together. *She said she still wanted to see you. So what if you can't have dinner with her? It's fine!*

Lauren tried hard to keep her voice even as she told Quinn that she would wait up to see her later. But still, she felt sad and slightly annoyed.

In addition to being let down, she also had to work in the morning. Staying up past midnight was not something Lauren did on a work night.

Not everyone is a party animal like you, Quinn. Lauren grumbled to herself. She downed the glass of wine and immediately poured herself another. She sipped the wine, savoring the acidic sweetness, and tried to calm herself. *Alright, Lauren, just pull yourself together and make yourself dinner. You bought all of this food; you may as well create something out of it.*

Lauren tried to move forward with her food prep, but now, it just seemed pointless. All of the joy and excitement that she possessed ran out of her like sand in an hourglass. Instead, she hopped herself up on the kitchen counter and opened a bag of potato chips. *I am so not in the mood to cook any longer.*

Feeling sorry for herself, she continued to drink the wine, but this time, she took a swig right from the bottle.

Sammy strolled into the kitchen and curiously meowed at Lauren. She looked down at her pet from her perch on the counter. "Looks like it's just you and me tonight, buddy." Lauren looked over at the bundle of flowers, mocking her with their vibrant colors.

She took another swig from the wine bottle and allowed the hot tears to roll from her eyes.

∾

QUINN HURRIED into her office at Lix to gather her belongings before heading out for the night. The club had been relatively quiet, especially in comparison to the evening before. It was generally a mellower crowd, and for the most part, the guests were more interested in using the pool and the playrooms as opposed to dancing and drinking. On Sunday evenings, there was no DJ; Quinn decided it would be better to cut costs and save the bigger headliners like DJ Collette for Fridays and Saturdays. Instead, Quinn played a Spotify mix of popular EDM mixes, just to add to the ambiance. Overall, it was chill night, and Quinn was grateful to be heading out early. There was no need for a front door person any longer. She looked at the clock; it showed the time at 11 pm. *Awesome!* She thought to herself. *I'll make it over to Lauren's sooner than I thought!*

As she got ready, she texted Lauren.

Hey, doll! I am leaving Lix now. I can't wait to see you soon.

Quinn left the office and did one more check through the club, saying her goodbyes to the staff who were still working.

Quinn rechecked her phone. There had been no reply from Lauren. *Hmmm,* Quinn thought to herself. *I sent that text 20 minutes ago. I hope Lauren is still awake.*

Quinn texted Lauren again, an uneasy feeling rose up the back of her neck.

Hi Lauren. I just wanted to let you know that I am heading out the door. There is less traffic on the roads now, maybe 30 minutes?

Quinn walked outside en route to her car. She rechecked her phone. Still no answer. Quinn's chest started to ache. Earlier in the night, she was filled with excitement and energy. She couldn't wait to see Lauren.

Whatever guilt and sorrow that usually filled Quinn's heart lessened, replaced with a strange yet freeing feeling of vulnerability.

Quinn opened the door to her car and sat inside. She looked at her phone once more; still nothing. The time read 11:35 pm. Quinn knew it was late, but she was desperate to hear back from Lauren. She decided to call.

The phone rang four times, followed by Lauren's voice mail. *Hi, you have reached the voicemail of Lauren Harte. I can't come to the phone right now, but if you leave a brief message, I will return your call as soon as possible.*

"Uh, hi, Lauren. It's Quinn. I am just leaving Lix now, and I was headed over to your place. I just called to make sure you were still awake. If you get this within the next 30 minutes, please call me. Thanks." Quinn left a message and hung up. Quinn ran her fingers through her hair and thought about what she should do next.

I need to see her; I need to try at least. What if she is just in the bathroom or something? Quinn revved her engine and headed over to Lauren's apartment in Encino. The roads were clear as she sped along the Laurel Canyon Boulevard, merging on the US 101 highway. As she drove, Quinn's longing to be close to Lauren grew, fear no longer occupied her heart. Quinn wanted Lauren to know that she would be willing to go the extra step-and drive the additional 29 miles- to prove that she valued Lauren in her life. Quinn had decided that she wanted to explore more with Lauren, and as soon as that notion occupied her mind, there was no stopping Quinn.

The car arrived in front of Lauren's building and rolled into a visitor's parking spot. Quinn burst through the lobby door, deciding to skip the elevator, she ran up a few flights of stairs until she reached Lauren's door, number 402.

Quinn knocked softly at first. "Lauren," she called out. "Are you there?" Quinn knocked again, harder this time. "Lauren!" Quinn checked her phone. There were no messages from Lauren. Quinn breathed heavily with frustration. *Oh no! Man, I fucked up. I guess she doesn't want to see me at all.* Quinn made one final attempt and knocked feebly on the door.

Crushed, Quinn stepped away from the door. The hallway started to spin slightly. Quinn put her head in her hands. She felt as though she had just lost something incredible, something that had slipped through her fingers in the same way that Angela did. Accepting her fate, Quinn walked down the hallway; regret and rejection crashed over her like a wave. She stopped in the middle of the hall and looked back at Lauren's door. She knew what she needed to do.

20

Lauren woke up with a start, her mouth was dry, and her head was pounding. At first, she didn't recognize where she was. She looked around, confused. *Did I sleep on the couch last night?* She smacked her lips; they felt sticky. Red wine! As she sat up, the memories from the night before flooded her mind. She looked at the clock on the wall. The time read 2:45 am.

Lauren's gaze traveled to her kitchen. It was a mess of unpacked groceries, half-eaten vegetables, and potato chip crumbs. An empty bottle of wine was poised on the counter. She noticed a few flower stems had fallen on to the ground.

Lauren rubbed her head. *God, I must have drunk the whole bottle of wine and passed out on the couch.* Feeling shaky, Lauren stood up and gathered her thoughts. Suddenly, alarm ran through her blood, sending shock waves throughout her body. Quinn!

Hurriedly, she checked her phone. She noticed three new text messages and four missed phone calls. *Oh shit!*

She must have tried to call me! Lauren listened to her voice messages. *Oh my god, I slept through her calls and messages. No!* Lauren sobered up immediately and scurried about her kitchen in a frenzy, trying to clean up the mess while continuing to piece together her night.

She remembered getting a message from Quinn earlier that afternoon, she felt sad. She had a glass of wine, then another. She had attempted to make dinner but lost interest as she became tipsier. Eventually, she had made her way to the couch and had fallen asleep in a drunken slumber.

As she continued to sweep and wipe down her counters, she called Quinn. There was no answer. She sent Quinn a text message.

Quinn! I am so sorry. I crashed out last night on the couch. I am sorry I missed your calls. Please call me back right away!

Lauren could not believe her luck. She covered her face with her hands and cried out in frustration. Yesterday, she was thrilled at seeing Quinn, but as Fate had it, she had missed her chance. *No!* She shook her fists in the air. *No, Quinn, come back!*

She tried calling Quinn again. Still, no answer. Feeling frantic, Lauren ran to her front door. She wanted to run to Lix, in an attempt to find Quinn. Upon flinging open the door, Lauren noticed a large bouquet of flowers and a card beneath her feet. Confused, she picked up the package, looking both ways down the corridor. The hallway was empty. *What the heck?* She examined the parcel. *God, I hope I am not taking someone else's gift. Who would have brought these?* Then, she noticed that the front of the card was addressed to her. She brought the package inside.

Puzzled, Lauren opened the card. It displayed a beautiful graphic of a rainbow cascading over a waterfall. She opened it up. The card was blank, but there as a note tucked in. Lauren caught the letter as it attempted to flutter to the ground.

My beautiful Doll

First, I want to say how sorry I am for messing up our plans last night. You have no idea how badly I wanted to see you and how excited I was. I truly thank you for being so sweet and understanding that I needed to go into Lix, but at the same time, I felt awful breaking our plans. I'll understand if you never want to talk to me again, but I need you to know that I am sorry for hurting you.

Meeting you for the first time at Lix was incredible. I was mesmerized by your beauty, charm, and wit. I thought about you after that first night. Almost immediately, I knew you were someone special. I so wanted to express that to you, but I didn't have the words. Honestly, I am not the best at telling someone how I feel, and now that I have lost you, I am filled with regret over not telling you sooner.

I want you to know that you never did anything wrong. I am the one with the problem. When Angela died, something inside me died too. I didn't tell you at first, but Angela committed suicide, and I was there. I could have saved her life, but I was too late. Her death haunts me every day, and ever since then, I have felt unworthy of love. You are right; I do have a shell; it was something I had to build to survive the loss of Angela. I had never felt the same about any other woman until I met you. I know you are angry with me, but I want to thank you for coming into my life, regardless.

I know that we probably won't see each other again, but since I can no longer tell you in person, I wanted to write you this note. Thank you for bringing beauty and light into my life. Thank you for helping me to feel again. You are a gift, and I would give anything to see you again. I respect your decision for space; I don't blame you. I just hope that one day, you can find it in yourself to forgive me. You are so precious and deserving of so much more.

Love, Quinn xoxo

Lauren leaned against the wall and slid to the ground, note in hand. An intense combination of love, sadness, and relief washed over her. Lauren held the note to her chest while tears streamed down her face. She was moved beyond belief at Quinn's transparency, her vulnerability. She felt deep sorrow for Quinn and her terrible loss. Lauren also was surged with happiness over Quinn's revelation of love and care. She felt overwhelmed with emotion. Quinn had wanted to be with Lauren as much as Lauren wanted Quinn. Lauren needed to talk to Quinn right away.

She dialed Quinn's number. No answer. Quickly, she texted Quinn.

Quinn! I just received your flowers and your note. I need to see you! I feel the exact same way. Please call me back. I want to see you. I am not angry at you. Xoxox

Lauren waited a few minutes to see if Quinn would respond. The time on her phone read 3:40am. Lauren needed to go to bed. She had work in the morning, and the events of the day and evening had drained her.

Lauren crawled into her bedroom and drifted off to sleep, taking comfort in knowing that Quinn truly cared about her. She knew that she would see Quinn again. Soon, they would be together.

∼

LAUREN UNLOCKED her door and entered her apartment after a long shift at the office. She had begun her morning in a bright and energetic mood; her heart was on fire with love and longing for Quinn. However, as the day progressed, her mood grew dark and sullen. Quinn had not returned her phone calls or message. Lauren started to feel confused.

What is going on? Why hasn't Quinn gotten back to me? If she doesn't want to talk to me, then what was that note all about? To play games with my heart?

Lauren angrily dumped her belongings on the ground, and absentmindedly opened the fridge. She felt insatiable, but at the same time, she had no appetite. She continued to pace around her apartment when suddenly her phone buzzed. She raced over to her purse to retrieve it and checked her messages.

Hi, Doll. Seems like we keep missing one another! I'd love to see you. I am happy to hear that you are not angry with me and that you got my flowers and note. I am doing inventory at Lix tonight. We are closed to the public, but you are welcome to stop by. I hope you do. I miss you. Xo

Breathless with excitement, Lauren cried out for joy. Quickly, she threw a frozen dinner in the microwave and scarfed her food down, before heading over to Lix. I am coming, my love.

LAUREN ROLLED up the entrance of Lix in an Uber and rushed to the front door. She knew it would be locked, so she texted Quinn to come and open the door. Lauren's heart was beating fast in her chest. She was bursting with excitement, eager to wrap her arms around Quinn.

Seconds seemed like hours while Lauren waited. Finally, she heard a bolt unlock and a tiny creak as the door opened.

Quinn peeked her head out and smiled widely. "Come in, my little one."

Lauren snuck in while Quinn bolted the door behind her. Immediately, Lauren jumped into Quinn's arms and wrapped herself tightly around Quinn's long torso. Quinn threw her arms around Lauren in a tight and warm squeeze. Lauren felt like she had come home; being with Quinn is where she belonged.

They held on to one another tightly, for many minutes. Neither of them spoke, both wanting to savor the moment. Whatever they needed to say to one another was channeled through their embrace. They both knew what the other was thinking, words were not necessary.

After what seemed like an eternity, Quinn released Lauren and looked at her intently, her eyes sparkled with pure bliss. Quinn bent down to kiss Lauren passionately. Lauren strained her neck to deepen the kiss, smashing her lips against Quinn as their tongues danced together.

They separated for a moment. Quinn grabbed both of Lauren's hands, giving her the once over. Lauren had never seen Quinn look so ecstatic. "How was your day, Lauren?" Quinn asked quietly as she smiled.

Lauren's face beamed with joy. "It was great, Boss. How was yours?" Quinn laughed. "Ok, first of all, please call me Quinn. You don't need to call me boss anymore... unless we are in the dungeon!" Quinn winked mischievously.

Lauren chuckled. "Ok Bo-I mean, Quinn. I love that name." Lauren searched Quinn's face, feeling honored to witness the walls around Quinn's soul crumbling around them. "That said, feel free to keep calling me Doll. I have grown quite fond of that nickname, actually!"

Lauren and Quinn shared a knowingly laugh. Quinn looked around at the empty club. "Well, as you can see, my night is just getting started, but it's time to take a break." Quinn pulled Lauren closer. "Do you want to take a dip in the pool with me?" Lauren melted on the spot. She would go anywhere with Quinn. "That sounds like the best idea ever. I'd love to."

Quinn looked at her and said coyly, "No bathing suit?" Lauren responded and shook her head. "Nope, no suit. I guess I will just have to go skinny dipping!" Quinn replied. "Good answer. I can't wait to get you out of these clothes." The pair kissed again, passion rising within them. Quinn drew her face back and whispered in Lauren's ear. "Lauren, I want you. I want to be with you. Everywhere. Here. Outside of here. You have me completely if you want me."

Lauren nodded her head, the breath of Quinn's whisper tickled her earlobe. "Quinn, that is what I always wanted. Yes, I am yours, all yours. I just want to love you. Please let me."

"I will, my little one. My Lauren. My Doll. Welcome to my heart." Quinn held Lauren tightly. "Come on, let's get wet!" Quinn and Lauren walked quickly together, hand in hand, down the corridor, towards the patio. They peeled off each other's clothing, punctuating each moment with deep kisses. Simultaneously, they plunged into the warm, salty pool.

Lauren emerged first, wiping the refreshing water

from her face. She looked around. Quinn was swimming like a fish underwater; her long, sinewy body snaked along the pool's bottom. Lauren felt Quinn's body brush against her legs, and she giggled with glee. Quinn finally surfaced, rising like a glistening statue from the water.

They kissed again while their bodies intertwined together in the water. Their hands felt each other's supple muscles. Quinn cupped her hands around Lauren's breasts while Lauren slid her hands down Quinn's back, grabbing her firm ass. They continued to make out, gasping for breath, while splashing about, grinding against one another.

Lauren was beside herself with desire. She needed to be inside Quinn, and she craved Quinn's fingers and tongue in her. Spitting water from her face, she asked, "Quinn, can we take this above water? I want you so bad. I want to lay under the sky and make love to you." Quinn shook the water from her head and ears. "I want you to, Lauren. Yes, let's grab some towels and lay down in the grass."

For a quick moment, Lauren looked around nervously. "But what about...what about the staff?" The sun was starting to set in the sky, but it was still light out. They were visible to anyone who came out on the patio.

Quinn brushed Lauren's concerns aside. "Don't worry about it, my love. The staff have seen it all. Besides..." Quinn said slyly. "They know you are here. They will give us privacy." Quinn put a hand to her mouth as if to shush them. Lauren laughed. "Wow, you really think of everything, don't you?"

The couple grabbed a few fresh towels from the shelves and laid them out on the grass. Quinn fell on her back, and Lauren mounted herself on top of Quinn's naked and wet body. Quinn was entranced with Lauren. She looked so beautiful against the backdrop of the sun setting low in the sky.

Lauren leaned her body against Quinn and softly kissed her neck, her lips traveling down Quinn's chest, stopping to suck on Quinn's perky nipples. At the same time, Quinn moved her hand between Lauren's legs, finding the warm, wet mound of silky lips. Lauren kept her legs apart, straddling Quinn, with her ass in the air, bending over like an arch so that she could continue to trace her mouth along Quinn's torso.

Quinn reached further, finally entering Lauren. Lauren lifted her body and rose up so that she could ride Quinn's hand. She rocked her hips back and forth, and Quinn moved her fingers harder and faster against Lauren. Lauren moaned, crying out to the night sky in ecstasy. She came hard and fast for Quinn; it was a well-needed release.

Lauren threw her naked body back, screaming with pleasure as her entire body flushed with an intense orgasm.

"Quinn, oh my god, Quinn. I love you, Quinn!" Lauren blurted out, overcome with emotion, and with tears. She fell on top of Quinn, shaking with post-orgasm spasms. Quinn wrapped her arms tightly around Lauren and smoothed her wet hair with her hands. "I know, Lauren. I know. I love you too." Quinn said in a whisper.

"Quinn, I want more of you. I need to taste you." Moving from a cowgirl position, Lauren straightened herself out and slid her body down to position herself between Quinn's legs. Quinn laid her head back, permissively allowing Lauren to have her way.

Lauren looked at Quinn, admiring how the folds of

skin opened back like delicate flower petals. Lauren looked up seductively at Quinn as she extended her tongue, tracing Quinn's soft lips and teasing her with long, smooth strokes. Quinn sighed with pleasure, grabbing Lauren's hair.

"Lauren, Lauren..fuck, please don't stop. Don't stop!" Lauren located the pearl of Quinn's clit, which was now engorged with arousal. Lauren quickened her speed, stimulating Quinn as Quinn bucked against her face, crying out with joy. Lauren slid two fingers into Quinn, and she felt Quinn's muscles tighten around her fingers.

She fucked Quinn harder, pushing her fingers in and out, her fingers slippery with juices. She felt Quinn tense up completely and cry out while tiny veins in her neck popped out. Quinn squirted hot liquid all over Lauren's fingers as her body started to soften.

Lauren lay her head on Quinn's chest, listening to the sound of her heartbeat. Quinn held Lauren close as they embraced a timeless moment of bliss. Lauren peeked her face at Quinn and smiled lovingly. Quinn touched Lauren's cheek. Finally, Quinn spoke.

"Lauren, I know that I am not the best person when it comes to words, but I want this time to be different. I know what I had asked you before, the last time we were here." Quinn paused. "I need you to know that I want all of you, all of the time, everywhere. I want us to be together. Really together." Quinn looked at Lauren. "Is that what you want too?"

"Quinn, you know I do." Lauren passionately whispered. "I want to be yours...I want to be your girlfriend." Lauren said shyly. "I know you have suffered a terrible loss, and I want to be the person to ease your pain. I want to share all of life's moments with you, the good and the bad. I want to be with you at Lix, and I want us to create a life together outside of the club."

Lauren looked down. "I know that I can't replace Angela, and I would never want to. But I can love you, Quinn. I can be your rock so that you don't have to be so strong all of the time."

"That makes me so happy, Lauren. You make me so happy!" Quinn laughed and tickled Lauren; together, they squirmed and giggled. Lauren untangled herself from Quinn and sat up on the towel. She sighed deeply. "So, now what?" She shrugged and laughed.

Quinn stretched out her body, lifting her arms to the sky. "Well, I say that we go inside and see if Chelsea can make us a drink. I think we need to celebrate. After that, I do need to get back to our counting our inventory." Quinn stood up and extended her hand to Lauren, pulling her upright. As Lauren stood, Quinn continued. "You are welcome to stick around if you want?"

Lauren replied. "I will take you up on that drink. But I will leave you to finish your work." Lauren brushed herself off. "I should get home." Lauren glanced at Quinn. "Maybe tomorrow, we could grab dinner together?"

Quinn beamed. "You mean like a date with my new girlfriend? I would love to. I will pick you up and take us out, like the gentleman I am." Lauren laughed and came at Quinn for a final hug.

Arm in arm, the couple headed back inside for a final nightcap.

As they approached the bar, Chelsea was working hard, wiping down bottles and measuring the contents. She was writing down her findings when she saw Quinn and Lauren approach.

"Hey, you two!" Chelsea turned her attention to

Lauren. "I saw you come in, but then you disappeared to the pool. I don't think we have formally met." Chelsea extended her hand to Lauren. Lauren took it and shook Chelsea's hand warmly.

"Chelsea, I would like you to meet my girlfriend, Lauren." Quinn smiled proudly, and Lauren's leg felt like jelly. It was official, and it made Lauren feel so warm inside.

"Congratulations!" Chelsea exclaimed. On Quinn's nod, she pulled out three champagne glasses and a bottle of Moet.

"Cheers," Quinn said. "To my beautiful girlfriend, Lauren."

Lauren smiled as she sipped the dry bubbly champagne. She finally felt at home at Lix, and for the first time in many years, so did Quinn. "Welcome to the family, babe." Quinn kissed Lauren on the cheek and threw her arm around Lauren. Tranquility filled Quinn's being; she knew she had a long way to go, but she felt at peace.

THE END

GET Book 2 of the Lix Club Series, Her Desire. See what happens next for Lauren and Quinn. They take a vacation to New York to explore the NYC kink scene and their own desires. Can they make their relationship work?

Click on the link or type the following text into your web browser: getbook.at/Lix2

THANK YOU FOR READING!

I really hope you enjoyed these stories! If you would like to continue reading and you missed the links earlier you can find Book 2 in the Forest Vale Hospital Series here: getbook.at/TDR

∿

You can get Book 2 in the Lix Club Series here: getbook.at/Lix2

(Or type the link text into your web browser)

∿

FREE BOOK:

Check out my Super Hot Summer Holiday Romance for FREE by joining my mailing list (you can leave at any time) https://BookHip.com/KARVZC

~

All my books are available on Amazon either to purchase or to read for FREE on kindle Unlimited. Gradually my books are being done for Audible- there is a selection on there now if you enjoy Audiobooks.

~

If you would like to check out one of my super hot recent releases, see below...

What happens when the dominant older woman you met on a dating app for casual sex turns out to be your new boss?

Find out in Assistant to the CEO getbook.at/ATTCEO

Printed in Great Britain
by Amazon

72372412R00393